ALSO BY DEXTER PALMER

The Dream of Perpetual Motion

VERSION
CONTROL

VERSION CONTROL

Dexter Palmer

PANTHEON BOOKS, NEW YORK

Copyright © 2016 by Dexter Palmer

All rights reserved. Published in the United States by Pantheon Books,
a division of Penguin Random House LLC, New York,
and distributed in Canada by Random House of Canada,
a division of Penguin Random House Canada Ltd., Toronto.

Pantheon Books and colophon are registered trademarks
of Penguin Random House LLC.

Library of Congress Cataloging-in-Publication Data
Palmer, Dexter Clarence, [date]
Version control / Dexter Palmer.
pages ; cm
ISBN 978-0-307-90759-2 (hardcover)
ISBN 978-0-307-90760-8 (eBook)
1. Married women—Fiction.   2. Physicists—Fiction.   3. Quantum theory—Fiction.
I. Title.
PS3616.A33885V47 2016 813'.6—dc23 2015018879

www.pantheonbooks.com

Jacket art from the series "Failed Memories" by David Szauder
Jacket design by Janet Hansen
Book design by Maggie Hinders

Printed in the United States of America
First Edition
2 4 6 8 9 7 5 3 1

We are children of time, not its masters; we can act upon time only by acting within it.

—ERNST TROELTSCH, "The Essence of the Modern Spirit"
(translated by James Luther Adams and Walter F. Bense)

How sad that this generation imagines that the form, colour, name and sound are enough to capture the essence of something!

—*The Book of Chuang Tzu*
(translated by Martin Palmer with Elizabeth Breuilly)

Knowledge is a big subject. Ignorance is bigger. And it is more interesting.

—STUART FIRESTEIN, *Ignorance*

CONTENTS

PART II The Shadow Brought Backward

PART I

THE POINT OF FAILURE

1

THIRD EYE

Nothing is as it should be; everything is upside down. That is what Rebecca Wright thought.

For months now, Rebecca had felt what she could only describe as a certain subtle wrongness—not within herself, but in the world. She found it impossible to place its source, for the fault in the nature of things seemed to reside both everywhere and nowhere. Countless things just felt a little *off* to her. Sometimes she would fork a thick eggy chunk of French toast into her mouth during a Sunday brunch to find that a faint taste of soap lay beneath the flavor of maple syrup; sometimes when she kissed her husband his breath smelled of loam, as if he'd been surreptitiously snacking on top-grade soil. Sometimes the setting sun seemed to her to be hanging in a slightly incorrect place in the sky, to be a slightly inaccurate shade of red.

And take the President, for example. Sometimes, when Rebecca would see him on television, giving a speech on the pleasures of austerity or making a cameo appearance in the reality show that detailed the lives of his two teenage sons, she'd think: *Something's a little wrong. He seems like the wrong person.* Not because he didn't deserve to run the country, or because he was some sort of impostor, but because when he stood behind a podium with the golden presidential seal framing his head like a halo, he seemed to be the wrong person in the wrong place, a misunderstood character in a misremembered history.

When Rebecca had finally confessed her weird, persistent unease to her husband a week ago, it had done little good. Philip Steiner was

not a man who readily comprehended the irrationalities of humans—
they puzzled him to distraction on those rare occasions when they
manifested in his own behavior, and when he observed them in others he usually figured they could be exorcised easily enough with
judiciously chosen language. "You're not making any sense to me," he
said to Rebecca when she woke up just after he'd come home from the
lab at six a.m., after she'd told him she just felt like something was,
well, *wrong*, with *everything*.

"Just listen," Rebecca said as she sat up in bed, the old, oversized
Stratton University T-shirt that served as her sleeping wear hanging
loosely off one shoulder. "It's like—you know, that feeling you have
when you walk into a room intending to do something, except when
you get there you forget what it is you came in there to do. I feel like
that all the time now. I just woke up from a dream where I had that
feeling. But that's all I can remember about it."

"I don't know what you're talking about," Philip said, removing
his left shoe by pushing at its heel with his other foot, then doing the
reverse. "I don't ever have that feeling."

"Or like when you put your keys down when you come in the house,
and fifteen minutes later you reach for them where you thought you
put them and they're not there. Then you spend two hours turning
the whole place upside down, even though you don't have anywhere
to go right then, because until you find them you'll feel like there's a
fishhook stuck in your brain. Tugging."

"I've never felt like that, either," Philip said. "My keycards move
from the nightstand to the right front pocket of my slacks when
I leave for work. They only leave my pocket when I need to open
doors. When I'm done they go back to my pocket. At the end of the
day they return to the nightstand." He tossed the little bundle of
rubber-banded RFID cards there, by example. "It never fails."

"Oh Philip you're *worthless*." Rebecca slipped beneath the bedcov-
ers and yanked them up to her chin.

Philip stripped down to his undershirt and boxers and sat down on
his side of the bed. "It doesn't make sense," he said, half to himself.
But it was at moments like these when, for all that he and Rebecca
had been through, he still felt conscious of the satisfaction of being
half of what most people these days called an "old married couple."
After ten years together, Rebecca's behavior still occasionally took

him by surprise, but with each passing month, the methods of modeling her mind became clearer, the proper procedures for response more plainly evident. Philip found that if the cause of her distress wasn't something obvious, like a sliver of a mirror's glass lodged in the palm of her hand, or a printer in the kitchen that was turning out misshapen forks and spoons, then asking her if she was upset often yielded positive results.

"Are you upset?" he asked.

"I'm *not* upset," Rebecca said, turning over and burying her face in the pillows. "Christ, Philip. You always ask me that." Her voice was muffled.

Philip frowned at her as she lay prone beneath the bedsheets. All he could see of her was a tousled mass of chestnut-colored hair, a month-old dye job betrayed by its scattered gray roots.

He quietly slid in next to her, kissed her tentatively on her ear, rolled over, and fell asleep within seconds, snoring lightly.

Rebecca soon drowsed again as well. She dreamed of tomatoes that hung heavy on thorn-laden vines, juicy, ice blue, and ready for harvest. She dreamed of sprawling mansions that rested on skewed foundations.

■

That was last week, and though that feeling of a fishhook lodged in her brain still lingered, Rebecca had decided to stop thinking about it. She was hosting a party of sorts this Saturday night—Philip had invited his colleagues and a few of the post-docs and grad students in his lab over to watch a show on television—and the preparations for it would distract her. The program was going to be on the Pscience! network, one of those half-dozen cable channels that broadcast sensationalist science and nature programs twenty-four hours a day, an endless procession of flashy animated renderings of Jovian orbiters, and experts on supernatural phenomena, and lions tearing out the throats of their prey.

One of the shows on Pscience! this evening was due to have a segment about the project that Philip had been working on for eight years. Philip would have preferred to receive his applause from his colleagues in the field, rather than from some television announcer who just read whatever she saw on a teleprompter—he had little interest in the opinions of laymen, and considered speaking to them about his work to be a waste of his valuable time. But the fact was, after nearly a decade of constant labor, on the rare occasions when his work was mentioned by other physicists, it was usually over one too many drinks at a hotel bar on the night before a conference, as an object lesson in how to avoid a research path that was likely to lead to a career-ruining dead end, or as a criticism of the habit of certain organizations of handing out grant money to anyone who could fool a panel of bureaucrats into thinking he was a legitimate scientist.

So when the television show had come calling, the rest of his lab subtly, gently convinced him that some attention, no matter its provenance, would be better than none. He'd suffered the intrusion of a film crew into the sacred space of his laboratory, the cameramen galumphing about while the custodians of boom mikes chased behind; he'd submitted to an interview by the show's hostess who clearly didn't know a thing about science, and managed to rein in his usual impulse to bark at everyone besides his wife who asked him to explain himself. It was hard to know how the result would turn out—given the tenor of the other shows on Pscience!, it was probably wise to expect something that was mostly truth-like rather than strictly true, perhaps with footage of an explosion spliced in somewhere—but Rebecca thought that it would be good nonetheless to gather the gang together so they could cheer, and pat each other on the backs, and watch the proceedings with an appropriate degree of ironic distance. A little party would be just the thing.

Though few of the physicists who would be coming by this evening were exactly conversationalists, she was looking forward to seeing them all together, and to taking vicarious pride in their work. There would not be many other women there—the only female post-doc in Philip's lab, Alicia Merrill, was a person Rebecca found it difficult to get along with—but Rebecca's best friend Kate from back in the day would be showing up early to help out, full of her usual mischief and sass. ("Will Carson be there?" Kate had texted that morning. "Has he said hes coming?" Carson Tyler was one of Kate's exes, and though they were still on good terms, as Kate usually was with her exes, she still wanted to be prepared. "Dont know," Rebecca had texted back. "He doesnt reply to invites. Just shows up.")

Kate arrived ninety minutes before the shindig was set to start, a small, ginger-haired thing in a slinky black dress that seemed to be woven from vapor. She steadied herself on shoes with three-inch heels and open toes, and she wore an odd style of makeup that had briefly been in fashion fifteen years before: her eye shadow was faintly dusted with a few specks of silver glitter, just enough to catch the light when she blinked, just enough to draw a drifting gaze back to her face; her cherry-red toenail polish matched lipstick that Rebecca foresaw leaving imprints on the rims of her glasses, and requiring soaking and scouring by hand once it set. (But Rebecca was determined for this to be a real party, and a real party needed real glasses made from glass, not flimsy plastic cups extruded from a printer.)

Kate gripped a bottle of booze in each fist. "This is for *now*," she said, handing Rebecca a bottle of Australian Shiraz, "and this is for *later*," doing the same with a two-thirds-full handle of coconut rum whose label featured the visage of a grinning pirate.

Rebecca hadn't had a drink in two years, and even when she had been drinking she'd never had much of a discerning palate. But the unadorned, pale blue label pasted on the bottle of Shiraz seemed tasteful enough—not too baroque; not too silly—so she figured she could serve it without causing offense to those who cared about such things. However, the rum was best spirited out of sight. The taste of that was something she remembered clearly enough, and with it the rhythm and comfort of ritual—in late afternoon, when she was in the house alone, before the school bus disgorged her strange and charming charge, when shadows settled in the living room's corners, and women known only by their first names appeared on television to interview up-and-coming starlets and the anguished authors of memoirs. The pull of the hand to the bottle, the clink of the ice in the glass, the burn at the back of the throat, the repetition, the repetition. This is how it is done. You drop four pieces of ice in the pint glass; then you pour in the rum until it climbs just short of halfway up the side. Then you fill the glass to the top with Diet Coke. Then you knock it back and you do it again. Then you refill the ice tray just as the boy comes home, gaily hollering his greeting in the hall—

"So," said Kate. "First. Do you need help with anything. Second. Boys. Besides Carson, I mean. Who." There wasn't much to do besides spot cleaning, since these guests would be easy to please—

salty snacks and hoppy beers would do. Rebecca was also cooking scallops wrapped in strips of bacon, but more because she liked them herself than because anyone else would, and the only time she seemed to come across them was at weddings. There was something supremely decadent about the marriage of pork and mollusk that implied the dish should only be served at events of moment and gravity. But Rebecca figured that this night was probably at least half as important to Philip as a wedding would be to someone else (though he was making a big production of pretending he didn't care), so it was a fine enough excuse.

Kate sashayed into the kitchen, her bottom swaying like a pendulum's bob, and for a moment Rebecca saw a younger, brace-faced version of the woman in her bedroom, practicing that same walk in front of a mirror, perhaps with a social-studies textbook balanced on her head. Women usually only walked like that in movies, when cameras were pointed at their behinds—again, Rebecca felt that certain subtle wrongness, as if all the substance of the world were shot through with error. Even though she had known Kate since her twenties, she couldn't shake the feeling that her gait was not supposed to be theatric vamping, that her mutton-dressed-as-lamb makeup and her flirty demeanor were not supposed to be quite like that.

She followed Kate into the kitchen, wishing her friend hadn't brought the rum. The gesture was tone deaf: the wine would have been fine enough. But the occasional inconsiderate act was the price one paid for having someone like Kate as a friend—if she was not always as empathetic as one might like, she was faithful and dependable, and she'd answer her phone on the second ring. For all her flaws, she was good, or tried to be. You could say a lot worse about a lot of people.

As they washed and dried wine glasses that had accumulated a thin, sticky film after years spent in the back of a cupboard, Rebecca wondered if there was anyone coming tonight that she had a chance of setting Kate up with. Signs pointed to no: those scientists she knew whose behavior was closest to normal were either taken, or married to their work (on her bleaker days, Rebecca counted her own husband among this number), or had long-term, long-distance relationships with other academics in other states or countries. And poor Carson—it was a shame that didn't work out, but when Kate lost interest in a man she was never left wanting for a pretext to kick him to the curb. He was slow to respond to texts and IMs; he never carried a phone; and (okay, this was fair) he rarely talked about anything except his work. (Once Rebecca had said to him, placing a gentle hand on his shoulder after he'd gone on for ten minutes about some new device he was building for the lab whose name ended in -*ometer*, "Hey. I want to talk about something else now." He wasn't offended in the least—he was nice like that, and sarcasm probably would have been wasted on him anyway.)

As Kate and Rebecca chatted and caught each other up, the party's preparations came together—the still sizzling scallops were pulled from the oven and placed on plates; the wine glasses were set on a table in two neat rows; the plastic coverings were removed from sushi platters that Rebecca had picked up from a supermarket that afternoon; bags of tortilla chips were emptied into large bowls, with smaller bowls of salsa placed nearby. (Rebecca could already see herself on hands and knees, cleaning red flecks and spatters off the carpet. But if chips and salsa weren't here, Philip would leave the party and drive to the nearest convenience store to get them himself.) Rebecca turned on the living room's television, which displayed a program about the supposedly real science that lay behind a big-budget space-opera flick appearing in theaters that weekend. The show's host, a square-jawed male-model type in jeans and a leather jacket, walked toward a slowly retreating camera while delivering a monologue on the basics of spacecraft propulsion, investing his words with a phony, jittery urgency. For a moment Rebecca could see his face as it really was, its pockmarks and beard stubble mercilessly depicted in ultra-high definition; then his voice hitched as the TV's real-time graphics editing algorithms kicked in, smudging away his wrinkles and facial blemishes, outlining his head in a faint bloom of light.

Philip arrived with his compatriots Dennis and Carson in tow just as Rebecca and Kate were finishing up, the three physicists deep in the midst of a gossipy conversation about someone else's project, their inscrutable tales of laboratory politics punctuated with occasional bursts of laughter. The women greeted Philip's colleagues: portly Dennis, who grasped Rebecca's small hand in his huge one and bellowed her name with a joyous *basso profundo*, and Carson, who hung back behind. You could look at him and see that as an adolescent he'd never quite grown into his skin, but was one of those men who only start to find their looks once they slip past thirty. Time had sculpted his cheeks and hewn a pair of matched divots between his brows, and favored his face with lines that told a history of frequent unself-conscious smiles. He was, as always, sharply dressed, unlike his colleagues, who tended toward the proudly rumpled and thread-bare: a forest-green sweater vest and a tie to match; charcoal slacks with creases you could cut yourself on. Philip could stand to take some fashion advice from him, Rebecca thought.

"Carson," Kate said softly, lifting up on her toes and kissing him on the cheek as he shyly cut his gaze away from her. She made a little kissing noise: "M-*wah*."

"Hey, sweetie," Rebecca said to Philip *sotto voce*, sidling over to him. "Nervous?"

"What do I have to be nervous about?"

"Oh yes you are," she said, patting him on the shoulder. "Look at you."

"But I don't have to *do* anything. It would make more sense for me to worry if I had to *do* something, and I hadn't prepared enough. When I gave that talk at Frascati, and I'd only just finished the sec-ond draft on the plane over—then, I was nervous. When I was stand-ing at the lectern I felt stark naked. But all I have to do tonight is sit, and listen, and watch myself on television."

"You're *famous*." Rebecca smiled.

"Rebecca. Don't be ridiculous." But he tried, and failed, to stifle a grin.

Meanwhile, Dennis had plopped himself down in front of the tele-vision, seating himself tailor-style on the floor with a large bowl of tortilla chips nestled in his lap and the salsa beside him. Rebecca glanced at Kate, who raised an eyebrow, but that was the kind of thing you expected Dennis to do, and he was so guileless and good-natured that it was hard for him to cause true offense. He was careful to tap each chip with his index finger as he held it over the salsa bowl, fastidiously dislodging any potentially wayward drips.

On the screen, the show's host was now seated in a leather-upholstered armchair, leaning eagerly into the face of the woman opposite him. According to the words dancing across the bottom of the screen, she was the film's "scientific consultant." "So what you mean," the host said, "is that faster-than-light travel could become a reality. That we could soon open up trade routes to the stars, with all the mystery and the danger and the wonder that might entail."

The woman squirmed in her chair. "Well, there are certainly some major barriers that would have to be overcome, but—I mean, I guess you can't prove a negative—"

The image cut quickly to the host staring directly into the camera, once again alone. "You can't prove a negative," he said sagely. "Humanity is not in the *business* of proving negatives. And we will soon leap over those barriers, just as if they had never even been there. The first step in that epic journey begins exclusively in theaters, this weekend."

More people started to show up now, and a few of the men had brought their wives and girlfriends along. Female physicists were a relative rarity, in Rebecca's experience. On the occasions when she'd come across them during her relationship with Philip, she'd found them to be cold and impenetrable—she felt a flinty edge to their personalities that made her uncomfortable, with challenges in their greetings and dismissals in their goodbyes. Their sentences seemed to spring from their mouths fully composed, with no slips of the tongue or midstream shifts in thought. Kate wasn't like that, which was why, despite the occasional instance of obliviousness, she and Rebecca could be best friends—she was comforting and small, and she talked about things that normal people talked about, and you could be around her without being constantly reminded that there were things you didn't know, and things you couldn't do.

Alicia Merrill arrived alone, and it was once again time for Rebecca to play the hostess: Kate was busy talking to Carson, over in the doorway between the living room and the kitchen.

"Have we met before? A couple of times, I think," Alicia said, even though Rebecca was quite sure they'd met more than just a couple of times. "I saw you at a Christmas party once." A handshake from her, not a hug. A firm squeeze of the hand. Swallowed up in a baggy knit sweater, Alicia couldn't have weighed a hundred and five soaking wet. She wore a pair of beaten-up Nike running shoes, and in her heels Rebecca had a full six inches on her. But Rebecca still found the woman slightly disconcerting, with her whippet-thin build and pinpoint gaze.

Alicia shifted her grip. *She probably keeps one of those springy hand exercisers in a desk drawer,* Rebecca thought, *preparing for moments like this.* "You're well?" Alicia said.

"I'm doing okay. A little nervous. It's Philip's big night, you know."

One side of Alicia's mouth twitched upward. She still clasped Rebecca's hand.

"So can I get you a drink?" Rebecca said, the last word of her question blurred by a skittish half laugh. "What are you having?"

Slowly, Alicia pulled her hand away.

"I rarely drink," Alicia said. "And I'm running tomorrow: training for a mini-triathlon. So. Seltzer water. If you have it."

■

"So are you gonna give me a hug or what?" said Kate. "Like I'd let you get away with hiding in a corner. Come here." But Carson's embrace ended before it began, his hasty withdrawal somehow managing to precede the tentative touch of his fingertips on her bare shoulder blades.

"You look good," Carson said.

"So do you," Kate said, though she didn't really think he did—the same features that meant maturity to Rebecca signaled simple age to Kate. His eyes had a flat, distant gaze, and his brow seemed clenched in a constant frown; his ensemble struck Kate as natty rather than stylish, better suited to someone fifteen years his senior. And he needed to eat something, so his face wouldn't look so pinched. "How are you these days?"

"Good. It's been crazy at the lab lately. A lot of stuff going on."

"Sounds like it."

They sipped their wine, saying nothing.

"So what about you?" Carson said quietly.

"No, I don't have a boyfriend," Kate replied, wondering why her mouth was making those odd shapes and noises. "But I'm okay with that." *Kate to self—stop talking.* "I mean, online it's always the same ten guys, and, yeah." *Kate! Zip it!*

"Me too," said Carson. "Okay. With not having a girlfriend." There was no hint of bitterness or falsehood in his tone; he was perfectly nice, like he always was.

They simultaneously downed half their glasses.

Then Carson sighed. "Well, okay. Except that—I've got that thing going where I feel like my life is a total waste sometimes. This work is my life, and right now my work is awful, so . . . Q.E.D."

"Everyone thinks their job is awful sometimes. That's why it's a *job*."

"No—not like that! Not like, *But what I really feel I'd be best at is traveling and seeing the world.* Not exactly. Take other people, right? A lot of them have regular hours they're at work, and they sell their time for the money that lets them make the most of the time they have left over. But most people don't want to—don't laugh—most people don't want to *change the world*, right? They might, you know, go out and vote or something, but for the most part they're happy to live in the world like it is. And there's nothing wrong with that. But stupid me—I have *ideals*."

"But—"

"And I'm not even bragging about it!" Carson interrupted. "Because ideals aren't *good* for me. They aren't *healthy*. Ideals are for *suckers*. All they do is let guys like *that*"—and he motioned toward Philip in the living room with a nod of his head—"get over on me."

"But that's good about you, that you've got principles," Kate finished. "Really. I like that about you. Liked it." *Christ, Kate.*

"But see—okay, look. Every once in a while, actually a *lot* lately, it gets to be around six o'clock, and not only am I still in the lab, but I probably have about three or four more hours of *being* in the lab to look forward to, working on a project that hasn't gotten me more than third-author credit on a few papers in some journals that aren't that spectacular to start with. That's it. And there's probably zero real-world application for this stuff, and maybe it's never going to work. So I'm still in the lab when sane people are knocking off for the day, and I think—like if I were a normal person? A normal single guy? I'd come home and pop dinner in the microwave, and maybe play some video games, and then go out to a bar. But instead I'm going to be in the lab, parsing code and taking another set of measurements on machines that aren't working the way they should. And I start to think about maybe hanging it up.

"But it's like, even when he's in his office with the door shut, he can *tell* when someone in his lab is having second thoughts. It's like he's a telepath. Because that's when he shows up. He'll just start talking to you, kind of idly, in the kind of voice he never uses except then, this kind of voice you'd use to read a bedtime story to a kid, not necessarily even talking about the project, and you can look in his eyes and just tell how much he believes in capital-S *Science*. And after about ten minutes of this, I go from thinking 'Man, I could go for a drink right now' to 'You know, he's going to be here later on tonight trying to figure out whether our Planck-Wheeler clock needs recalibrating, and it'd be a shame to leave him here by himself. And if we can confirm that there's nothing going wrong with the clock, maybe then we'll start to be able to figure out why we're not seeing the results our models say we ought to see. So I just need to stick with it a little longer. In fact, I should just run down to the sporting-goods store the next time I get a chance, and pick up a cot. It'd be nice to have a cot in the office, for quick little naps.' Because I have *ideals*, see. Same as he does—he's got the same disease. And he knows it. And he *exploits* it.

"Yeah, sure, he's brilliant," Carson said, nodding toward Philip again. "And you could say he hasn't gotten his due. But sometimes I can't stand the son of a—"

"Kate? Carson?" Rebecca said from directly behind them. Carson's mouth clamped shut.

"Hey, girl," Kate said.

"They're getting ready to start, I think. It's time."

■

In the living room, Alicia and Philip stood apart from the rest of the crowd, who were now seated around Dennis, gazing up at the television. Alicia spoke low and fast, repeatedly cutting her eyes back to the rest of the physicists, dispensing for a moment with the slightly deferential tone she and the other post-docs normally used with Philip when they were in the lab. (At work she called him Philip instead of using his title, of course, but post-docs had a way of speaking their adviser's first name with the subtle intonation of an honorific.) "I'm going to be honest," she said. "I don't like this. Everyone else might, but I don't. It's not as bad as announcing results before you've verified them, not as bad as the stuff that NASA's dragged people into by teasing a press conference like it's some kind of movie premiere, but it isn't good. We're going to be embarrassed."

"But we're really close," Philip said. "Maybe another year. Eighteen months on the outside."

"We've been a year away from sorting this out for years now," Alicia said.

Philip winced. "I think you're making too much of a big deal about a cable show that no one watches."

"Well, *someone* has to. I can't believe you let them talk you into this. I mean, sure, everyone in the field thinks we're a joke, but fortunately we were able to find people to fund us who get a kick out of comedy. Granted, I'd rather *not* be on that particular payroll if I could help it—"

"Excuse me?" Rebecca said, standing behind Alicia.

"*What*," Alicia said flatly, turning toward her.

Rebecca looked at Philip quizzically. His expression was a whiteboard wiped clean.

"Would you like to join the rest of us in front of the TV?" Rebecca asked hesitantly. "It's time."

■

If you had never watched that much television, then you might wonder how it was that the President of the United States had found the time to record a video introduction to every program that appeared on every one of the hundreds of available channels—not just a generic twenty-second speech that gave his imprimatur to the program about to commence, but a short monologue that always seemed to be tailored to the program's subject matter, linking it to some larger political or spiritual meaning. But keen-eyed viewers knew that the President repeated himself: he almost always delivered one of a finite number of canned speeches, perhaps tweaking a word or two in a halfhearted effort at personalization, and anyone who viewed a variety of programs for long enough was bound to see a prologue for a telecast of an English soccer match repurposed a few months later for a stream of a *StarCraft III* tournament final.

This repetition was easiest to notice for fans of science documentaries. For programs like the broadcasts of mega-church Sunday-morning services, it wasn't uncommon for the presidential preamble to mention the same book of the Bible that would be the subject of the minister's sermon. But for science documentaries, the relationship of the monologue to the program that would follow was usually tenuous at best: in fact, as the presidential seal appeared on the screen at nine o'clock sharp, Dennis and Carson began to try to guess which address they were about to hear.

"It's going to be the one about Mendel," Dennis said. "Where he talks about Mendel and his peas, except he calls them beans."

"Nope," said Carson. "We're going to get the talk about science and empire. You know the one. The one that's supposed to make you feel good about doing science when you hear it."

"Wanna bet?" said Dennis. "Twenty says it's Mendel and beans."

"And twenty on science and empire," Carson said. "But no payout if it's something else."

"Get your Gipper ready, then," Dennis said, and then the image of the presidential seal dissolved to reveal the man himself, sitting in an armchair whose frame seemed to have been carved from a single hunk of redwood. Rows of vintage leather-bound hardcover books with matching spines lined the shelves behind him; the flickering lighting discreetly implied a fireplace just offscreen.

"Good evening!" he said. "I'm glad I have this chance to talk with you. Now, before we start, I want to tell you something: I want to give you something to think about while you watch. You know, I remember—and this is back when I was a kid, growing up in Newark—I remember that in my parents' house, the word *empire* used to be a *dirty* word."

"Damn it," said Dennis, and got out his wallet.

"And my mother—you wouldn't believe, looking at me now, that I was her son—she was always going on about how we'd been making all these mistakes as a country, how the government just couldn't do anything to satisfy her, and she'd wind up these little rants by saying, 'You know what this is? This is what happens when a nation turns into an *empire*.' And the way she said it, it sounded like the foulest swear word."

"Look!" said Dennis, pointing at the TV. "There's something wrong with the President."

"Because that word, *empire*—that word was loaded with all the histories of all the empires that came before us, right? Rome, and the Turks, and the British—all of them, declining and falling."

"I don't see what you're talking about," said Kate, sitting down on the opposite side of the group from Carson, and that was when the President leaned forward in his chair, closer to the camera. "But let me tell you this," he said. His right eye was its usual brown, but his left, for a moment, sported an iris of shimmering indigo. Then he blinked, and the purple disappeared.

"Huh," Carson said. "Interesting."

"Look at American history," the President said, both his eyes brown again. "Think about the way that Americans rose up and just shrugged off the chains of the British. But they weren't just strong— they were smart, too! Because after that, the Founding Fathers immediately sat down and proceeded to *invent* a new kind of nation. Our wisest men came together, and studied all the histories of all the nations that had come before us, and saw what mistakes they'd made, and *invented* a new nation that would not repeat those mistakes."

"I still don't see what you people are talking about," Kate said, and then the President's visage changed again: this time both of his eyes turned purple and then, as if to prove a point, a third eye opened up in the middle of his forehead, colored a gleaming goldenrod. "And if we got *that* right," he said, "and I think we can all agree that America got that right, then why couldn't we do what no country on earth had done before us, and get empire right?"

"I told you," said Dennis.

"Yeah, okay, oh em gee," Kate said.

"It's the TV," said Philip. "The 'shopping chip in the TV. It's having trouble resolving his face."

"I'll tell you one of the things that makes me think we are getting empire right. Look at the strength of American science." The color of the President's tie shifted from red to blue to green and back to blue. His eyes and nose disappeared for a moment, leaving an empty stretch of skin marked only by a moving mouth; then they blinked back into being.

"Rebecca, turn off the 'shopping," Philip said.

"But then everyone'll look *gross*," said Kate.

Rebecca brought up the TV's remote-control app on her phone and pressed the button that seemed most likely to get something done. The image on the TV screen became overlaid by a menu littered with cryptic hieroglyphics, the myriad branches of a decision tree blooming in three dimensions. Tint and tone; aspect ratio and time delay. "Look at history," the President said, "and you'll see that when empires start to fall, the science and the art are always what go first. In a dying empire people can't innovate anymore; they can't think new thoughts; they can't see the world for what it really is."

"Rebecca," Philip said, "turn off the 'shopping."

"I heard you the first time." She pressed a couple of other buttons, and the audio of the President's monologue switched to the Spanish play-by-play of a soccer game.

"That's not right," Philip said.

"Well since *you* know so much why don't you—"

"Because I'm not the one who watches this TV: you do."

"Hey, girl," Kate said softly. "I have an idea. Maybe we can just watch it like it is? It'll be funny, to see Philip on TV without a face. It'll make things seem not so serious. Isn't that a good idea, Carson?" Kate looked directly across the room at him.

"Um," said Carson, pinned by Philip's glare. "Yeah."

The audio switched back to the President's voice as the screen's menus twirled and expanded.

". . . Romans and philosophy, or the Turks and their math," he said. "But you can look at science shows like the one you're about to watch, and see that even as we aim to do all the things those past dead empires tried and failed to accomplish, and even as we succeed in those aims beyond the dreams of the Founding Fathers, the state of our science is strong! We are getting empire right!" There were two extra mouths on his face where his eyes should have been, and they were widened in surprise.

"If you can't get it straight," said Philip, "we'll just have to watch it like it is."

"Ten physicists in here and not one of you knows how to operate a television, I guess," said Rebecca.

"I don't watch TV except when I'm at someone else's house," said Dennis, munching on tortilla chips.

"Shh," said Kate quickly. "Wait—there it is. Rebecca. Look. *Revert to factory settings*. Just try hitting that."

"I make my sons watch science shows," said the President. "I sit them down in front of the TV, and I make them watch. Because I want them to believe in this."

The menu's branches collapsed into themselves and vanished. The screen brightened considerably and the audio's volume increased, but the surreal artifacts decorating the President's face quickly winked away.

Philip said nothing as Alicia leaned over to whisper something into his ear.

"Hey, you got it," said Kate to Rebecca. "Now sit down with the rest of us and watch the show. And relax!"

As Rebecca made her way around the group to sit down next to Philip, with Alicia on Philip's other side, the President finished his monologue: ". . . and I would ask you to have this thought in front of your mind, always. Say it aloud if you feel like it. Don't be ashamed to say it.

"We are getting empire right."

■

Philip's project would be the subject of the second of the show's three segments; the first, according to the show's narrator, who slid her rimless eyeglasses up the bridge of her nose, was about "collective intelligence." The screen switched to footage of a flock of thousands of birds in flight, over a lake whose mirrored surface reflected the snowcapped mountains rising above it. "Collective intelligence," the announcer breathed huskily, and all at once, as if in response to an angel's unseen signal, the direction of the flock's flight snapped from west to north.

"She sounds like she's in a porno," said Kate. "And she needs to button her blouse."

"I think that's the point," Dennis said.

"I doubt she has any idea what she's reading," said Alicia.

The image cut to a headshot of a scientist explaining the principle of collective intelligence in a laconic drone. "One way to explain this that's not perfectly accurate, but at least has the benefit of being easily understood by the general public—"

"He sounds so condescending," said Kate.

"I'm sure he doesn't mean to come off that way," said Rebecca.

"—is that the information of collective intelligence is contained in the gaps between the birds of a flock that's in flight. It allows a group of myriad discrete entities to present the illusion of behaving as a single mind, with a single purpose." Footage followed of thousands of bats flying forth from the mouth of a cave, rising to swirl in a perfectly formed midair spiral, backlit by the morning sun. Then the birds again, switching direction as if choreographed from on high.

Now they were seeing the interior of a laboratory that looked the way labs used to look in summer blockbuster movies, everything clean and polished and angular, the lighting harsh and the contrast high. Technicians in spotless white coats walked purposefully down white-walled corridors, on their way to perform astonishing feats of intellectual endeavor.

"Not a roll of duct tape to be seen there, I'd bet," said Carson. "No empty soda bottles. No takeout boxes."

"The Defense Agency for Pure and Applied Science," the announcer said. "Created by the merger of a division of DARPA with divisions of Homeland Security and the Department of Energy, it is now one of the most well-endowed patrons of scientific research in the world."

In three-quarter profile, an Army two-star general in a service uniform, his left breast sporting three rows of insignia. "That collective intelligence project—that's a call I helped to make that I'm really proud of. Let me give you a little background. Look back to the twentieth century, and you'll see that universities used to have the money to support science that didn't have any apparent real-world application—cosmology; string theory; you know, sense-of-wonder stuff. But those times are gone—state schools are strapped, and just about all of the second-tier private universities have reorganized into for-profit organizations. You see the same thing with corporations— once upon a time they'd make donations to pure science just for the PR, but now they're busy trying to add that last few miles to a car's range before its battery needs a charge, so they don't have time for this final-frontier business.

"But defense is always doing well financially: I wouldn't say we have more money than we know what to do with, but when we pick projects to back, we don't have to be too risk-averse. We can throw money at research that might seem esoteric, or even crazy. Because you can never tell what pure research will turn out to have some kind of military application in the long run. And if that project that everyone else thought was useless pays off? It will pay off big. Big enough to pay for all the research that didn't have potential for military use, that just advanced science for its own sake.

"Collective intelligence, that bird project—that was one of our long-shot bets. We couldn't even see how to make it work at first—we just had a hunch. And it paid off."

On a clean white table, what looked at first like a small, silvery mound of sand. The camera moved closer to it, closer still, switching seamlessly at some unidentifiable point from digital video to a computer-generated image. Magnification revealed that each of the seeming grains of sand was a strange little robot; the tiny, insect-like devices crawled friskily over each other like fire ants in a bed that had just been poked by a stick. Each had a pair of telescoping antennae, and six legs that ended in needle points, and two wide, translucent wings that nervously flicked open and shut like Japanese paper fans.

"Nanobots," purred the announcer.

"Now what we can do at DAPAS," the general said in voiceover, "is take research from several different highly specialized fields and combine it together to create new applications. Collective intelligence? Wasn't much use to us on its own, but when we put it next to nanorobotics, we developed some prototype nonlethal weaponry that's showing a lot of promise. It's done well in the field when deployed against the Dakotan secessionists, and soon we'll be shipping these out to our troops in the Middle East."

A cut to computer animation of an unmanned reconnaissance drone, flying low over a barren landscape. A hatch in the drone's belly slid open and ejected a vacuum-sealed plastic bag that burst as it collided with the ground. The camera quickly zoomed into the swirling cloud of dust that emerged—Rebecca saw the same nanobots, now arrayed in hundreds of purposeful phalanxes, like squadrons of Allied planes in the final act of a World War II movie.

"We can control the swarm by remote from the rear," the general said. "Their size makes it nearly impossible to defend against them—seriously, your chances would be better against a horde of wasps. But they can work together with a single purpose that's far larger than their size. We can tell them to clog the barrels of enemy weapons. And if the enemy isn't wearing a nanobot-secure helmet, which is prohibitively expensive for a lot of the people we're going up against, that gives us lots of additional options for nonlethal incapacitation. We can send the swarm down the nose to play havoc with the respiratory system; we can tell it to enter through the mouth and start working on their digestive tracts. We can tell them—and this is absolutely fantastic for interrogation purposes—to work their way beneath an enemy's eyelids. Watch this."

The image looked like surveillance footage of a camera mounted to the ceiling of a holding cell; a superimposed digital clock jittered in a corner of the screen. In the cell was a pale, shirtless, emaciated, screaming man, probably not more than twenty-three; across his hairless chest was tattooed, in a neat sans-serif script, the phrase MAGNETO WAS RIGHT. He moaned nonsense as he staggered across the floor and swatted at the air before his face, his eyes squeezed shut, his face pulled into a grimace. "We loaded about eighty thousand of those things in there with him. Gave him pure hell." A tear tinged with blood ran down his cheek, and in a moment when he opened his eyes and stared directly into the surveillance camera, Rebecca could see that they were now colored a featureless, shining silver.

Rebecca tried to imagine what that would be like—even an eyelash trapped beneath a contact lens was enough to drive most people crazy. But hundreds of those little things, so small you couldn't make them out without a microscope, crawling all over the surfaces of your eyes. Digging into the flesh of your eyes with their little needle legs until you said the secret thing to make them stop.

"Collective intelligence," the general said in voiceover. "Beautiful stuff."

"Fucking *awesome*," said Dennis.

The program cut to a commercial.

Philip stared at the floor.

■

As the second segment began, Rebecca reflected that Philip wasn't coming off quite as coldly as she'd feared he might. It helped that in addition to getting him to sit for an interview, the crew had shot a good deal of additional B-roll footage of him working in the lab, and though it was clearly staged, it served to humanize him. ("They asked me," he said in high dudgeon after coming home from the lab one evening, "to sit at a desk, a clean desk with nothing on it, and write. On paper. With a *pencil*. They said: *Don't look at the camera. Just make up some equations or something. Throw some Greek letters in them, and maybe we can get a shot of the paper, too.* It was laughable, Rebecca. It was fatuous." But fatuous or not, here was Philip sitting at his desk, dutifully scribbling away, looking like a dinner-theater actor playing the part of a scientist.)

"Here at Stratton University in New Jersey," the announcer cooed, "Philip Steiner and his small but devoted team are hard at work on an idea that has captivated the imagination of humanity since the novelist H. G. Wells first conceived of it in 1895."

"Oh, no," said Alicia. "Oh no."

"Philip calls it a causality violation device," the announcer said.

Sitting next to Rebecca, Philip bristled. "I call it that because that's what it is!" Rebecca reached over and patted his hand.

The screen showed Philip in the lab, speaking past the camera to someone out of the field of view as Carson fiddled with machinery in the background. "There's Carson," said Dennis. He had finished the entire bowl of tortilla chips and wiped the bowl of salsa clean.

"I must have removed and reattached that robotic arm a dozen times in front of those guys," Carson said. "That's not even from our lab. We got it from another building."

Onscreen, Philip was wearing a lab coat. He never wore a lab coat. It looked fresh from its packaging. He was cradling a robot in both arms, an eight-legged contraption of steel and plastic with a digital clock strapped to its back. "This is Arachne," he said. "Our little causality violation detector. For all the work that's going into this experiment, the central concept is actually pretty simple."

"You're doing good here," said Rebecca. Despite Philip's protestations before the party that he was generally unconcerned, he was clearly worried—he'd gone pale and tight-lipped.

"So," the onscreen Philip continued, "Arachne's clock is synced by radio to the atomic clock in Boulder, Colorado, one of the most accurate timekeeping devices in the world. Here's the idea: We send Arachne into the causality violation chamber, retrieve her a few moments later, and see if the clock she's carrying is still synced to the clock in Boulder. If Arachne's clock is running faster—and if all works perfectly, we'd expect her clock to be about an hour faster—then that'll mean that she's existed for a longer period of time relative to the scientists who are observing her. Which would mean, in turn, that we had successfully created a causality violation."

"In short—" the announcer said.

"Oh no," said Alicia.

"—if Philip Steiner is successful, he will have built—"

"She's actually going to say it—"

The announcer gasped. "The world's first *time machine*," she said.

"God*damn* it," Alicia said. "I knew they'd take that corny angle."

They saw a rapid series of clips from twentieth-century movies: an open-shirted Rod Taylor rescuing Yvette Mimieux from a rubber-faced Morlock; the USS *Nimitz* appearing in Pearl Harbor a day before the fateful attack; Michael J. Fox stepping out of the gull wing door of a modified DeLorean.

"This is so embarrassing," Alicia said, while Philip quietly clenched his fist and the rest of the physicists stared at the television in despair. "And oh hey *look*, without even telling us, they went out and got an interview with Anne Lippincott for this dog-and-pony show. Ridiculous."

Anne Lippincott, according to the banner displayed at the bottom of the screen, was a representative of the Committee for Ethical Restraint in Science. "Well, of *course* it's unethical," she said, gesturing wildly with one long-fingered hand while she brushed a flaxen lock of hair back behind her ear with the other. "If these positively *amoral* people are going to go and honest-to-goodness rip a hole in the spacetime continuum, then that's something that affects everyone—we all have to live on this planet together, and it's something they shouldn't even think about doing without first consulting the American people, so we can put it to a vote. You got all sorts of stuff going on now that's unethical, that's amoral—you got that business with the stem cells, you got people eating steaks that didn't even come off a cow—and now we've got these absolutely reckless people who just can't imagine that there is even one piece of knowledge that God just *might* have chosen to place off-limits for a *reason*, that maybe God made space and time the way they are for a *reason*—"

"Turn this *off*," Philip growled. "I don't want to see any more."

Rebecca quietly pressed a button on her phone. The television burped a little ditty and went black, shutting off Lippincott's rant in mid-sentence.

"That's it," Alicia said to the rest of the silent group. "We're screwed."

2

GOOD CATCH

The next morning, Rebecca came up out of another series of disquieting dreams (capsizing ships; snakes with human faces) to find Philip already out of bed, grunting his way through his daily exercises on the floor nearby. For the next few days, until he placed that disastrous television appearance at the back of his mind, he'd be more difficult to deal with than usual.

For as long as Rebecca had been married to Philip, he had started his day by scooping four heaping tablespoons out of a tub of low-fat vanilla yogurt and plopping them into his mouth, dropping to the floor wherever it was convenient, and doing push-ups to the point of failure. His record before collapse was fifty-five.

Rebecca stared at the bedroom ceiling, listening to her husband mutter numbers through clenched teeth. "Nnnng: thirty-nine. Nnnn: forty. Nnnn! Forty-*one*." His arms were probably trembling already. She had pointed out to him more than once that he ought to rest for a day or two between his workouts, so that he could give his torn muscles time to knit themselves back together, bigger and stronger. He'd nodded at her and continued to do things the same way he always did, year after year, his pecs and triceps always sore.

"Hnnn-nn: Forty . . . *five*—" The breath went out of him as he dropped to the floor wheezing.

Rebecca had figured that there must be a good reason that Philip put himself through this. (Strength training was not her choice: she'd never been fond of the idea of doing crunches or lifting hunks of iron until pain and fatigue got the better of you. Philip had tried to tell her that that post-workout ache was a "good ache," but that couldn't be a clearer example of an oxymoron.)

Perhaps Philip was just not interested in becoming stronger; perhaps it was not the exercise itself that mattered to him, but the experience of it. Maybe he wanted to set the tone of each morning by always trying, and always failing, the consequent band of pain across his chest serving as a reminder of that failure to carry him through the day.

Still breathing heavily, Philip clambered to his feet and shuffled out of the bedroom, wincing and shrugging his shoulders.

∎

As Rebecca drifted in and out of a light doze, she heard the usual series of sounds of Philip getting ready for work: the hiss of the shower-head; the *thunk* of the refrigerator door shutting; the voice of an NPR newscaster muted to a tranquil murmur even as she related details of the most horrific events. Rebecca remembered the other morning noises that, a few years earlier, would have provided a counter-point to Philip's: the clink of a spoon as she deposited it in their boy's cereal bowl; her gentle but continuous harangue as she coaxed him into dressing and tried to teach him to match his shirt and pants. But sometimes an incipient tantrum she had no time for meant that checks and stripes were the order of the day. "Have fun at the circus," she'd say to Sean's back as he ran out the door to catch the bus.

Rebecca also remembered mimosas. This is how you make mimosas. You put the bottle of Prosecco in the back of the refrigerator the night before, after your husband and your son are asleep. You aren't hiding it, exactly—it's just that the back of the fridge gets colder than the front, and in the morning you want the bottle to be nice and chilled, right? After the house is empty the next morning, you uncork the bottle and pour Prosecco into a wine glass until it's two-thirds full. Then you fill it almost to the rim with orange juice. Then, yes, you take the first sip, yes, and that cold tart effervescence never fails to shock your tongue, the sweet citrus flavor chasing just behind to soothe it. Prosecco goes flat quickly; best to kill the bottle by afternoon—

She heard the front door shut, sat up in bed, and sighed. Corn-flakes and black coffee for breakfast. Then work.

■

A person who saw Philip entering his non-autonomous car at his home each morning and getting out of it at his lab twenty-five min-utes later might think that he'd perhaps been replaced by an actor, one who'd been hired to play the part of Philip based on his resem-blance to the man and not his talent. It seemed as if on his way over to the laboratory that the set of his jaw changed ever so slightly, that the blue of his eyes changed from water to ice.

The transformation was not entirely unconscious; at times Philip was not even sure that it was necessary, though by now it had become a habit that, like his morning push-ups, he could not do without. He did not feel that he had to become a different person in the lab (and in fact, the experience of watching himself on television last night, of seeing himself perform himself, had discomforted him even more than he had expected). He merely thought that the proper discharge of his duties required that certain aspects of his personality had to be brought to the forefront, while others were temporarily suppressed.

It was perfectly natural. Humans are always transforming, even when sitting still. At a family gathering a few years ago Rebecca's mother, Marianne, had told Philip, as if it were fact, that all of the atoms in a human body replaced themselves every seven years, and that this was clear evidence for a constancy of consciousness that was so near to the idea of a soul that it might as well be called by the name. Under Rebecca's glare, Philip had managed to refrain from mention-ing radiocarbon studies that had demonstrated the persistence of the material that made up tooth enamel: he sometimes forgot that what he saw as simple truth others viewed as pedantry. But to be fair, aside from her needlessly theological conclusion, Marianne had been more right than wrong: inside of a year, almost *all* of the stuff of which you were made got regularly switched out for other stuff as you ate and drank and breathed, and yet if you said you had the same identity you did a year ago, no one would think to call you a liar. Being is always becoming; people change and stay the same. What is true for bodies is also true for selves: even the most honest person has many faces, none of which are false.

The fact that Philip Steiner loved Rebecca as much as he loved doing science was an indication of the depth of his devotion to her, not of its absence (even if declarations of his affection went unspoken more often than they might have; even if the science never fully left his mind). But if those twin loves were equal in degree, they were greatly different in kind and in the nature of their demands. The face with which Philip looked upon his wife was not one he could present to the beautiful device that occupied his days: it wanted a colder gaze.

By the time he arrived at the lab he had changed from Philip to Philip. Processor cycles that, at other times, were dedicated to parsing Rebecca's mood, or mentally replaying Rush's song "Fly by Night," or imagining possible lives for the absent boy in timelines other than this, were retasked to a single purpose. When he passed through the door he was ready to give all of his attention to the machine, and for it to favor him in return with its unending stream of maddening, wonderful questions.

■

Her breakfast finished, Rebecca was now on the treadmill, its pace set to a walk; she wore a T-shirt and loosely fitting gym shorts, with monitor shades on her face, a headset stuck in her ear, and a single-hand keyboard strapped to her left forearm. All of this gear communicated wirelessly with the desktop computer in the next room: maybe it would've been more practical just to be in the room with it instead of on the treadmill, but if she spent her whole day sitting there she'd just get fatter. As it was, a slight extra roll of flesh still crept over the band of her shorts, but a few pounds picked up ounce by ounce over a couple of decades were nothing more than evidence of a life lived well. For those women without golden genes, the choice as you headed toward forty was either this or that tough, stringy look that came from twice-daily ninety-minute gym sessions, followed by meals of rice cakes garnished with kale leaves. Like Alicia Merrill. Philip's post-doc. She'd be like that not long from now. Always with the running, and the yoga, and the water, and those awful insect bars. Carrying around a stainless-steel water bottle with her all the time, telling you she needed to stay hydrated. When you get to this age your body becomes your history. You could look at her and see she'd had a joyless life.

It had not taken long for Rebecca to learn how to operate the sixteen-key keyboard and the thumb-powered nubbin that pushed the cursor across the screens of her monitor shades—she could handle the controls while moving at a slow walk, not so fast that she might get winded while on the phone. Rebecca worked part-time as a customer service representative for Lovability, the online dating service where, eleven years ago, she'd actually met the man who was now her husband (and where Kate had first met Carson, come to think of it). The people who called her were generally in deep and barely disguised distress, their complaints about double-billed charges and dropped connections serving as proxies for other, deeper grievances. It was not unusual for Rebecca to find herself dragged into an interminable conversation about the fickleness of the human heart, or on the receiving end of a rant that sounded as if it had been lifted from a Jacobean revenge play. It would not do, in the midst of one of these conversations, to have to catch her breath. Hence the slow walk, better than sitting still.

The first call came in three minutes after she logged on, a thirty-nine-year-old divorcé on the Silver Plan (which guaranteed priority customer service: she'd have to turn on the charm, since her electronic masters might be listening, measuring the pitch of her voice for the modulations that indicated the appearance of pleasure in conversation. Flat affects earned red flags on your record; too many and a supervisor told you you were done for the day).

"Lova-*bil*-ity, this is Re-*bec*-ca," she sang, then dropped into a purr that came from the back of the throat and seemed to promise special unmentionable services for Silver Plan customers: "How can I *help* you?"

"Hello!" the customer screamed, and Rebecca dialed down the volume of her headset. His profile came up on her shades, blurry at first, but snapping into clear 3D as she tapped a temple and settled them on her nose. PhilPhilliesFan1984. There was half the problem right there: profile name too long and confusing; gave away his age right off the bat. His photo hovered next to his vital stats. Class-B health care from his employer. He could get a wife with that alone if his standards weren't too crazy, a pretty woman in her thirties with asthma or scoliosis, some kind of flaw you'd never really notice.

"I have a problem!" PhilPhilliesFan1984 said.

"Just a moment while I pull up your file," Rebecca said, buying more time. His photo was horrible. A lot of people with profiles on Lovability hired professional photographers, who spent three hours in Photoshop for every one behind the camera. But this guy was using some candid photo from a wedding reception, with a heavily pixelated toupee added to his pate. Poor bastard might have even 'shopped it himself, unskilled and unaware.

His profile message was entirely in capital letters. Screaming online just like he screamed on the phone. At least it was accurate.

"GOOD CATCH"!

I AM A "GOOD CATCH". I AM A KIND AND LOVING MAN WHO MADE SOME BAD DECISIONS WHEN I WAS YOUNGER. BUT NOW I AM READY TO MEET THE "LOVE OF MY LIFE"! OTHER THAN MY BABY GIRL, HEHE. SHE JUST STARTED SIXTH GRADE SO SHE IS NOT SUCH A BABY GIRL ANYMORE, HEHE! SHE LIVES WITH HER MOM MOST OF THE TIME BUT SHE IS STILL THE "APPLE OF MY EYE".

I LIKE BASEBALL (GO PHILS!!) AND MOVIES FROM "BACK IN THE DAY" (ARNOLD!!) AND HANGING OUT WITH MY DOG RUDY (HE IS A "MUTT" FROM A SHELTER.) AND I LIKE JUST KICKING BACK WITH SOME BEERS OR EVEN A BOTTLE OF WINE. I HAVE BEEN EMPLOYED AT THE SAME PLACE FOR THIRTEEN YEARS, AND I AM A GOOD PROVIDER.

I AM LOOKING FOR A WOMAN WITH NO "BAGGAGE" WHO LIKES TO BE TAKEN CARE OF (BUT NO "GOLDDIGGERS" LOL!) IF YOU WANT TO MEET RUDY AND MY BABY GIRL, SEND ME A SMILE! P.S. PLEASE, NO "NEGRESSES". I AM NOT A RACIST BUT I CANNOT HELP THE WAY MY HEART THINKS.

Hm.

"I have a problem!" PhilPhilliesFan1984 reminded Rebecca.

"Okay," she said, opting for perkiness rather than seduction. "I've got your profile up. How can I help you?"

"I am on the Silver Plan. And this lets me give out one hundred Smiles, and get back a hundred and fifty Smiles."

"That's the monthly allowance on the Silver Plan, yes."

"And this month I have given out all one hundred of my Smiles!"

Quickly, moving her thumb on the keyboard's nubbin, Rebecca

pulled up a trend analysis of his clickthroughs on other profiles. Several graphs sprang into view, with dozens of images of women floating behind them in illusory three-dimensional space. As she expected, there was a huge discrepancy between the profile of the kind of woman he declared he'd most like to meet (between ages thirty and forty; Christian or "spiritual but not religious"; looking for new friends) and the average profile he was actually likely to spend time viewing and messaging. Not one of the women he'd checked out for more than thirty seconds was older than twenty-three. Pinched kissyfaces; midriffs sporting pierced navels; bolt-on boobs tumbling out of tank tops. Webcam bait. Half the profiles were probably fake.

"I gave out all one hundred Smiles this month, and I only got back one, from someone I didn't even send one to! And she had something wrong with her head, it looked like. Not mentally, but the shape of it! That doesn't seem right. Is there something wrong with the way my account is set up?" She could hear the hope in his voice.

This would be tricky. "Well, I'm looking here at your profile, and first off, I have to congratulate you on your taste. You are going after a lot of gorgeous women here."

"I like to think I've learned how to pick 'em," PhilPhilliesFan1984 said.

"If you're going to step up to bat, you might as well swing for the fences, right?" She followed the baseball metaphor with a conspiratorial chuckle.

"You got it! You got it. Man, I tell you. Women get that. Men don't always get that."

"But see, the thing is, women at this level are going to have about a hundred guys coming after them too, right? And sure, half of them are losers, but these ladies log on and open up their Smilebags and see a hundred Smiles in there, and chances are against you even getting a clickthrough to your profile in the first place. A lot of these women will look at all those Smiles and just give up and not click on any of them at all, much less send a Smile back."

"That has *got* to be the problem."

Surely.

"It's the kind of stuff you learn when you've got the God's-eye view of the whole thing," Rebecca said. "I mean, and I'm not really supposed to talk to customers on this personal level, but I'm looking at your profile right now, and you *are* a good catch." She flinched as soon as she said it. Too much, too soon?

"Well, I like to *think* I am! Thank you. You are really nice. Just really nice."

Perfect.

"What's your name again?"

"Rebecca."

"Rebecca," he repeated.

"I'm thinking," she said. "Thinking about how I can maybe help you out here."

She paused for a beat.

"Give me a chance to pull something up."

Another beat.

"Hmm. This isn't going to—well, it might. Have you ever considered the Gold Plan?"

"The Gold Plan?" He sounded a little suspicious, but not too much. Easy to recover.

"See, here's the thing. It's not just that with the Gold Plan you can send out two hundred Smiles and receive three hundred, but when a Smile from a Gold Plan customer appears in a Smilebag? First, it's got a little gold star next to it, and second, it shows up at the very top of the queue, instead of being buried in the middle somewhere where no one will see it. And see, we had this offer that just expired where Silver Plan customers could get a free trial month of the Gold Plan to see if they liked it. Which would have been perfect for you. But I'm thinking . . . let me see if I can get in touch with my friend Lindy in Accounts. Maybe I can have her set you up as a last-minute thing."

Absolute delight. "That would be *excellent*. That would be just fine."

"I got Lindy and her fiancé a pair of Phillies versus Mets tickets for her birthday, so she owes me one." Gilding the lily, maybe, but why not.

"You are a fantastic lady," PhilPhilliesFan1984 said.

"Okay . . . okay. I just IMed Lindy and got the go-ahead. So I'll just change you over to the Gold Plan myself. Your account should refresh in a few minutes, and you'll see the updated allowances and additional privileges." This was not a man who read license agreements, Rebecca thought. He might not even notice the eventual steep increase of the automatic monthly charge to his credit card; he might not even be able to follow the elaborate procedure necessary to cancel the upgrade after that first trial month (which involved finding a light gray link displayed against the white background of your profile page before you could even begin). No need to mention any of that.

"You seem like a really nice person," PhilPhilliesFan1984 said.

Uh-oh.

She drained all the music out of her voice; by now the modulation monitors wouldn't care. "Can I help you with anything else?"

Silence on his end, then a cleared throat. Oh no. Here it comes.

"This may seem inappropriate to you," PhilPhilliesFan1984 said. "And maybe kind of sudden. But this is how good things happen, right? Suddenly! And I can tell just from your voice that you are a great person. And I was wondering if we could talk again. Just about baseball, with a fellow Phils fan, or whatever—"

One last delicious lie: "I'm black," she said, and disconnected.

A few minutes later she received an automatically generated e-mail congratulating her on her twentieth upsell to the Gold Plan this month. It came with the usual gift certificate that could be cashed in at any of the pseudo-ethnic chain restaurants that lined both sides of Route 1, huge as warehouses and filled with families that had screaming toddlers in tow.

She'd give the certificate to Kate, like she often did. Maybe the two of them could have a girls' night out: it'd be good to be distracted for a bit, to have a reason not to think of the way her husband's personality had lost some of its shine as he'd grown older, or the late-afternoon silence that screamed the news of Sean's absence, or the troubling memories that still sprang on her from the empty house's shadows.

3

CRACKPOT THEORIES

After Rebecca knocked off her shift at Lovability (the final tally: three customers upsold from Silver to Gold; two more from Bronze to Silver), she watched TV for a while, flipping idly between three different channels that were all showing reruns of hour-long crime shows, featuring coroners performing autopsies in dimly lit morgues who then traded their lab coats for bulletproof vests in order to go out on stakeouts. Philip came home earlier than expected—eight thirty—with a bag of Mexican takeout for the both of them, which he'd forgotten to inform her about by phone beforehand. She chose to read the meal as a silent apology for his anger of the night before, and so she quickly slipped back into the kitchen where pasta was on the boil, shut off the heat, and tossed the half-cooked spaghetti into the compost, collateral damage from a harmless marital miscommunication.

He'd brought her chicken and cheese enchiladas with green sauce. (She eyeballed the meal in its foil tin. Maybe a pound more when she stepped on the scale tomorrow morning. But still within spec. Would be nice to be taller. Amazons eat what they want.) She transferred the food to dishes so they could eat like civilized people at the kitchen table, and after he devoured the first of three soft-shell tacos in silence (not a snacker, he hadn't eaten since noon and was starving), she said, "Any crackpots?"

"Two crackpots. Fewer than I expected. I thought my inbox would be running over today, but: just two. One was a cease-and-desist order from some guy who claims I 'stole his research.' He's been working for fifteen years on a device called the Zybourne Clock— has nine patents pending, he says. The journals are afraid to publish his work because it would mean an end to our erroneous belief in the scientific method."

Philip bolted down a fourth of another taco in a single indecorous mouthful. "He had a phone number on it, so Alicia handled it just for kicks. Called him up and said she was a lawyer from the firm of Dewey, Cheatham, and Howe." He paused, gazed into the middle distance for a moment, and smiled. "There's something beautiful about a sustained tirade from a woman with a gift for foul language. Those harsh Anglo-Saxon consonants, but her voice gave this nice lilt to it. Wouldn't be the same from a man." He snapped back to the present and took another big bite from the taco.

Philip and Rebecca finished their meal in quiet communion, neither of them particularly wanting to discuss Rebecca's endless parade of lovelorn callers or Philip's troubles with lab management. "The second crackpot tract is in my briefcase," he said once they were done. "Overnighted to the lab by FedEx. It's special. It's spectacular."

It was an eight-hundred-page hardcover book, bound in leather, with its pages edged in gold and a pair of red silk ribbons sewn into its spine. Rebecca opened it: English on the right-facing pages, Arabic on the left. Each page was decorated with splashes of color: columns of text wove their way between indecipherable graphs with unquantifiable measurements on their axes. "An expensive production," Philip said. "The author comes from oil money, a dilettante intellectual. They got copies at the labs in Frascati and Perth, too."

"It's beautiful," Rebecca said.

"It's tacky. It turns out that I've been wasting my time. Because the design for the *time machine*," Philip said, "is already coded in the Qu'ran. The Qu'ran is a perfect text that is directly revealed by God and therefore contains all information; however, we are flawed, imperfect people, and so the full import of its meaning will be obscured from us forever. In short, the smart bet is to start spending my grant money on religious studies."

Rebecca turned to an elaborate four-color diagram that portrayed the flow of time as an infinitely large tree, its branches forking into a multitude of possible worlds. Clinging tightly to several of its limbs were strange animals with reddish pelts, and the long, coiling, striped tails and wide, liquid eyes of lemurs, and the fangs and muzzles of foxes. Angels with rainbow-colored wings held hands and danced in circles at the tree's base.

"Once we complete the time machine, which we can do with the assistance of that book," Philip said, "we can send a group of sentinels back in time to stand guard at important junctions in the time stream. Thereby hastening the Day of Resurrection."

"To give credit where it's due, he's ambitious."

"Alicia said it reminded her of when she'd tried to read the Bible as a teenager. She said it has all this best-selling hype, but once you get into it, it's full of continuity errors and plot holes and *deus ex machina*. Worst novel she ever read, she said. She put it down halfway."

"She's certainly funny," Rebecca said, in the tone of voice she usually reserved for parents who insisted on boasting to her about their particularly ugly toddlers.

"She's good to have in the lab," Philip said. "She's smart and she's good for morale. It seems weird that you have to think about morale in a laboratory—it's not a battlefield—but you do. Happy scientists are smarter scientists."

"I'm sure they are," Rebecca said, allowing herself just enough ice in her voice to satisfy herself without making Philip ask whether something was wrong, or whether she was upset.

■

Later that evening, Rebecca's father called. "When's Philip around?" he said. "It's time for single combat." *Single combat* was Woody's term for the conversations on religion that he insisted on having with Philip as a playful condition of Philip's continued marriage to Rebecca. ("He came to me and asked for your hand," he'd said. "He should have known I was going to set terms. Especially since he came to me with no dowry. Has that wastrel yet brought me a cow, or a goat? Not one cow, Rebecca. Not one goat.") Philip, for his part, pretended exasperation, and liked to claim he only put up with Woody to humor Rebecca, but he inevitably recounted their dialogues to her after the fact like a football fan reliving the final quarters of a close game, repeating the times when he felt he'd boxed Woody into a corner, or coming up with staircase retorts to the times when Woody had stymied him. It was good, thought Rebecca, that, in their way, they got along.

"He looked exhausted this evening," Rebecca said. "But I'm sure that later on he'll be happy to make the time for you."

"Good. I want him in top shape, so he won't have any excuses. And what about you? How are you doing?"

Rebecca knew the right answer here. "I'm okay. I've been thinking about Sean."

"I'll worry when you don't," Woody said.

And it was true that Rebecca had been thinking about Sean—she always did, in the back of her mind, in the same way that dull, constant pains in the joints of former athletes were ever-present reminders of decades-old injuries. But what was at the front of Rebecca's mind at that particular moment, and had been ever since dinner, was margaritas. Really, there was nothing like the margaritas at the Mexican place where Philip had picked up the takeout. They served them out of a slushie machine, and the recipe was simple—off-the-shelf margarita mix with a corn syrup base, mixed with the kind of tequila that came in plastic bottles designed to survive the clumsiness of plastered college kids. But there was something magical about them nonetheless, the naughty concoctions served in thirty-two-ounce plastic glasses with salt-coated rims. The salt hit your tongue first, followed by the sour sweetness of the margarita with its lovely texture of finely ground ice. You didn't even taste the tequila—you just felt a little lightheaded afterward, a little more disposed to good cheer, a little more aware of the world's color and light, and when the twenty-two-year-old woman with the spray-on tan asked you if you wanted a second, you smiled back and said—

"Rebecca. Have you heard a word I've said?"

"Yeah! You were talking about—" She took a guess. "Emerson."

"Augustine." Woody sighed. "Same number of syllables, though. Good try. That's okay, though: Philip will pay attention to me, when I am tearing him apart in single combat. He will say: *Goodness, this timid minister is giving me a most unpleasant intellectual thrashing. These Unitarians can certainly be some disputatious folk! Look: my nose is bleeding. Suddenly metaphor has become fact.*"

"I'm sure he will."

"Don't tell him I'm bringing Augustine into things. I don't want to alert him."

"I will be sure not to bring Saint Augustine up as a conversation topic with my husband in the near future."

"Good. I'll be by to see him one evening in a few days."

"Okay. Love you, Dad."

"Love you too. Bye."

4

PROXIMITY MEDALLION

Rebecca watched bubbles of carbonation climb the inside of her glass of Pellegrino. Before her sat a half-eaten bowl of penne pasta, slathered in a congealing cream sauce: the serving that the restaurant thought proper had been large enough for three. Across the table from her, Kate was telling some sort of catty story about a coworker or an old boyfriend: Rebecca had lost track. The details of Kate's rapid-fire tales started to blend together after a while, but Rebecca knew the general structures of her stories and how they tended to go. As long as she laughed at the right moments, she could zone out sometimes; moreover, she suspected that, on this particular evening, Kate expected her to be a little inattentive, and had chosen not to mind.

Kate had texted her at nine thirty that morning, insisting on a girls' night out right that evening, and beneath Kate's claims that she had super-important news, Rebecca sensed Kate's desire to give her a chance to get out of the house, away from Philip, where she'd feel obligated to talk, about Sean. Talks with Philip about Sean never went well—usually, they were more defined by the gaps between their words than the words themselves. And on this particular day of the year things were generally worse because she felt she *had* to talk about him, rather than merely dealing in silence with the nagging presence of his absence.

This morning, Rebecca had woken up to hear Philip going through his usual exercise routine, the grunts that accompanied his push-up counts perhaps a bit more anguished than was ordinary. He collapsed on the forty-seventh and lay there on the floor for a minute or so, face down; then he came to his feet, stretched his arms and rolled his shoulders, and was on his way out of the bedroom when Rebecca called to him.

It took a second or two for him to turn around.

"I miss Sean," Rebecca said from the bed, trying not to think that the truth of the feeling she had at that moment (and it *was* true, it was: how could it not be?) was somehow diminished by the compulsion she felt to perform it.

Philip's lip twitched. "Me, too," he said, his voice barely audible, and before Rebecca could say anything further, he turned and left.

■

Rebecca and Kate were having dinner this evening at a big-box Italian restaurant on Route 1. Its homey decor was at odds with its gigantic space: the place could seat five hundred, and the seemingly handmade one-off knickknacks tacked to the walls—thirty-year-old concert posters; rusted signs that advertised soft drinks in glass bottles—generally had exact duplicates mounted thirty yards away.

Rebecca and Kate sat by a window; through it, Rebecca could see cars whipping down the highway with the smallest of gaps between them, the traffic brought to a relative crawl and the vehicles spacing out only when they were forced to negotiate around the rare driver who still insisted on using manual steering controls. She found it difficult to concentrate on what Kate was saying, even when she could put her thoughts about Sean and Philip in the back of her mind. The noises of families and gaggles of college kids collected in the restaurant's cavernous ceiling, whose exposed beams were surely made of steel sheathed in paper-thin wooden paneling. At the table to Rebecca's left were a group of women in their forties, Jersey born and bred, free from familial obligations for a night and all dolled up for each other; one of them tossed back the dregs of her appletini and loudly declared that she "still knew how to party." On Rebecca's other side was a table of four: a mother and father, a screaming toddler in a high chair, and a four-year-old whose parents had given up on trying to get him to stay in his seat. He wore a large plastic medallion around his neck with an LCD display that featured a minimalist representation of a smiling bear's face; the necklace appeared to be some kind of proximity detector meant to reassure multitasking guardians. Whenever the child climbed out of his chair and wandered away from the table (the father fiddling with his phone; the mother dutifully trying to slide spoonfuls of risotto between the baby's defiantly pursed lips), the bear's face lost its grin; if the boy got more than fifteen feet away, a three-note chime sounded and the device sang, in an infuriatingly earwormy way, "It's time to come back to Mommy and Daddy. Mommy and Daddy are too far away! Come back, come back to Mommy and Daddy: this is where you should stay." Clearly the child liked the tune, and wanted to hear it as many times as he possibly could. He would cartoonishly tiptoe one step away from his parents, then another, and then, very slowly, another: then when he finally took the step that tripped the proximity alarm he'd clap and giggle.

"What do you think would happen if the kid actually left the restaurant?" Kate said after she and Rebecca had suffered through the jingle for the ninth time. "I bet that thing around his neck would start playing Metallica and pop him with five hundred volts."

Rebecca clapped her hand over her mouth to stifle a snigger.

"Yeah," Kate continued, "and then when he was writhing around on the ground with his eyes rolled back and foam coming out of his mouth it'd say: *Justice is done!*"

■

"So you said you had some super-important news?" Rebecca said as Kate tapped the touchscreen implanted in the middle of the table, ordering a cup of coffee for herself and another little bottle of Pellegrino for Rebecca. The touchscreen displayed an animation of a waiter with slicked-back black hair and a pencil mustache scurrying off to a kitchen, leaving tracks and smoke in his wake; then it resumed its display of a series of images of vaguely Italian-American subjects: a movie poster advertising *The Godfather Part II*; the album art for Frank Sinatra's *In the Wee Small Hours*; a red-checkered gingham tablecloth rippling in a light wind.

"Well," said Kate, "you're not going to believe this. But I've been hanging out with Carson again. After your party, we got in touch—I got in touch with him—and we talked a bit—e-mailing and IMing, mostly—and we hung out a couple of times."

"Hung out?"

"You know: *hung out*, hung out. I guess we hooked up once."

"Hooked up?"

"*Hooked up*, hooked up. I ended up staying over the other night."

Rebecca rested her chin on a hand propped up by an elbow. "Staying over?"

"Ha fucking ha, Becca."

"Ah, *that's* the word you were looking for."

"You're impossible."

"It was you who decided to break it off with him the first time, right?" Rebecca said as a harried server dropped off their drinks. (The server quickly reached over Kate's shoulder to tap the touch-screen in the middle of the table as if he were tagging the next runner in a relay race, and the cartoonish Italian waiter appeared with a comic-book-style speech bubble over his head that read, "96 seconds! That's-a A-OK!" The server left the table without a word, heading back to the kitchen at a jog.)

"Yeah, the first time," Kate said.

"I doubt he's going to change whatever convinced you to call things off before, just because you lured him back into your arms with your feminine wiles. Irresistible as they may be."

Kate sighed. "See," she said, "there's the thing. I didn't really dump him because he was slow getting back to me when I sent him a text, or because he always seemed distracted when he was around me, thinking of his work instead. I think that was just something I told myself. It's certainly what I told everyone else. Even though it sounded kind of, I guess, flighty."

"So why'd you dump him, then?"

"You're going to think I'm awful."

"Probably."

"No, seriously!"

"Okay." Rebecca lost her playful smirk. "Tell me what happened."

Kate took a breath. "Well, I'll just say it. When we were first going out, I was really into him! He wasn't the kind of guy who usually answers my profile—he could write in complete sentences, for one thing."

"Which is rare," Rebecca said. "I look at these profiles, and I see so many people do so many terrible things to English."

"Yeah! And when I met him, he was weird, a little, sure, but nice! I mean, kind. And how many times had I gone out with a guy a couple of times to find out that he was all peaches-and-cream online, but a total asshole in real life. So there was that. And he was successful, too—honestly, when you say to people, *Oh, by the way, did I mention, I'm dating a scientist*, it sounds pretty badass. Not like, *I'm dating a mattress salesman*, or something like that.

"So I was really into him, but—and I feel bad about this—in the back of my head, the whole time, once I started to feel kind of serious about him, I was thinking: *How am I going to bring this guy home to my parents?*"

Rebecca put down her glass of sparkling water and looked across the table. "Kate. Seriously."

"I know, right? And it wasn't like I would even have to! My mom died three years ago and my dad is in a home! And this is the twenty-first century: we basically live in the future. But it was just the *idea* of it, in my head. The idea of my parents. I thought about them and it was like I went back in time. And it was like they were still sitting at this dinner table, both of them, waiting to judge. And I just . . ." She let the sentence trail off and protectively drew her arms across her chest, her nails digging into the palms of her hands. "You know. You know you're thinking something stupid, and you know it's stupid, but it doesn't stop you from thinking it anyway."

A server holding another tray of fruit-laced martinis for the increasingly raucous women on their girls' night out deftly avoided the hyperactive four-year-old, who was now running up and down the aisle as the medallion around his neck continued to sing.

"Have you told him any of this?" Rebecca asked.

"Oh hell no."

"Do you think he's guessed?"

Kate thought about it. "Honestly: probably not. It's not the kind of thing he would think about. Head full of science and all."

"Well, it might not be a problem, then," Rebecca said. "I mean: you look at it one way and yeah, okay, it's a problem. But look at it like this—you were into this guy. You had a conversation with your-self about him, and you made a bad decision. Now you have a second chance. That conversation with yourself happened entirely in your head, right? Well, you told me about it, but what you tell me goes in the vault and stays there." She pinched her thumb and index finger together and ran them quickly across her lips. "So it might as well not have happened. So just let it go and stop beating yourself up about it. Easy."

"Yeah, you're right," Kate said. "And I think maybe I just wanted you to tell me something I already knew was true. And I do like him. I guess . . ." She sighed again. "I want to make sure that I think I like him because I like him, not because I'm guilting myself into liking him. I don't want to do it so I can pat myself on the back for being"—she raised her hands to trace scare quotes in the air—"conscious."

"Kate, for real—if this is the worst problem you have, you're having a good run right now."

Kate gasped. "Oh, Rebecca, I didn't—"

"That didn't come out right. *The worst problem you have with Carson*, I meant to say."

"I still didn't—"

"I know."

"I've been doing all the talking."

"Of course you have!" Rebecca forced a teasing smile.

"You're great, Becca," Kate said, reaching out and clasping her hand.

"You, too," said Rebecca.

■

For a moment, not knowing how to transition into a lighter conversation topic, Rebecca and Kate both looked at the table's touchscreen, which was displaying a portly illustration of a chef with a thick black mustache, joyously flinging an expanding disc of pizza dough into the air. But suddenly, the image disappeared, replaced with the presidential seal on a field of navy blue.

The volume of conversation in the restaurant quickly fell to a murmur.

The medallion around the wandering boy's neck continued to declare that his parents were too far away. At the table with the rest of the boy's family, the father stopped poking at his phone, staring at it with confusion; then he tapped it gently against the table's edge a couple of times, as if there were a component inside that needed to be joggled to get it to work again.

The President's face appeared on the touchscreen in front of Rebecca, staring blindly up out of the table. From Rebecca's point of view his head was upside down. "Kathryn Mullen!" the President said. "Hello!"

"Hello, Mr. President," Kate said as the diners at other tables greeted their touchscreens in unison.

"Kathryn, I just wanted to take a little time out to say hi. It's good to see"—the image of the President stuttered slightly—"a mother and daughter having dinner together out on the town!"

Rebecca looked up at Kate and mouthed: *Mother and daughter?* Kate silently pointed at Rebecca's glass of water. Oh: that was it. Kate's drinks on the bill would have alcohol and Rebecca's wouldn't—it was a fair guess that one of them was underage, and a party of mother and daughter was the fairest guess from there. (Though what gave him the idea that they were both female? Cameras concealed in the ceiling? Sensors in the seats that could detect your gender based on the shape of your butt? Maybe only women ordered penne pasta with cream sauce?)

"These are times of austerity," the President said. "It's important to keep up those female bonding rituals."

"Of course," Kate said.

"Though I was just thinking." The President narrowed his eyes conspiratorially. "We can't be tightening our belts all the time, can we? This is still America. We can still have a little fun sometimes. And I was just cleaning the house and found some change under the couch cushions and I was thinking: why don't you ladies let me treat you to dessert?"

A cheer rose from the tables throughout the restaurant. "That would be lovely," Kate said.

"You two just go ahead and get anything you want. One dessert each. It's on me. Have a good night."

The President's face faded to black as the father at the table next to Rebecca went back to thumbing his phone.

"I feel like the President should know that I go by Kate instead of Kathryn," Kate said.

"I feel like the President should know that I'm not your daughter and I'm pushing forty," Rebecca said.

"Did you vote for that guy?"

"Yes, and I regret it now."

"You'll change your mind once you have the crème brûlée."

■

"So what is Philip up to this evening?" Kate asked, sliding a fork into an obscenely large slice of chocolate cake.

"Dad's talking to him," Rebecca replied after swallowing a spoonful of crème brûlée, which *was* pretty good, if a little too sugary. "It's funny. Philip never wanted to go to a therapist or anything like that after what happened with Sean: I think partly because he thought that going to one was like admitting you were crazy or something. And he's an atheist, but he's happy to talk to a theologian, as long as Dad frames the conversation like it's an argument. And after these little talks, Philip always looks like he has a lot less on his mind. So I'm happy to stay out of it. I don't ask questions."

Nearby, the four-year-old boy was screaming his head off, yodeling long wordless wails of pure anguish. Rebecca could see what the problem was: while the other three people at the table had desserts in front of them—mother and father had both opted for the cake, while the baby had a bowl with a single scoop of slightly runny ice cream—the boy had none. Tears spurted from his eyes, and his cheeks were dotted with troubling arrangements of red and blue blotches. The kid was crying so hard that beads of sweat had broken out on his forehead. The bear's face on the medallion around his neck wore an expression of abject panic, its eyes jittering from left to right as if it were frantically searching for an avenue of escape.

"You know what happens when you have sweet things after six o'clock, Dyson," the mother was saying. "The sugar wakes up the gremlins that live in your body, and they take control of you and make you get into mischief. But Chelsea is too young for gremlins. And Mommy and Daddy do not *have* gremlins: we *killed* the gremlins that lived inside us, long ago. So this is why we can have sweet things at night and you cannot. We'll have something special for you when you get home. How about a glass of the special milk? The tasty two percent milk, not the skim milk."

Dyson took a deep breath, held it, and let it out with an ear-piercing holler.

"You guys over there are parents of the year," one of the drunken women shouted.

Dyson's mother looked up, her face gone incandescent with rage.

"It might be time for us to get the check," said Rebecca.

"No: I'm not leaving this cake until I can't eat another bite." Kate scarfed down another forkful. "I'll do some time at the gym tomorrow. Besides, Carson might appreciate an extra half pound here or there: somewhere nice to put his hand."

"So what have you guys been doing together? Other than, you know, hanging out, or whatever you want to call it."

"Rebecca."

"Just playing."

"Well—he made dinner a couple of times. And he's a pretty good cook! By which I mean he's really good at following directions. His kitchen looks more like a chemistry lab than, like, a kitchen. I just turn the oven on to whatever and cook whatever it is until it looks right. But he's got, like, a centrifuge! And this set of hardcore cookbooks in its own Lucite case—he's super careful not to spill anything on them. But the stuff he puts on a plate is to die for. I could get used to that.

"And he wants to bring me out to the lab to show me what he's working on."

"Ha! You're meeting the family."

"Stop it."

"I'm serious! When Philip and I were going out, the day I came to the lab was a big deal. Though he tried to pretend it wasn't. He got all haughty about it." Rebecca pulled her face into an exaggerated frown. *"You're going to need a basic understanding of my work if we are to be serious about seeing each other romantically.* You know how he can get when he wants to."

"But he just wanted to show off his hot new girlfriend."

"Absolutely."

"Well, I'm looking forward to seeing the time machine I've heard so much about."

"Kate, whatever you do, please do *not* call it a time machine when you go over there. Philip will be livid. He will absolutely lose his—"

"*What* the—"

While Rebecca and Kate had been talking, dessert-deprived young Dyson had left his chair, stealthily sneaking up behind Kate's. He'd sprung up beside her, plunged a chubby hand directly into her half-eaten slice of chocolate cake, ripped out a hunk of it, and shoved it straight into his mouth.

His mother was right behind him. "Dyson!" she shouted. "The gremlins! The gremlins! God*damn* it!"

"That, right there?" Rebecca pointed at the mutilated cake. "That was worth sticking around for."

"I'm so sorry," Dyson's mother said, wrestling with the boy, who had frosting smeared all over his mouth. "His terrible twos have been going on for three years now."

"Don't worry about it," Kate said, looking at the woman placidly, as if this sort of thing happened all the time. Rebecca had seen this before: Kate had this way of being able to chill people out just by handling them the right way. She had a face for it: she could just look at someone and calm her down.

Dyson's mother staggered as the keening boy clasped her legs. "Can I get you—"

"Don't worry about it!" Kate repeated, her voice full of bonhomie. "In fact, let me—" She held an index finger in the air: *Hold it.* Then she removed her purse from where it had been hanging by its strap on the back of her chair and began to go through it. "I carry these little candies with me, for when I get a craving," she said. "They're sugar-free!" She looked the mother directly in the eye. "May I give one to Dyson?"

Still holding on to his mother's legs, Dyson turned to look at Kate, sniffling back a string of snot.

"Sugar-free," Dyson's mother said suspiciously.

"Yeah! I get them at this place online. Do you have any idea how hard it is to find stuff like this?"

"They put sugar in *everything*. They squirt it all over cereal and green beans and hamburger buns. Kids today grow up not knowing what real food tastes like."

"I know exactly what you mean," Kate said. "Hey, Dyson," she whispered loudly, proffering the piece of hard candy in its nondescript brown wrapper. "This is for you."

Quickly, Dyson snatched the candy off Kate's palm, unwrapped it, and popped it into his mouth. "Ha!" he said to his mother, then left her to climb back into his chair, as polite as could be.

"You're a very nice lady," Dyson's mother said.

"Oh, gosh, thanks," Kate replied with a smile.

On the way out to the parking lot after they'd settled the bill, Rebecca said, "I didn't know you had it in you. You're like some kind of baby whisperer."

Kate laughed. "You know that candy wasn't sugar-free," she said. "Also, it had a coffee bean in the middle. Watch for that mother doing a perp walk on tomorrow morning's news."

"Kate! That's horrible!"

Kate paused and thought about it. "Yeah!"

They shared a good long belly laugh over that, and then as Kate caught her breath she said, "Okay. Seriously. Are you okay?"

"Yeah," Rebecca said. "I'm okay. I'm good."

■

On Route 1 the lane in front of Rebecca was empty for fifty yards: her car's red license plate marked it as a vehicle under exclusively manual control, and so the automatics with their green plates gave it a wide berth. Strangely, the drivers of automatic cars could be just as rude as if they'd actually had to steer them; there were occasional beeps behind her, and as one car pulled by on her right, its driver rolled down his window, stuck both fists out of it with their middle fingers extended, and yelled, "Learn to drive, you stupid bi—," the wind snatching the last word out of his mouth as he passed.

But so what, Rebecca thought. So what. If other people wanted to get angry about something that didn't matter, about ten seconds of inconvenience, then let them get angry. She felt good, really good, and she had a clear road in front of her, all the way home.

5

BLACKOUT SEASON

In the midst of what Rebecca had thought of, thirteen years ago, as her "blackout season," there had been no such clear roads ahead. But at the time, when she'd been deep in it, that hadn't seemed so bad: such was the season's peculiar character. The blackout season made you feel that it was perfectly fine to be in darkness for a while; that it was good to sit and wait for the light and the path to reveal themselves in their own time. It was good to sit still, to close your eyes, and wait, and listen—

■

"Rebecca. Have you heard a word I've said?"

"Yeah! You were talking about—" She recalled half of what she remembered him saying and took a guess. "Thoreau."

"Emerson," her father said. "Close enough."

Woody took a drink of whisky from his glass (the Scotch Ardbeg, the glass Waterford crystal—in this area he was a stickler for niceties and details) and continued to pace the living room floor in front of Rebecca, who was seated in a recliner with her laptop, idly flicking back and forth between three different browser windows, each displaying a feed from a different social network. There wasn't much going on this Thursday afternoon: mostly posts and reposts and re-reposts of others' status updates, and videos of pets and photos of toddlers. Minor slights were rendered as major tragedies ("out of Bloomin Onion at Outback FML!!!"); impending off-the-cuff social engagements were treated as reunions with long-lost relatives ("Can't wait to GET MY DRINK ON w/Kimmy and Jules tonite!!"). But still, it was hard not to immerse yourself in that constant drip-feed of information without feeling that *something* was going on, something nebulous and hard to state, but nonetheless deeply profound. Every page refresh promised the little dopamine kick that came from the shock of the new. Meanwhile, Dad was trying to hammer out the superstructure of Sunday's sermon, but if she got out of bed on time she'd just hear it then. (Though if you were going to be a preacher's daughter, you might as well reap the benefit of being a Unitarian preacher's daughter, and sleep in now and again.)

Woody liked to link the sacred to the secular whenever he could; he also had a strong distaste for prosperity theology, or any sort of optimistic theology in general, and felt that he wasn't properly doing his job unless, about two-thirds of the way through the message, he didn't sense a little disquiet in the congregation, a dash of despair. ("The name-it-and-claim-it crowd has plenty of venues," he'd say. "Someone has to be a bulwark against the tide.") Lately he'd been thinking on the Transcendentalists. "Here's the thing about Emerson. You look at those early essays and addresses, and time after time you see this distrust of books and libraries. True wisdom lives in nature; that's where you go for the hot new information. Budding branch and newborn butterfly and all that. While books are dead and static. But how do you get Emerson's message? Through a—Rebecca. For fifteen points, and the lead."

"Um. Book."

"Exactly. It's a paradox. It is, how do the kids say it, meta? And does he ever address the paradox? As far as I know he just leaves it on the table. *Distrust all texts*, he says, *including this one*. Which you could say is also the message of Ecclesiastes. Now *there's* the hook. You can never have enough of Ecclesiastes. Nothing like Ecclesiastes to put a real pall on proceedings. A quick glimpse into a godless world that's sure to chill the spine. Full of doubt and contradiction. I could lead from there into the Emerson, and maybe move from there into a *charming personal anecdote* about how my adult daughter Rebecca spends way too much time online and way too little out in the world. Among nature."

"This is nature," Rebecca said. "It's just, you know, electronic."

"What I'm saying, Rebecca," Woody said with just a touch of fire and brimstone, "is that in general, you could stand to be a little more Emersonian—hint: *self-reliant*—and a little less sitting-around-the-house-and-surfing-the-net-all-day-ish."

"Time for this week's lecture from Dad. FML," Rebecca typed quickly, updating her status and closing her laptop.

"I admit I can see the pleasure in living one's life as the heroine of a film loosely based on a Jane Austen novel, doing little or nothing except waiting for a suitable husband. But Austen's times died with Austen, and even she was joking. College was more than a finishing school for you, my dear. You've been out for three years now. It's time, as the kids say, to get paid."

"Nine point five percent," Rebecca responded; the beats of this conversation were familiar enough that she didn't have to spell out to her father that this was New Jersey's present unemployment rate.

"Nine point five is for the people who—"

"Plus the ones who aren't counted in the stats anymore because they've been out of work for ninety-nine weeks. Call it twenty percent to be conservative."

"Twenty percent of the population who could stand a little Emerson in their lives. You know what he was about? Other than the business with the trees and the butterflies? Being a *doer*. Didn't matter what everyone else was doing with their time. You had a duty not to squander your human potential. You were supposed to go out and shape the world in your image. Just—"

"I have a bachelor's degree in English. I can recommend books for people to read if they tell me the kind of thing they like. And Amazon does that for free."

"—just get out there and *do*. You know? When you're here you spend, what, five, six hours a day on that laptop?"

"Looking for jobs. And I am *out there*. Just in a different way."

"Screwing around on Myspace—"

"Multitasking. And everyone moved to Facebook a year or two ago. Stop being old, Dad."

"Maybe you'd do a little better with the job search if you went out and knocked on some doors."

"It's not like when you were a kid—"

"You're twenty-five!"

"—everything's done online now. You don't just go up to people and talk to them: only crazy people do that. If you show up at some company unannounced, they call security."

"I still see Help Wanted signs in windows."

"I didn't get a college degree from Livingston State so I could get stiffed on tips when the diners hate the baba ghanoush."

"Graduate school?"

"In debt enough already. Also, I'm not a *sucker.*"

Woody swallowed back what he was about to say next. Then he sat down on the floor near the recliner, looking up at Rebecca. His shoulders slumped, and he suddenly looked drained: oddly tired and childlike, strangely unfatherly. "I just want you to do something," he said. "Other than sit here and string together babysitting jobs and give up. I feel like you're giving up."

"Maybe Emerson's times died with Emerson," Rebecca said, hating herself for slinging his words back in his face like that. But why let an English degree go to waste?

Then the front door slammed: Mom was home. "Woody!" they heard from the foyer. "I have been training this new hire at the library all day today. He's autistic! Granted, he can shelve books like nobody's business, but otherwise: *whoo!*" Her voice moved into the kitchen. "Man alive. He drove me to drink. Literally. As in: first I drove home, and now I'm drinking. Bam." They heard the rumble and clink of the icemaker's dispenser ejecting cubes into a tumbler: next would come the cranberry juice and the vodka.

From the recliner, Rebecca looked down into her father's upturned face. "How, my dearest, only daughter, do you bear the burden of our parentage?" he said. "It must be intolerable."

"I do my best." She forced a smile.

"We only want the best for you."

"I know." She reached down and gently placed her hand on his shoulder; he placed his own hand on top of it.

■

Dad's problem was that he didn't understand the nature and the purpose of the blackout season, never having had one. Really, "blackout season" was just Rebecca's label for it: there was no real name for that phase in the life of many suburban millennial Americans during which they moved back in with their parents after college for a while, and waited—maybe for a few months, maybe for several years—until an opportunity came along to take up the mantle of adulthood.

In Dad's day, when you graduated from a four-year school, you magically found a forty-hour-a-week job that let you take on a mortgage if you wanted. But the paths to success were not so well marked out for Rebecca's generation, and so with diplomas in hand they returned to their old bedrooms for a period that was part extended adolescence, part premature senescence. The period did not have a name, because to name it would be to acknowledge its existence, which would in turn lead to an admission of failure—of the promise of higher education, or of methods of parenting, or of such vague concepts as the System or the American Dream. If you did name it, you kept the name to yourself, and you only spoke it in confidence. (Rebecca's BFF Kate would say, now and again, that she was in her "twilight time"; their college friend Jen would occasionally blurt after a couple of ladies' night mojitos that "this is the best time of my life," but Rebecca would hear the pose of defiance in her voice, and the desperation beneath it, and know what she really meant.)

Rebecca looked for jobs, like everyone did—during the first few weeks after graduating from college she'd really thrown herself into it. But there was a certain dispiriting monotony and automation to the process. You filled out online forms. It was presumed that the forms were examined by humans, but probably not—what probably happened was that an automated routine searched for keywords in the submissions and flagged certain ones with signs of priority, or, more often in Rebecca's case, lack thereof. You could probably beat the system if you knew one of the people controlling the switches, but she knew no one who could speak her name at a meeting, or place an appointment on a superior's calendar. (It was about here that Rebecca realized that she might have missed out on at least some of the point of college. She'd spent most of her time there mooning after boys and partying—she hadn't really networked, or joined any of the college clubs that were the ersatz versions of the nameless real-world clubs that really mattered.) So there she was with her laptop, auto-completing fields and attempting to guess the secret words that would open the doors.

Sometimes she got interviews, but strangely, she felt the same way during those as she did when she was filling out the online applications: there'd be some human resources person staring at her across a table, not trying to figure out whether she was smart enough for the job, but merely waiting for her to say whatever his manuals or computers told him was the correct answer to an unstated question. ("I'm very *self-motivated*," she'd state with an assertiveness that she didn't quite feel in her gut, and the HR guy would look down at the paper in front of him and then back up at her blankly, as if to say, *No, that's not today's password*. Then she'd follow with something like "I'm also *committed to life-long learning*," and the response would be dead silence. A few days later, she'd get a no-reply e-mail expressing perfunctory pro forma regret, telling her the spot had been filled and wishing her the best of luck.)

In the meantime, she got her beer money from the shadow economy of the blackout season. The little town of Stratton was never short of babysitting opportunities, at fifteen an hour paid under the table. The money to be reaped from a freshly mowed lawn was mostly locked down by teenage boys and bands of landscapers, but every once in a while she'd get a gig from a landlord, cutting a patch of grass behind a duplex. Envelope stuffing and door-to-door canvassing for local political candidates during primary season; customer service for retailers during holiday sales: even if you couldn't get a steady paycheck, you could always hustle something, if you were willing to suffer the slight abrasion to your dignity, day by day.

When you'd spent enough time filling out job applications, and you'd had the required amount of family time, then you hung out. Hanging out occurred in coffee shops in the morning and afternoon and bars in the evening, or in parks or forests when the weather was warm. Or you hung out online, reading forum posts on random trivial subjects, or tracing the sprawling webs of social network friendships to see where they led you. It was then that you felt the full force of the blackout season, and what it did to time. It made time pliable; it smudged the lines between hours on clock faces; it sent hands spinning at twice their normal rate or stopped them altogether.

Sometimes you'd wake up too early, before the sun was up, before it was reasonable to expect someone to take up the task of facing the day, and so instead of getting out of bed you'd lie there for a while, and drowse, and slip into a dream in which, for instance, you were an ice skater. This is the thing you can *do;* when you slip on the skates you are a doer instead of a mere dreamer. Your blades carve lovely loops and spirals in the ice; when you twirl in midair your body is a blur. A talent scout selects you out of a crowd at Rockefeller Center one December day (easy to do, since amateurs have cleared the field for you to work your magic). Before you know it, you have a free trip to Disneyland, flight and hotel paid for. Once there, you're escorted to a secret labyrinth beneath the amusement park; at the heart of the labyrinth is a candlelit hall; in the middle of the hall sits a cryogenic chamber in which Walter Elias Disney, the man himself, is kept alive and, horribly, *conscious.* ("If he leaves the chamber he will die in moments," the scout says. "It's a miracle he hasn't gone insane in all these long years. This form of immortality is a curse, not a gift. But he makes this sacrifice of his own free will for the children of the world. To guarantee their happiness.") You are ushered before the chamber's window, and an acolyte with a pair of plastic Mickey Mouse ears sutured to his shaven head wipes away some condensation on the glass, so that the man inside can see you. His eyes widen and his agitated voice comes tinnily through a speaker mounted on the chamber's side. "She is all the princesses!" he shouts. "She is all the princesses. She is Cinderella; she is Sleeping Beauty; she is Ariel and Jasmine and Tiana. Put her in *Disney on Ice* posthaste!" "I knew you were destined for gainful employment," says your father when he suddenly appears; then you wake up to find that only five minutes have passed. The day with all its little reckonings has not come much closer, though the dream has tired you down to your bones.

Or: it's eleven a.m. You have filled out enough job applications for the day and it's time for a quick break. Check Facebook: Kate wants you to look at a YouTube video of this local band that she's trying to get a group together to go see Friday night. They're called the Dancing Axolotls, and they're some oddball amalgam of Celtic punk and industrial—Pogues and Dropkick Murphys crossed with beats lifted from Ministry and Nine Inch Nails. Who knows where they came up with that name—what the fuck is an axolotl? It doesn't sound Irish— but they rock! You watch three videos from their live shows (and the dance floor is full of guys, too, jumping up and down with their fists in the air. This could be the best night *ever*: bare minimum, you hook up with a dude in a ratty green T-shirt that says SLÁINTE!). And in the list of other videos that YouTube seems to think you might also like is one that appears to feature . . . some sort of animal? It's underwater and half translucent, with a face like a child's drawing of a smiling man. Looking at it is like getting kicked in the face with cute. It is so cute that it looks like something is wrong with it. It is an axolotl.

You have been down this rabbit hole before—once you watch the first YouTube video of a cute animal, there's no turning back until you're sated. From axolotls it's on to potbellied pigs, and cats that paw at the dancing lights of laser pointers. The whole subcategory of videos of cats grows by thousands a day, and they never, ever get old. Here's one that's been tinkered with through film-school visual-effects wizardry. A cat is toying with a plastic mouse that has guts of mechanical gadgetry—despite what should have been a series of stunning blows, the thing keeps moving, lying on its side while its legs writhe in the air. Then the cat looks directly into the camera and speaks with a human voice, its computer-generated lips moving in perfect sync with its goofy baritone. "Mousey-mouse should be dead," it says. "But it ain't! Why ain't it dead?" It is hard at these times not to be overcome with a sense of wonder, at all the centuries of technological advancement that brought humanity to a point where a photorealistic image of a talking cat merits little more than a quick glance. What better place to live than here? What better time than now?

And now you look up and it's three o'clock: most of the day has gone by. Mom'll be home soon, mixing the vodka and cranberry.

Thus time shrinks and stretches; thus your twenties are whittled away.

■

There were four women in what Rebecca and her friends called the "core group," the girls who made it a point to hang out together at a moment's notice, who understood that girls' night out was a standing weekly appointment, even if it wasn't explicitly declared as such, even if the core group pretended otherwise. (A sample e-mail sent from one member of the core group to the others with a couple of extra ladies cc'd, its subject line EMERGENCY: "It's an emergency b/c I haven't seen you guys in FOREVER ["forever," in this instance, being four days] and we SERIOUSLY need to hang out. The Glow Club at 9: don't be an asshole." The core group would be there at nine on the dot. But the others would fail, as their cc'd status had implied from the start.) The three girls in the core group besides Rebecca (who, when among them, became Becca for short) were Britt (short for Brittany and not Britney as Britt would insist, taking time to spell out the difference), Kate (short for Kathryn), and Jen (short for Jennifer). Other women came and went, but didn't have the necessary sticking power: either they didn't get the core group's pop culture references and inside jokes, or their own witty sallies fell on dead air, or they got steady jobs or serious boyfriends, both of which placed too heavy a demand on their time to maintain real membership in the core group.

The core group was into guys, in theory, in the abstract—when they went out to bars or clubs, one of them (usually Kate) would note with approval or disapproval the male/female ratio of the clientele, and whether the guys on offer were of sufficient cuteness or hotness. They didn't identify so much with the women of *Sex and the City*, though with them being a foursome of singles, that might have seemed the obvious call—for one thing, they all lived with their parents in New Jersey instead of in apartments with stellar views of the Manhattan skyline, and with a persistent recession under way, even an ironic appreciation of conspicuous consumption wasn't in the cards. They thought of themselves more as gender-switched versions of the dudes in bromance movies, who shared strategies about picking up chicks while sitting in front of the TV playing *Madden*. If they were having a long adolescence forced on them by circumstance, it wasn't necessarily a *bad* thing, and if men appeared in their lives it was on the periphery of the frame, the better to throw the true and inviolable nature of female friendship in sharp relief, to affirm its seriousness and depth. (A chain of texts copied to all members of the core group, beginning with Britt's: "I wanna go out to a club tonite but fuck guys I just wanna dance." Becca: "Yeah lets just get in a circle & put our purses on the floor & dance our asses off." Kate: "& if any guys get up in our grills well tase em!")

If one of them did meet a guy at a club, it would be made clear, if it wasn't already, that he was a supporting character in the tale of the core group, someone good for a three- or four-episode story arc, but someone who wouldn't (or shouldn't) stick around. One-night stands were thus tacitly approved of, if not encouraged—hookups were generally followed by a trio of snarkily congratulatory texts from the other members the next afternoon. Speed relationships were okay, as long as they had a quick, predictable three-act structure (the meet-cute and subsequent hookup; the whirlwind romance tinged with the suspicion that things were perhaps not what they seemed; the breakup and return to the fold, to the three comforters who could always be depended on, no matter how fickle men were).

The Rebecca Wright of thirty-eight, thinking back to the blackout-season Becca of her mid-twenties, would recall that the assignations of the core group were the performance of love, rather than the thing itself. But for Becca, back then, all romance was performance. Once you realized this, Becca thought, once you understood that the inherent falseness of courtship wasn't necessarily a *bad* thing, that it in fact served a useful purpose, then you understood that there was no need for these mating rituals to be long or elaborate, especially in the twenty-first century, when news could travel from one side of the world to the other in seconds. There was no rational reason that a quick wink couldn't serve the same purpose as a love song.

And so you got used to, and actually came to enjoy, these love affairs that were compressed in time, from years to days or even hours: the glance across a dance-hall floor, the hand on the shoulder, the third drink, the grind, the makeout session in a darkened booth. Maybe you traded digits, though Kate liked to give out fake numbers ("So he was like, I want to see you again, and I'm like, okay. Here's my number. Got your cell? Okay. It's: nine, four, five, eight, nine, one, nine, nine, nine, *nine*, NINE!"). Maybe you exchanged a couple of desultory text messages afterward ("u doin anything tonite?"), and maybe those led to a couple of one-on-one things. But more than one or two of those would start to attract warnings from the other girls, and it was hard to keep secrets from them. The combination of smartphones and BFFs meant that you didn't have much privacy— one or another of your friends pinged you every hour or two from waking to sleeping, and the group as a whole took silent note if you dropped off the grid. Even a few hours' absence was cause for curiosity. ("Someone wasn't answering texts last night. I'm not naming any names, but I'm just saying that if I was in the middle of hooking up with some guy I'd only met at a bar a couple of days before, and *my phone rang* with *our special chime*, then I would take a quick break to text back. Because, priorities.") Two or three days without a text from one of the girls constituted an emergency, and called for happy-hour bonding.

Because after everything—after the failed job searches; after the harangues from your parents; after the hookups, after the breakups, after every fucking thing the blackout season threw at you—the core group would still be there for you. In troubled, nebulous times like these, it was important to have some dependability, some stasis. And if maybe you got a little bit tired of seeing the same women's faces now and again, if Britt's constant management of your social life started to grate a little (but it wasn't like you had much of one anyway—you might as well let her handle it), if you got a little bit tired of Jen's constant habit of telling you how long she'd been unemployed, or how she hated living with her parents, or how she couldn't figure out what to do with her life (though if you ever wanted someone else to complain to, you could be sure you had a willing ear), if you got a little annoyed by Kate's characterization of their lives as not just adolescence, but a second childhood laced with a wistful irony (though it was hard to turn down a text message that read "yay yaay come and play," especially when you knew that it would involve vodka shots and potent weed)—if you got a little bored with all this, if you felt a little stuck in life sometimes, then that was a small price to pay for the comfort of a reliable social circle. Dependability was good. Stasis was good.

■

Who broke up the core group in the end? Britt, that's who! She met a dude on the Internet!

Britt was the principal organizer of the core group's social life; her nickname among the rest of the gang was "Julie the Cruise Director" (though if pressed, none of them could have sourced the reference without pulling out an iPhone). When they got together, it was usually because Britt had messaged them all and blocked out spots on their empty calendars; they all agreed that was Britt's job, so they didn't have to think about it. So it took a while longer than it would have otherwise for someone to notice that Britt was more or less missing in action lately: only when Kate texted Becca ("Have u heard from britt?") did Becca realize that her days had been a little emptier than usual, that she'd been spending a little more time than usual around the house, listening to Dad work out his drafts of next Sunday's sermons and watching reality shows on the couch with Mom. (Rebecca's drink of choice during these mother-daughter bonding moments was a glass of Australian Chardonnay poured from a one-point-five-liter bottle; Mom stuck to her traditional vodka and cran.) It took three days after that first text message for Kate to clear her throat and declare an emergency, and two days after that until Britt could say that she was "available."

Serious business. They splurged on appetizers at this classy seafood place in Haddam that was BYOB; when the server sniffed at the straight-up *jug* of Carlo Rossi Chablis that Kate had picked up at a grocery store on the way over, Kate smiled and said, "Don't worry: we're drinking this ironically. If you don't have wine glasses, just bring us four straws."

After they'd had a couple of drinks, Jen popped a morsel of calamari in her mouth and said to Britt, her voice coy and melodic, "So what's *uuuup*?" If you heard that question asked in that way, with the word *up* slithering down through three tones of the scale, you couldn't help but spill the beans out of reflex. It turned out that late one night a couple of months ago, after the core group had closed down the bars and gone their separate ways, Britt had been screwing around on the Internet at three in the morning because she was too wired from Red Bull and vodka to go to bed and she was still a little drunk, and just to see what would happen, she had opened up a profile on one of those dating sites and put up a couple of cute pictures of herself. And she got some winks and some messages from some guys, and she started messaging back and forth and flirting with some of them, and going out on dates with a couple of them, and lately she'd been hanging out a lot with one of them. And she really liked him. He was really, really cool.

"What the actual fuck," said Kate, after Britt had told them all this. "Have you noticed that you're hot? Dating sites are for women who are *not* hot. And in the profile they go on and on about how nice they are, and how they like the same books and movies that nerds like, and when you look at their picture all you see is, like, half of one ear. And that has a zit on it."

"I know!" Britt said. "I know! I didn't go on it because I was *desperate*. I can meet guys in real life whenever. And I was just screwing around for fun at first. But later on it started to make more sense to me. Look: meeting guys in real life is okay if you just want a casual thing, but I'm not twenty-one anymore! I'm tired of hookups and I want something that at least could *maybe* be serious. And for that kind of thing it's a lot better to meet guys online.

"The thing you don't have to put up with online is the *talking*. Like, you meet a guy for a coffee at Starbucks, and you're sitting at this little table, and you're both totally *there*. It's *intimate*. He's looking at you and waiting for you to say something. And the whole place is quiet because everyone is on their computers, so whatever you say sounds like the whole world can hear it, even though everyone else in the place has earbuds in, so it shouldn't matter. Whenever I'm in a situation like that, especially with someone I've only met once in a bar, I'm like: *Shields up!* I don't like it! I want to say: Do you mind if we just put headphones on and sit here and drink our lattes, and we can just text. How am I going to get in an actual serious relationship if I have to be in these intimate situations from the very beginning?

"But when you're meeting people online, you're not totally *out* there at first. You can take baby steps. First somebody winks at you, and you look at their profile, and if you like what you see you wink back. Then they send you a little message—Hey—and you send one back. And you message each other for a little while. Then you can go offsite and switch over to IMing, which is like talking in person, except you can edit yourself: if you find yourself about to say something stupid, you can just delete it and say something better.

"So by the time you actually meet a guy in person, you've laid all this groundwork. And you're ready to graduate to having a real conversation, where you have to say what you think and there's no takebacks."

"I don't know how people got along before we invented the Internet," Kate said.

"I know, right? And the other thing is—you know this—even with going out to bars and stuff, it's harder to meet people than it is when we were in college. I can go for days and days and not meet one new person, much less a guy, much less a guy I'd want to date. But online there are scads and scads of people. And because there's so much choice, you don't have to settle. Like, if you had to stick to the two or three people you'd meet shopping for groceries or standing in line at the DMV or something, you'd think, 'Well, this guy is alright, even though I won't be able to wear heels when I go out with him because I'll look like a giant.' But online there are so many guys, you can just shop for a tall one."

Britt's new beau had lied a little about his height, actually. Everybody lied a little in their profile, though—an extra inch; a couple of years shaved off the age on your driver's license; a book you claimed to love that you'd been given as a gift and you placed on the shelf unread. You learned to correct for that pretty quickly, though; you were willing to wave away a couple of initial white lies because you'd done the same thing too.

And this guy she'd met—his name was Victor—was pretty cool! He worked in the marketing arm of a pharmaceutical corporation, introducing a new antidepressant to South American markets. Britt and Victor texted and IMed all the time, and she'd been staying over at his place a few times a week. "I might go down with him to Brazil for a week in the fall," she said. "It's moving fast, but it feels right, and this guy is really, really awesome. Like, I can't believe my luck."

"We're really happy for you," Becca said, and the rest of the women agreed, clinking their glasses.

"It was cool that we were able to get together like this," Britt said. "Just like old times." *Old times*, in this instance, being about a month ago.

"Totally," said Jen.

"We should do this again soon," Britt said, the regretful tone of her voice indicating that, no, they probably wouldn't be doing this again soon.

The next day Rebecca logged on to Facebook to find that Britt had changed her profile picture. Her new one was a snapshot that looked like it had been taken in a hotel ballroom, a spacious hall suffused with golden light. She stood next to beaming (and handsome!) Victor in his made-to-measure suit; she was smiling, and slouching ever so slightly in her Audrey Hepburn LBD.

■

And then there were three. But bereft of Britt, the remaining members of the core group quickly found that her borderline-neurotic organizational skills and her endless chatter had made her the glue that held them all together. None of the rest of them was as motivated to get people out on the town, so nights in bars and restaurants began to happen less often. And when the ladies did come out, their conversations didn't have the rambling garrulousness they'd had before—sure, Britt had had a habit of turning dialogues into monologues, but in her absence the rest of the gang realized that she'd been dutifully filling up the empty spaces between their exchanges until they felt like speaking again. Without her they silently sat in a row at the bar, people watching and sipping on their drinks. Awkward.

It wasn't much longer—a few weeks, maybe—until Jen noticed that Kate had dropped off the face of the earth, the same way Britt had before. At the subsequent emergency conclave that Jen convened, Kate casually mentioned that she'd opened up a profile on a dating site as well. "I figured, it's like throwing pearls before swine, but what the hell," Kate said. It was exhausting replying to most of the messages she got—"to be good at it you have to treat it like a job"—but she was already going out to dinner with guys a couple of times a week. "I'm not going to lie," she said, "it's nice to be taken out for a meal when you're broke. Granted, I've told the same stories so often that I'm starting to get bored being around myself. But once you get past that, it's fun! Not being serious about it, like Britt is now: just, you know, dating around. And I get what she was talking about—it's maybe mean to say it's more efficient than leaving the house and trying to meet people in person, but it is.

"Anyway. Sorry I haven't been around much lately. But this was fun. Let's get together and do this again soon!"

■

And then there were two, and Becca was pretty sure that they would never be a trio again. Without Britt's bubbliness and Kate's constant snark, Becca would be left to listen to Jen be Debbie Downer.

Becca and Jen went out for drinks once, just the two of them—they'd tried messaging Kate and Britt, but they were both indisposed, probably on a double date or something. And Becca didn't like just sitting there at the bar with Jen: it didn't feel right. Everything that

Jen said circled back to the subject of her own regrets; somehow even her mere presence managed to lace silence with despair. Even after a drink things didn't loosen up between them, and when the bartender gamely asked them if they wanted a second round, Becca cut Jen off to call for the check.

So that was that. After the group broke up, Rebecca spent a lot more time at home in the evenings. Not that this made her parents any happier: "How about putting down the phone for once," her mother said, playfully patting her cheek as if she were trying to wake up a knocked-out boxer. "You're here but not here. Quit talking to ghosts." It was an old person's way of seeing things. Really, it wasn't that she didn't hang out with her friends anymore—at least this is what Rebecca told herself—it was that the whole idea of meeting someone in a physical place, to talk to them in real time, was so *twentieth century*. It was no wonder that she didn't really want to get together with people—the skill of spoken conversation was one that people of her age and her technological savvy were evolving out of, like writing in cursive, or making popcorn without a microwave oven. Even if the gang didn't meet up anymore, and Kate was the only one left that Rebecca even texted with, social networks carried the news—she could easily figure out what was going on by looking at Britt's feed (photo after photo of her and Victor), or Kate's (lots of guys friending her whom Rebecca had never heard of—clearly dudes from dating sites), or Jen's (suddenly, a bunch of pictures of her family's two basset hounds and the labor-intensive meals she was cooking).

To call them ghosts was to miss the point: face-to-face conversation, what her mother naively thought of as "being here," was for people who still needed constant confirmation by glances and nods that they were being understood. But one of the benefits of the Internet, for people like Rebecca who had been born after it, was the merciful elimination of that need. Just as you could log on to the site of your choice and listen to everyone you wanted to at once, the never-ending streams of tweets and status updates blending into a mélange that portrayed all your friendships and acquaintances and hates and curiosities as a whole greater than the sum of its parts, so could you speak at those same places and at least be certain that, no matter what you said, you were always being heard.

Even if you looked lonely, you felt free.

6

PERFECT INFORMATION

If, thirteen years later, Rebecca did not exactly feel free, she at least felt . . . okay. She had reconciled herself to the fact that this was the life she was living and not another, no matter how much she wished that things had turned out otherwise. She was not one of those people her age who, after a divorce or a dismissal from a long-held job, drew smiles across their faces and spoke of "starting over." She had been dealt her own peculiar tragedy, and she'd come to terms with it in her own way (even if doing so involved realizing that she would never *not* be coming to terms with it; that even though she'd gotten past it, she'd never be able to get over it).

When she returned to the house after dinner and entered the living room, she found Philip and her father deep in conversation, as expected. But there was something weird about it—the two of them seemed unusually nervous and restless. Philip sat perched on the edge of his chair, leaning forward as if he were preparing to spring out of it at a moment's notice; Woody, on the sofa opposite him, squinted at Philip from beneath eyelids made slightly heavy by whiskey. A bottle of Elijah Craig bourbon and an empty shot glass sat on the coffee table in front of him. He poured himself a shot and said, "You're putting words in Popper's mouth now. He said falsifiable statements were what made science *different* from other ways of thinking. But he didn't say they made it *better* than other ways of thinking! That's something else!"

"But I'm not saying that falsifiability makes science better; I'm saying it makes science *good*."

"Which is just a way for you to make this belittling comparison without owning up to it! You can't just dismiss unfalsifiable claims out of hand as unworthy of serious thought, which you've been trying to do one way or another for half an hour now. If you do that you're just a machine; you're just a bunch of numbers."

"How have you guys been getting on?" Rebecca said, repeating the question when Woody and Philip did nothing in response but glower at each other.

"We're fine," Philip replied eventually. He sipped from a mug of freshly brewed hot tea. Black, Rebecca saw: he'd be tossing and turning tonight, trying to take the sheets for himself.

She considered sitting down to join them, but then there was that odd mix of emotions she felt roiling under the ostensibly antiseptic nature of their dialogue: frustration and rage and machismo. She sensed testosterone in the air and thought better of intervening: let the men hash this one out. "Well, I'm going to go on to bed, then," she said. "You two have fun. Dad, don't let Philip drink too much tea."

"I won't," said Woody warily to Rebecca's back as she headed down the hallway to their bedroom.

The click of the bedroom door's latch set Woody off as if it were the crack of a starting pistol. "Look here," he said. "If the blessing of being human is sentience—the ability to actually know things and to reason instead of just relying on brute instinct—then the curse of being human is the constant awareness of how much there is to know, and how little of it we *do* know. Or even how little of it we *can* know. And I don't mean stuff that goes on in a lab! I'm talking about things like what's going on in someone else's mind. Whether she truly feels the same way about you that you do about her. What would have happened if we'd done one thing instead of another. What your friends say about you when you aren't around. If we were always consciously aware of that lack of knowledge, we'd go nuts! We wouldn't be able to leave the house for pure paranoia, or getting lost in imagining better alternate histories for ourselves, or wondering exactly what our significant others are thinking when we're lying next to them in bed."

Philip glared at Woody, who nonetheless pressed forward. "So that's why we need unfalsifiable statements. They let us navigate an unimaginably complex world, with these stupid hunks of meat inside our heads that'll never let us get even close to perceiving perfect information. Sure, you don't *really* know what's going on, but you can say to yourself: *She still loves me, even though she hasn't said it in a while.* Or: *God exists, and He rewards good and punishes evil.* Or: *I live in the best of all possible worlds.* Even if you can't prove these things are true, you act as if they are, and they help you get through the day without having to deal with these paralyzing existential questions every time you take a step. They're really useful! They're indispensable. If you intend to stay sane, that is."

Philip took a breath. "I'm trying not to be angry about what you're saying," he said, "but you're making it hard. You're trying to lump all of these kinds of claims into a category—whether someone loves someone else with whether a God exists or not—and say they all ought to be treated equally, and you're also trying to say that these claims are neither better nor worse as a category than the kinds of claims that make the scientific method as powerful as it is. But that's preposterous! Surely some unfalsifiable claims don't merit consideration because they're inherently ridiculous, right? If someone told you there was a teapot orbiting the sun, you'd instinctively say it was silly! You wouldn't even stop to think about it!"

"Some philosophers might."

"Well, some philosophers waste their time thinking about all sorts of useless things. But my point is that if someone comes to me with this claim that there's some guy, with a beard, who lives in the sky, who knows everything, who can read my thoughts, who cares about the moral and ethical positions I take, and who will reward me after I die if I take the positions he prefers—it's just a silly story on its face."

"Again with this tired boilerplate rhetoric now. Is this a dorm room I'm in? Am I seventeen? I brought my *good* whiskey over here for this. First of all, it doesn't make any sense to argue about the *chance* that an unfalsifiable claim is true, because unfalsifiable claims can't be verified as true or false in the first place! It's a waste of time. The only thing I can legitimately concern myself with is the effect that *belief* in an unfalsifiable claim has on someone's actions. Like: say I'm walking down the street and someone's trailing me, thinking about picking my pocket. But he decides not to. What business is it of mine what goes on in his head when he makes up his mind? Why should I care whether he's afraid of God's punishment or the state's? What matters is that I still have my wallet, right? If you get your credit cards stolen, you're not going to say, 'Well, I hope the thief was at least an *atheist*.'"

"Oh, like religion's never been responsible for any evil—"

"Is this the part where you bring up the Crusades and the Spanish Inquisition and I bring up Stalin and Mao? Look. You're free to deny the existence of God all you like! I don't much care. I don't think the statement that an atheist can be morally good is one that needs to be defended. But to ridicule someone else's belief in God, to dismiss someone else's way of working their way through the world because their basic premises just seem inherently implausible to you—well, there's nothing else to say about it but that it's pure ethnocentrism. An occupational hazard to which scientists, in particular, seem to be singularly susceptible."

Philip placed his empty mug down on the table in front of him and looked Woody in the eyes, unblinking. "I can tell you this," he said. "I can tell you that what makes me able to get up and go to work every day is knowing that I'm playing some small part in doing what humans were put on this earth to do—"

"Interesting phrasing."

"—knowing that I'm doing my part to help uncover the universe's underlying logic. And sure, maybe my one mind can't see it all alone, but all of us working together may be able to, if we're careful thinkers and we leave clear records for those who'll follow us. That's science. And science works. And it's good."

"Do I have to point out the nature of the claim that the universe has an underlying logic that humans can ferret out if they think hard enough?"

"If you're saying that I'm motivated by unfalsifiable beliefs like everyone else: well, maybe so. But I choose the beliefs I have because they don't feel like failure. Even if it really *is* true that I can't know everything, saying so is failure. It's giving up."

■

Rebecca woke up when Philip slipped beneath the sheets next to her. She checked the time: one thirty. "I drove your father home and took a cab back," he said. "His car's autonomous, but I insisted."

"It sounded like you two were a little wound up," she said. "Are you okay?"

"Your father is an unrepentant sophist," Philip said, his voice still displaying lingering traces of bitterness. "He wants to argue just for the hell of it. I don't even know if he believes what he says, or if he takes positions just because he wants to provoke me."

"He's always been like that."

"And he doesn't know how scientists use language, either. I'm very careful when I speak. The things I say are unambiguous. But he takes my words and twists them and throws them back at me, and tries to make me mean something I didn't."

"Of course."

"It's fatuous. It's laughable."

"You should hire a referee next time."

"Hmph."

Rebecca closed her eyes and turned over on her side, her back to Philip. As she began to drop off to sleep, she felt him move close to her, spooning her while sliding his hand beneath her nightshirt to rest it gently on her breast. In another, earlier time, she might have gently pressed back against him in encouragement, but it seemed to her that this evening he wanted not sex, but simple comfort.

She thought back to the way that Philip and her father had looked when she'd walked in this evening, all wired and on edge. What conversation had been going on beneath their conversation? For what unspeakable subjects had their airy discussions served as code?

No way to know. But it seemed that somehow her father had done a minister's job, as irritating as her husband might have found him. These days she and Philip could literally go for weeks without touching each other. She had forgotten how starved she was for simple contact. It felt good; it made her feel human.

They lay still, listening to each other's breath, feeling each other's heartbeats, taking in each other's warmth.

"Tough day today," Rebecca whispered, placing her hand on his.

"Yeah. Tough day."

"I really miss Sean."

A ragged sigh tore out of him. "Me too."

7

SILENT WORLD

There came a time, a few months after the core group broke up and its members went their separate ways, that the Internet began to lose its hold on Rebecca's attention, and the never-ending river of chatter from forums and gossip sites and social networks acquired the flavor of over-chewed gum. Despite her best efforts, she fell prey to that rarest of twenty-first-century emotions: boredom.

And so, as a mild winter shaded into a premature spring, sending shoots of grass up early and befuddling the buds of wildflowers, Becca sometimes found herself closing her laptop, divesting herself of her phone (and feeling strangely naked without it), and spending her afternoons wandering alone in the world, hoping perhaps to hear the news that her father and Emerson had said was out there for those who had the ears to listen.

The nature of the towns that dotted the Northeast Corridor had changed so much since the empty summers of her college days. To drift through places like downtown Princeton or New Brunswick on weekday afternoons, when responsible people were at work, was to live in a strangely muted world. Sure, there were plenty of *sounds*— car engines; the rhythmic clicks of heels on sidewalks; the tinny *wub-wub* of dubstep beats leaking from a teenager's headphones— but these sounds had nothing much to declare; there was little of the noise in the streets and public places that, as recently as five years ago, would have indicated that humans were speaking to each other, changing each other's minds and making new meanings. The coffee shop in Princeton that would have once been filled with the raucous clamor of graduate students arguing about esoterica was now somber, the scholars' faces underlit by laptop screens as they listened to music through their earbuds. Björk was playing over the coffeehouse's speakers; the baristas were the only ones who could hear it, and the woman who poured Rebecca's coffee sang along to "Human Behaviour" in a caterwauling, unembarrassed mockery of an Icelandic accent.

Sometimes Becca could hear halves of exchanges barked into the air by men with Bluetooth headsets, or women who concealed them beneath their hair; stripped of their complements, their declamations seemed half mad, or at least as if it would have been best to make them in private. (One afternoon, she sat on a bench next to a matronly woman with clunky eyeglasses and rouge ground into the wrinkles of her cheeks, who spoke as if she were a medium hosting a séance. "I need to talk to you," she said, her voice quivering. "I need to talk to you, and not to your machine. My feng shui consultant has made his report: my walls have too many pictures of men. That's maybe why the polyps. That's maybe why the dreams.") These messages spoken to the ether were less likely to occur in bars, which were somehow still a bastion of twentieth-century customs, but even there, around two o'clock, after the lunch rush, you'd see some red-faced former alpha male bellying up to the bar, ordering a pint of stout, and placing his BlackBerry in front of him as the sigil of his authority. If the phone didn't ring or beep by the time his beer was half drained, he'd ring someone else himself, straightening his back and throwing out his chest as the connection completed. "Rick! Rick. I wasn't expecting to get you! I was expecting to get sent straight to your voicemail. I got a lot of stuff going on right now, but I just wanted to run something by you since I had a couple of minutes. . . . Yeah, I know! Modern times, right? . . . What do you mean you're letting *me* go? I called *you*."

There were still as many people in the silent world as there had been before; they had not been raptured. Nor had they been zombified or made dumb by their devices, as her parents would have sarcastically said: if anything, there was more intelligence in their gazes when they stared at their phones or laptops than when they lifted their eyes to look past their screens into the world beyond. Their minds were merely elsewhere, absconded to new and shining places with strange geometries.

It was the service staff of the old world that kept its secret as they kept it running: the nature of their jobs meant they *had* to stay here, at least until the ends of their shifts. When they caught Becca's eye and saw that she, like them, was entirely *here* in the old world with them, they'd often share a sign of commonality or collusion with her, something as small as a smile that lasted long enough to let her know that, unlike all the others that had been granted to customers, this one was genuine. Sometimes, if business was slow and they got the chance, they'd try to make her linger at the counter, and they'd want to just *talk*, about whatever was on their minds. Once she stopped into an empty chocolate shop to purchase a fifty-cent morsel, and the cashier delayed her for ten minutes while she told her a tale of a failed wine bar that her husband had tried to open up in Sarasota, Florida. Once she had gone into a Mediterranean restaurant and bar that had two-dollar tapas if you bought a glass of wine, and as she tucked into a little bowl of albondigas, chasing each morsel of lamb with a swallow of Merlot, enjoying one of the surprising little pleasures of being alone in the silent world, the French-immigrant bartender tipped her off to an iPhone app that would let her download free recordings of lectures on the philosophy of mind from a professor at Berkeley. Once she was in a long coffee shop line, and she saw the woman at the register roll her eyes in exhaustion at a customer in front of her who was attempting to place a detailed order while simultaneously carrying on a cell-phone conversation with someone who seemed to be in another country, her request for a vanilla latte with a triple shot and her list of the amenities of a Cairo hotel blending together into an unintelligible mishmash. Rebecca and the barista shared a fleeting smirk; later, when she received her cappuccino, she found that a smiling face had been drawn in the foam that floated on its surface.

Sometimes you saw visitors return to the silent world, here for a quick trip to discharge the duties that their bodies or traditions demanded. It was so strange that here, you could see two people you'd never met and infer their past histories with such certainty and ease: not like in the new world, where everyone seemed so blurred around the edges. There's a man sitting at a table with a young girl outside a Panera at nine o'clock on a Sunday morning: he's clean-shaven in a button-down shirt, leaning forward solicitously while speaking quiet endearments with a voice unused to subtlety; she slumps in her chair, her baby fat still clinging to her arms and cheeks as she begins to head into her teenage years, her leg jittering restlessly as her gaze avoids the man's eyes, preferring instead to trace the paths of sidewalk cracks. You see all this and you instantly know: father and daughter. He is willing time to slow, counting the hours before his allotted custody ends. Her dancing leg is still burning off the sugar from the cakes and chocolates he'd proffered the night before, sweets intended to stand in for unspoken love, tendered in the knowledge that her mother surely only served her dishes piled high with taste-less green things. Beneath the table the father unconsciously slides his thumb over the leather cover of his smartphone, as if it is a com-forting totem. Always, even now, the new world calls him back.

The online daters meeting in person for the first time are always the easiest to spot. The man always shows up first, five minutes before the top of the hour, nervous and eager, staking out a space at the bar with an empty chair next to him, draping his arm across it as if asserting his future possession of the woman who will soon appear.

The woman always shows up ten minutes later, moving with slow alertness into the space of the bar, looking at all of the men while trying not to look like she's looking, attempting to map the photo-graphs she remembers onto one of the faces of the people around her. Then there's that weird moment of mutual recognition, when people who may have exchanged the dearest of confidences in the new world realize that here, in the old one, they are still strangers to each other. Half the time they bobble that first greeting, his lips colliding clumsily with her cheek as she hastily turns it to him, their subsequent embrace halfway between a handshake and a hug. "It's so nice to meet you finally," the woman says, withdrawing tactfully, unsure if what she says is true.

■

Becca still saw Kate every couple of weeks. She was doing okay for herself, picking up shifts as a server at two different restaurants in Hopewell, and planning to move out of her parents' place soon, split-ting the rent on an apartment with another waitress. "It's going to be just like a TV sitcom," Kate said. "All we need is a hot guy next door who'll be forever unable to decide which one of us he wants to sex up. It'll be platonic, but with *tension*! In the final episode there's a three-way."

It seemed like every time Rebecca met up with Kate, her hair had changed color, going from platinum blond to ash brown to auburn and back to a different shade of blond, perhaps with a single strand of bubblegum pink that could be tucked out of sight when she wanted to present as respectable. "Here's the thing," she said to Rebecca over drinks—this particular Monday evening she was letting her pink lock dangle in front of her face. She was still deep into the online-dating thing. She had three different profiles on three different sites now: the photos she had of herself sporting different hairstyles had given her the idea. "They've all got sort of different personalities—I mean, they're all *like* me, but I talk more about different parts of my life. Like, Kathy is all into being athletic—don't message me unless you think you can beat my time in a 5K—and Katie is all into music, with this long list of albums she likes by Lard and Fishbone and Refused, and Katharine is total nerdbait: Oh, boo hoo, it's been ten years and I'm still not over *Firefly* getting canceled. And sometimes I'll hear from the same guy on all three profiles! And not even the same message! Like, he'll tell Kathy all about how he can run a seven-and-a-half-minute mile, not world-class, but pretty good, and Katie gets to hear how cool it is that when you see Fishbone live Angelo Moore plays like five different horns including a bass saxophone, and for Katharine he drops this little anecdote about he went to a con and ended up having drinks at a hotel bar with Jewel Staite, who told him about all these cool ideas that Joss would have put in the second season if the show had gotten renewed. I'm like, you looked all this stuff up on the Internet. It's still fun, though. In real life it isn't so easy to spot the bullshitters and the nonstarters."

When Kate asked Becca if she was ever going to fill out a profile, Becca demurred. "I haven't been online as much lately. I've just been kinda, you know, bumming around. Outside."

"Oh, yeah," Kate said. "I did some of that too, for a little while. *Screw this computer: I'm going to get some air. I'm going to be around humanity.* You know what the problem with the real world is?"

"What?"

"It's *lonely.* Because everyone goes online the second they get the chance! The real world is awesome if you want to be by yourself, though. Maybe that's your thing now."

■

How many profiles on these sites were filled out by still-intoxicated people on weekend nights, after they'd struck out yet again in the bars? At two a.m. on Sunday morning their servers probably glowed red-hot.

And that was when Rebecca finally took the plunge. She hadn't been out looking to meet guys—she'd just made a Saturday-night appointment to catch up with Britt, whom she hadn't seen in person in months. But Britt's boyfriend Victor had shown up at the local brewpub as well, the uninvited third. (Later, Rebecca would reflect that had she not hidden Britt's messages in her Facebook news feed, she would have seen this coming—Britt sent mash notes to Victor via status update every six to eight hours, and it should have been obvious that a girls' night out like the ones in the old days was no longer an option. Victor's presence should have been assumed.)

Rebecca sat by herself on one side of a booth, watching Britt and Victor canoodle. They were feeding each other French fries! And they always had their hands all over each other, though they tried to pass it off as horseplay. It was ridiculous. And Britt's constant chatter was all about them, never about her. ("Our friends have just *totally* given up on us: they call us 'Brictor' now!" She giggled. Victor grinned and rubbed her thigh.) And she kept floating these trial balloons about their future together, in the form of idle comments about how the real estate market was turning around, or teases about Victor's poor culinary skills ("I'd have to do all the cooking for both of us or he'd poison himself!"). It was absolutely nauseating. Rebecca couldn't wait for it to end.

But Britt looked so *happy*, was the thing. And Kate was right—the real world *was* lonely now. If you wanted to do what humans did, you had to go where humans were.

So when she got home that evening, Rebecca said good night to her parents, shut herself up in her room, and opened up the screw-top bottle of Cabernet Sauvignon she'd stashed in her closet. (Okay: *stashed* was overstating the case. She *chose to keep* the wine there, in the closet, behind some stuff.)

After a couple of drinks, Rebecca reached that perfect moment when booze casts a pleasant haze on everything but doesn't really impair you or make you feel stupid. As boring as surfing the net could seem when you were sober, there were few things in life more captivating than goofing off online while drinking. Intoxication mixed well with the way the web provided chains of distractions nested within other distractions. Even just a drink or two could suppress that need for information to be *fulfilling* in some way, the desire that made browsing such an unsatisfying time-waster sometimes— without that, you could get into a groove and see the larger shape of things, see the Internet the way it saw itself. With diminished inhibitions you could leave yourself open to its suggestions, letting it show you things that'd tickle your hindbrain or give you a nice surprise. You could let it try to divine your wants from the trail of data you left behind as you bounced from site to site.

For instance, the Internet knew, better than Rebecca did, that what she wanted to do right then and there was open up an account on a brand-new dating site called Lovability. It showed her three ads for Lovability within a half hour, in fact. The first appeared when she checked her Gmail account, the text above her inbox claiming that Lovability would let her "find a match through twenty-six axes of compatibility!" The second showed up during a quick binge of clips from old *Simpsons* episodes on YouTube (a photo of an ambiguously ethnic woman with curly hair and clunky black eyeglasses, sitting across a table from an equally ambiguously ethnic man with hazel eyes, a shaven head, and a sweater vest; both had the self-satisfied look of people who were glad they were themselves and not someone else. They probably both had apartments that got lots of sunlight. "Twenty-six axes of compatibility!" read the caption beneath them). The third came when she was scrolling through a catty comment thread on the Huffington Post, the woman here an aggressively freckled redhead who was getting a piggyback ride from a square-jawed guy who looked like he'd stepped off the set of a soap opera. That one was the charm. She clicked it, and when she saw how easy it was to get started—you just needed to give them your gender, age, e-mail address, zip code, and a couple of other things—she figured: hell, why not. Curiosity killed the cat; satisfaction brought him back.

■

The next morning Rebecca woke up in the house alone, the clock on her nightstand reading ten thirty, the empty wine bottle on its side next to her bed. Mom and Dad must have already left for church, letting her sleep in.

She sat up, feeling like her skull had been stuffed with cotton. Pancakes and black coffee would stave off the incipient headache—the stuff to make them was already in the kitchen. But first she opened her laptop to take a quick look at Facebook and Twitter and e-mail.

Oh.

Oh yeah.

She didn't *not* remember doing that—it was just that seeing the Lovability web page, its muted blues decorated with tastefully playful pink accents, reminded her of what she'd been up to before falling asleep. She'd apparently filled out forty percent of her profile. She'd answered a few questions (things she was good at: laughter; sleeping late; receiving back rubs. Things she couldn't do without: family; friends; electricity. Wasn't she more interesting than this? This part would need work if she was going to be serious about it, which she wasn't—she was just goofing around). She'd uploaded a couple of cellphone photos from when she'd been out nights with Britt and Kate and Jen. She was making a duck-faced pout in one of them, her face harshly lit by the phone's flash in the darkened bar, but so were Kate and Britt—surely the irony came through.

A heart pulsed insistently in the upper right corner of the screen, with a numeral 2 inside it: she had messages! Already, she had messages. But the first was just a link to a video welcoming her to the site, featuring Gaia Williams, the Lovability CEO. Gaia was a woman who'd probably always look thirty, with a slender face, a long modelly swan's neck, gorgeously lissome legs, and a wide, welcoming smile. "Now it's time for the magic to happen!" Gaia said, going on to talk about the "efficiency," "precision," and "effectiveness" of Lovability's proprietary personality-matching algorithms. "The more you tell us about you, the more we'll be able to help," she said, clasping her hands and winsomely cocking her head to the side. "So fill out that profile, answer some of the questions in our super-fun quizzes and compatibility surveys, and let's get going!"

The second of Rebecca's two messages was from one Jonny9266, and read, in its entirety:

hnnghnnnnggghh

To be fair, she had only filled out forty percent of her profile, so perhaps preverbal grunts were all she could expect in return. But Lovability promised a custom match for her if she brought her profile completion rate up to fifty percent—for now, the face of her potential beau was a featureless silhouette hiding behind a hovering question mark.

Just a few more stupid questions. Hell: why not.

■

A couple of days later, working on and off, she'd gotten the profile as good as she could get it. She'd listed a selection of books she liked that would make her look smart but not eggheaded; she'd said she loved to laugh (trite, but true, and everyone else was saying it, so she didn't want to seem like the girl who sits in the corner at a party with a frown on her face). She said she liked peace and quiet, but also the energy of clubs or a night in the city. She'd scattered a few emoticons through her text even though using them made her feel like a failure when it came to using the English language, but again, all the other women were doing it, and she didn't want to seem humorless. She said she loved a nice glass of wine.

For some reason she found it difficult to express herself, like she could have in an e-mail or even a text message. There was some intangible thing about the site itself that made everyone seem sort of the same. It wasn't that they were boring, exactly (if anything, people were always going on in their dating profiles about how they were the exact opposite of boring, even as they all listed the same five things they wouldn't be able to do without in life). But they weren't nearly as interesting in their descriptions as they would probably be if you met them by chance out in the world. It was as if the questions that were meant to serve as conversation starters, or allow the site's elves to begin plotting your personality on its compatibility axes, worked instead to make everyone seem equally bland and anonymous.

Were there fads that dictated the content of profile photos, certain poses and features that were thought to be more alluring for one reason or another? Almost all of the thumbnails of women looked similar—cropped tightly to avoid providing an initial hint of the shape of the body, their faces cocked in coy three-quarter profile.

Many of them had their lips pursed (and Rebecca, noticing this, quietly deleted the photo of her making duck faces with the rest of the old gang). If you clicked through to look at a portfolio of photographs, you could generally get a little more of the story: those women who considered themselves in shape posted shots of themselves hiking, or assuming yoga poses, or, in one particular instance, curling a twenty-pound dumbbell; others had photos of themselves draped in fabrics that confused the eye and obscured their curves, or displayed their bosoms if they had them to show.

Some of the profiles were clearly fake, jokes set up by teenagers to bait the lonely—stock photos of nubile babes reclining on beach towels with drinks in their hands. The fake profiles usually spoke boldly of sexual proclivities; real women tended not to talk that forthrightly about that sort of thing, though you could sometimes tunnel down into the data of the ladies who seemed the most demure to find they'd blithely answered questions in quizzes like "Do you like the taste of semen?" or "Would you consider acting out a rape fantasy with a partner who asked you to?" The whole site was set up to get its users to yield up their privacy, one way or another. It put Rebecca on guard, but as Gaia Williams cheerfully cautioned her in somewhat different words, guarded people didn't score on Lovability. Guarded people ended up forever alone.

Once Rebecca started getting messages from guys (and it took about three days for them to start arriving in force, four or five a day), she started to understand why the profiles of some of the women she'd looked at before she filled out her own were so bizarrely defensive— surely it would have been easier not to have a profile on Lovability in the first place than to spend thousands of words describing the kinds of guys you *didn't* want to talk to. ("let me just state this right upfront before you start reading about me because I do not want to waste your valuable time. do NOT message me If you are OVER 35, if you are MARRIED, if you are just looking to have a good time because I am NOT a good time girl, if you are not 5'11" or taller, if you are not white (I am not racist, my parents did not raise me that way), if you are not living in your own place with your own job, or if you cannot write REAL SENTENCES in REAL ENGLISH without using f***, b****, or c***.") If the men's profiles were generally unappealing to Rebecca on first glance (with a photo from a senior prom, the guy's date cropped out of the image except for a disembodied, bracelet-clad arm draped across his shoulder; or a shot taken by pointing a phone's camera at a bedroom mirror, one hand lifting up the hem of a sleeveless T-shirt to reveal a scrupulously maintained six-pack), then the messages they sent were truly awful. They seemed to have been written by men who had learned what little they knew of women by watching James Bond movies through a scrim made of cheesecloth.

There were the nonsensical gruntings, and the f and the b and the c (meant, Rebecca was sure, with endearment). The messages that were longer and more coherent either showed signs of being sent en masse to every new woman who showed up on the site, or were mistakes made by guys who probably had multiple browser windows open. It was news to Rebecca, for instance, that she wore eyeglasses, and it was further news that for some guys, girls with glasses was, like, a *thing*?

Heyyy youre really hott! Ever since I was a kid I have fetish for girls with bad eyesight. I like to think about when were in bed together and I take her glasses off and hide them and its dark and she cant see and she gets a little scared. Would you tell me your prescription? I am -4 in both eyes. You look like youre at least -5 which is super hott!

Then there were the guys who must have been watching reality shows about pickup artists on cable, and thought it would be a good idea to lead with an insult:

Don't take this the wrong way—I don't mean to be critical—but I can tell from your profile that you really think you're hot shit. Arrogant, and pretentious, too. But I like that in a woman. You aren't going to find many guys around here who are willing to deal with arrogance. (I am going to go out on a limb and predict that with an attitude like yours, you haven't had much success on this site so far.)

If you want to try to convince me that you're something other than what I think you are, reply to this message, and we'll talk. But you probably won't write back. I know when I've hit a nerve.

How this whole thing had worked out for Britt and Kate was a mystery—one had met the love of her life right out of the gate, and the other had more guys than she knew what to do with. It was hard to imagine them having the patience to deal with all this stuff. And yet the whole experience was somehow compelling. If you could keep in mind that what people were communicating with wasn't you, but a stripped-down version of yourself, a little marionette made out of data, then the things that other people said to your puppet became amusing rather than insulting, and the act of puppetry became a game instead of something that mattered. Once you got it straight in your head, the whole thing became, in a weird way, fun.

■

Eight days after opening her profile, Rebecca struck gold—or, if not gold, something that at least held the promise of a precious metal, a shining glint of a vein:

> Hi! My name is Bradley, and I've just moved out to the New Jersey area from Los Angeles, where I worked in entertainment law (don't hate me!). I took a pay cut for my new job as a corporate consultant on copyright law, but the decrease in my cost of living makes up for it, and my hours are better. However, I don't know many people here, and I'd like to meet someone new!
>
> In my free time I like to go biking (twenty-five miles on a temperate spring day is not unusual for me). I also like board games (my Scrabble scores come in at around 325–350 when I'm playing seriously and sticking to the official dictionary; my chess Elo rating is around 1600, which isn't too shabby).
>
> I'd like to invite you to check out my profile! Let's talk if you like—you seem really cool, and I'd love to hear from you.

Okay. So there were some things about the note that were a little off. The information about taking a pay cut was, she supposed, meant to make him sound selfless, but it came off as self-congratulatory. And all the numbers gave the impression that he was maybe a little anal-retentive. You got the idea that you'd be playing Scrabble one evening, and he would lay down some bullshit two-letter word like ZA for thirty-three points, and if he saw you roll your eyes he'd throw a fit and say he really didn't think this relationship could continue. And though he said he thought she was cool, he didn't say *why:* he gave no real sign that he'd even read her profile in the first place. This might be a batch message, like so many others.

But it was so well written: it was amazing to her that she'd come so quickly to find proper grammar and spelling to be a turn-on, but here she was. Look at that properly nested series of punctuation marks after "don't hate me." That's hot. Look at that semicolon! Bradley might have been the first guy to message her who'd used a semicolon.

And the message was polite, too. It didn't just assume that she wanted to screw. Maybe she just wanted to be friends. Maybe if it turned out that she had a chess rating around the same as his, he'd call it a win.

And he was cute. His profile pic showed him with his bike, one of those expensive bikes that required special shoes that attached straight to the pedals. He had, it had to be said, the perfect body for spandex bike gear. And a bright smile (though his cleanly shaven head was likely meant to disguise a receding hairline). And a totally ripped upper body. And . . . yeah. Yes, I will. Yes.

She clicked the pulsing heart at the top of the screen, and it quivered as a window sprang open with a text box for her reply to his message:

> Hey, Bradley! Nice to e-meet you. I'm new here, too. (I mean new to Lovability, not new to New Jersey—I haven't been able to escape here, and can't figure out why anyone would come here voluntarily. But maybe you'll be able to explain that to me.)
>
>   I have a confession to make: one of the proudest moments of my life was when I was able to play QUADRANT in a game against this guy, and it covered two triple-word score squares.
>
>   Entertainment law! Did you meet any famous people? I rode on a subway with Christopher Walken once in NYC. You would think he'd take cabs everywhere, but there he was, just like the rest of us. Everyone was trying to look like they weren't staring at him.
>
>   Thanks for getting in touch!

He wrote back within a few hours (his favorite Scrabble play: SYZYGY with a blank for the third Y; his most memorable celebrity encounter: Marty with Bobby D). And after a flurry of e-mails during which they exchanged all manner of trivia about themselves (the first R-rated movies they'd seen; their favorite alcoholic drinks; their preferences in ethnic restaurants), they decided to just skip the intermediate step of talking on the phone, and meet for a happy-hour drink after Bradley got off work on Wednesday.

Bradley picked the place, a sports bar in Princeton, which wasn't the most intimate place for a conversation—it was baseball season, and Mets and Phillies games were blaring from the dozens of HDTVs in the place. But Rebecca figured that Bradley was a sporty kind of guy—he was probably planning in advance for the opportunity to flick his gaze over her shoulder occasionally to check a score. And indeed, when he showed up, the first thing he said, before he even greeted her, was that games in Citi Field were a lot more interesting since they moved the left field wall twelve feet closer to the plate.

"It's nice to meet you finally," Rebecca said as Bradley seated himself at the bar (no kiss, no hug) and loosened the knot of his tie. She felt that strange confusion she'd seen displayed in others' faces during her wanderings through the silent world, as she tried to reconcile the breathing, living man in front of her with the pictures of him she'd seen online and the texts and e-mails he'd sent. The rumpled lines of his suit disguised the shape of his body, but she suspected from the stubble of his hairline, which sat farther back on his head than she'd expected, that that shot of him with his bike had been taken a few years ago, at the beginning of the end of his prime.

"Guess how old I am," Bradley said, as if he'd noticed her quick glance at his forehead. "Go ahead."

His profile had said he was twenty-eight; she figured thirty-four, though he looked a little older—the lines around his eyes suggested time spent in the sun. "Well, you said in your profile that you were twenty-eight," she said.

"That was maybe a bit of a lie."

She pretended to mull it over. "Thirty?"

"Thirty-*four*," Bradley said gleefully. "But I don't look like it! That's the crappy thing about these dating sites—they make age into nothing but a number, and they penalize you for having good genes and aging well. If I don't *look* thirty-four, I shouldn't have to *say* I'm thirty-four, at least at first. When I'm sixty I'm going to look forty." He placed his hand on hers: it was a little cold, but she repressed a flinch. "That was the only lie I told on my profile, and I just confessed to it. The rest of the data I provided you with is correct. Total honesty from here on out."

She forced a laugh. "Everybody lies a little," she said.

Over the next half hour, as she nursed her gin and tonic while Bradley drained his Miller Lite, Rebecca would have ample cause to reflect on the slight strangeness of what he'd said: *The rest of the data I provided you with is correct.* Bradley was a man made out of numbers; nearly every sentence out of his mouth bespoke his belief in the quantifiable life. He talked about how his move to New Jersey from LA had shortened his commute. ("Forty-three minutes to eleven, on average. So thirty-two minutes each way, times two: sixty-four minutes. A little over an hour a day; five hours a week. You can do a lot with five hours.") He went on about his change in income, though in a concession to tact he spoke in terms of percentages gained and lost rather than absolute values. ("When they made the offer, I did the math and saw I'd see a drop in income of twenty-eight percent. But my expenditures could easily drop by thirty-five percent, and I'd be able to maintain roughly the same standard of living. My apartment's square footage is actually slightly larger, in fact.") Every once in a while, when he looked up at one of the TVs to see a batter he knew at the plate, he'd cut himself off in mid-sentence to say something like "Oof, that guy is on the interstate" or "He's just making absolute hash out of his PECOTA projections—good for him."

"It's time to transition to more intimate subjects of discussion," Bradley announced as soon as the bartender brought his second beer, and though said subjects of discussion were, Rebecca supposed, nominally more intimate, they were still primarily data-driven. He described his eating habits ("If I come in above 2200 calories by the end of the day I feel like crap the next morning. Miller Lite: 128. With gin and tonic you're probably ringing up around 200, by the way, depending on the pour: it's not the booze you have to watch out for, but the sugar"). Oddly, he mentioned his success on Lovability ("It's trending upward, though it's not at the level it was when I was on the sites in LA. When I first joined I averaged between zero and one date in a given week. Now it's upticked to between one and two. Closer to two"). Even more oddly, he related a statistic he'd heard that he found surprising: that ninety percent of adult Americans got cold sores. ("It's amazing that, given its prevalence, people treat oral herpes as such a scandalous thing. If you get to a certain age and you've lived an active social life it's a practical inevitability!")

As Rebecca's opinion about Bradley shifted from amusement to boredom to active distaste, her responses to his statistical declamations decayed from curt *mmm-hmm*s to silent nods to blank indifference. Bradley responded by pulling an iPad from his briefcase, loading up a Scrabble app, and placing the tablet in front of her without a word. They played a quick game and he cleaned her clock, 330 to 175. ("You need to learn how to count tiles so you don't make mistakes like that," he said near the end of the match, his tone more in sorrow than anger.) Then he settled the bill, they shook hands (awkward!), and parted in silence.

■

Late that night, Rebecca received a message from Bradley that was a hell of a thing.

Dear Rebecca—

You may have picked up on my growing disappointment with you this afternoon as our first meeting progressed. I have to say that though you seem quite personable in your electronic communications, in person your behavior is a little lacking in some of the traits that would let you get from a first to a second date with regularity. If Lovability had a rating system, I would award you 2.5 out of 5 stars; however, if it used a scale that only allowed for integral values, I would unfortunately be forced to round down to two.

Here are some suggestions for what you could do to improve the initial impression you make. I am speaking here as a veteran of the online dating scene in LA, which is MUCH more intense than New Jersey's—there, you are competing with aspiring actors and actresses, and a professionally produced headshot and a warm demeanor are the bare minimum necessary to get in the game. By the end of my first year in LA my askback rate (the rate at which my first dates with women led to second dates) was a remarkable 68%. So I know what I'm talking about. I hope you take this constructive criticism in the manner in which it is intended.

1. Vary your responses to inquiries. When our conversation began,

you seemed quite cheerful and animated, but as it progressed you became much less so. I asked you a series of questions that were intended to give you opportunities to reveal more about yourself, but you offered only binary answers, and then, troublingly, no answers at all. If you want your date to go well, you need to display more interest.

2. Direct the flow of conversation. Dialogue is collaborative! One consequence of your reticence was that I was forced to propose all of the topics of discussion, both before and after the transition to more personal subjects. If you contribute topics of your own then it will make you appear more engaged: you should aim to bring up one new subject for every one introduced by your date.

3. Take control of the path of the date. If you want the initial meeting to extend beyond the planned drinks, there are many ways you can go about doing this. You can directly say, for instance, "So I wasn't thinking about this when you showed up, but . . . do you have any plans for dinner? I'm starving, and I could really go for some pad thai." Or you can make a vaguer, more general statement such as "After this, I'm up for whatever," or "Hey, I don't really want to go home yet, Bradley: I'm having a lot of fun." Again, this comes down to a general lack of engagement on your part. Without your feedback I was left to offer a game of Scrabble, which was not the best way to end the meeting.

4. Don't lie about your ability in Scrabble. I won't go into an analysis of your strategic and tactical errors here, in the interest of brevity, but your amateurish playing style was quite evident.

Now, despite my reservations as expressed above, I really do feel that we had some chemistry. So I would like to give things another chance. Would you respond to this message within the next three days, with a suggestion of a place you'd like us to visit together, or an activity that you believe we would both enjoy? I would be forced to construe a delay of more than three days as an unfortunate sign of indifference.

I hope to hear from you soon.

Best, Bradley

Well.

After reading through the whole missive again, the better to get herself good and angry, she poured herself a glass of Chardonnay and prepared to spend about an hour composing a message that would *really* tell this guy off point by point, because holy shit. But then once she opened the text box and began to type, she looked at the wall of words she was replying to, and opted instead for five quick keystrokes of netspeak:

tl;dr

Too long; didn't read. She fired off the message, belted back half the glass, and shut her laptop. Jesus fuck. Human beings.

■

The next morning Rebecca woke up late (not really with a headache, it wasn't a headache, she'd merely stayed up late watching most of a season of *Archer* and killing the half-full bottle of Chardonnay in the fridge and, okay, starting on the bottle of Cab in the bedroom closet. She hadn't drunk the whole bottle, but enough to make for a poor night's sleep: she'd snapped awake at a quarter to five, unable to drop off again. Of course she was going to feel a little muzzy after that, a little fuzzy). She figured that a Belgian waffle with a slab of Canadian bacon on the side would set her straight, so she walked into town and ordered up the meal at a little café. (Her developing habit of downing most of a bottle of wine at night now and again and chasing it with a big syrupy breakfast the next morning was starting to make for a muffin top, but it'd be easy to get that weight off whenever she wanted. Not a problem.) Rebecca was the only person in the place without a phone or a laptop—even the couple at the table next to her both had iPhones in their hands, their heads bowed as if in silent prayer.

When the server brought her food over to her table, she lingered for a couple of seconds. "Enjoy your breakfast," she sang. "It's got a special ingredient!"

"What?" Rebecca asked suspiciously.

"Love," the server said. She smiled, pivoted neatly on the ball of one foot, and returned to the kitchen (and Rebecca glimpsed a flash of the fifth-grade girl still inside her, doggedly going through her routines at the barre).

As Rebecca devoured her waffle, she saw the other customers poking away at their devices, and imagined the flat, blurred faces of their digital identities hovering before them like gossamer masks. She'd spent so much time on Lovability that walking around Stratton by herself evoked a constant sense of déjà vu: she was confident, for instance, that the guy at the table on the other side of the café was in fact SureShot26, whose collection of profile photos was mostly composed of shots taken before fraternity formals. For all she knew, her server might now be checking the messages of OliveOyl782. Perhaps in the new world their eyeless avatars were bumping up against each other in blind confusion, while their creators sat here with only a wall and the custom of the country to separate them.

Perhaps in some other timeline, SureShot26 does not have his headphones on when OliveOyl782 brings him his challah French toast; instead of starting in on the food without a word when an anonymous, disembodied hand places it in front of him, he looks up, into her eyes. And it's just like in the movies. Sparks fly, literal sparks that singe an array of tiny black dots into the paper napkin in which his fork and knife are wrapped. An unspoken, unspeakable message arcs like an electrical charge from mind to mind of the customers in the restaurant; all the electronic devices in the café short out at once and melt into lumps of slag and plastic. OliveOyl782 begins to weep. "You don't understand how many mistakes I've made," she sobs. "All the wrong steps I've taken; all the lies I've told and chosen to believe in turn. But in spite of this God has still seen fit to show me grace."

SureShot26 stands up and quietly embraces her. He doesn't know what to say, but both of them are confident that the right words will come in their own time; their whole lives together are ahead of them, and they will have plenty of time to speak to each other with care and truth. But silence, now, is best.

8

LABORATORY TOUR

We're going to need to get you a temporary security badge," Carson said to Kate as he ushered her through the sliding glass doors of the building that housed the Steiner lab. "Security here is a pain ever since we started taking funding from DAPAS: they call more shots than we'd like. With their money come these paranoid security measures. Our badges have RFID transmitters. And there are monitors through this whole place that check for human-shaped heat signatures: if there's a signature that doesn't correspond to an RFID signal, it raises the alarm. And we've got ceiling-mounted cameras, like this is a casino or something."

"Sounds very high-tech."

"And completely unnecessary. Anybody smart enough to know what to steal from this lab deserves whatever they can take. Maybe the physicists at the Frascati and Perth labs would know how to find their way around this place, but that's it. Most people would just go for the laptops."

Carson and Kate approached a desk at which two security guards sat, one with his chair propped back against a wall as he turned a page in a yellowed paperback book. (Kate glanced at the novel's title: *Mind of My Mind*.) The other guard was not even bothering to disguise the fact that he was checking Kate out from top to toe. Remembering what Rebecca had said about her first trip to the lab being like an introduction to the family, Kate had opted for an ensemble that was conservative but still cute, the sort of outfit that a dame in need of services would wear to Philip Marlowe's office: a long gray pleated skirt, a simple white blouse, and black pumps with modest heels. She meant men's gazes to slide off of her today, not stick, but the guard at the desk looked at Kate, then Carson, then back to Kate again. He beamed. "Carlton!" he said.

"My name's Carson."

"Oh, yeah: I keep forgetting," the guard replied. Kate looked at the two of them in puzzlement: this seemed like an iteration of a running joke on the guard's part that Carson did not want to explain.

"Are you going to need a temp badge for your lady friend?" the guard said, still staring. At least he was looking at her face now.

"I'm showing her around the lab," Carson said, and then, a bit more quietly, "This is Kate."

"It's nice to meet you," Kate said, feeling a little awkward as she stepped forward and extended her hand. The guard clasped it with an unexpected tenderness. "Spivey," he said. "It's a real pleasure to meet you, too. We don't get to see much beauty in here: just a bunch of machines, and ugly people like this guy," indicating Carson with a nod of his head.

The other guard turned a page in his book, his face stoic.

"Oh ha-ha-*ha*," Kate laughed as she withdrew her hand, injecting some clear phoniness into the chuckle for Carson's sake.

Spivey reached down to riffle through a drawer of the desk, extracting a blank keycard. "Show me some pearly whites, please," he said to Kate in a bass that put her strangely in mind of butterscotch. He swiveled around the laptop on his desk, tapping the tiny camera mounted above its screen.

Kate smiled as Spivey slotted the keycard into a little color printer and pressed a button on the laptop's keyboard; a few seconds later, he withdrew the card, which now featured a pixilated image of her face. Somehow the card also had her full name (with her given name spelled "Kathryn," not "Kate"), her birth date, and the last four digits of her Social Security number.

"Now this is good for eight hours," Spivey said, fastening the keycard to a lanyard and handing it to her. "After four the picture starts to fade. When it's gone that means we don't want to see you anymore: we don't care how pretty you are." He looked at Carson. "Though if you're *lucky*, maybe we'll be able to set you up with a permanent one of these." Spivey's grin had something strange sitting behind it.

But Carson was already withdrawing, with a gentle hand on Kate's shoulder to steer her away. "Thanks, Spivey."

"Good luck, Carlton!" Spivey said after him, a little loudly.

"It's Carson," Carson replied over his shoulder.

"Oh, *yeah*," Spivey said, louder still. "Slipped my mind."

"What was that about?"

"Spouses of lab employees get permanent IDs, with pictures that don't fade," Carson said, in a tone implying that any further questions she had were best dropped.

■

Once through the door, Kate found herself in a long, narrow, dusty, harshly lit corridor lined with doorways on either side, featuring an imposing set of double doors at its end. "Why are the doors taken off the hinges?" Kate asked. She could see straight into all the rooms as she and Carson passed.

"It was Philip's idea," Carson replied. "He says it fosters community. But he also probably thinks we'd sit around playing video games all day if we could close our doors. Though Philip gets his own door, of course." Carson indicated it at the other end of the hallway, with its window of frosted glass. "The privilege of power. He might be playing *Dwarf Fortress* right now."

Peering through one of the open doorways into the office beyond, Kate saw Dennis sitting on the floor with his legs folded up beneath him. All the chairs in the room held stacks of books and papers and journals that threatened to topple. Wrappers from granola bars were strewn around him; next to him sat a half-full two-liter bottle of Diet Coke. He was staring up with rapt attention at an insect-like quadracopter hovering in the middle of the room, its red and blue lights blinking as its rotors buzzed. He clutched its remote controller in his hands. He wasn't piloting it; he was just *looking* at it.

"Hey, Dennis," Kate said. "Haven't seen you since the party at Rebecca's. How are you?"

"Hello, Kate," Dennis said, his eyes still on the quadracopter. "I'm good." His usual overbearing bonhomie was altogether absent.

"Whatcha up to," Carson said.

"Debugging. The galaxial drift subroutine."

"We were going to have to get around to taking a closer look at that eventually: no point in putting it off."

"It's a pain in the ass." Dennis's miniature quadracopter quivered briefly in midair.

"Well, keep at it."

"Will do. It's good to see you, Kate."

"Nice to see you, too," Kate said, and the two of them left him to his meditation.

"He *was* actually debugging, by the way, not slacking off," Carson said in response to Kate's unspoken question. "I've never seen anything like it. He'll stare at a screen of code for a few minutes with the font shrunk down to six points; then he'll go into his office and play with the helicopter. Then he'll come back to the computer, delete the entire block of code he was looking at, and retype it from scratch. And it'll *work*. He can't—or won't—write comment code either, so good luck trying to figure out the rationale behind what he does."

"Comment code?"

"Extra lines that show your work in plain English, so when someone else looks at your program, they'll be able to tell at a glance why you did what you did. Philip *loves* comments, and I've seen routines he's written himself that literally had more comment than code, huge blocks of explanation that go way beyond what most people would expect to see. But whenever he goes after Dennis about not writing enough comments, the guy just shrugs and says, 'Well, it works, doesn't it?' It's like he thinks if he gave away his secrets he'd make himself dispensable."

They reached the double doors at the end of the hall. Carson waved the ID card hanging from a lanyard around his neck in front of a scanner attached to the wall, as did Kate. A lock disengaged with a throaty, heavy *ka-chunk*, and the doors swung open to reveal a chamber beyond, spacious and full of afternoon sunlight. "Behold," Carson said, lowering his voice theatrically as he gestured in welcome. "The time machine."

"Don't call it a time machine!" a woman shouted from deep inside the room. Alicia.

"Sorry," Carson said, and then, speaking more quietly to Kate, "We're going to make a run this afternoon. It'll probably be boring to us—I think we're up to run 328, and it's highly likely that it'll turn out more or less like runs 1 through 327—but it might be interesting to you to see how things work around here."

The room they entered was two stories high and maybe forty feet on each side; it gave the impression of being hastily occupied, rather than settled by researchers with any sort of a long-term plan. The walls were bare except for a few science-related posters that seemed intended for college classrooms. In the center of the room was an enormous metal column that reached up to the high ceiling; a single door was set into it at its base, tall enough for a man to enter. Thick electrical cords snaked from the cylinder across the floor in all directions, and picking her way through the coils of cables as she crossed the room reminded Kate of that scene in *Raiders of the Lost Ark* where Indiana Jones had to tiptoe gingerly through a nest of snakes.

Desks had been placed throughout the room so that a person sitting at one of them could face the looming central column. There was also a scattered collection of mismatched chairs: a knockoff Aeron whose base was held together with duct tape; an old recliner that had stuffing poking through a rent in its cushion; a folding chair that would have been more appropriate at a poolside. Almost every square inch of the desk surfaces was covered with laptop computers and stacks of papers; more cords led from the laptops, making for more of a mess.

In a space near the central metal chamber that had been cleared of cords and debris, Alicia Merrill sat on the floor along with a bespectacled graduate student, the two of them huddled over an eight-legged robot whose brightly colored gears could be seen inside its translucent plastic body. Near them was an MP3 player plugged into a pair of speakers; from it came some hip-hop song that Kate figured was a little before Alicia's time, and definitely before her own. Kate bent over to look at the player's screen, whose scrolling message proclaimed that she was listening to ALICIA'S NEW JILL SWING MIX!!! PEBBLES! TYLER COLLINS! JODY WATLEY!

"We take turns picking the music for the lab," Carson said. "Philip doesn't want us wearing headphones: too isolating. Today it's Alicia's turn to play DJ."

"That's Michel'le," Alicia said, presumably to Kate, though she still stared intently at the conglomeration of brightly colored gears that made up the guts of the robot spider. "'No More Lies' was her biggest hit."

"She sounds great," Kate said.

"That squeaky speaking voice isn't a gimmick," Alicia said indifferently. "She really talks like that." Then she extracted a snapped belt from the robot's interior and said to the graduate student, "Randall, we've made significant advances in the field of physics since the days of Isaac Newton, discoveries about which you appear to be unaware. Later on I'll recommend some texts for you to look through."

"So what's the robot for?" Kate asked Carson hastily, even though she still remembered the TV segment from Rebecca's party a few weeks ago: Randall looked uncomfortable, and she figured she could spare him a further tongue-lashing if she changed the subject.

"That's Arachne. We send her into the causality violation device. In a perfect world, where everything worked as it should, the area in there would basically join two sections of spacetime that would normally be non-contiguous. To us, with our limited ability to observe objects and events, it just looks like a big tube, but the space inside there is, I guess you could say, *connected* to a point in spacetime that's about eight years earlier than now, in the place where this lab used to be, back then."

She looked up at the giant cylinder that seemed to be emitting a subsonic hum, something she felt in her chest rather than heard. "That must have been a hell of a thing to pack up and move."

Alicia snorted. Kate turned to look at her, but she was busy dismantling Arachne with a screwdriver, and seemed to be suppressing a laugh.

"Let's see, how to say this," Carson said, and Kate felt a slight bit of shame as she heard him try and fail to stifle a sigh. At least he wasn't completely condescending. "Part of the problem we have here, the PR problem—you saw some of this in that TV program—is that what most people think they know about time travel—"

"Don't call it time travel!" Alicia said. "If Philip hears you, he'll disembowel you and make you clean up the mess."

"—they learned from science fiction," Carson continued. "And most of the time science fiction makes this kind of thing look really easy. You jump in your phone booth that's larger on the inside than it is on the outside, you pull some levers, and you're back in the 1840s or wherever. But in real life, connecting two naturally non-contiguous points in spacetime such that a corporeal object can move from one to the other is extremely difficult! And it's not really moving through time that's the problem: moving through space is the problem."

With Kate following, Carson went over to a desk and cleared a small space off of it, consolidating two stacks of papers into one large pile. "You ever watch hockey?" he said. "Okay. You're on the ice, and you want to shoot the puck to your teammate. But the other guy is moving, right? So you can't just shoot the puck to where the guy *is:* you shoot the puck to where he's *going to be* in a couple of seconds. It's instinctive, but what you're doing is making a calculation about the other player's path through spacetime, and then shooting the puck such that its path through spacetime will intersect that of the player. If you shoot at where the player is at the moment you take the shot, you'll miss, because you forgot to think about the path the player would take through space as time passed. Got it?"

"I think you just explained to me why I sucked at soccer in middle school," Kate said. "I was always like: Hey, I'm trying to kick the ball to you! Stand still for a second!"

"Okay. Now, the calculation you have to make to send an object backward in time is similar to the instinctive one that a hockey player makes before he shoots the puck to his teammate, except that it's a whole lot more complicated. Also, you have to make the calculation—obviously—in reverse." From a dingy coffee cup filled with writing implements, Carson removed two ballpoint pens and, holding one in each hand, stood them up on the desk, side by side. "Let's say you have a time machine. It's like this little thing that you carry around in your pocket. And it'll let you go back in time by, I don't know, two hours. So you want to use it to go back to the same place you're standing right now, but two hours earlier. It shouldn't be that hard, right? Two hours is nothing.

"But look what happened between the time you want to go back to and the time where you are. First," and Carson moved the pen in his left hand away from the one in his right, "the earth rotated on its axis. And the earth also moved in its orbit around the sun. And that orbit isn't a clean ellipse, like you see in diagrams in middle-school science books: there are chaotic variables that influence that movement, so even though the earth is never actually going to *fly away* from the

sun or anything like that, there's a relatively small but still important random element in the path it takes." Carson dragged the pen
across the desk again in another direction, jittering it as he did so.
"And in the meantime the Milky Way drifted away from the center
of the galaxy." He moved the pen again. "And the universe continued to expand, as it has since the Big Bang." He moved it again, this
time completely off the desk. "So if you tried to go backward in time
without making the proper corrections to account for your relative
movement through space, you'd be lucky if you could glimpse earth
from deep space in the few seconds before you suffocated."

"Jesus," Kate said.

"The calculations are extraordinarily difficult. And this contrib-
utes to the sharp limits on what we can do. A lot of fanciful sce-
narios from science-fiction stories are right out. We'll never be able
to send a human being back in time to Hitler's bunker in 1945, or
the Texas Book Depository in 1963, because the data that would tell
us how the earth moved through space between then and now is lost
to time, and can't be reconstructed. But what we *were* able to do—or
at least what we believe we may have done, if only we can get this
thing to work properly—is construct a wormhole, a discontinuity in
spacetime. It has one fixed end and one moving end, like so." Again,
Carson held the two pens up on the desk in his hands, and began to
pull one slowly away from the other. "One end of the wormhole is
fixed at the point in spacetime we call Point Zero, the point where
we first started constructing the causality violation device; the other
end of the wormhole is in our present, and travels along with us as
we move through space and grow older. And the thing that makes
all of this work is a mechanism we installed in the device eight years
ago at its conception, called the Planck-Wheeler clock. You can see
it there." Carson pointed up to a featureless black sphere mounted in
the side of the column, about halfway up its side. "Philip's research
into gravitational wave detection in the early years of the century
indirectly led to its design—he doesn't like to talk about that period
of his career for some reason, but even if the research into causality
violation turns out to be a dead end, his name will be in the history
books for his contribution to the Planck-Wheeler clock alone."

"So what's the clock do?" Kate asked. She was trying not to let on
that her head was starting to swim a little, especially since Alicia,

who was still fiddling around with her robot, seemed to have an attitude problem with those who didn't get all this stuff. God forbid that someone shouldn't take to this like a duck to water.

"The Planck-Wheeler clock measures its own movement through space and time relative to the point in spacetime when it was activated. It accounts for the earth's orbit, the universe's expansion, and everything else. And it's remarkably precise: the unit of time it uses is the period it takes for a light wave to move its own length. Basically, it keeps our computers informed about where both ends of the wormhole are."

"So why can you only go back to this point in spacetime you call Point Zero?" Kate said. "It looks to me like if you have this clock that's been doing all these measurements since you started, then you've got all the data: it's not like if you tried to go back to the Kennedy assassination, like you said earlier. Shouldn't you be able to go back to any point in time you wanted after you turned the thing on?"

"That's a good question," Carson said, and Kate sensed that his comment was meant as much for Alicia as for her. "The thing is that a wormhole isn't like an interstate highway, with a bunch of different entrances and exits along a line. It's more like a roller coaster or a tunnel, though analogies to familiar three-dimensional objects are obviously going to be inadequate in this case. And to be honest, the thing has weird properties: we have theories about what we've got here, but we're not entirely sure.

"We're almost completely certain that any object that enters the causality violation device can only exit at either end of the wormhole the fixed end that's in the past, and the moving end that's in our present. We can't send an object to where the moving end of the wormhole once was at a point in the past, or where it'll end up in the future. There's also a restriction placed on us by the law of conservation of mass and energy. If an object enters the wormhole at our end, it has to come right back to the point in spacetime from which it left: otherwise, the amount of mass in the universe wouldn't remain constant. You can cheat the law temporarily—for a certain, rather unusual definition of the word 'temporarily'—but you can't cheat it permanently. Though the nice thing about the way the device works is that when we perform runs like this, we get the results literally instantaneously."

"Even if the results are null," Alicia cut in, "again and again and again." She'd finished repairing Arachne and replaced her plastic shell. "Carson, we're just about ready for run 328."

"Isn't Philip going to be here for this?" Kate asked.

"Not this one," said Carson. "He only watches the runs every once in a while: most of the time he stays in his office while they're happening. I asked him about it once: he said that the odds of any given run being successful were so low at this point that his time was better spent doing research; and even if a given run did work, we wouldn't actually see the causality violation happen, because from our point of view there'd be nothing to see. We'd only be able to observe the result. And there was no real value to getting the result as soon as you could: the news would be the same fifteen minutes later. Keep in mind that we're talking about the same guy who claims not to understand why you'd spend three hours watching a football game when you could just check the score online as soon as it was over.

"Of course, this doesn't mean that his loyal underlings don't have to execute every run and observe it firsthand. In the lab we've gotten used to Philip's philosophical arguments possessing a certain . . . expediency."

One song on Alicia's stereo ended and another began. "This is SWV," she announced. "SWV stands for Sisters With Voices." She'd placed the robot spider on a desk, where Randall was fastening an LCD digital clock to its body with a pair of plastic zip ties.

"For all the equipment we've got here," Carson continued, "the conception of the experiment is actually pretty simple. We've strapped an atomic clock to this robot—well, it's not really an atomic clock in and of itself, but it receives a signal from a real atomic clock located in Boulder, Colorado: it's the official time clock for the United States."

"Have you ever sent a person in there instead of a robot?" Kate asked. The idea dawned on her by the time her question was halfway finished: "I want to look in there!" Her right foot was already taking an eager step toward the device, as if of its own accord.

Alicia looked up from the robot. "Are you a physicist?"

Kate stopped and turned; she meant to inject a note of sarcasm into her response, but even in her own ears her voice sounded too much like pleading. "Well, *no*, but—"

"Then stay away from the causality violation device, please. Physicists touch. Tourists look."

Kate quickly cued up a couple of sharp-tongued retorts—oh, she had something in mind to say that would age the woman three months when she heard it—but when she saw Alicia's steely, unblinking squint, what actually came out of her mouth was a whiny, "Well, I just wanted to see what it was *like* in there."

Alicia's silent return to her robot was somehow more damning than anything she could have actually said. Kate glanced at Randall, who suddenly became deeply interested in the zip ties that attached the clock to the robot, making sure they were extra tight.

"Kate," Carson said softly after a few moments, in a tone that Kate found irritatingly conciliatory, "the thing is that it doesn't actually look like much of anything in there. Because even though our instruments say the thing is working, at least most of the time, direct observation indicates that it isn't. You'd think that if you were to enter an area that for all practical purposes exists at two different points in spacetime, you'd see some kind of *effect*, like some trippy lights, or a doubled image, or something. Or at least you'd think that you could close the door to the chamber in the present and open it again to look out on the past. But nothing happens. Philip's been in there; Alicia's been in there; I've been in there. Some of the people from DAPAS who are paying for these shenanigans have been in there. We've never seen anything interesting. You go in the chamber; you close the door; it's dark; you open the door and see the same thing you saw before. It's about as exciting as entering a dressing room in a department store." He tentatively placed a hand on Kate's shoulder, a gesture she found hard to read. "Sorry to be so anticlimactic.

"Now. The robot, with the clock attached. We send it into the causality violation chamber, which is set—or should be—so that within it, time's arrow is pointing toward the past end of the wormhole. It leaves the chamber and exists in the past for an hour; then it returns under its own power. Its reentry into the chamber trips a mechanism that should make time's arrow within the wormhole point toward us, here in the present. When it comes out again, its clock should show that an hour has elapsed, even though to us it'll look as if no time has passed at all. And we should receive confirmation of our firsthand observations when Arachne's clock has to re-sync with the clock in Boulder. Simple enough."

Meanwhile, Randall had swiveled open the door to the causality violation chamber, and Alicia had placed the robot on the floor before it. "Beginning run 328," she said, as the graduate student began to type figures into a spreadsheet on his laptop. "The time display on the robot's clock is fifteen eighteen and thirty seconds."

"Sync with the U.S. time clock is exact," Randall said.

"This is all very exciting," Kate said.

"I'm glad you think so," said Alicia. "Sending it in."

She flipped a switch on Arachne's spine, and the robot jerked to life as the colorful gears inside her transparent plastic shell began to turn. With the nervous jitteriness of a bride walking down the aisle, the robot marched toward the causality violation chamber, bearing the clock on her back. Even though Carson had said that the interior of the chamber was nothing special, when Kate looked inside it she thought that it looked *too* dark, as if some smoky malevolence out of a fantasy novel were living in there, swallowing all the light that fell on it.

Arachne disappeared into the blackness of the chamber, and the door slammed shut behind her.

"Now the rest is automatic," Carson said. "By the time I started speaking this sentence it had already happened. If everything worked correctly—and there's always a chance that it did, however small—our computers interfaced with the Planck-Wheeler clock to open up the past end of the wormhole; the robot exited the causality violation chamber into the past, where it spent an hour; then it reentered the chamber and returned to the present."

"Chamber door's opening," Alicia said.

Arachne emerged from the chamber, stumbled forward on her legs, and came to a stop.

Alicia checked the time on the robot's clock. "The time reads sixteen nineteen and fifteen seconds."

Randall dutifully typed the figures into his laptop. "Sync with the U.S. time clock is still exact," he said. "Sixteen nineteen fifteen."

"And that's run 328! Good night, folks: you don't have to go home, but you can't stay here."

"That's it?!" Kate said incredulously. "How is that even an experiment? Nothing happened! The robot went in and came out and that was it! That's like nothing!"

"They're so cute when they're young," Alicia said, picking up Arachne and carrying her away, cradling her as if she were a newborn child.

"One perception that nonscientists often have," Carson said with a patience that Kate couldn't help but find infuriating, "is that science always *succeeds*. And you only ever hear about the successes, so from the outside, scientific progress can look like nothing but a string of triumphs. But most people aren't aware of what an astonishing amount of failure is involved in scientific research. We screw up day after day. And the worst thing about it isn't the failure in and of itself—it's that from the point of view of the general public, or even the places where we publish, on which our careers depend, there's no point to failure. Success they're happy to hear about; failure you'd better keep to yourself. Even though failure is something you can learn from: common sense would tell you that it's almost as valuable to know what *not* to do as it is to get things right.

"So when we fail, which is often, the social pressures, or sometimes our own shame, can make us stay quiet. The failure becomes invisible. And the illusion that science is nothing but a series of successes is preserved."

Carson paused for a moment, distracted; then he snapped back to the present. "So what we'll do now is what we always do," he said. "Check and double-check everything: the Planck-Wheeler clock; the robot; the atomic clock; the causality violation chamber; and especially the software that runs everything. And Dennis will make further revisions to the code. Maybe run 329 will be the magic number. Or 330. Or 331. You can always hope."

He reached out and took Kate's hand in his, and the simple gesture went a long way toward ameliorating her frustration with him and her outright anger with Alicia. She looked over at Alicia, who was silently tinkering with her robot again.

"Hey," Carson said gently, drawing Kate's gaze back to him. "I could stand to get out of here for a little while. Do you want to go get some tacos with me before you head home?" He placed his other hand on his stomach. "Suddenly I'm *starving*."

9

VERY INTERESTING

Online dating makes you jaded really fast, even if you're not serious about it (and this is what Rebecca still told herself, even though she'd logged on to the site every day for months now: that she wasn't serious about it). You go on enough dates where you find out within ten seconds that the guy you've been messaging has lied about his age, or his height, or his number of chins, and it starts to wear you down. And then if you can get past that, there are all the little nasty human things about a man that could never be captured in the profile photos or the questionnaires: his wheedling, lisping voice, or the way he insists on splitting the bill even though you're only going out for coffee, or the light film of spit he leaves smeared across your face after what will be his first and only kiss.

No, rushinazz69, I am not into punching guys in the groin, Rebecca thought as she scrolled through this evening's messages. Not that she begrudged others their particular predilections. But it wasn't like they were even bothering to *try* to imagine another human being on the other end of the line.

NJBoukis, it is nice to know that you are specifically looking for a smart, funny, leggy brunette with a C cup or larger. At least he listed the personality traits first before he went on to specify the bra size.

triathlete08542: oh, look, and in his profile pic he's got a medal around his neck to prove it. Have coffee with this guy and all he'll want to talk about is his sweet five-grand bike with its carbon-fiber body. Next.

Richard127: likes "watchin TV, hangin out w/friends, laughin, and generally havin good times." Well, you're out of luck, 'cause I hate doin all of those things. Next.

There was one thing Rebecca was willing to agree with Kate on, when considering this whole sorry mess: it really did make it simple to eliminate suitors who clearly weren't your type. If you met these people in person, they might come off as okay at first, and it'd take weeks or months of being around them to figure out that you didn't like them, that it wasn't going anywhere, that you were going to have to have an awkward conversation. Or worse, you'd fall for a guy, and after you dated him for a while you'd end up convincing yourself that his need to spend thirty hours a week raiding in *World of Warcraft* was just a quirk that made him more lovable. Whereas if you met that guy online first, reading his profile at one o'clock in the morning with a gin and tonic in your hand, you could weed him out right off the bat because his screen name was WoW_RULES, and in one of his profile pictures he was grimacing at the camera while brandishing a sword with a yard-long blade. Got to be kidding me with that. Next!

Thanks, russellthemuscle, but I'm not going to date a married guy. "I dont want to disrespect my wife, but you seem like a really spectacular lady and I just had to reach out to try to get to know you." Christ.

But what's this? What's this one?

The screen name was apparently just the guy's real name, first and last: PhilipSteiner. He was outside her age range by a few years: thirty-six. But his picture didn't look bad, even though it would have been more appropriate for an ID card than a dating site: looking straight into the camera, unsmiling. He definitely wasn't a kid anymore, but he looked seasoned, not used up. There was a shining star next to his screen name with the word NEW! written inside it in red: he'd opened the profile just this week.

She clicked; the window opened. She topped off her drink and read.

Dear beccabeccabecca:

You seem interesting to me. I am outside your preferred range of ages by several years, but I am sending you a message anyway in the hope that you will ultimately find such concerns relatively immaterial. I have never been married; I have no children.

I am an experimental physicist at Stratton University who specializes in gravitational waves and the structure of spacetime. I am also intrinsically multidisciplinary: my other interests include regular exercise and musical performance.

I have attached links to two videos in lieu of writing more about myself. (Viewing images of a person in motion conveys more information than looking at photographs; my hypothesis is that it will reduce the amount of cognitive dissonance you would encounter if you were to meet me face to face.) Would you take the time to watch them? If you find them informative or engaging, please write me back. I believe I would enjoy conversing with you further.

Yours, Philip (PhilipSteiner)

Below this were two links to videos on YouTube. The first had fewer than a hundred views: its title was "Steiner Lecture on CTCs and the Novikov Self-Consistency Principle." Oof. Tough sledding—it crossed her eyes after three minutes, and she couldn't comprehend why this guy seemed to think the average person he'd find on a dating site would have the background to understand this stuff. Though standing behind the podium, talking about billiard balls that could be sent on trajectories that carried them back in time so that they collided with themselves (what?), he did seem rather—well, virile. He sported an artfully tousled mane of dark brown hair, and his voice had a rich depth that lent the aura of truth to what he said (though she got the strong impression that he genuinely knew what he was talking about: a bullshit artist would have used a baritone like that to beat his audience into submission, while Philip's sonorous and gently non-confrontational tone implied his belief that his facts were strong enough to speak for themselves).

She skipped around the video here and there, paying a little more attention to the argumentative Q-and-A at the end. ("Certainly, piling theories on top of more theories is the *safe* thing to do if we want to preserve our careers," he said to an audience member out of the camera's view, coming close to raising his voice. "But at some point we're going to have to find out whether the universe is willing to back up our speculative claims. We don't have the technology now. But we'll have it soon. And now is the time to start planning to use it.") Then she cued up the second video.

He seemed at least a few years younger in this one, though that might have been because of what he was wearing: an old pair of jeans and a black T-shirt that read I'M UNCERTAIN ABOUT QUANTUM MECHANICS. He was sitting behind a drum set and clutching a pair of sticks in his hands; behind him was a featureless white wall. Off to one side of him was a stand that held some sheet music, along with what appeared to Rebecca to be a metronome. "Drumming is very interesting!" Philip said. "You might think at first that it isn't, since its principal purpose is to allow the other musicians in a band to keep time, but a talented human drummer can do all kinds of other things with the instrument while simultaneously accomplishing the primary task. He can add occasional extra beats on top of the basic beats that dictate the tempo, or incorporate little improvisational riffs called 'fills,' and so on. Now, Neil Peart is a particularly interesting drummer—quite highly regarded within his field as both a musician and a lyricist. I don't want to go into an analysis of his philosophical leanings right now, but I want to try to show you why it is that his drumming is considered notable. Here's my interpretation of the drum part of the Overture from Rush's '2112' suite. Wait a second."

He reached over to the stand and started the metronome to ticking. "There's an unmistakable Objectivist influence on 2112, granted," he said. "But like the best thinkers, Peart takes from Rand what he believes is most useful, and jettisons the rest. Anyway. Overture. This lasts for about four and a half minutes, after which Geddy Lee sings 'And the meek shall inherit the earth.'"

Philip then proceeded to launch into what sounded to Rebecca like a whole lot of noise. At first he would stare intently at the metronome, then he'd suddenly beat out a quick stuttering tattoo on the drums; after about a minute of this, he started wailing all over the place. Without the other instruments providing context, it was hard to make any sense out of what he was doing, but Rebecca felt sure that they were playing in his head, perhaps in a fantasy in which Neil Peart developed a crippling case of food poisoning in the middle of a live set and Philip heroically ascended the stage from the front row of the audience to replace him.

She clicked back to the message. The whole package, with the formality of his introduction and the weirdness of the accompanying videos, was so bizarre that it was doomed to failure—his admitted handsomeness aside, it was hard to see how any woman could read that note, and watch the lecture and the unaccompanied drum solo, and be attracted to this guy. And yet, Rebecca thought, you could tell that there was something inarguably good-natured about him, something a little teddy-bear-like. He probably made strangers happy by being around them. And out of the hundreds and hundreds of guys she'd come across on Lovability, she didn't think she'd found one who was this clearly guileless and unguarded and unembarrassed. Even if she didn't feel the slightest bit of chemistry with him, she *liked* him; she wanted things to turn out okay for him. Maybe if he stuck this online dating thing out, maybe with just a little bit of polish—not full-on phoniness, mind you, but just a little finesse—he'd find some nerdy-cute mathematician girl who played bass guitar, and together they could be a rhythm section.

It would be pretty cool to help this guy out, thought Rebecca. She opened up a reply window.

> Hi, Philip—
>   Thanks for your very sweet message. I don't think I'm the woman for you, but you seem like a great guy! I do feel like your profile doesn't really show you in your best light, though—I hope this isn't a cruel thing to hear from a stranger.

She thought back to that long, tedious, tone-deaf message she'd gotten from that guy Bradley, fearing that she was becoming what she had once beheld. But she checked her heart and was sure it was in the right place.

> If you are open to it, and if you wouldn't find it presumptuous, I would love to give you a little bit of advice about sprucing up your profile. It wouldn't take that much effort at all. I feel like someone wonderful is waiting out there to hear from you!
> Yours, Rebecca

Hoping she didn't sound too condescending, she sent the message to him, idly surfed the net for a little while longer while she finished her drink, and turned in.

■

She got a reply back from him a couple of days later.

Hello, Rebecca—

Thanks for writing back to me, and thanks for offering me advice. I don't know how much longer I'm going to participate in this site, actually—I've sent four messages to women (the only sufficiently interesting ones I could find) and yours is the only response I have received. In most other aspects of my life, people generally reply promptly to my e-mails.

I did a rather extensive amount of research into sites like this before opening an account. (Hard data is difficult to come across, because all of these sites treat their matching algorithms as proprietary information; however, I recommend Finkel et al.: "Online Dating: A Critical Analysis from the Perspective of Psychological Science." I can suggest other papers if you find that one interesting.)

Research indicates that one is more likely to succeed in this endeavor if one shifts conversation off the site as soon as possible: the longer that communication is mediated by a third party, the more likely it is that one of the persons communicating will become susceptible to either of the phenomena of "choice overload" or "assessment mindset." (See Finkel et al.) To that end, would you be willing to e-mail me privately? (You say that "[you] don't think [you're] the woman for [me]"; I don't think you have enough information yet to make that judgment conclusively. I still find you interesting.)

—Philip.

P.S. The only things I've thought about today that are as interesting as you are leather shoes. Shoes made from synthetic material tend to have a shorter life than those made from natural materials, but an additional expense of leather shoes derives from maintenance—polishing, resoling, and so on. But leather shoes conform over time to fit your feet, while synthetic shoes do not—sufficiently aged leather shoes are more comfortable than new shoes of either natural or artificial materials. This means that leather shoes are valuable not merely because of their components, but because they are *superior repositories of information.* P.

■

Dear Philip [Rebecca wrote in her e-mail to the address he supplied, wondering what the hell she was doing]:

I must say that this is the first time that a man has offered me a compliment by comparing me to an old pair of shoes. I find that quite fascinating.

Thank you for the link to the paper. I will read it when I have the time to spare.

I'm really certain that I'm not the woman for you—the main thing that stands out to me in our brief conversation is our clear incompatibility. Insisting otherwise won't change things. I do sincerely wish you good luck in your future endeavors, whether or not you choose to stay on Lovability—if you do, my offer to give you advice on rewriting your profile still stands. (By the way, you might consider finding more specific synonyms for "interesting" when writing your messages—you use the word a lot, and it makes you seem like you're not trying. "Charming," "funny," "scintillating": these and hundreds of other complimentary words are possible options.)

It was nice to talk to you. Best of luck!

Rebecca

■

Hello, Rebecca—

Thanks for e-mailing me.

I insist on things when I know that I am right about them—there's no possible way you could have gathered enough information in our brief exchange to eliminate me as a potential romantic partner. There's just not enough bandwidth here, so to speak.

"Interesting" is the word I use to describe you because it is the right word! If I had wanted to say you were charming or funny, I would have used those words instead!

You're very interesting. Here is a proposition: we should meet at the Grounds for Sculpture in Hamilton next Saturday afternoon. That'll give you plenty of time to read the Finkel paper so we can discuss it. If you meet me in person, you should quickly be able to make an acceptable decision about whether we are potentially romantically compatible, a decision I am willing to abide by.

Surely it must have once been the case that you communicated online with a suitor who seemed initially promising, only to be gravely disappointed later when you found your first impression was mistaken. If this is true, the converse can also be true. You are in a logical bind now. Is this something you can live with?

I would like to hear your suggestions on how to improve my Lovability profile as well. A fruitful line of conversation might be possible if I pretend that I am socially awkward, and allow you to give me advice about my behavior. We might learn a lot about each other that way.

I hope to see you Saturday!

Philip.

■

As she pulled into the parking lot of the Grounds for Sculpture a few days later, Rebecca decided to chalk up her decision to meet this guy to simple curiosity—she was sure there weren't any romantic possibilities here, but at the least she'd be able to determine whether this guy's e-mails were a joke, or whether he was actually like that. She thought it could go either way: he could be a comedian or a weirdo. If he was a kook, then it was easy enough to fake an emergency with a cellphone. But if it turned out that he wasn't, maybe they'd end up being friends. And there was nothing wrong with wandering around a sculpture garden on a Saturday afternoon, on a cloudless day that was warm but not too hot.

The Grounds for Sculpture had been founded late last century by Seward Johnson, one of the scions of the sprawling pharmaceutical empire that had a home in nearby Princeton. But Seward had never had much interest in Band-Aids: after dropping out of the University of Maine, spending a stint in the Navy during the Korean War, and getting fired from a management position in the family company by his uncle, he ended up learning bronze casting, and found he had a love for it, though his legions of critics would be quick to point out that a love was not the same as a knack.

While most sculptors who worked in bronze tended toward the kind of abstract designs that happened to be in demand for the lobbies of office buildings, Seward, who had never attended art school other than the odd adult education course, and who also had virtually unlimited funds to back his work, began to drift toward the direction of troubling the real. His pieces traded in pranks and illusions; the question of whether they were in fact even art was not entirely settled. What was one to make of the twenty-six-foot-tall statue of *Seven Year Itch*–era Marilyn Monroe that stood in a Chicago plaza, with passersby shielding themselves from the rain beneath the enormous swooping canopy of her updraft-caught dress, staring up at the endless white expanse of her panties? Or the equally gigantic reproduction of Grant Wood's *American Gothic* that Rebecca had seen as she drove down the road that led into the sculpture garden, with a suitcase at the feet of the dour agrarian midwesterners, festooned with oval country decals from China and India? If they were kitsch, or knockoffs of the works of true masters, you couldn't deny that they drew the eye. (On the opposite side of the road from the giant faux Wood stood a life-size statue of a father and son, the father pointing up at the monstrosity before him in shameless awe.)

It would have been unfair to say that Seward Johnson founded the Grounds for Sculpture solely so that he'd have a place to show his own work. The acres of carefully manicured landscape held a comprehensive assortment of pieces by artists who might well consider themselves lucky to display their efforts in spaces like these, with shimmering lakes as backdrops or culs-de-sac of hedges that made their sculptures into secrets. (Though when one wandered through the park, the true interests of the garden's patrons were difficult to ignore: while the art that advertised itself as such earned sidelong glances and occasional moments of reverent appreciation, it was Seward's work that drew families who lingered to examine it in detail, squinting at the individually painted hairs in a beard, or running fingers over the pleats of a pair of trousers.)

Rebecca had agreed to meet Philip in the gallery near the visitors' center. He was easy to find—except for the guy sitting behind an information desk, he was the only person in the capacious, warehouse-like space. The entire gallery had been given over to the sculptures of an artist whose work Rebecca found singularly disturbing: it looked like the stuff of a botanist's nightmares. Though the floor was completely barren save for a couple of stone benches that sat in the middle, the walls were decorated with gigantic renderings of natural objects—wishbones; pine cones; something that looked like a rotted pig's snout—whose size alone placed them in the realm of the grotesque. The twisting silver tubes of air conditioning ducts that ran across the ceiling supported slowly twirling mobiles, from which dangled strange fruits that seemed to hail from a future full of mutations: furred peapods as long as a man is tall; distant cousins of apples and oranges that had developed drooping tendrils and neon tumescences; a slumping, eyeless homunculus made from tree bark, deep in a dream of being human.

The man sat on one of the benches with his back to Rebecca, wearing a white, long-sleeved, button-down shirt despite the warm weather. She spotted him by his tousled head of hair and his ramrod-straight posture. His head was darting from side to side as he looked at the conglomeration of sculptures above him. In most cases, when Rebecca showed up for dates, the guys looked nervous if she happened to see them first: usually, though, they were watching the door, and had on their genial game faces as soon as she made eye contact. But this one seemed like his mind was elsewhere altogether.

"Philip?" she said softly, not wanting to startle him.

"Rebecca!" he replied, still not turning to look at her. "I'm glad you could make it."

Then, instead of standing up and walking around the bench to greet her, he lifted up both feet, spun around on his behind while using his hands to brace himself, and dropped his feet to the floor again once he was facing her. It was an oddly childlike gesture from someone of his age.

He looked almost as she expected (and she thought that he might be right after all when he said that a person's appearance in the real world was less of a surprise when you'd seen images of them in motion first). The only feature of his face that she hadn't anticipated was his eyes: though they were a glittering blue, they were deeply set beneath his heavy brows, and without his kindly smile to mitigate their appearance, the first impression he gave would have been somewhat sinister.

But a warm grin spread across his face. He slid sideways on the bench and gently patted the empty space he'd vacated. "Come here!" he said. "Sit down."

She did so, smoothing her flowery pastel sundress over her lap, clasping her hands together in mock primness. "Philip, it's nice to meet you."

"It's nice to meet you, too!" He gestured at the artwork around him. "Isn't this place unsettling!" he said excitedly.

"It certainly is," Rebecca replied.

"Did you get a chance to read the Finkel paper I sent you?" he asked eagerly, and then, before Rebecca could respond that she'd intended to get around to it but hadn't been able to fit it into her busy schedule, he said, "Because the thought that goes into the design of online dating sites is very interesting! Listen. Consider this. Imagine there is an online dating site that works nearly perfectly. It was coded in a garage by a couple of college dropouts. You open an account, you answer some questions, and within three days it matches you with the love of your life. It is amazing! It is so amazing that it attracts investors. The garage becomes an office. Now the coders are surrounded by men in suits. Now the service that was once free requires a subscription; now the terms of service are quietly altered, and the data the site gathers is sold to corporations that do who knows what with it. Money changes everything! A man in a suit says to a whiz kid: 'People who visit this site find true love in three days. But after this, they become less interested in the site: they stop updating their profiles, and when they log in it's only to observe, not participate. Stale profiles are unreliable for our own data-mining purposes, and of less value when sold to others. Information is money, and we are leaving money on the table. What if you made a slight alteration to your algorithms, so that the site matched people with their soulmates in an average of five days instead of three? What would be the harm? In fact, it's clear that we are deeply undervaluing true love here. Is active participation on our site for seven days, or ten days, or six months, too much of a price to pay for what we offer?' When the possibility of profit enters the situation, the engineering problem changes. It is no longer: What is the best way to introduce people to strangers with whom they are highly likely to fall in love? It becomes: How can we best maximize revenue? And yet: imagine an online dating site that *never* matches people together successfully. Customers log on to the site and open profiles; they visit the site for some period of time; they lose interest because it offers no hope of providing the service it promises. Word of mouth spreads; revenue falls; the site dies because it is too inefficient. So the goal is not maximum efficiency in pairing mates, but *optimal inefficiency*. The site maximizes revenue when it takes as long as possible to make matches without taking so long that its members give up and stop using it. And once you realize that inefficiency is coded into the design, that the site's true purpose is not to match you with a mate, but to keep you actively participating in the site for as long as possible, then you can take steps to mitigate that inefficiency. The key to success, I think, is to treat the site as your *opponent*, not your *facilitator:* it's like the house in a casino. You should strive to take any communications off-site as soon as possible, for one thing: when routing them through the site both parties continue to be susceptible to the phenomenon known as *choice overload*. Now, choice overload works like this: Imagine that I offer you a choice of one of three delicious cakes for dessert. You will say, 'What good fortune,' and select one. But what if I offer you a choice of one of eleven cakes? You will become temporarily paralyzed by the magnitude of the choice; you will realize that selecting any one of them deprives you of the potential experience of ten others. It will take you *longer* to choose; you will choose more *inefficiently*. Now, notice that every page loaded by Lovability features a reminder of how many members are on the site. Hundreds of thousands of members! Think of all that choice! Notice that next to a profile picture are links to eight other profiles, of people who are similar but not the same. Surely one of these other eight must be better than the profile you're reading now. The promise of a more suitable mate is only a click away, perhaps with an unexpected interstitial survey to deal with, a minor nuisance at best. You see? The mediator that promises you a valuable service does not in fact have your best interests at heart. Best to cut it out of the chain of communication as fast as possible; best to move quickly to meet in person. Which is what we have done. We have outsmarted the house by leaving the casino. I'm very happy to see you! Rebecca," he finished, slightly short of breath, "I would greatly enjoy it if you and I went for a walk together in the sculpture garden."

■

And so Rebecca and Philip went for a long, leisurely amble through the Grounds for Sculpture. Philip found the abstract works in the garden as engaging as most of the other visitors found Seward Johnson's attempts at realism: he seemed drawn to the clean, perfect math of their arcs and lines. Unless a given work had a sign next to it strictly forbidding contact, he'd get up close to touch it, in a way that Rebecca found endearingly intimate: running his finger along the inside of a swooping curve, or knocking with a knuckle to hear the timbre of an echo. When the sculptures featured red plaques dissuading human touch, Philip looked as if he felt cheated.

He talked a lot, about random vaguely science-y subjects: the physics that governed the trajectories of golf balls and the benefit provided by their dimples; why the bubbles in a freshly poured pint of stout appeared to float downward instead of upward; the enormous amounts of metadata in which Twitter messages were wrapped. His mind was pleasantly magpie-like, alighting briefly on one subject or another for a quick explication, and moving on once it got restless. If he didn't talk much about himself, he also avoided the nonsense that guys usually pulled on first dates, the coyly dropped hints from which you were meant to infer their salaries or their sexual prowess. Listening to him talk was a little like watching over someone else's shoulder as they surfed the Internet, but someone who knew how to go to cool out-of-the-way places and read about cool things, not someone who just stuck to screwing around on Facebook.

Eventually they sat down at a lakeside table to take a break from walking. The table was one of Seward Johnson's tricks: it had places set for four for dinner, with china plates and silver utensils and folded cloth napkins and poured glasses of red wine, but all of it was fashioned from bronze and resin. A pair of peacocks strutted together along the shore, lazily trailing a riot of blues and greens behind them. Rebecca was pretty sure that this was the first time she'd ever seen one of the birds up close. They were shockingly, sublimely beautiful: photos didn't do them justice.

Philip placed his chin on his hand, grasping the stem of the wine glass in front of him as if he were about to lift it to drink, even though it was permanently riveted to the table beneath. "A counterfactual," he said. "We are at dinner. The lighting is nice—on the table there are candles or something. Now: I remember something I read in a foolproof guide to picking up women. If I follow its precepts, it promises to turn me from a *zero* into a *hero*. It says at the beginning of one of its chapters: Remember to show some interest in your date! It's not just about you! So I ask you: What do you do?"

"What do you mean, what do I do?"

"How do you spend your days? How do you earn a living? For instance, if someone asks me this, I have responses with differing degrees of granularity: I might say, 'I am a physicist,' or 'I am an experimental physicist,' or 'I'm mainly concerned with problems of spacetime.' So: What do you do?"

"Oh, I'm just a local girl."

"*Local girl* is not something to be preceded by *just*. Most of the women I come across these days are scientists: local girls are a novelty to me. Second: *local girl* is what you *are*, not what you *do*. It's a good thing for you that I'm so socially clumsy: otherwise I would be picking up on a certain reticence here."

This is why it was hard to go out on dates with guys older than you! Not because you'd be into different music, or because an older man's joints could forecast the weather, but because at this particular point in history, the difference between being in your twenties and being in your thirties was often the difference between having a blackout season and not having one. Most people Philip's age were actually *doing* something, because they'd had more of a chance to try.

"Well, I'm kind of in between things right now," she said.

"Between what and what?"

Jesus! "Between graduating from college and whatever will let me move out of the house where I've been living like a teenager, pretty much." It sounded more snappish in her ears than she'd intended, but she felt better once she owned up to it. "My mom is a librarian. My dad is a Unitarian minister."

"Hm," Philip said, in a tone perhaps a little less damning than Rebecca expected, considering that she'd gone ahead and dropped all her bombshells on him at once. "Yeah, it's pretty ordinary," she continued. "I work odd jobs here and there so I don't just sit on my ass, but it's been really hard to find something steady, with an English degree. No one will hire you unless you have experience, and without a real job that has a guaranteed paycheck every two weeks, you can't get anything that people want to call experience. It kinda sucks."

"I can imagine."

"I feel like a failure."

"That's a thing we have in common then," Philip said. "I felt like a failure just yesterday. And the day before that." He thought about it for a moment. "The day before that, too."

"See, but you're just being nice! This is like *next-level* failure: I can't even get anyone to give me the chance to do something so I can be bad at it! I can't even call it frustrating anymore, because to be honest, I've kind of gotten used to it. I mean, for a lot of people of my generation—that's not what I mean—"

"Please continue."

"—it's kinda what you do now. It's not like your life is like: something great happens, then something bad happens, then something awesome happens. It's just a constant, low-level samey-same feeling that's not that good."

"Some more pessimistic types would say that you have exactly described the day-to-day feeling that often comes from doing science," Philip said, quietly placing one of his hands over the wrist of the other. "I'm serious! I have what most people would consider to be a rather prestigious job. It is not an exaggeration to say that I am on the cutting edge of human knowledge. But being on the cutting edge means that I'm confronted each day with my own incredible ignorance. Some days—and sometimes these can be the best, most promising days—I leave work knowing slightly less than I believed I did when I arrived! If I understand one thing that most people don't, it's how little I actually know. I have good days. Sometimes what I do is exhilarating! But I'd be lying if I didn't admit that sometimes it's not."

"Well. Here we are, a couple of failures, then. Though I feel pretty sure you're underselling yourself." Impulsively, Rebecca reached out and touched Philip's hand. "You want to go get a drink?"

■

They had a drink at a little place on the sculpture garden's grounds called the Peacock Café: one of the restaurant's namesakes was placidly preening itself in front of the entrance. Philip got a can of Dr Pepper. Rebecca ordered a Corona with lime, and she didn't realize how tense she'd been, and how intimidated she'd felt by this guy, until she had a drink. Just the slight shock of the bottle's cold glass touching her lip made her loosen up a little. And it had been hot out there, too—a good long gulp, and another, and she felt refreshed. She started to feel, well, interesting.

She began to regale Philip with tales of the little ignominies of the blackout season, while he drank his soda through a straw. There was the time she worked retail in a department store, selling designer shoes until she couldn't take it anymore. She remembered kneeling before an angry dowager, the woman's foot naked in front of her face, its gnarled, spotted toes as long as fingers. ("She says, 'Young lady. Young lady. These shoes made my feet bleed. It's an absolute outrage.' And she's waving around a pair of Ferragamos that have little flecks of blood inside them. And I'm thinking: The problem here is your feet are totally *prehensile*. You'll be better off heading over to Accessories and getting a nice pair of *gloves*.") She told him about the time a couple of years ago when she'd picked up work going door to door for the U.S. Census, getting the info from stragglers who'd failed to fill out the form. ("And someone would answer the door, and they'd be drunk or high or whatever, and I'd say, 'Okay. I'm from the Census, and I need you to count the number of people in your house and tell me the answer.' This one guy, I could smell the weed on him, he opens the door and he's got a half-eaten Hot Pocket in his hand. He looks at me and takes this *huge* bite out of his Hot Pocket. I give him the spiel, and he says, 'Yeah, okay,' and he points at himself and says, 'One.' Then he takes another *huge* bite of the Hot Pocket: finishes it off. Then he licks his fingers and goes back in the house. Just leaves the door wide open. I stand there for maybe three minutes, I don't know what's going on, and then he comes out again, with this big smile on his face like he's just figured out how to cure cancer. And he says: 'Two.' ")

Philip listened to her stories with rapt attention. "That was interesting," he'd say (and Rebecca was thinking that on their second date, which she was already taking as a given, she'd gift him with a thesaurus as a well-meant tease). Finally, when she told him about a job she turned *down*—the details she'd found out were vague, but it was an opportunity that had been relayed to her by Kate through one of Kate's friends, something about three hundred dollars cash if she showed up at this particular house in a nice neighborhood, wearing a Catholic schoolgirl skirt—Philip shook his head in wonder and said, "Your life: it is very interesting to me. Do you like food?"

"All of it. I eat all of the food."

"I'm an excellent cook. Name something, and I'll prepare it for you."

"That's a bold offer, Philip."

"Yes."

"Shaving cream."

"Things are going well between us: I'd rather not injure you."

"Panda."

"Nor would I prefer to break the law. I may have exaggerated slightly in my offer."

She made a show of sighing. "Okay. Salmon."

He nodded. "Salmon is perfectly fine. When?"

"Wednesday?"

"Perfect. Come by my place then: seven thirty."

"Will do. Looking forward to it."

On their way out of the garden Rebecca and Philip passed a final Seward Johnson sculpture, a three-dimensional, life-size copy of the photo that one guy took at the end of World War II, the one with that sailor smooching a surprised nurse in the middle of Times Square. "Unconditional Surrender," its plaque read.

■

On their second date, Rebecca went over to Philip's apartment for dinner, a cozy two-bedroom place in a faculty complex whose rent was subsidized by Stratton University. Picking salmon turned out to be a good call, because Philip's cooking was about as good as his drumming: serviceable, but perhaps not as good as he thought it was. And salmon is a dish that's hard to screw up unless you have malicious intent. To his credit, he'd opted for ease and simplicity: in the kitchen's recycling bin, she saw the empty jar that had once held ready-made bruschetta topping, but said nothing.

She'd brought wine along, a liter bottle of Grüner, and after two glasses to his half of one she said, pouring herself yet another glass in what she considered to be the most obvious of hints, "I'm a little too tipsy to drive right now. Can we just hang out for a bit?" "I have a collection of classic films we could watch," Philip replied, and they repaired to his living room, where he pointed out his floor-to-ceiling shelves of DVDs and Blu-rays. His collection was composed almost entirely of science fiction and fantasy movies: you'd look in vain for a rom-com or a Disney flick. Rebecca hadn't seen many of them, either, which Philip found incredible: "You haven't seen *Enemy Mine*? You haven't even seen *2001*? Seriously: you haven't seen *Krull*? Liam Neeson and Robbie Coltrane were great in that!" "No, no, and no," Rebecca said. "If it has a gun that shoots lights instead of bullets, I probably haven't seen it."

"Well, we're going to have to fix that," Philip said. He spent ten minutes looking at the spines of the disc cases on his shelves. ("I don't know where to start," he said. "I don't even know.") Eventually, he decided on *Blade Runner*: he had a special edition of the movie that came in a futuristic-looking silver briefcase, along with some photos of scenes from the film, and a little toy car, and a little origami unicorn. "The problem with watching *Blade Runner*," Philip said as he pulled out a folder full of Blu-rays from the briefcase and began to look through them, "is that there are five different cuts of this movie, and none of them is perfect. They all have strengths and weaknesses. So what would probably be best is if I do a sort of curated exhibition of the movie: every once in a while I'll switch from one cut to another, and explain what the differences are between versions. You'll get a lot more out of your first experience if you watch it that way."

"Hey, can we just hang out on the couch and talk?"

"But I really want to show you *Blade Runner*."

Rebecca poured herself another drink.

The subsequent viewing experience severely tried Rebecca's patience. Whenever she started to get into the movie, which was about a young, handsome Harrison Ford hunting robots in the future, a subject that didn't appear to be in particular need of scholarly exegesis, Philip would pick up his remote control and pause the film to explain some plot element in excruciating detail. ("Now pay attention here. When Deckard walks into Bryant's office, Bryant says there are 'four skinjobs walking the streets.' And later Bryant says that six replicants escaped from the off-world colony and two have already been killed. The math is fine. But in all other cuts of the film but this one—the Final Cut—the math is incorrect! In the earlier cuts Bryant says there are *four* replicants loose on earth, *six* escaped from the off-world colony, and *one* has been killed. Which raises the interesting question: Who is the missing replicant? Many fans of the film insist this is clear evidence that *Deckard* is a replicant, but a moment's reflection should show that this makes neither formal nor thematic sense. It's safe to say that the dialogue of the Final Cut results from a quiet correction of a continuity error that persisted through the other, older versions of the film.") How was it that Philip wanted to deliver a dissertation instead of getting his bones jumped? She was doing everything but drawing him a diagram! Finally, when he paused the movie to explain that in some cuts this one character who was the lead of the gang of outlaw robots said, "I want more life, father," while in other cuts he said, "I want more life, *fucker*," Rebecca said, "Speaking of," extracted the remote control from his hand, and tossed it across the room. "Stop talking so much," she said. "I like you."

They hooked up during the movie's third act (though annoyingly, Rebecca occasionally saw Philip peeking over her shoulder to watch Rutger Hauer chase Harrison Ford through an abandoned apartment building). The whole thing was rather clumsy—she got a crick in her neck while turning her head to kiss him, and one or the other of them seemed to have an extra limb that kept wedging itself between their chests.

Doing her best to keep her frustration out of her voice, Rebecca eventually suggested that things would go much better if they repaired to Philip's bedroom, where it became clear that he hadn't remotely considered the possibility that he might get laid this evening: the bed was unmade, and a sad, discarded pair of tighty whities lay at its foot, gone loose and gray. They tumbled in a tangle onto the mattress, where it turned out that Philip, perhaps a bit overeager as a result of his unexpected good fortune, was what Kate, when hearing this story later, would laughingly call a "two-pump chump." And yet there was an expression on his face the whole time that sat halfway between confusion and delight; it was neither the smug smirk of a man perhaps excessively sure of his skills in the sack, or the pinched grimace of a laborer stolidly setting about his assigned duties. There was something genuinely sweet about the way he collapsed next to her, blissful, loose-limbed and silent, after the barest effort.

She curled up next to him, pulling his arm toward her and draping it across her, listening to his breath slow and even out. He was, essentially, a good person—it was easy to tell this already. And for all his awkwardness and eccentricity, he provided the certainty that he was what he appeared to be. All his words and actions betrayed his absence of artifice. This was a guy you could let your guard down around; you probably even had to. You'd feel like you were cheating him if you kept it up.

In time, she could knock a couple of the rough edges off him. She could buy him a couple of cookbooks and a set of bedsheets, maybe; the sex could be worked on. But in the meantime: this was nice. This held promise. This was something she could get used to.

■

Later, when things started to go wrong between them, Rebecca would look back to those first dates and wonder if, in fact, she'd missed something, some sign in his behavior or his personality that would have signaled how he'd change.

You can't tell what history will do to a person. In those early days, before he'd conceived of the causality violation device, his company was a constant delight: he was easygoing and cheerful, kind and guileless, childlike without being childish. And if he was a genius, he wore the mantle effortlessly: though he had a self-confidence that sometimes shaded into arrogance, the flashes of hubris in his speech were only occasional, and gone before you'd think to remark on them. And there was something charming about the way he leapt from subject to subject in his conversation, his tangents birthing other tangents as he teased out the structures of information that lay beneath the surfaces of things.

His intelligence, back then, was wider than it was deep, but that wasn't the kind of intelligence that got you remembered, and it was clear to Rebecca that Philip had the same ambitions as any other person in his position would have. But what wasn't clear to Rebecca was what the eventual choice to focus on a single grand project would do to him over time: she hadn't known that the effort to accomplish what Science demanded of him would replace his beaming smile with a straight slit of a mouth, and drape his gleaming eyes in shadows, and slowly smother his beautiful magpie mind.

■

As Rebecca and Philip spent more time together, the weeks of their incipient romance becoming months, Rebecca's log-ons to Lovability became less frequent, and eventually nonexistent (though the once-single electronic version of Rebecca still persisted on the site's servers, never growing older, never changing its tastes and desires, a representation that continued to beckon strangers even as it lay stranded in the past).

In turn, Philip began to introduce her to his friends, who were mostly his colleagues in the physics department at Stratton. When he was around them, for an after-work meeting at a bar, or a backyard barbecue thrown by a senior faculty member on a Saturday afternoon, he changed a little—it wasn't so much that his personality altered, but that certain features of it that usually remained submerged when he was alone with Rebecca rose to the surface. He became a little more aggressive in his speech; he lost the unself-conscious grin that bloomed on his face whenever he thought of something interesting, and his rare smiles flashed across his face with a strange flint in them that stopped just short of meanness.

In general, Rebecca found something strange about the way his colleagues spoke at first—their language just seemed somehow *flat* to her, in a way she found it difficult to pinpoint. But as she got to know them better, she realized that they'd been socialized into a culture that valued precision in language above almost all other things. And so their speech was often stripped of the components of casual conversation that usually greased it: vague generalizations; idle chatter to fill the air; bullshitting and spitballing. A couple of times, Rebecca made some sort of trivial comment like "Hey, I haven't heard this song in years," or "Literally *nobody* liked that movie," and the response would be a flatly stated "That must be false," or "That is highly unlikely," or "That is untrue," delivered not in a particularly accusatory manner, as if she were thought to be a liar, but in a sorrowful tone, as if her careless talk deserved the kind of brief chastisement merited by a minor failure of character.

Arrogance: that featured among Philip's colleagues, too, though that was more a matter of mien than anything else. If there was one subject about which they tended to be cavalier, it was the ease of doing anything in life besides physics. They were quick to let you know that, in addition to practicing that best and most worthy of all the sciences, they were, as Philip said about himself, "intrinsically multidisciplinary": they'd casually mention that they'd just cycled their first century, or were doing a show with a local band, or were nearly finished with building a kiln. It was as if the stereotype of the physicist as a bespectacled dweeb was something they felt it was their duty and obligation to strive against. And though they never seemed to be quite as skilled at their extracurricular activities as their pride in them might have indicated, if they were perhaps unlikely to play in professional orchestras or chalk up record-beating times in marathons, then it was even more unlikely that top-level violinists and athletes were doing science on the side, as a hobby. Rebecca was never sure whether there was something about physics as an occupation that made it a magnet for the arrogant, or whether the process of becoming acclimated to the culture of physics involved developing a certain conceit about oneself if one was to succeed, but either way she got the impression that arrogance was often a benefit to physicists, rather than a liability. Hence the steely stare that Philip assumed when he entered a room full of his colleagues; hence the slight hauteur. It was something else she had to get used to, and she was glad, in those early days of their courtship, that she got to see him alone often enough to let him divest that arrogance as if it were an overly warm and heavy cloak.

And over time, Philip's peculiar use of language came to make sense to her. If the worst thing a physicist could say about a statement is that it was "false," the best thing he could say is that it was "interesting." This was different from saying it was true: most true things were, in fact, uninteresting. Interesting statements lived on the twilit boundary between fact and question; they held the promise of revealing something unexpected and new about the world, and thus were to be treated with respect. The physicists Rebecca met always seemed to be on the lookout for something interesting, a claim or proposition that seemed to possess some kind of rare interior light.

Rebecca came to understand that Philip's constant repetition of the word "interesting" meant that he was offering what he saw as the most precious of compliments. And for someone who was in the depths of the blackout season (but who was perhaps coming out now, perhaps seeing a haze in the air that foreshadowed daylight), to be thought "interesting" in that way, considered worth the time to think about by a man who seemed to value thinking more than life itself, was . . . well, it felt good. Great, really. When the two of them were by themselves, and Philip suddenly got that look on his face of wide-eyed wonder that preceded *finding something out*, something unexpected and amazing and new: there was nothing like it. Strange, but you couldn't have a guy look at you like that and not fall for him hard and fast.

■

So she did, and it was fantastic. They both dove headlong into the dozens of minor, tender negotiations that presaged falling in love: the restaurants at which they liked to eat together (he, anything but Greek; she, anything but sushi); the time they spent in contact (no, she didn't need to hear from him *every* day, though she wouldn't have minded, it wouldn't have hurt); the positions in which they slept on the nights they shared his bed (spooning made his arm go numb; sleeping back to back seemed too unfeeling. He slept on his back; she slept on her side to face him). They traded the contents of their minds and catalogued their scars.

It did occasionally occur to Rebecca that Philip preferred to talk about what he thought to be interesting things, rather than about his own life—granted, her general mode of discourse tended toward funny anecdotes rather than little factoids, but she never got stories out of him about things like the first time his parents let him drive the family car alone, or the enchanting Hungarian woman he'd met while backpacking abroad, from whose company he'd regretfully had to part. It didn't bother her much, but it did have the effect of making him something of a cipher. (Though if he was a cipher, he was one about whom she had no suspicions—she could talk to him about whatever was on her mind, or simply spend time with him in companionable silence. If he had a past history of secrets that he wasn't yet ready to reveal, then that was fine.)

And so Rebecca consigned herself to, not ignorance, but a judicious incuriosity: she decided, for the time being, to live with the constant, cryptic reminders that the scope of another person's soul could never be fully surveyed. In sleep he squeezed against her as his breathing hitched, and as he mumbled disconnected, nonsensical syllables that might have been snatches of scientific jargon or confessions of nameless sins, she slid the soothing tip of a single finger gently down his forearm, across the back of his hand, and along the faded scar that shot horizontally across his left wrist, keloidal and thin as a thread.

10

SERIOUS QUESTION

Terence had been working at the security desk in the Steiner lab for eighteen months now—it was a good, steady gig, and he wanted it to last a while. A lot of the jobs he worked, he got laid off after a year, or he had to work two of them at the same time to cover food and rent. There had been a few months a little while back where he'd done a full eight-hour shift at a grocery store in Trenton, then driven out to New Brunswick to spend another six hours sitting in a bar's front doorway, looking mean and bouncing drunk-ass college kids; then he'd head back home to Trenton when the bars shut down around two. Nights like that, he figured he was lucky he made it to the bed before he collapsed. His wife and his daughter (now in fourth grade) didn't talk to him much during that time, needless to say: he was either sleeping or gone.

By comparison, this security job was great. First of all, it was a real full-time job with benefits. It had pretty good health care, the kind that meant you could leave the house without wrapping yourself in bubble wrap. (That Affordable Care Act from a while back had been a good thing while it lasted, but over the past few years the insurance and medical industries had gotten so many changes made to it that you couldn't call it "affordable" anymore without laughing.) Second, he was technically a Stratton University employee, which meant that if he stayed on long enough, another year and a half, his daughter Harlie would get preferential treatment when it came time to apply for college: good financial aid, and maybe a free ride if her grades were good enough. It'd be good to have that in your hip pocket.

The one really bad thing about this job was the hours. For most other security gigs he'd done, at department stores or nightclubs or concert venues, the hours were at least *predictable*, even if they weren't the same time each week. But in this university lab they were working on some heavy-duty stuff, apparently: word was that it was at least partly military-funded, and these guys insisted on all sorts of protocols. First of all, there had to be two guards at the desk, at all times, twenty-four/seven. Second, they didn't want either the guards or the people in the lab to get *too* comfortable with each other, because when you saw the same guard at the same time every day, five days a week, you'd strike up a friendship, and that was when you'd relax a little, maybe, and that was when equipment and design documents would start walking out. So the shifts were completely randomized, and Terence never knew what duty he was going to pull until he got the text message forty-eight hours before. It was good to have a full-time job in this economy, but he was always on call. And he never knew who he was going to get paired up with for the four-hour shift, not until he came in to work. And your shift partner mattered. They didn't want you screwing around on your phone, or listening to your music, or anything like that: you had to be aware and paying attention the whole time. You were allowed to bring in a book and that was it. And even if you brought a book in to read, you were constantly conscious of this other person who was there in your space with you, breathing and making noises and having stuff on his mind.

It looked to Terence like there were seven or eight other guards in the rotation, though they would come and go. Most of them would bring books along too, and that meant he'd be left alone to read, which was great. (Lately he'd been working his way through some novels by this woman Octavia Butler. He'd found some paperbacks at a yard sale priced at a dollar each and picked them up for the hell of it. Wild-ass stuff, and maybe a little too touchy-feely for his tastes—he was more of a Don Pendleton guy—but he was kind of into it.) One guy, who he guessed was some kind of off-brand minister, would sit at the desk with a King James Bible and *The Oxford Bible Commentary* open in front of him, his back straight as a board, only moving when he turned a page in one of the books. Another had a different paperback in his hand whenever Terence saw him, and every single one had a picture on the front of either a zombie or a vampire. Then there was this one Brazilian woman who was about forty-five and had these big broad shoulders and completely jacked biceps, like back in her teenage years she'd put a serious hurting on a pommel horse, and instead of reading a novel or something she'd just *sit* there, not saying a word other than *hello* or *goodbye* for the whole shift. That was weird, but Terence could deal with that: at least she understood the value of peace and quiet.

But there was one thing that never failed to make Terence swear under his breath, worse than drawing the shift from midnight to four on a Saturday night, and that was pulling duty with Spivey. Terence liked this job because it wasn't the least bit dangerous, and it gave him a chance to spend some time in his own head: during the first couple of shifts where he wasn't allowed to have a phone or a tablet he got fidgety as hell, but he got used to it, and came around to liking it. It turned out he liked quiet: he had just never really had the chance to find out.

But Spivey did not like quiet! The man would not let you alone. He *had* to talk, and he had the gift of gab. If you put Spivey in solitary confinement he'd *talk* his way out: he'd just sit there running his mouth about every damn thing he could think of until the very prison walls said *Fuck it* and crumbled. And he wouldn't take a hint, either: Spivey couldn't care less. Ten minutes into the shift he was guaranteed to say, "Hey. Hey Terence. Put that book down for a second. Put that book down for a minute and help me bullshit."

■

Spivey was older: fifties, maybe, hard to tell, but he was headed toward being one of those retired guys who did nothing all day but drive slow down back streets in a land boat, wearing a track suit and a trucker cap, flagging down anybody he knew on the sidewalk to shoot the shit, burning away the day. He was the only other black guy in the rotation, and Terence figured that because of that, Spivey felt like they had something important in common.

Terence thought that was very old-fashioned, very twentieth century, this idea of all black people being brothers and sisters by virtue of their race, sharing the same blood and language. He guessed that he was "conscious" of his racial identity, whatever that meant these days, but not in the same down-to-the-bone way as Spivey. Terence's daughter Harlie, however, seemed not to be "conscious" at all about these matters, in a way that concerned Terence a little sometimes. (For example: lately Harlie had been playing this game on her tablet that all the kids in her classes were into. It was one of those games that tricks you because it says it's free: then when you start playing it, it nickel-and-dimes you for this and that and then you've dropped a Reagan on the thing before you know it. It was a popularity contest, basically. The whole thing was set in a school, and every time someone said hi to you in the hall or you answered a question right in class, you got a coin, and with enough coins you could buy things in the shops for your character, like cute little bows for her hair, or sparkly dresses. Then if you had a printer you could send it a file and it'd make a little doll that looked like your character, and wore the same stuff it did in the game. The thing is—and this is where the bastards got you—if you played this game all day, you *might* get ten coins for free, and even a little plastic bracelet for your character cost two hundred coins, minimum. *Or:* you could go get Daddy's credit card, and buy all the coins you wanted! Ten thousand coins for fifty dollars! It was a bargain! A lot of the other kids did that, it looked like, but when Harlie came to Terence, begging and pleading for him to spend his hard-earned money on a bunch of voxels, he said hell, no. If she wanted to trick out her character with doodads she could earn the money in the game fair and square. Terence figured it'd teach her perseverance—either that, or she'd figure out the game was a scam. So one day Terence was looking over Harlie's shoulder while she was playing this game: she fired it up every day as soon as she got home from school, and all the other kids did, too. God knows why she wanted to spend her free time pretending to do something she already had enough of in real life. On the tablet's screen there were a bunch of kids sitting in this classroom, with old-fashioned wooden desks and a chalkboard at the front, and Terence felt a little bad for Harlie at first because all the other kids in the class were wearing top hats and diamond tiaras while Harlie was just sitting there in jeans and a T-shirt, but the kicker was that while the other kids' characters looked like cartoon versions of real children, the skin of Harlie's character was straight-up green. It had pigtails like Harlie liked to wear, and hazel eyes like Harlie, but it also had this shimmering green skin that twinkled like an emerald with light shining through it. Terence figured he was going to have to sit her down and have a talk with her about how there was no shame in being black, and how she was beautiful no matter what the TV said sometimes, but when he just casually asked her, *Hey, why'd you make that girl look like that?* Harlie looked at him like he was a moron and said, "I made her look like that because that's what I look like!" Terence was so puzzled he left it alone. What the hell did that even mean?)

Truth be told, Spivey's idea of blackness made as little sense to Terence as his own daughter's sometimes. Like a lot of black men of that older generation, Spivey had two voices, a private and a public one. The public voice was a buttery baritone that he used to welcome people (who, yes, were mostly white) into the lab, asking after their health and getting them to pose for ID photos. The private one, on the other hand, was melodic and slangy: that one he saved for when he and Terence were alone on the graveyard shift, and Terence was helping him bullshit. It was a voice for black folks, a voice for Us: Terence could hear the capitalization in the pronoun when Spivey said it.

Which of Spivey's voices was real, and which one was performance? Maybe the voice that was meant for Us was the real one, and the other one (what Terence's mother would have called "talking proper") was intended to set white people at ease, to convince them to accept him as one of their own for long enough a time to do business. Or maybe it was the other way around: maybe his public voice was the true one, and when alone with Terence he laced his speech with shibboleths to avoid getting called out for "talking proper," like Terence's mother would have. Terence couldn't say.

Or maybe that was asking the wrong question. Maybe both of Spivey's voices were put-ons, the one as well as the other. Maybe when he slept he dreamed in Portuguese, or German.

■

Helping Spivey bullshit didn't involve much more than listening with impartiality, if not agreement, to his limitless supply of anecdotes and strong opinions. He talked a lot about his sister Rita in Camden, with a mixture of love and disapproval. (Recently her diabetes had gotten worse. "Two weeks ago Rita calls me, crying up a storm. I say what's wrong, girl? She says: The doctors are gonna *take my leg*. And

I feel sorry for her—it's my own sister—but damn if it didn't make me angry, too. *The doctors are gonna take my leg.* Like she didn't have anything to do with it. Like the doctors *loaned* her her own leg and now they're taking it back, like repo men coming to get a car you quit making payments on. You go to Camden and you see plenty of people on the street, missing fingers and toes and legs that the *doctors took.* People young as you! But see, the only thing they eat comes out of a fast-food place or a bodega. Because damn if you can find a single green vegetable for sale in Camden: broccoli doesn't make it into that town. Oh, *everybody* gets the sugar: then the doctors come and take. I drop what I'm doing and I go right over to see Rita. And there she is sitting on the couch, watching *Price Is Right,* holding: guess what. A bellywasher. A *soda.* And she looks at me and says, *Spivey, the sugar got me.* Like sugar is as sure to come as death. I was so mad I couldn't even figure out who the hell to be mad at.")

And sometimes he talked about current events or politics, on the occasions when they entered into his life. ("I got another one for you. I was on the phone with Rita: I'm in the middle of a sentence and the line gets quiet and you know who cuts in? Yes. The President! 'Oh, hello, Spivey, this is the President of the United States, and I just want you to know that I appreciate the moral support you are offering your sister as she recovers from her diabetic complications. It's important to remember that families need to bond together in difficult times.' Interrupting jackass.") But most of his monologues eventually came back around to the people in the lab who walked back and forth past him on every shift, his assessments of their true natures and his speculations about their secret lives.

He didn't like most of them. Dennis was too weird, too in his own world. Philip, in his opinion, "had a stick up his ass." But the one who bothered him the most, the one he kept returning to like a tongue relentlessly probing the tender gap left behind by a freshly extracted tooth, was Carson. "You know who I can't figure out?" he'd say to Terence. "Carson. I can't figure that guy out." Then, in a rare occurrence, Spivey would trail off into silence, staring with puzzlement into space. Terence would take the opportunity then to knock out another couple of paragraphs of Octavia Butler. But it was clear that Spivey was working through whatever it was about Carson that got under his skin, thinking of a way to talk about it.

Oddly enough, it was Terence's book that let Spivey find a way into it. "Hey Terence," he said one evening, right on time, fifteen minutes into their four-to-eight-a.m. shift. "Terence. Whatcha reading? Tell me about it."

Terence handed the paperback over to Spivey, who peered at the back cover. "Science fiction," Spivey said, with faint distaste. Then: "Black woman?"

"Yeah."

"I figured. Otherwise they wouldn't have bothered to put a picture of a black woman on the front."

He handed the book back. "Science fiction: never been much for it. Dreams and cartoons is all it is."

"You don't say," said Terence.

"It's ridiculous," said Spivey. "Nobody takes that stuff seriously! Even these physicists coming in and out of here know that, and they don't know much about anything besides machines and numbers! You know what they're trying to build back in that lab, right? You saw the TV report?"

"A 'causality violation device,' is what their boss calls it."

"Ah hell you know they're trying to build a time machine back there! And they don't want to call it that because when you think of time machines you think of science fiction, and if they call it what it is no one is going to take them seriously, and rightly so."

"But even if that's true! A lot of good inventions showed up in science fiction first, right? Cellphones? Elevators? Even just the idea of going to outer space?"

"That's different. Those things are different. Those things, you can see how they would help people, or at least not hurt people. But a time machine? Going back in time? You lost me there. I do not see the point of that at all. I don't see why you'd spend the time and effort.

"And here is what I don't get about that guy Carson," Spivey said. "Here is what I don't understand at all. For the life of me, I can't comprehend why any black man with even a *lick* of sense would have the *slightest* bit of interest in time travel. Going backward in time? A black man? You have got to be out of your mind.

"Why are you laughing? This is serious business. I am telling you the truth now. You give a white man a time machine and he's gonna think about going on vacation! He'll think it might be fun to go check out the 1960s, or ancient Rome, or something. He will jump in that time machine, and start twisting dials, and he will have himself a grand old time. He'll fit in just about anywhere! But can you imagine some crazy black man doing that? Some Carlton Banks–looking jackass strolling up to this time machine with a sweater tied around his neck, toting a picnic basket, thinking this shit is a joke? Next thing Carlton knows, he's on the Middle Passage! Hundreds of men chained in the hold of a ship, constant wailing and moaning. The guy on one side of him just died two hours ago; the guy on his other side is saying, 'When I had land beneath my feet I was a prince. Now I am at sea, and I am less than a maggot. When I am taken up to the deck for food and fresh air, I will throw myself over the side, and I will sink beneath the waves. When my feet touch the ocean floor I will become a prince once more.' Carlton is all shackled up and ready to shit himself, and he's going, 'Oh dear me, the conditions of this cruise are most intolerable! Where is the all-you-care-to-eat buffet? Where is the family-friendly stand-up comic? Rest assured I will be writing a stern letter to the proprietors as soon as this is over.' Hell with that.

"I'm telling you, Terence: time travel is something only a white man would think is a good idea, and he is welcome to it, as far as I'm concerned."

■

The one person in the Steiner lab who Spivey loved without qualification was Alicia Merrill, who he thought was "absolutely badass." "Weighs a buck and small change, but kick her and you break a toe, put your hand out to her and you just might draw back a nub! My girl, right there."

And for whatever reason—Spivey's reasons for his actions were generally inscrutable to Terence—Spivey favored Alicia with his "private" voice when he spoke to her, not his "public" voice: that is, as long as Alicia and Terence were the only other ones around. Why was she granted such honorary status? Terence suspected it was her taste in music: "They all get to choose what they listen to while they're working," Spivey said. "A lot of those guys just listen to piano, you know, or bloop-bleep-bloop, but when Alicia gets hold of the mic she takes it back to the old school! Put your hands up in the air and wave 'em like you just don't care; bang to the boogedy beat. Stuff your mama had on *cassette*." Or maybe it was because Alicia liked to take breaks from work sometimes to knock out quick six-mile runs, and when she strutted past the security desk with her small, trim body clad in spandex shorts and a sports bra, she was hard not to look at.

She arrived at seven o'clock: lately she'd been training for a marathon, and she'd been getting up at five to go running before she came in to work. She preferred to get into the office early: she liked to get as much done as she could before others started showing up. She walked past the security desk, wearing a simple outfit of a white T-shirt and jeans, her cheeks still slightly ruddy, her hair damp from the shower, and Spivey beckoned her: "Alicia! Come over here a second. Terence and I are having a discussion. And we require the knowledge of a scientist to help us answer a very serious question."

Alicia approached the desk. "I'm a scientist," she said.

"Good!" said Spivey. "I was just talking to Terence, telling him about that time machine you're building back there."

Alicia looked around her with a show of slyness, as if to make sure no one else was overhearing. "Go on," she said.

"And I said to Terence that any black man would be out of his mind to use the thing: if he said he wanted to get in it, you need to take away his belt and shoelaces and put him on suicide watch."

"This is true," Alicia said.

"Yes! Now, here is my question. I can see a white guy jumping in there, easy enough. But can you imagine some kind of a crazy white woman thinking a time machine is a good idea? This is a serious question."

"I'm going to need to do something first before I can give you an answer to that." Alicia extended the thumb and little finger of her right fist and placed it next to her face, thumb next to her ear, pinkie in front of her mouth. "Hello?" she said. "Hello. You're not going to believe this, but I've got a code thirty-seven. . . . Yes. . . . Yes! His name's Spivey. . . . Yeah, that's him. . . . Yeah. Okay. . . . Okay, thanks. I'll catch you at the potluck on Tuesday." She dropped her hand. "I just wanted to get clearance to speak for all Caucasian women on this issue," she said. "You can never be too careful. Now. First of all, time travel is real: you just have to believe. Second, when we get that machine working, I'm going to be the first one to use it, because you know what I'm sick and tired of? Reliable birth control and the right to vote. Just absolutely fed up."

"Old times were great, weren't they? You got an apron on and a bunch of squalling kids hanging on your legs, your husband just died from some damn disease hasn't even been discovered yet, you bite into a boiled turkey drumstick and it pulls out two of your front teeth."

"Then your mother says, *I warned you: this is what happens to a woman when she turns twenty-three.*"

"Seriously, to hell with time travel."

"I don't even know what I'm doing here. Have a good morning, you guys."

"What're you spinning today?" Spivey said to Alicia as she walked away.

"Mostly stuff from '87, '88. Some Ultramagnetic MCs; some tracks from *He's the DJ, I'm the Rapper*; some Public Enemy to keep it honest."

"Elvis! Was a hero to most—"

"But he never meant shit to me!" Alicia said over her shoulder as the door to the lab closed behind her.

"I told you," Spivey said to Terence. "My girl."

■

Carson came into the lab about an hour later, just as Terence and Spivey were getting ready to get off shift. Terence had that loopy feeling you get when your body clock goes out of whack—if he was lucky and the traffic was good, he could be in bed by nine thirty, and he'd wake up in the early afternoon in time for a ravenous brunch.

Spivey was sitting at the desk when Carson approached. "I don't know if you need this back," Carson said. He proffered a white plastic rectangle attached to a lanyard, which Spivey plucked from his hand: it was Kate's temporary ID. Over the last day the image of her face had faded from it, Cheshire-cat-like: nothing remained of it but the ghost of a single, pale blue eye and a washed-out smudge of red that had once been a lip.

"Thanks," Spivey said, and then, with a stand-up comic's timing, waiting a beat for Carson to turn away: "Carlton."

Carson took a couple of steps away from the desk, then stopped, his shoulders sunken. Then he turned and said, with a voice that sounded louder than it would have if he'd shouted, "Look. You need to stop calling me that. I get your little joke. *Now this is the story all about how my life got flipped, turned upside down.* I get it. But it isn't funny, it never has been, I'm not in the mood to pretend it is, and I'm sick of hearing the same tired little insult whenever I set foot in this place. I get it. Now leave it alone."

Before Spivey could reply, Carson stalked away, letting the door to the lab slam shut behind him.

Terence looked at the back of Spivey's balding head over the top of his book. Then, as if he could feel his gaze on him, Spivey turned to face Terence, and in that quick moment Terence caught an expression on Spivey's face of despair and confusion.

Then Spivey brought forth a tortured guffaw. "Hoo *ha!*" he said, with unconvincing bonhomie. "Did you see that? I tell you I had my doubts about him, I had my doubts about the man, but I figured if I poked at him enough he'd show me he has a little fire in him after all."

11

ATMOSPHERIC NOISE

Philip proposed to Rebecca about a year after they started dating, and a couple of months after she'd moved in with him. His request for her hand in marriage came in a way that made it seem like it was a surprise even to himself, and when Rebecca later tried to puzzle out the chain of events that led to it, she decided that its principal cause was her gift of the wristwatch.

Since Rebecca and Philip had started seeing each other, she'd gotten a pretty decent idea of what he was doing as a physicist. As a graduate student and post-doc, his primary interest had been gravitation, but when you started to deal with the really big concepts in physics, like gravity and space and time and light, you soon found that they were all inextricably linked together, and the more you pondered one, the greater the chance that you'd find yourself mixed up with another. Hence Philip's somewhat vague description of his work to nonscientist strangers as "an investigation into the nature of spacetime."

Rebecca knew a little more about his research than could be gleaned from that imprecise summary, though, enough to know that he tended to keep it imprecise unless he was pressed because he didn't want to sound like a crackpot. At the moment the lab he supervised at Stratton University was engaged in the development of a device called the Planck-Wheeler clock, which would make all sorts of incredibly accurate measurements across space as well as through time. But the clock was only part of a larger project that Philip had just begun to seek funding for, writing grant proposals to send to various government agencies and private organizations. He called it a "causality violation device," but part of his problem was that the people who held the strings of the purses he wanted to open usually weren't scientists. So the grants had to be written in plain English instead of a specialist's jargon; unlike the precise scientific language he favored, in which each word had a single, agreed-upon definition, he had to use words of a common culture, words that necessarily came freighted with other, older meanings. And anyone who considered Philip's idea for more than a couple of minutes, written out in that plain manner, was likely to decide that what he was actually doing was looking for money to build a time machine, which was deep into crackpot territory.

It was easy for Rebecca to see that rejection after rejection was bringing Philip's spirits low. And so she decided that a gift would be good for him, a pick-me-up meant to show she still believed in him. Lately she'd landed a temp job doing secretarial work at an architectural firm. The gig wasn't great, but it was as steady a paycheck as she'd had recently, and she figured she had enough disposable income for the moment to afford some largesse. God knows he'd taken her out to dinner enough times when she was broke.

The perfect present nearly jumped out at her when she walked past it, sitting beneath the glass of the jewelry counter in Macy's. Amid the selection of men's wristwatches, which ranged from the austere to the egregiously complicated, with dials marking off every unit of time from days to tenths of seconds, sat a timepiece whose face was completely transparent—you could see the assemblage of gold and silver gears beneath it, driving its hands forward tick by tick. It was mesmerizing.

The slim, bird-boned saleswoman behind the counter saw where Rebecca's eyes were pinned. "A lovely, lovely watch," she said. "Completely mechanical: powered by stored kinetic energy. Accurate to plus or minus, say, one minute per week. But higher accuracy, in a fully mechanical watch? Brand-new cars are cheaper! This one is a bargain at two hundred."

Rebecca didn't care about the accuracy—she thought the watch was super cool. With a digital watch, you couldn't really see how it worked, and so the ability to measure the passage of time seemed like a mundane task that took place at the heart of a microprocessor. But there was something about seeing a mechanical device work that spoke to everyone, not just electronics experts. It made the mere act of marking time look like some kind of magic. Two hundred dollars was a good deal steeper than what she'd planned to spend when she stepped through the store's doors, but she was so sure that Philip would love it that it was worth the cost. She heard her credit card squeal in anguish when the saleswoman ran it through the reader.

■

Later that week, Rebecca and Philip had dinner at an Indian restaurant on Route 27, one of those ethnic holes in the wall that turned out to be much more promising inside than its dingy facade would suggest. The two of them were the only white people there, which was a good sign to her—it foretold food that would be spiced without fear of offense. Philip had ordered the lamb biryani cooked "medium": even so, he kept spooning yogurt onto his food and removing his napkin from his lap to wipe his damp forehead.

Rebecca saw that Philip was clearly not in a good mood—another grant rejection must have come in today, or the day before. Her sallies at idle conversation died in the air; questions about his work were met with grunts.

She waited until the server brought two bowls of irresistibly sweet gulab jamun to fish the jewelry box out of her purse. When she placed it on the table and pushed it across to Philip, he picked it up with cautiously extended fingers, as if he feared it would electrocute him. Once he sensed its weight and confirmed that it was too heavy to hold a mere band of gold, he relaxed. He popped the box open, peering at its contents; then he closed it and shook it vigorously to set the watch's gears twirling. He reopened the box and stared inside for a moment.

The smile that Rebecca expected to see on Philip's face, the one she depended on to soften his default expression and remind her of the gentle personality that lay beneath his gruff exterior, did not materialize. "It's a wristwatch," he said.

"Yeah!" Rebecca said. "Because, you know: time."

He looked at her blankly.

"I thought you'd appreciate it," Rebecca said. "I just—I was thinking about you, and I saw this. And."

He looked down at the watch again.

"It doesn't have to be a special occasion to get a gift for someone you care about. If you care about someone, a lot of the time you just get them little gifts whenever." Maybe that was a touch resentful, a little passive-aggressive. So be it.

"I already have plenty of ways to tell time," Philip said. "I usually carry a phone. And I can't help but be near a computer during most of my day. It's hard for me *not* to have an idea of what time it is. And Rebecca, this looks unnecessarily expensive: especially given its probable lack of accuracy relative to a quartz watch, which would have cost you next to nothing—"

"Damn it, Philip, I didn't get you the watch so you could tell time!"

She watched Philip stare into the middle distance, presumably riffling through possible responses. "It's a very nice present," he said finally, his voice distant and muted. He extracted the watch from its box and clasped it to his left wrist; then, as if he'd been quietly waiting for the little tiff between the two diners to end, the server appeared with the check.

■

Rebecca pretty much forgot about the incident until a month later, when she got the flowers. They showed up at the architectural firm where she was working, her job primarily consisting of fielding complaints from angry callers who'd gotten hold of the phone number for the front desk. The architect's designs were the sort that could not have been conceived in the days when blueprints had to exist on paper instead of in a computer's memory: houses with walls at seventy-three-degree angles from each other; roofs with swooping, asymmetric domes. While their interiors looked spectacular, with wide-open, light-filled spaces, their outsides looked like the kind of shapeless things a six-year-old would make by mashing together a bunch of Lego bricks. Most mornings the first phone call of the day was from an elderly woman already in mid-rant when Rebecca picked up the receiver: this *thing* that's being *thrown up* in this *historic neighborhood*, it's *appalling*, it's *outrageous*, it has *no respect for our community*, for God's sake it's *taller than our church*. In her heart of hearts

Rebecca sympathized with the callers, but she couldn't very well say that—the most she could do was say she'd be sure to pass their grievances on, and then forget to do that.

So the flowers were nice when they showed up around eleven a.m., a simple arrangement of a dozen roses with an accompanying note:

Hello, Rebecca:
 I was just thinking of yuo!
 —Philip.

The message was sweet in its plain sincerity, and even if it had something of a taint of duty—she imagined Philip sticking a Post-it note to his monitor at work that read "show appreciation for girlfriend at random times"—it was better than nothing at all. In his somewhat distracted way, he cared. The typo in the note was a little negligent, but it was the thought that counted.

The strange thing was that when Rebecca called Philip that evening to say thanks, there was a moment when she could have sworn he didn't actually know what she was talking about. "Oh, yes!" he said. "That was—that was just a thing. It seemed like a good idea."

"Well, it certainly was, sweetheart." Positive reinforcement.

"Yes!"

She shifted to another subject, and didn't think about Philip's seeming forgetfulness again until two months later, when another assemblage of flowers showed up at the office around nine thirty, dropped off by a delivery woman who shrugged quizzically as Rebecca signed for them on a proffered clipboard. The bouquet was perhaps more appropriate for a funeral than a display of affection, a spray of pale lilies and carnations mounted on a slender tripod. Rebecca removed the little card from the ivory envelope attached to it and read:

Hello, Rebecca:
 Just wanted to say hi!
 —Philip.

It wasn't as completely surprising as the first time she'd received flowers from Philip, and people coming into the office today would probably stop to offer condolences, but she still appreciated the effort. She'd have to make him a nice dinner or something, she thought.

An hour later, a different delivery person from a different flower service arrived, holding a crystal vase containing two dozen daisies. "Rebecca Wright?" he asked as he stood at the office's entrance, and when Rebecca approached to receive the flowers from him, he saw the funeral arrangement already standing next to her desk and looked at her briefly in confusion. But he declined to ask questions.

Another envelope, this one periwinkle, was attached to the end of a slender plastic stick lodged in the vase along with the daisies, and Rebecca read the note inside:

Hello, Rebecca:
I was just thinking of yuo!
—Philip.

Something was definitely weird about this. Philip had never been the type to get sentimental. And yet despite the irregularity of the situation, the two bouquets didn't quite seem like *mistakes:* they came from two different flower shops, the arrangements themselves were different, and even the notes were different. There was something *off* about the whole thing. She had it in mind to call Philip to see if he was okay, but then the phone rang with an irate Kingston resident who wanted to give her an earful for twenty minutes ("This is ghastly. This is *ghastly.* I'm calling my lawyer. I'm *calling my lawyer.*") and then it was time for her to go out to a local pizza place for lunch with the rest of the office.

The third bouquet showed up about a half hour after she got back, brought by the same woman from the same service that had delivered the funeral flowers that morning. The dozen roses had been placed in a white ceramic vase. When the delivery person placed them on Rebecca's desk next to the daisies, she leaned over and said *sotto voce* to Rebecca: "It's not my business, but I just want you to know that I'm really sorry about whatever it is. Unless your boyfriend or husband or whatever is apologizing for screwing up, in which case, you give 'em hell."

"Thank you?"

"We had one customer get *eight* dozen roses in a day once. I think that's the record."

The note that accompanied the roses read:

Hello, Rebecca:

    I was just thinking of yuo!

        —Philip.

What in the hell? She dialed him up at the office, let it ring until it went to his voicemail, hung up, and immediately dialed again. He picked up on the sixth ring. "I'm really busy, Rebecca," he said, without a greeting.

"Philip! Honey! What's going on?"

"We've got some interest in funding the development of the causality violation device. An eccentric millionaire kid. Teleconference in an hour. I have to go—"

"Philip! Don't hang up. You sent me three bouquets of flowers today. What is this?"

"I . . . what?" he said, after a moment of stunned silence.

"I'm looking at them. I've got them right here. It doesn't make any sense at all."

"Just a second, Rebecca. Just a second." She heard the furious clacking of a keyboard. "I didn't need this right now. Just a second." More typing. A pause, and then a quick flurry of keystrokes. Then: "Oh God. I'm a moron."

"Philip?"

"I'll explain this evening. I really have to go now. But I have an idea: we'll have a candlelight dinner this evening. That'll be very romantic. I'll order pizza—half pepperoni, half cheese, per usual. Would you go by some kind of department store and pick up some candles on the way home? Thanks." And before she could tell him that she'd already had pizza for lunch, he disconnected.

■

Philip was in a better mood over dinner. It looked as if he'd secured some grant money, from a young investor named Edmund Taligent, whose father's company, Taligent Industries, specialized in the construction of robotic prosthetics for amputees. It wouldn't be nearly enough to finance the construction of the causality violation device entirely, but it would be enough to pay for some initial computer modeling, develop a plan and a timetable for building the device, and establish "Point Zero," the point in spacetime that Philip called "the fixed end of the wormhole." Once Point Zero was established, Edmund Taligent would see how things were going, and decide whether to fund the rest of the project.

"To be honest, the man is kind of a kook," Philip said after he folded a slice of pepperoni pizza in two, shoved the end of it into his mouth, and took a large bite. "He's like a twelve-year-old kid bouncing around in an adult's body. But he appears to have a nearly infinite amount of money and a willingness to spend it. He doesn't even want to draw up a contract—he says it'll ruin things.

"But I feel optimistic about him. And this is the most optimistic I've felt about the whole project in a while. You don't know what it's like, to have a new truth in your head that you feel so *sure* about, that you want to bring out into the world so that others can know what you know. But then just when you make that first attempt at describing it to someone, they look at you and they say: Oh, you're crazy. Or worse: You're too ambitious. Your reach is exceeding your grasp. Like there is such a thing. Only a person who had already reconciled himself to a life of mediocrity would even say such a thing.

"But then you connect with the right person, who's actually on your wavelength. And now your idea lives in two minds instead of one. This is a beginning. If it lives in two, it can live in four. And if it lives in four it can live in eight. There's hope. You're on your way."

Rebecca left the discussion of the multiple floral bouquets until after dinner, though the unresolved conundrum nagged her so much that it killed her appetite. Despite Philip's comparative good cheer, the essential wrongness of the whole situation seemed worse with each passing minute. When she finally broached the subject, she figured it would be best to pitch her tone toward drollery. "Philip," she said, "as I may have mentioned earlier today, I couldn't help but notice that you sent me three arrangements of flowers, which arrived at my office an average of two hours apart. I'm deeply flattered, but an explanation would not go amiss."

Philip bit his lip and looked at the floor, fidgeting like a child being chastised. "Well, it's a funny story," he said distantly, after a moment. "It's interesting. It's interesting! I'd been thinking about something you said when you gave me this wristwatch. Which I've been wearing every day, by the way." He held it up to show it to Rebecca. It could have stood to have a link removed from the band, and it looked like it was running slow. "You said that people who care about each other give each other gifts at random times sometimes. And it occurred to me that though love is an extraordinarily difficult thing to re-create in a computer model with a meaningful level of sophistication, the act of random gift giving is actually relatively easy to model. In fact, a sufficiently savvy programmer could whip something up, much like a lovelorn poet of an earlier century would write a sonnet for his sweetheart. It seems to me that the pleasure of a sonnet comes in mastering the restrictions of the rhyme scheme, in the service of self-expression. Programming has similar restrictions! That's interesting, isn't it?"

"I . . . can't say I've ever looked at it that way," said Rebecca. "But go on."

"Here's what I did!" Philip said. "I set up a means for generating random numbers that were derived from the frequencies of atmospheric noise. True random numbers: not pseudo-random. I just want to point that out. And atmospheric noise is very romantic: it's radio noise, you see, largely generated by lightning strikes. Lightning: very romantic. So. I tuned a radio receiver to static, connected it to a computer, and wrote a program that used the static to generate a random series of values. If those values stayed within a certain band for a sustained period, this would trigger a script that randomly contacted one of a selection of online flower delivery services, selected one of a number of flower arrangements constrained by expense, appended one of a selection of accompanying notes—one of which apparently had a typographical error; sorry about that—and paid for the delivery with funds I had placed in a dedicated account at an e-commerce site. I coded the whole thing in a few hours. I was clearly a little careless. First there was the typo. But I also should have added a line that prohibited the purchase of a bouquet within, say, ninety-six hours of another purchase, even if atmospheric noise conditions were satisfied multiple times during that period. The chances of that happening the way that did, three instances of satisfied conditions within such a short time frame, are—I can't even figure them offhand. Was there some sort of meteorological anomaly today? It's worth looking into. At any rate, the code was sloppy. A poet writes a sonnet with a rhyme that is a little forced and doesn't sound quite right, but he's forgiven because he made the effort. But write a program with a couple of glitches in it and suddenly it's a huge problem!"

"The world is unfair," said Rebecca.

"I know! Here is the problem. Here is my problem. I think about you all the time. Well, not all the time, really. Not literally. You're like a little process running in the background, snatching cycles here and there. Sometimes it occurs to me that I think about you more than I ought to think about anything besides physics. Look at Nikola Tesla. Invented alternating current; died a virgin in his eighties. You should thank him every time you flip a light switch. If you have the gift of a mind like his, it comes with a duty to humanity that trumps your own desires, doesn't it? And yet. And yet. As much as I might like to be, I am not the man he was. I sit at my desk and my mind drifts back to a memory. Something trivial. Like your smirk or your instep. I find myself considering my future histories instead of thinking about my work, and all those that have you in them seem to be brighter than those that don't. Don't you see that I don't have time to think about this? But there are so many possible futures in which I look back on the past and see that I made a terrible mistake, through neglect or through inaction. This is a problem. This is a very interesting problem.

"I'm working through this. Here's what I propose. You and I should just go ahead and get married. This is what we should do. It will relieve me of the peril of living the rest of my life without you, and it will relieve you of the peril of living the rest of your life without me. This is one of those rare cases where the most optimal solution is also the easiest. It'll be great! We can save on taxes."

■

"And the next morning," Rebecca said to Kate one afternoon over drinks two days later, "he e-mailed me this Excel spreadsheet showing that, yes, we would actually save several hundred dollars on our returns under the current tax code if we tied the knot. That's just the kind of guy he is."

Kate sipped her gin and tonic through its slender black straw. "It's hard for me to know how to react to this," she said. "You seem really happy."

"I *am* really happy!" said Rebecca, close to bouncing up and down in her chair. "I am. I am."

"But I can't help but feel—and I wouldn't be being honest with you if I didn't say so—that there's something really weird about this guy that you're sort of ignoring. I mean, you told me this story about the wristwatch and the flowers and all that, and the way you tell it, it sounds sentimental and cute. But look at the facts. This is a guy who figured he'd have more time for his work if he wrote a computer program to pay attention to his girlfriend instead of doing it himself. Isn't that actually kind of horrible? And then when he got caught—because don't think you would have ever found this out if he hadn't gotten caught—he didn't even apologize: he was like, 'I put a lot of work into writing that program, and you should understand that computer programs are really just like poetry.' I mean, if you look at it that way, it's one of the most terrible things I've ever heard."

"But it's not like he meant anything *bad* by it," Rebecca said. "I got three bouquets of flowers out of it. That's really, really sweet. As for the computer software—he's really rational! Which means that sometimes he might not see the world the way the rest of us see it. And he's not the most, you know, socially adaptable person. But he's *good*! A really good person. His heart is totally in the right place."

"Rebecca," said Kate, "I think you're overlooking a lot of real problems here! And I think you've been overlooking these problems for so long that you've just gotten used to it. First of all, I think you're being forgiving of this guy because he's passing off this kind of disaffection for human beings as *geekery*, like he's got Asperger's or something and he can't help it. I mean, that comment he made about the two of you getting married so he could save you from a mistake. What the hell kind of thing was that to say at one of the most important times of his life?"

"Kate, that's just his sense of humor! It's really understated, really dry, really self-mocking. It takes some getting used to."

"Like, oh ha-ha, isn't it funny how I'm *not actually joking*? Ha-ha? Is that the kind of sense of humor we're talking about? Now. The second thing. And the nerd stuff is kind of minor, but this is a serious concern, if you're talking about marriage. I know you were over the moon when you met this guy. And he's brilliant, yes, and he's really successful. But I can tell from the way you talk about him that he's starting to change, that he's not the person you met even a year ago. That he's getting obsessed with this project he's working on, spending more and more time with it, worrying about it all the time. And what I'm afraid of, and what he all but directly told you himself, is that this is a guy who is going to put his own precious ideas ahead of your well-being if he's forced to make a choice. And maybe he's even right that humanity needs people like that in order to progress. And maybe he even *is* one of those people, even if saying so is just incredibly, *unbelievably* arrogant. Good for him, he's a genius, and without people like him we'd still be trying to make fire by banging rocks together to strike a spark. Great. But is this the kind of person you want to be married to?"

"Kate, I wanted to tell you this and now you're—"

"And it's not like you've ever been on your own, either. Have you, Rebecca? Really? The closest you've even been to living on your own is college, and there we were all taken care of pretty much night and day. And then you moved back in with your parents, and you went from there to moving in with this guy with no time by yourself in between. All I'm saying is: don't rush into this, when you haven't really lived life yet—"

"Kate, what the fuck. I wanted to share this great news with one of my oldest friends and you're just—"

"Oh, Rebecca. I'm sorry."

"What the *fuck*. God—"

"I didn't mean to make you cry, Rebecca."

"I just—I just—"

"I'm so sorry. I was way out of line."

"How many times. How many times have I listened to you say you met some great guy on the Internet or whatever, and three days later you're telling me you dumped him because of stuff he wanted to do in bed, or he didn't wash his car often enough, or some stupid shit like that. Because he wasn't *perfect*. If you hold out for perfection you'll end up alone.

"And Philip is great. He's wonderful and he's brilliant and he's funny and he's amazing. And when he proposed to me I felt like the luckiest woman in the world. And I'm not going to let you ruin that. I won't."

"Becca, you're right to say this. You have every right."

"Kate—"

"I take it all back. I don't know why I said all that. I don't know what got into me. I take back everything I said."

Rebecca said nothing as her sobs subsided. Her eyes stung; the back of her throat tingled.

Kate reached across the table and placed her hand on Rebecca's. "I take it all back," she said again. "I feel like I've ruined our friendship. Will you forgive me?"

Her eyes squeezed shut, Rebecca quickly nodded.

"Thank you," Kate said. "I'm really happy for you. Really. I mean it."

12

MODERNIST CUISINE

The thing about memories wasn't that many of them inevitably faded, but that repeated recall of the ones you remembered burnished them into shining, gorgeous lies. Rebecca clearly remembered what Sean was like at the age of five or six, with a precocious light in his eyes even though he came a little late to his early childhood milestones, like walking and toilet training and speech. (His pediatrician regularly hinted that he might turn out to be on the spectrum, but Rebecca chose to ignore him: her son was perhaps a little eccentric, and maybe a touch slower than the other kids of his cohort, but in a couple of years that was sure to even out.) She effortlessly remembered the times when he'd been rapturous over some simple pleasure like a piece of candy given as a surprise, or when he'd recoiled in comical displeasure after curiously licking the terminals of a nine-volt battery, or when he'd made some cute remark that betrayed a misunderstanding of the adult world that he'd someday enter. But she had extraordinary difficulty remembering Sean at seven months, when he was a little defecating machine. Those times did not come to mind unbidden. ("All he does is piss and crap and puke and cry," Philip had said, marveling at his son's furious transmutation of mass to energy, though when changing time came he was nowhere to be found.) The part of her unconscious that was responsible for calling up memories of the strange boy at random times was a careful, prudent censor. In her mind her son was always clean and smiling, with the wonderful man he would become lurking in wait behind the boy's shining eyes.

Not only did Rebecca's mind perform careful elisions of Sean's history to make him seem like some kind of Platonic ideal of himself, but lately—and she thought this had started in earnest around the time she also began feeling that there was something a little wrong with the world, that everything was upside down—she had found herself imagining what Sean might look like now, as if she were peering through a rent in the thick velvet curtain that divided the timeline in which she existed from all the others that were possible. Even now, as she was driving down Route 1 with Philip beside her in the passenger seat, she could almost see some older version of Sean behind her, a little blurred around the edges, gleaming even as he was swaddled in darkness. He would have been nine now. Nine is the age of wearing T-shirts silk-screened with the images of toys you love (and the thing portrayed on Sean's slender chest morphed from a winged robot with missile launchers slung beneath its armpits, to a Tyrannosaurus rex wearing gauntlets and greaves, to a currant-eyed rodent wreathed in lightning). Nine is the age at which you can stretch out in the backseat of a car and touch one door with your hands and the other with your feet (and while Rebecca saw him lounging there, the hem of his shirt riding up to expose the soft flesh of a stomach that begged for a startling tickle, he was also curled there in a fetal position, attempting to shield himself against some secret and trivial terror). As protean as the vision seemed, Rebecca was half inclined to ask Philip if he saw the boy back there as well. But there was no way to bring up the subject without sounding like someone who didn't know how to put an end to grieving.

Philip and Rebecca were on their way to Carson Tyler's apartment for dinner. Kate would be there, too—it'd be just the four of them. Though Carson had extended the invitation and was doing the cooking, Rebecca sensed Kate's hand in it—she didn't see Carson as the type who'd propose something so domestic and double-datey. "Please don't bring anything," he'd said in the e-mail, but no one ever means that—on the way over, Rebecca had insisted on stopping by a grocery store to pick up a half-dozen freshly baked red velvet cupcakes, each topped with a spiraling mountain of cream-cheese frosting and dotted with pastel sprinkles. No matter what Carson made, there would be something to look forward to at the end of the meal. It was impossible to say why red velvet cupcakes, in particular, tasted so good—"red" was not a flavor—but without the coloring, they'd be unremarkable. Something about their deep crimson hue made your eyes tell your tongue that you were eating something special.

Philip held the clear plastic container full of cupcakes in his lap, staring silently at the road in front of him. Rebecca knew that things had been increasingly going wrong at work between him and Carson: Philip seemed to think, or possibly fear, that Carson was becoming disinterested in the work and burning out. ("I heard him complaining about tweaking," he said over what was Rebecca's breakfast and his . . . dinner? What meal did you have at seven a.m. when you were coming back from work and you were just going to go to sleep afterward? "At the edge of the field ninety-nine percent of experimental physics *is* tweaking. I saw worse than this in my early career, far worse. He doesn't know how lucky he has it.") Rebecca figured that Carson would not be inclined to invite his boss (and his boss's wife!) over to his apartment for a home-cooked meal. But Kate would not be aware of such lab politics; even if she were, she would probably find them trivial, especially when compared to the fun that she and her girlfriend Rebecca would have, putting their feet up while a dude cooked for them.

Philip had turned the car radio to NPR (Rebecca had given up on teaching him the custom that the driver had the privilege of selecting the radio station). The subject under discussion was a new and as yet unnamed psychiatric syndrome that seemed to be spiking sharply in the tri-state area: psychiatrists were dealing with a number of patients who weren't feeling *depressed*, exactly, so much as feeling—

"That something's wrong with the world!" Rebecca shouted, bringing Philip out of his reverie.

"—that something's wrong with the world," the psychiatrist being interviewed continued. "Lately one out of three patients who come into my office, they say something like, 'I don't know how to describe this, and I don't know what the name is for it. But I have this feeling that I'm not what I'm supposed to be.' Or they'll say, 'I have this weird feeling that the shape of everything is wrong.' I even had one who came right into the office and pointed at *me* and said, 'You aren't right. You're not right.'"

"Listen!" Rebecca said, pointing at the radio.

"What I want to suggest," the psychiatrist continued, "is that the reason we can't readily identify this disorder is because it is new and peculiar to the twenty-first century. It is the first genuinely new disorder of the Information Age, directly caused by the lifelong pervasiveness of communication technologies."

"Nonsense," Philip said. "This is the kind of thing that's dreamed into existence by doctors and hypochondriacs."

"If you consider human history in its entirety," the psychiatrist said, "for most of it we had only a passing knowledge of what went on beyond the borders of our town, or even past the fences that defined our property. But now in nearly every room we enter, there is some kind of screen, of a computer or a phone or a tablet, that acts as a window on a much larger world. And as we sift through that constant flow of information, we develop the illusion of control. We believe that since we know so much *more* about the world than our benighted ancestors, we have a far greater capability than they did to direct our own destinies."

In the backseat of the car, Rebecca saw Sean snoring indolently, and feverishly manipulating the joysticks of his portable gaming console, and kneeling in the seat so he could look out the rear window at the headlights of the car behind them.

"Now, consider that the group of people now coming into middle age are the first in history who can't really remember a time before the World Wide Web. They have always viewed the world through these electronic windows; they have always had that false feeling of control. And, for all of us but the most fortunate or the least introspective, middle age is the time in our life when we look back on our past and begin the long process of coping with regret. For these children of the Information Age, who have grown up feeling that they had an unprecedented ability to shape the world and their place in it, but who have also been made acutely aware of all the other directions their lives could have taken—because you only have to spend five minutes online to prove to yourself that someone else out there in the world is living one, or all, of your possible lives—wouldn't that feeling of regret be greater still? Wouldn't it metastasize into some other dysfunctional psychological phenomenon for which the word 'regret' just isn't adequate?"

"Okay, now that part's just pop psychology," Rebecca said. "I never felt like I could change the world when I was younger—if anything, it was the opposite! If there's anything I regret from that time, it's the hours and hours I wasted holed up in my bedroom in my parents' house, drinking cheap wine and browsing online. But the rest of it—I don't know. I think there's something there. That there's some sort of disease that technology has something to do with. That makes perfect sense."

"It's just hysteria," Philip replied as Rebecca turned off Route 1 and onto a smaller, less congested two-lane road, her shoulders relaxing. "Fear of technological change brings these things on. Thirty years ago it was fear that radiation from mobile phones was microwaving our brains. Now it's this. In three years we'll have forgotten all about it."

Neither of them spoke until they arrived at Carson's sprawling apartment complex in Plainsboro. Like many similar abodes in the Jersey hinterlands, the place was a maze, full of little alleys named after flowers and trees and dead presidents, and parking lots with spaces numbered out of sequence. When they finally found the building, Philip was a little clumsy getting out of the car and ended up jostling the cupcakes inside the container, turning one of them over entirely and bouncing several others so that they left smears of frosting against the lid. But Rebecca figured they'd at least still taste the same.

She felt the tiniest pang of guilt as she locked the car doors and walked away, as if she were doing the kind of carelessly awful thing that landed you on the eleven o'clock news. But she wasn't, clearly. There wasn't anyone left behind in the backseat; there had never been anyone there.

■

Kate greeted the two of them at the door to Carson's apartment, overdressed in a vaguely ball-gowny thing with a slit in the side that went to the thigh. In her hand she cradled a crystal tumbler two-thirds full of Pinot Grigio. "Carson doesn't like to drink while cooking: he says it dulls his edge," she said. "He treats it the same way he treats one of his physics problems: deadly serious about it. But *someone* has to drink while the food's on the stove because of tradition, and *I like drinking.* So. Q.E.D."

Kate led them into the apartment, slightly unsteady on too-tall heels. The outfit was a bit much, and Rebecca began to suspect that Kate was in that phase of her relationship with Carson where she convinced herself that she was really going to make a go of things. This phase usually came just before the one in which Kate suddenly called it off. Lately when Kate talked to Rebecca about Carson, her comments indicated a general unease about how things were going, one that didn't seem to have a clear cause. ("i dunno," she'd said one evening by IM. "not sure about the overall vibe.") Though the closest she got to anything specific was saying that he "didn't seem motivated sometimes. i say hey let's hang out and he's not like, awesome! he's just like yeah ok. wanna go to the movies? ok. wanna hook up? yeah ok. maybe he's not the kind of person who takes initiative. you know?" Rebecca could easily recall times when Kate had said the exact opposite about a man— too driven with respect to his work; too controlling; too eager to jump in the sack—but when Kate was casting around for reasons to cut loose from a man, it wasn't the details of the excuse that mattered so much as the fact of its existence.

Carson was in the kitchen, his back to the rest of them as he huddled over the stove. Rebecca immediately surmised that bringing the store-bought desserts might have been a mistake—the kitchen looked like a chemistry lab. Had the cupcakes not been in Philip's hands, she would have tried to spirit them back to the car under some guise or other, but it was already too late for that: Philip was stepping forward to hand them over. Rebecca looked at Philip and sensed that he knew that something was a little off as well, but it was too late for him to pivot to another script.

"We brought some cupcakes!" Philip said, his tone halfway between apology and command.

There was no other noise in the kitchen besides the whirring of the centrifuge that sat on the granite countertop. Carson turned from his work to look at the half-dozen cupcakes, at the pale smudges of icing on the inside of the lid. Once again Rebecca reminded herself that she was going to have to take Philip out for a wardrobe refresh, even if he didn't want to spend the time: Philip's plain white button-down shirt, with its limp collar and its frayed cuffs, made a poor contrast to Carson's shirt in a tasteful lavender, his deep purple tie, and a pinstriped chef's apron that seemed like it needed its own apron: it was too nice to get stains on.

Behind Rebecca, Kate went toward the refrigerator to retrieve the bottle of wine.

"I told you not to bring anything," Carson said quietly, assiduously avoiding Philip's gaze.

"Cupcakes!" Philip barked, shoving them forward.

Carson took the cupcakes from Philip and placed them on the counter. They looked sad, and he looked sadly at them. "I'm sure we can integrate these into the meal somehow," he said, smiling weakly.

■

The first course was a caramelized carrot soup—Carson had been spinning one of its ingredients in the centrifuge when Rebecca and Philip arrived. "A centrifuge opens up all kinds of possibilities in the kitchen," he said. "You'd be surprised. I didn't have the room for the one I wanted in this apartment—that's a priority when I move into a larger place. But the chem lab will let me borrow their equipment whenever I want to separate a liter of something, or spin something really fast. Have you ever had pea butter? It's wonderful!"

"No, I've never had *pea butter*," Kate said, her wine sloshing around in her tumbler. "I've never had *butter*, made out of *peas*." She was the only one at the table who was drinking, really: Rebecca and Philip had goblets filled with sparkling water, and though Carson had a glass of wine in front of him in order to keep Kate company, he'd barely touched it. Rebecca got the impression that Carson felt as if drinking in front of Philip would be like drinking in front of one's own teetotaling father.

"Well," said Carson patiently, "if you take a pea puree and spin it in a centrifuge, it'll separate out into three discrete layers: the juice at the top, the starch at the bottom, and a thin layer of bright green fat in the middle. A pea is about three percent fat. Now, if you siphon off the juice and remove that middle layer of fat, you'll be able to treat it much as you would butter. It's a great spread on toast!"

"That's weird," said Kate.

"Carson, this soup is very tasty and smooth," said Rebecca.

■

The second course was something that Carson referred to as "American barbecue": each of their plates held six parallel strips of boneless pork, coated in a transparent sauce. "Did you use a centrifuge for this, too?" Philip asked, delicately cutting at the meat with his fork and knife.

"Tomato confit, brown beef jus, malt vinegar, a dash of maple syrup, a little bit of rendered bacon, and some other ingredients, reduced and spun for an hour at 27,500 gs," Carson said, sounding a little like a bright student who was overly eager to prove himself. "It's clear, but if you spin off and discard the solids that would provide the color, the remaining solution has a strong and unique flavor. I had to cheat a little here and there with the rest of the recipe—I don't have a proper hot-smoker—but with a ceramic grill you can do a lot of surprisingly sophisticated things with temperature control. Slow-roasting is a lot easier than you'd expect."

"You're funny," Kate said. "I mean, you do all this research in order to make simple barbecued ribs, when I'd think that'd be the one recipe that'd be in your blood, you know?"

Carson looked up at Kate, frowning slightly.

"I mean, that's the kind of thing where I'd figure you'd come out of the kitchen with, like, a *platter*, and the ribs would be *hanging off the edge* and *dripping with sauce*, and when we asked you how you did it you'd say, 'Aw, you know how we *do*: I just got back there and threw together a little something-something.'"

"I just remembered that I have a Cabernet I meant to pair with this course," Carson said, getting up to go into the kitchen.

"How are things at work?" Rebecca hastily said to Philip.

"Great!" Philip said, perking up suddenly. "Oh. Oh! I have a funny story to tell all of you. I have a story about Alicia Merrill."

"Is this about the calibrator?" Carson yelled from the kitchen.

"Yes!"

"She was in rare form," Carson said, returning from the kitchen with a bottle of red and two empty glasses.

"So one of the instruments we use in the lab is a calibrator for the causality violation device. Some parts for it are off the shelf; some are printed; some we have custom machined to our specifications. But the whole thing has to be hand built and hand maintained. The calibrator basically ensures that certain elements of the CVD are behaving as they should, and that the readouts it's giving us are accurate. Now, the design for this was a collaborative project—Alicia and I designed it, with Carson making a few vital contributions—but Alicia is the only one of us who has actually built one of these."

Kate opened the bottle of Cabernet and poured a serving of it into her tumbler along with the dregs of the Chardonnay. She swirled the wine around, smirked at Carson, and said, "Rosé."

"Now there are two other labs attempting to build a CVD right now: one's in Frascati; the other in Perth. And if any one of the three of us succeeds, it will be a massive step forward for human knowledge. But at the same time, I would greatly prefer that *my* lab build the first working version of the device, because I am human. And I'm sure that the physicists at Frascati and Perth feel the same way. It can be difficult to hold both these contradictory positions in one's head at once, and yet in a way, that tension between collaboration and competition is what drives good science.

"So because we collaborate, we've published the schematics for this calibrator along with instructions for assembly: not just the construction, but where to order parts or get them machined, the templates for those components that can be printed, and so on. And we're happy that Frascati and Perth have been able to build calibrators that are accurate enough to verify the validity of our design. But we cannot help but be pleased, perhaps guiltily, but still pleased, that the other two labs have failed to produce calibrators as accurate as the two that Alicia built for us, even though they followed our instructions to the letter."

Carson laughed.

"Alicia and Carson composed the design document, and it's as precise and careful as can be. We're not leaving out some sort of secret ingredient: we really do want Frascati and Perth to succeed, if only to have a stronger confirmation of our work. But there's a phenomenon in practical physics called 'golden hands.' Just as a Stradivarius violin has a unique sound compared to other violins because it was built by Stradivarius, so can an instrument function better because it was built by a particular person. One might suspect that a person with golden hands has picked up some additional knowledge in the lab through experience and instinct, something that is known with the muscles rather than the mind—the kind of thing you can't document because you don't even know you know it. At any rate, when it comes to building this calibrator, it looks like Alicia has golden hands. One of the calibrators she built for us gives readings that are accurate to four decimal places; the other is accurate to five. The calibrators that were built at Frascati and Perth are accurate only to three places at best."

"Even though they're supposedly following the instructions to a T," Rebecca said.

"Exactly. And unless the calibration is accurate to as many places as possible, you can't be sure if the causality violation device is failing because the fold in spacetime is misaligned, or because of one of a hundred other possible reasons."

"So we get this phone call in the lab a couple of months ago," Carson cut in, "and it's from Perth. And what they want to do, at their own expense, is fly a few members of their team from Australia to New Jersey, as well as sending us two sets of the components necessary to construct one of these calibrators. And they want Alicia to build one at a workbench, while a physicist at another workbench matches her move for move, and two other physicists watch. And they want to videotape this, too."

"It takes six hours to assemble one of these things, by the way," Philip said.

"So Philip tells Alicia this and she says, 'As long as we can get an extra calibrator out of the deal at no cost—because damned if I'm going to spend a workday building one of those things just to hand it over to the Aussies—then, sure, I'll do it. Send them over."

"Days later," Philip said, "the parts for this calibrator start showing up by FedEx, two by two. And soon after that the team from Perth is on its way over: they want to do this as soon as possible. They show up, take over one of the rooms in our lab, and set up shop: two long workbenches facing each other, with all the necessary components laid out on them identically, along with tablets that have PDFs of all the design documents. And they've got two cameras to film both of the tables. Because at this point they're thinking that there's something about building the calibrator that we didn't document because we didn't realize it mattered. Maybe Alicia licks her index finger before she touches a component, or maybe she turns a particular screw five times instead of six. Some stupid little thing like that."

"So they set this thing up," said Carson, "and at nine o'clock sharp, Alicia comes strolling in. She's actually got—she's wearing this red T-shirt with two golden Ws on it, like on the bustier that Wonder Woman wears. She brings a little stereo in with her, and she puts it down on her workbench. Then without a word, she turns it on—it starts playing James Brown; 'Mother Popcorn,' I think the song was called—and starts assembling this calibrator *without even looking at the schematic*."

"And I'll say it again," Philip continued. "We really do want these Perth guys to be able to build this thing. We really do believe that the transmission of as much information that is as accurate as possible is to the mutual benefit of all. But at the same time, we are human, and we would not mind, it would not kill us, if these people were forcibly made aware of what they were up against."

"So Alicia goes about putting this thing together, not saying a word to anyone. At one point one of the observers wants to stop her so he can ask a question, and as soon as he gets out a few words she gives him this *look*. And she stabs a finger at one of the cameras and says, 'I assume you brought *those* so you wouldn't have to *interrupt me* while I'm engaged in the *non-trivial task* of assembling a *causality violation device calibrator*. Or did you people spend twenty-four hours on a plane so you could *chat*. Do me a favor and stay quiet: save your applause for the end.' And except for Alicia's music it was silent in there for the rest of the day."

"And their guy who was supposed to be watching her while he assembled his own fell behind after about a half hour. He wasn't counting on her actually having the design *memorized*, right? Well, she helped design it, so he should have accounted for that. She finishes putting the calibrator together in about five hours—an hour ahead of schedule. She didn't even have lunch, except for a protein bar she'd squirreled away somewhere, and occasionally she'd take a drink from a water bottle. And she sits there for another hour with her arms folded, staring at this physicist from Perth while he finishes up. And of course he doesn't want to ask for help now—it's a matter of pride."

"And there was some gender stuff going on there as well, I think," Carson said. "And maybe some nationalist stuff, too. I forgot to mention that Alicia had her hair tied up in a ponytail with this scarf that had blue stars on it, to match the Wonder Woman T-shirt."

"So this guy finally finishes, and Alicia says, 'Well, okay then!' They take their calibrators into the room in our lab with the CVD. And Alicia's is well within spec—it probably won't turn out to be as good as the second one she built, but it's probably better than the first."

"But this Perth guy hooks his up, right? And—hell, I don't even know how this happened."

"I don't know, either. It was an inexplicable phenomenon."

"I don't—"

Carson and Philip both dissolved in laughter, while Rebecca and Kate caught each other's glances and shared a mutual rolling of eyes.

"He hooks his calibrator up—" Philip said once he recovered.

"And honest to God—" Carson continued.

"Smoke started coming out of it! Like the smoke that comes off the tip of a lit cigarette."

"And Alicia looks at the broken calibrator—which is displaying a bunch of Xs instead of actual numbers—and she says, 'Oh heavens to Betsy: that's not indicated at all. You'll notice that *my* calibrator, the one *I* built, did not *combust*. But we learn by doing. Maybe if you look at your tapes, you'll see something magical. Anyway, I'm going for a run. Enjoy the rest of your stay in America!' And she walks out of the lab and leaves these guys to pick their jaws up off the floor. It was amazing!"

"It was absolutely amazing."

"Alicia's great," Carson said.

"Alicia's really great," Philip said.

Meanwhile, Rebecca had finished her plate of barbecue, feeling only slightly less hungry than she had felt when she arrived.

"I've got to say," said Kate as she reached for the wine bottle—she'd polished off the mixture of white and red in her glass—"that I'm not one hundred percent with you guys on the whole 'Alicia's great' thing. I mean, Carson, when you brought me into the lab to visit, she came off as kind of a smartassed bitch, to be honest."

"She can initially present as perhaps a little severe sometimes," Philip said. "A first impression like that is understandable."

"I have to say I can kind of see where Kate's coming from," Rebecca said cautiously. "She's not someone I think of as having an excess of social grace."

"Shit, that's a polite way to put it," said Kate.

"May I hazard an explanation here?" Carson said, placing his hand on Kate's (and gently stopping her from lifting her glass to her lips, Rebecca noticed). Strangely, Carson was looking at Philip as if *he* were the person at the table whom Carson was most worried about offending.

"The thing to take into account here," Carson said, "is that physics is, and basically always has been, a field that's mostly male. The other pure sciences are different: in chemistry there are about as many women as men by this point, and in biology there have been more women than men for a while. And there are certainly more women in physics than there used to be, but there aren't so many that the presence of a woman in a lab doesn't instinctively seem at least a *little* unusual.

"So because physics is a field that generally has significantly more men than women, the style of discourse tends toward what we think of as masculine—physicists can often come off as assertive and blunt. So a woman who does well in the field, who gets socialized into the profession, may have, or might develop, I guess I should say, some personality traits that make her seem to be a little difficult to get along with at first. So I can see—"

"Oh, uh-uh, no," Kate interrupted. "Oh no no no. Give me a second to process this—see, my pretty little girly little head is full of unicorns and pink things, so it can take a while for men's serious thoughts to push through all that stuff sometimes."

"Kate, I didn't mean—"

"Wait: still thinking! Okay. Okay, I've got this now. Do you mean to say that the reason I've mistaken her for bitchy is that she's actually *assertive*? And this secretly makes me uncomfortable? Is that what you're saying? It certainly sounds like what you're saying."

"I may not have chosen my words well," Carson said.

"I mean, it was cool the way you covered up your mansplaining with some kind of pseudo-feminist jiujitsu, but the fact is, she's an annoying smartass who only opens her mouth when she wants to try to cut someone up with her tongue, and the only reason you guys are all members of her fan club is 'cause she's little and cute, so she can get away with shit. Trust me—I'm little and cute, too, and we know our own kind. Guys have always let me get away with all kinds of shit."

"Once you get to know Alicia better and she lets her guard down, she's really quite likable," Philip said. "And she's an invaluable asset to the lab. Invaluable! And I'm certain she's going to go on to have a spectacular career. When she leaves and gets her own lab she's going to be great for physics as a whole, but I'm not looking forward to losing her."

"You're both pussywhipped," said Kate.

"Hey, I could go for some dessert," said Rebecca.

■

Dessert was a strawberry gazpacho, and Carson served everyone with one of Rebecca's cupcakes, which sat next to the soup bowls on their own little matching plates. Kate was pretty well wasted by this point: with what she'd had to drink, she would have been more than tipsy even if this weren't the kind of meal where you were still going to be a little hungry afterward. Rebecca's stomach was screaming out for the cupcake—she felt like she could finish it off in three bites—but out of politeness she felt that she should first try the soup. It was reddish pink with half a strawberry floating on the surface, and the ceramic bowl in which it was served was smaller than Rebecca's fist.

"I'm just saying something," Kate said, swaying slightly in her chair. "Saying to say something. Saying *something* to say something." Carson had filled her wine glass with water.

"I really like this gazpacho," Rebecca said, and hoped she made it clear that she wasn't merely being polite. She would have liked it more if there had been more than three spoonfuls of it in the cup— the soup would be gone before she was able to become familiar with how it tasted. Still, when she got around to that cupcake she was going to punish it.

"Because how it *is*," said Kate, "is."

"You wouldn't expect the ideas of 'strawberry' and 'gazpacho' to go together," Rebecca continued. "And usually when someone puts gazpacho in front of me I think, *Ugh, this soup is cold*, and I want to throw it in a microwave for a couple of minutes. But this is really good."

Philip had somehow gulped down both the gazpacho and the

cupcake—poor thing, he must have been hungry too—and he was sitting ramrod straight in his chair, wringing his hands in his lap. He was ready to go.

Carson had provided everyone with forks that seemed too large to be salad forks but too small to be dinner forks—Rebecca would not have been surprised to find that they were called cupcake forks. He carefully extracted his cupcake from its paper wrapper, slid the fork into it and broke off a piece, and placed the fork in his mouth.

"Yeah," Kate said. "Yeah."

"Do you taste that slightly bitter note under the sweetness?" Carson said. "That's from the red dye. Most people think food coloring is tasteless, but if you put enough of it in a dish, it actually will change the flavor a bit. So using cream cheese in the frosting to complement that slight bitterness makes sense. Did you know the most common form of red food coloring is derived from petroleum?"

Rebecca didn't care about petroleum. She tore the wrapper off her cupcake and lifted it to her mouth. No need for the fork; no need, at this late date, to stand on ceremony.

"You know what would've been a really good dessert for this meal?" Kate said. "Watermelon. You could treat it if you wanted. With a process."

Carson looked at Kate, whose eyes were smiling even as she covered her mouth. "Actually, you can do some interesting things with watermelon," he said in a barely audible voice. "If you place it in a dehydrator for twelve hours, the result will be something that is very much like meat."

"Oh, goodness, I think we need to go," Rebecca said, putting her cupcake down untouched.

"A bulgogi glaze would go nicely with it," Carson said.

"Come on, Philip," Rebecca said, standing. "Time to go."

"Did I miss something?" Philip said.

"Just—I forgot there's some stuff I need to do at home. It was a lovely dinner, Carson," Rebecca said, removing her purse from where it hung on the back of her chair. "You're an excellent cook. If you ever get tired of physics I'm sure you could find a place in a fancy restaurant somewhere."

Carson looked up at Rebecca placidly. "Are you sure you can't stay longer?" he said, his voice admirably free of sarcasm.

■

Rebecca's phone rang the next morning at around ten thirty, interrupting a reverie in which she was thinking of Bloody Marys. (The tomato juice counts as nutrition, which is why it's socially acceptable to drink them in the morning. You pour the vodka into the glass first and then the tomato juice; then, as an afterthought, you pour in an additional half shot of vodka. But you never fail to leave room for the afterthought in the glass.) She did not hear garbled noises of play coming from the living room as she sat in the kitchen; she did not hear the nonsense syllables that Sean strung together to tell the stories of his lame and decapitated action figures. He was not pushing into this world from another.

Kate's voice sounded slightly hoarse, and a little sheepish. "Hey, Becca."

"Hey, Kate."

Rebecca patiently listened to the silence on the line.

"So it was nice of you and Philip to come over to Carson's last night," Kate finally said.

"He's a great cook," said Rebecca.

"So, hey," said Kate after a pause, "you're not going to believe this. But—okay. Before you guys showed up, Carson and I had had a cocktail, and then I had a glass of wine. And this morning when I went into the kitchen I saw one empty bottle of white, and a bottle of red that was only like half full. And . . . well, it looks like I drank almost all of that by myself. It was kind of ridiculous."

"You *were* drinking a lot," Rebecca said.

"I hope I didn't get too crazy. I mean, I woke up this morning with an *insane* headache. I don't even remember anything past, like, the beginning of the second course. I remember him getting ready to bring out those little plates of pork, and next thing I knew I was waking up in his bed this morning. Though it looks like I puked in his bathroom. And he cleaned it up. I feel like an ass."

"Really? You don't remember anything? You were that drunk? *Kate.*"

"Yeah, it's a blank. I guess I can't drink like a college kid anymore. I feel like I've been saying that once every couple of months for the past ten years."

"I know how you feel," Rebecca said.

"So . . . I don't know how to ask this."

"Just ask."

"Did I do anything stupid? Like, did I *say* anything stupid? Sometimes my mouth gets out of control when I drink."

"No," said Rebecca after a moment. "You looked like the same old Kate to me. I wouldn't have known you were blackout drunk if you hadn't told me just now."

"Oh, *good*. You know how it is—you can't remember what happened, and you worry after the fact that you made a fool of yourself."

"We've all been there."

"Carson was already gone when I woke up this morning. So I haven't had a chance to talk to him yet."

"You were fine."

"Awesome. It's really a relief to hear that. So what are you up to today?"

"I've got a Lovability shift from noon to four. Other than that—cleaning the house and other, you know, goofy homemaker stuff. And I'm making a beef stew for dinner in a slow cooker—you throw the stuff in the pot when you get up in the morning, and by evening your whole house smells good, like beef stew."

"That sounds *delicious*."

"It is. It's not like you need a chemistry PhD or anything to make it, but it's good."

"I am totally going to go out today and buy a slow cooker," Kate said.

"So, hey, as long as we're making confessions . . ."

"What?"

"I didn't embarrass you in front of Carson by bringing over cupcakes I got at a grocery store, did I?"

"No!" Kate said excitedly. "No, you didn't!"

"Because when we went in the kitchen and saw that Carson was making basically the fanciest dinner in the world, I looked at his food and I looked at my pathetic red velvet cupcakes and I was like, oh shit—"

"No no no! Don't worry about it! He loved those cupcakes! Because as soon as you guys left he totally scarfed down the one on his plate, and then ate the one you left on yours, too! He had this look on his face; he ate those cupcakes like he was *angry* with them—"

Kate cut herself off in mid-sentence, and both of them were mute for a few moments. Rebecca felt the time stretching, felt it trying to pry her mouth open to wrench something out of it. But she had no idea what she should say.

Then Kate said, "Okay. Bye, Becca."

The line went dead.

13

POINT ZERO

The limousine making its way down I-295 toward Stratton held four people in the back: Rebecca; Philip; Sean, who was a few months old and asleep in Rebecca's lap, snug in a baby sling; and, sitting across from the three of them, drinking champagne at eleven a.m., was Edmund Taligent, the millionaire who had been funding the development of Philip's causality violation device for the past several months.

Edmund Taligent was twenty-seven. He wore cargo shorts, a pair of Birkenstock sandals with soles that had been worn down to the cork, and a T-shirt that proclaimed in bold, fluorescent letters: SCIENCE! He was lanky and fidgety, and he boiled over with exuberance. "I feel really good about this," he said to Philip, sloshing his champagne around in its fluted crystal glass as he gestured. "I feel like today's your big day, like tomorrow you're going to look back on yesterday and think, *Shit, that was a big day.*" Today was the day when Philip and his team were to activate the Planck-Wheeler clock and establish Point Zero, the fixed end of the wormhole that was still an idea, rather than a thing. If all went correctly, and the Planck-Wheeler clock functioned as intended, the place that would mark the other end of the wormhole would travel with the researchers forward through spacetime as they continued their work. Eventually, at some point that was likely to be at least several years in the future, the physicists would figure out how to send an object into the end of the wormhole that stayed in their present, out through the fixed end that was anchored in the past, and back again to the place it had left, bearing evidence of some kind that it had taken the trip. Then the experiment would be considered a success.

Philip was a little bothered that Edmund had wanted to make this relatively uninteresting moment, the simple flipping of a switch, the metaphorical driving of a stake at an arbitrary point in spacetime, into a grand ceremony. There was no need for a limousine; there was no need for champagne. The science hadn't happened yet. But Edmund Taligent was footing the bill, and he demanded his amusements in return. "This is *big*," he'd said to Philip over the phone, his voice high and wheedling. "We're going to play this like it's big. Here's what I'm seeing. I pick you up in a limo like you're a *rock star*, and we go over there in *style*. In this lab there's the whatever it is, the Point Zero, and it's cordoned off by a velvet rope, the kind that stops guys who don't have arm candy from getting into clubs. And there's a bouncer. This big dude in a black suit, with a black shirt and a black silk tie and sunglasses. He unlatches the rope and he lets you in. Then you turn to everybody and you raise your arms, like a *priest*, because that's what you *are now*, you guys need to step up and *own that*, you are our *new priests*, the *priests of the secular*—"

"I'm not a priest," Philip had said. "I just want to do science."

But Edmund had barreled on as if Philip had not spoken. "You raise your arms—I'll have someone tailor a nice bespoke shirt for you for this, something special with a little give in the sleeves—you raise your arms and you say something like, 'With the activation of the Planck-Wheeler clock, we begin the next step in humanity's relentless endeavor to comprehend all knowledge. Behold. The future is, quite literally, now.' Then you flip the switch! And everyone applauds! And the next day we have a *press conference*, where I announce that I'm funding this project in perpetuity, until it's done. We'll put out a couple of really nice cheese plates for the press guys and the bloggers. You put a nice cheese plate in front of a blogger and he'll bark and clap like a trained seal—I've seen it before. We have this press conference, and I give you one of those big novelty checks for like a million dollars."

"This all seems a bit much."

"*Science!* Goddamn. I get so excited when I think about this stuff, you know?"

∎

In the limousine, Rebecca felt Sean shifting in his baby sling as he slept. She listened as Edmund Taligent told her how he made what he called his "mad money," the cash reserves he used to back scientific projects on a whim. He'd carved out a space for himself in the R&D division of his father's robotics company, Taligent Industries. "I'd walk around the halls and I'd hear people saying, you know, *Here comes the kid.* Thinking I was Dad's spy or something, instead of somebody who could think for himself. But then I cracked that problem with the baseballs and that shut the haters up. You know who figured out how to automate baseball production? *Me.* You probably didn't even know that up until recently, baseballs were made by hand! Because that was a difficult problem to solve—not just figuring out how to join these two pieces of leather together into the shape of a sphere, but telling a machine when to start and stop the stitching, and how to know when to vary the tension of the stitches so the cover won't tear. Engineers had been trying on and off to work this out for, like, sixty years. Anyhow, most baseballs, like the ones used in pro games, were made in Costa Rica—these guys in the factories there were *fast.* Like, they could make five or six balls an *hour.* And what looks like some hard-ass mathematics and engineering problem to an R&D division is nothing to these guys. They watch someone make a baseball, and then they can make one themselves. Simple.

"So here's what I do. I fly out to Costa Rica along with a bunch of smarties and some gear. Because the mistake these other engineers have been making is asking these guys how they make these things, or maybe watching them and taking notes and trying to, you know, quantify all this stuff. But these guys who make baseballs all day long don't *know* what they're doing, not in the way an engineer knows something. I mean, they don't know *consciously.* The knowledge is in their muscles and their instincts—that's what we have to get to."

In Rebecca's arms, Sean stirred and woke. His eyelids fluttered as if he were trying to clear his head of a troubling dream; then they sprang open as his mouth widened in what Rebecca hoped was joy and not the precursor to a tantrum. He was not yet a year old, and so he still seemed startled to be in the world instead of the womb (and Rebecca herself had just begun to feel that her internal organs had settled back to where they used to be, though it looked to her as if there were some parts of her that would be forever stretched and displaced). With one hand Sean stretched up toward the roof of the limousine; with the other he clumsily grabbed at Rebecca's breast, his doughy little hand already strong enough to pinch.

"So here's what we did," Edmund continued, rocking back and forth in his seat. "We got their ten best guys, the ones who'd been at this for decades, they damn near had images of baseballs burned into their retinas. And we got them to wear these gloves—very light, very unobtrusive, designed to impair motor control as little as possible. Specially fitted for each person. And these gloves had motion-capture sensors in them! We mo-capped these guys as they stitched about five hundred baseballs. And we took *that* data and fed it to this software that drives a pair of robotic arms—there's some fuzzy logic in there; there's some AI. And that's enough to get these arms to start learning how to make baseballs themselves. At first their failure rate was greater than ninety percent—we'd be lucky if what they turned out was even *round*, never mind it being something a major leaguer would want to touch. But that artificial intelligence, right? If you give it a chance and you program it right, it can simulate that knowing without knowing. Knowing in the muscle instead of the brain. The arms learned from experience; they got better. After a few weeks we had the failure rate down to thirty-five percent, which still sounds like a lot, but get this—while ninety percent of the handmade balls met specs at six balls an hour, sixty-five percent of the machine-made balls were perfect at *sixty* balls an hour. Do the math! It was worth it to Rawlings to license that tech from us, even with the increase in spoiled materials from the balls that didn't turn out right. And those poor Costa Ricans motion-captured themselves out of a job, but science marches on, right? You'd think hardcore baseball fans would have been up in arms—you know how they are, the stat junkies and the guys who get dewy-eyed whenever they hear 'Sweet Caroline'— but it turns out most people thought baseballs were already machine-made *anyway*. Fans couldn't have cared less! Everybody was happy, Taligent Industries killed it, I got some *respect* for once, and I got a little mad money to play with, to fund the kind of stuff I like to fund. Like this," he said to Philip. "Figuring out how to get a robot to stitch seams in a baseball—that's small-time stuff. But you? You are on the *bleeding edge*. Time travel! I cannot believe that in an hour, time travel is going to be real."

"I'm not building a time machine," Philip said evenly, though Rebecca thought his voice carried an undertone of alarm.

"Time travel," Edmund said distantly, shaking his head in bemusement and wonder. "In-freakin'-credible."

"Bluh-*gah*?" said Sean.

■

Strange how fast one's life could change—a little over a year ago Rebecca had been dating an older guy she'd gotten reasonably comfortable with, even though she didn't really see marriage in the cards. Now she was in fact married to that guy, with a newborn kid to boot. It was as if the nuptials had imbued her with something of Philip's inexorable sense of purpose: once hitched they (or perhaps he) saw a goal, the life they (or, perhaps, he) wanted to live, and progressed toward it with dogged efficiency.

No, it wasn't just Philip who seemed in a hurry—she was fast approaching thirty, and with that impending birthday the way she thought of her own life was beginning to change. When she was twenty, she thought of people in their thirties as, well, *old:* after all, they had lived as long as she had and half as long again, and so they must have been tired, with the beginnings of aches in their bones and the first intimations of their own mortality.

But the peculiar horror of growing older was not what she expected. In fact, she felt the same age as she had eight years ago, and twenty-eight years of life had managed to compress themselves into a life-span that once comfortably held twenty. It wasn't that she was getting older, but that the years were getting shorter, and were therefore more precious. You had to use them sparingly.

So you got married: you trusted your gut, and you didn't meditate on it much. The ceremony took place in your father's church: he performed it himself, spiking the plainspoken ritual with sideways winks and subversive flashes of wit. The reception afterward had an open bar, against your new husband's wishes, but damned if your parents were going to stay dry when they married you off. (Though your mother, who you expected would be the wild card in the evening's proceedings, was surprisingly well behaved: it turned out that the wife of one of Philip's groomsmen was a rare-books archivist, and once the two of them began to discuss strategies for the proper preservation of digital media, they were dead to the rest of the world.)

But near the end of the evening, Kate, your maid of honor, pulled you away from a tedious conversation with one of Philip's brothers to usher you to the men's bathroom: she assured you that the girls were on guard, and that while you were in there, no one else would enter.

The only occupied stall was carelessly left unlocked, so you slowly pushed its door inward and entered, careful not to trail the hem of your wedding dress on the tile floor. Your father was kneeling before the toilet in bleary-eyed communion; the acidic stink of vomit rose from the bowl. He wiped a rope of snot away from his nose as he turned toward you. "He's a good man," he said. "He came to me and asked for your hand, like a man out of another time. I appreciated that. I look forward to engaging him in single combat. I look forward to convincing him to think as I do.

"I'm glad you're happy. I'm really happy for you.

"But he's so fucking *weird*, honey. He's *so* fucking weird."

■

And you had a kid, because if the years continued to compress themselves and fly by faster still, you'd soon be forty and telling yourself you never wanted kids anyway, that you liked the independence, that there were already too many people on this earth, that egotism was the only thing that made people want to pass on their genetic code. You caught quickly, maybe a few weeks after you started trying: your marriage practically began with pregnancy, not the few years of hedonistic idyll and Saturday-afternoon sex that the twenty-one-year-old version of you imagined you'd have with a new husband. Time, as they say, flew—there were mere eyeblinks between the first missed period and the morning sickness, between the swelling of the stomach, the fluid in the feet, the water breaking, the rush to the hospital, the command to push, the pain so profound in spite of the drugs that it cast you back to a primal state of mind. Then you heard the boy's first panicked cry as instincts told him what his lungs were meant for—*just breathe, damn it, and we'll figure out the rest later.*

Then you looked up from your haze to see that father and son had the same startled expression on their faces. *Would you look at this*, they both seemed to be thinking as they gazed into each other's eyes. *This is what it is like, to be here in the world.*

■

When the limousine arrived at Philip's laboratory, there was little of the hustle and bustle that Rebecca would have expected: the odd grad student came and went through the doors of the building, but nothing more.

"There should be more *people* around," Edmund Taligent said as he emerged from the car. "Some fans or some protesters or something. I should have brought in some people to stand around with signs, and some other people to take pictures of those people: you know, for the optics. You'd think people would be more excited about time travel."

"I feel as if I should clarify that I'm not really interested in the possibility of human beings traveling through time," said Philip.

"Time travel is *awesome!*" Edmund said. "Just the *idea* of it blows your mind. *Pow!*"

There were eight people milling around in the lab when Philip, Edmund, and Rebecca entered, with Rebecca pushing the dozing Sean along in a stroller. A few were curious physicists from other labs who had come by just to watch—they were standing near a folding table that held a couple of boxes of donuts and a warm bottle of orange juice. Two of them recognized Rebecca and raised their hands in greeting before they went back to talking among themselves.

Edmund Taligent's personal assistant, a woman named Sinclair, had arrived at the lab in advance to make preparations. (Rebecca couldn't tell if Sinclair was her first or last name.) Sinclair's job had been to provide the donuts and set up a velvet rope that enclosed the causality violation chamber, but she had underestimated the circumference of the giant cylinder that squatted in the middle of the room, and so the assemblage of rope and stanchions only led a third of the way around it. (Fortunately, Edmund had either dispensed with or forgotten about the idea of a bouncer: that would have made the whole scene look even more pathetic.)

Besides Rebecca and Sinclair, there was only one other woman in the room: Alicia Merrill, a graduate student whom Rebecca had heard Philip mention once or twice, but whom she hadn't actually met. Alicia had walked around the stanchions with a complete disregard for the barrier they implied, and was keying in a series of codes on a panel attached to the chamber's side. Sinclair had produced a phone and was snapping shot after shot of her, the device repeatedly emitting the *snick* of a twentieth-century shutter. "Sinclair," the woman at the panel said, her fingers still flying over the keys. "Do you like the taste of apple? Because if you don't get that iPhone out of my face I'm going to make you eat it."

"Who's the little firecracker?" Edmund said to Philip.

"I think you're talking about Alicia Merrill, who had a sole-author credit on a paper in *Science* at the age of twenty-three. It was a revision of her senior thesis."

"Aw *snap*."

Alicia finished typing on the panel and closed its transparent cover; then she walked over to Philip, accidentally but probably-not-actually-accidentally knocking over one of the velvet-rope stanchions, leaving Sinclair to set it right again. "Philip," she said, "we're ready."

"Hello," Edmund said, stepping forward and offering his hand. "I'm Edmund Taligent, an executive director in the research and development division of Taligent Industries."

"That's nice," Alicia replied, leaving Edmund's hand hanging in the air.

"Alicia," said Philip, "I want you to meet my wife, Rebecca Wright."

"Hi!" said Rebecca. "And this is Sean." She pushed his stroller forward in greeting, though he still lay in an intense and deeply pleasurable slumber.

Alicia involuntarily took a step backward. "I'm sure he's a lovely baby. Philip, if we're going to do this whole ceremonial thing, you should get ready. It's eleven fifty-seven."

■

There was a moment, just after Philip walked past the velvet rope to approach the causality violation device but just before he turned to face his small audience, when Rebecca saw that he felt himself to be alone with the machine that he'd designed. With a tenderness that Rebecca found unexpectedly paternal, he quietly placed his palm against the cool steel wall of the giant cylinder. Rebecca felt a sudden surge of vicarious pride. This was the beginning of what was sure to be an arduous project, but for now, the future seemed full of promise. And the man she'd married was a *doer*. He'd actually *built* this damn thing. She'd married someone who wanted to change history, not someone who was content to sit still and let history change him.

In the stroller, Sean kicked his feet in sleep, his face pinched as if he'd sniffed something bad. If it was not wrong for her husband to respond to the machine he had designed as if it were a son of some kind, it could also not be wrong that she felt, at least in part, the same way about Sean that Philip felt about his machine. It was not just that Rebecca had been granted the precious charge of another human life, but that that life, or any human life, had so much *potential*. Her child made her feel like a *doer* as well—the first time, really, that she'd felt that way in her life.

After his quiet communion, Philip turned to face the assembly, standing on the other side of the rope. "I don't know what to say," he said. "I feel . . . I feel very optimistic about this. I feel like this is a good beginning."

"It's eleven fifty-nine," Alicia said.

Philip glanced at Alicia, who made a quick circular gesture with her hand: *Hurry it up.* "Okay, then," he said. "Without further ado." He checked his watch (the watch Rebecca had given him, which she knew was not even close to accurate: though he wore it every day he never corrected its time, and it was running ridiculously slow by now). Then, after a suitable pause, he said, "Ladies and gentlemen, we are now establishing Point Zero." And he pressed the bright red button displayed on a touchscreen attached to the side of the causality violation device.

The button didn't do anything functional—Philip had said before that he'd be crazy to trust such a crucial function as the activation of the Planck-Wheeler clock and the establishment of Point Zero to humans instead of electronics. The Planck-Wheeler clock was programmed to begin taking measurements of its own movements through spacetime automatically when the atomic clock in Boulder, Colorado, read twelve noon; the clock would have activated on its own even if no one had been in the room to observe it (and, in fact, it had quietly started working at around the time Philip had said, "I feel like this is a good beginning"). But Philip was not unaware of what Edmund Taligent called the "optics": he saw the need to make the abstractions of the science visual for those who didn't have the understanding that he did. So he and Alicia had spent a few hours the day before rigging up this little display: a red button on a touchscreen that would give the impression that something important was happening, and an array of LEDs that would illuminate when Philip pressed the button. The LEDs would, of course, communicate no other information of value besides the fact that they were functioning.

So Philip ceremoniously tapped the touchscreen, the LEDs began to twinkle in shades of red and green, and the group of people assembled outside of the rope applauded. (Edmund Taligent and his assistant were the only ones not in on the joke: Philip had told Rebecca about the LED panel the night before, and Philip's colleagues recognized it as a playful fraud on sight.) The rest of the physicists stood around for a few more minutes, chatting and eating the rest of the donuts; then, one at a time, they shook Philip's hand, congratulated him, and left the lab to return to their own work.

Meanwhile, Edmund stared intently at the causality violation chamber as if he were waiting for something, or willing some serious science to be done. After about ten minutes that yielded nothing more interesting than some blinking LEDs, he turned to Rebecca, his face downcast. Rebecca had lifted Sean from the stroller and was quietly dandling him: she had the sense that he was on the edge of a fit of temper for some reason, but she still had hope that enough rocking and cooing would bring him back.

"It's too bad," Edmund said. "I really believed in this. I really felt like it was going to work."

■

Twenty minutes later, when everyone had cleared out of the lab but Philip, Alicia, Rebecca, and Sean, Edmund approached Philip and sat down on his desk. Philip was staring intently at a laptop whose screen was displaying the initial data yielded from the Planck-Wheeler clock. "I haven't run a serious analysis," he said. "I'm just eyeballing it right now. But it looks good."

Philip looked up at Edmund, who was gazing down at him with inexplicable sadness. "It looks good!" he repeated.

"Philip," Edmund said, "I wanted to wait until everyone else was out of the room before I dropped this on you. But I'm afraid I'm going to pull the funding for this project. I'm really sorry about this."

Philip looked at him in utter confusion, tongue-tied.

"I'm pulling the funding," Edmund said, a little louder, as if Philip hadn't heard the first time.

"I heard what the—I heard what you said. I just don't understand it. I—this doesn't make sense to me."

"I just don't see the point in pouring my company's money into a project that's clearly doomed to failure. It's better for me to cut my losses now."

"What on earth are you talking about?" Philip fairly shouted as Alicia came over to join the two of them. "Twenty-five minutes ago you were as optimistic about this project as I was! As I am now! Look at this," he said, indicating the screen of the laptop in front of him. "We're only just starting to get data! It's a massive, *massive* understatement to say that you're being *really* impatient here. Don't you understand how science works? This is an experiment that won't yield results for years, or maybe even decades! Certainly not in *minutes*!"

"I don't appreciate your tone. I know you're angry, but that kind of condescension just isn't called for. I may not be a scientist like you, but I know how time travel works."

"You know how time travel works," Alicia said.

"Look," Edmund continued, "here's what was supposed to happen. You established Point Zero, which is a fixed point in spacetime, like a beacon. And the Planck-Wheeler clock allows you to track the movement of the causality violation device through spacetime relative to that point."

"Right," Philip said.

"And at some point in the future, you were supposed to figure out how to make a wormhole with a moving end, attached to the causality violation device as it traveled along with you, and a fixed end, anchored at Point Zero. The experiment would have been proven a success if you were able to move an object, like I don't know, a robot or something, through the moving end of the wormhole to Point Zero—which now, as we sit here talking, exists about thirty minutes in the past—and have that object return to the present with some kind of evidence that it had been in the past."

"Right right right! That's all right. Why are you—"

"Well, you see where I'm going with this, don't you? It's already obvious that this isn't going to work out for you. If the experiment was destined to be a success—in the future—wouldn't we have actually seen evidence to that effect here? Now? In the moment when you established Point Zero? Shouldn't the door to the causality violation chamber have opened? Shouldn't something—or someone—have come out?"

As Edmund looked up at the towering column of the causality violation chamber in the center of the room, he allowed himself to give free rein to his fantasies. "Like, for instance: the door opens. Three people come out. Holy shit: it's *us*, from the future. Me, and you, and Alicia. And the future version of you comes up to you and says, 'I don't have much time. But there is another team of duplicates of ourselves right behind us. You must not listen to anything they say. The future of humanity depends on it.' Then ten seconds later, the door opens *again*. Here come three *more* duplicates of ourselves, except they're wearing burlap sacks and they look like heroin addicts, and they have bar codes tattooed on their foreheads. And this *other* future version of you comes up to you and says, 'There are truths that man was not meant to know. You must abandon the attempt to build a causality violation device. The future of humanity depends on it.' And it's like: how did this happen? Which of these duplicates should we believe? And our minds get totally blown—*pow!*

"What I'm saying is that if this experiment was something that was going to pan out, we should have seen something that was, you know, all weird and paradoxical."

"Let me get this straight," Alicia said. "That's something you *wanted* to happen."

"Well, no, I didn't exactly *want* it to happen. But it would have been an awesome thing to see."

"With all due respect," Philip said, in a tone of voice indicating that he didn't think much respect was due, "I don't think you understand how the scientific process functions. Science often has a habit of refusing to confirm our suppositions about how the world works. You have a notional model of how things are, and then when you start to try to verify that model, the facts don't cooperate. So you have to find a new model. That's what's interesting! That's one of the reasons you do science—to find out what your illusions are, to get rid of them, and to find a new, and a better, and a more refined way of seeing the world. You don't throw in the towel when it turns out that your old way of seeing things is contradicted by the data. That's not when you stop. That's when you *begin*. Don't you see?"

"Philip," Edmund said patiently. "Philip. I know what's going on in your head. I've seen people even smarter than you go down this path before. You've been thinking about this idea your whole life, and your whole sense of identity is riding on your theory being proven right. And when the evidence starts to say otherwise, when people begin to *tell* you otherwise, you just ignore them. You go down this dead-end research path by yourself, and you tell yourself that if you pursue this for long enough, then you'll be able to show everyone how wrong they were. The more people criticize and denigrate you, the sweeter your victory over them is going to be in the end. Be honest. Isn't that what you're thinking right now?

"If you want to go down that path, I wish you luck. Maybe it'll turn out well for you. But I can't join you. And I can't throw good money after bad.

"Again, I'm really sorry about this."

Quietly, Edmund pushed himself off the desk and stood. He waved goodbye to everyone (Rebecca suddenly finding a reason to tickle and fuss with Sean; Alicia giving Edmund a look that could have curdled milk), and, without speaking, he left the lab, its heavy double doors swinging shut behind him.

"Screw him," Alicia said. "You don't need him. You can get a grant from a real organization, or, barring that, at least from someone less crazy."

"I just hope we don't have to find someone crazier," said Philip.

14

KNOB CREEK

Once again, Alicia placed Arachne in front of the entrance to the causality violation device. "Beginning run 368," she said. "The time is . . . twenty forty and fifteen seconds."

"Sync with the Boulder clock is exact," Carson said wearily, eyes on his laptop screen.

Except for the two security guards at the desk out front, Alicia and Carson were the only people in the lab this Friday evening. Philip was out with his wife—on his way out of the office, he had mentioned, with perhaps the slightest bit of resentment, a "date night"—and Dennis had somehow managed to leave the office at five sharp every evening since he'd started as a post-doc, which was the surest sign of all that he wasn't interested in academia in the long term. He'd quietly confided to Carson that he was already applying for positions in the civil service, one of the last places in American culture where a workweek longer than forty hours was thought to be unconscionable. ("Work to live; don't live to work," he'd say: as much as he seemed to enjoy it, the line that doing science offered so much pleasure that it didn't count as work held little traction with him.)

The robot dutifully began its march toward the open door of the causality violation chamber. One of its legs had a rackety jitter, and it was pulling slightly to the left; soon it'd need to be repaired yet again. In a lab you came to look forward to little repair jobs like that, though: they had clear goals, and clear paths by which those goals could be attained. You were practically guaranteed to get the satisfaction that came from doing something right.

After a gentle nudge in the right direction from Alicia (which Alicia then dutifully noted in her log), Arachne entered the causality violation chamber and the door sealed shut behind it.

Sitting at his desk, Carson's shoulders slumped slightly and his eyelids fluttered.

"Activating the CVD," Alicia said. "Carson, you look like hell. What's going on?"

From the speakers of the little stereo on Alicia's desk, Nas declared that some unspecified nemesis was a slave to a page in his rhyme book.

"Things haven't been going so well for me lately," Carson said. His face looked ashen.

"Sorry to hear that," said Alicia. "Opening the chamber." The door swung open, and Arachne limped out.

Alicia checked the time on the robot's clock. "The time is . . . twenty-one forty-one and five seconds," she said. "Carson, what've you got."

"What did you expect me to have? Twenty-one forty-one and five seconds. Sync with the Boulder clock is still exact."

Carson silently closed his laptop, lifting it and cradling it against his chest, his gaze elsewhere. "You know what?" he said, his voice cracking.

"What?"

"I don't know."

He held it out in front of him, opened his hands, and let the computer fall. Alicia heard a crack as shards of plastic from its case skittered across the floor.

"Okay," she said, unfazed. "First things first. Let's clean that up, and, I don't know, hide it somewhere, so Philip doesn't see it until we have a story. Then I'm going to take you out to a bar and get you drunk, and you're going to tell me what your problem is, and I'm going to solve it."

Carson's slight smile was at odds with his downcast eyes. "You're surprisingly confident about that."

"You should know better than to be surprised. Come on. Hop to it."

■

They went to a bar with good nachos, since they were both really hungry (and at least there was this persistent sign that they were doing exciting science—that even the most mundane chores related to the CVD could make you focus so much that you lost track of time and forgot to eat). Carson sat down in a dim corner at a wooden table with a slight cant, and Alicia went to the bar to get the drinks. While Carson waited he watched the President on the TV mounted over the bar: the volume had been muted, but the captioning that scrolled up the screen suggested that talks had broken down between state officials and the leaders of the occupying rebels in the Dakotas who were attempting to secede from the Union. Alicia came back with two glasses of ice water, along with smaller glasses filled with a dark amber liquid.

"I asked for a beer," Carson said.

"This isn't a beer," Alicia replied, setting the glasses down. "This is a double shot of Knob Creek single-barrel bourbon. I want to loosen your tongue." She pushed the shot glass across the table to him. "Drink down half of that and sip the rest."

She drained half of her own glass by example, and Carson (who may not have wanted to let himself get out-drunk by a woman he out-weighed by sixty pounds) did the same, wincing as the booze drew a thin trail of flame down the back of his throat and pooled in his belly.

"Not a whiskey drinker?" Alicia said.

"Not really," said Carson, suppressing a cough.

"I didn't know," Alicia said. "Otherwise I'd have gotten you something lighter and smoother, better for a novice: Basil Hayden's, or the like. But what's done is done. Now: talk to me."

Carson took a moment to get his thoughts together. Then he said, all at once: "The thing is, as sure as I am that we really are doing interesting science, even though it's hard to find too many physicists who'll agree, I'm starting to wish I'd never gotten mixed up with something so ambitious. Seriously, when I look at where I am career-wise, and where the rest of my cohort is, and I look at all the time I've spent generating null results while they've been publishing papers, I wonder where all the time went. Because a lot of the guys I graduated with hopped onto projects that were already up and running: they were working with experiments that had already been designed, or devices that had already been tested, and pretty much all they did was turn a dial on a machine to a setting it hadn't been turned to before. And that new setting generated a collection of results, and out of the results they got a paper, except before they sent it off they realized they'd be much better off if they split that into *three* papers, which would be three lines on their CV. Meanwhile." He threw his hands up. "Here I am."

"I sympathize. But—and this might be cold comfort—you have to accept that the things you're worried about aren't the purest parts of doing science. Hirsch numbers and impact factors and CV lines: that's all ancillary stuff. And humans worry about things like this because humans aren't perfect, but these concerns are about reputation, not about knowing. The rational part of your mind tells you that 368 sets of null results are still results, and those results tell you more about the world than you knew before you conducted the experiment. The part of your mind that has an ego, that likes to see your name on shiny things, tells you that a null result is the same as a failure. That part of your mind is wrong. The people who really *do* fail in science—the ones who give up—are the people who forget that."

"That's easy for you to say—you're the wonder girl who had a paper in *Science* at twenty-three."

"Wonder *woman*," Alicia said. "And yes."

"Which means you're arguing from the privileged perspective of someone who already has a strong reputation: it's easy for you to dismiss it. Whereas a lot of other young scientists have to deal with the fact that science is done by humans, as you say, and humans aren't as dispassionate as the scientific method is, and so reputation matters to them. You can see how it's easy to talk yourself into thinking that gaming the system is the same as doing good science: that you have to do the first if you want to do the second. And that idealism in science is for chumps."

"I can't speak for everyone, but the work I've done can speak for itself."

"I know, I know. You really are genuinely brilliant—seriously. And I'm not going to say you've been lucky, but I will say that you've been very skilled at making your own luck. And that's fine, and that's fair, and you deserve it. But when I look at your career so far—and I say this to you out of appreciation, not envy—I see someone who's going to land on her feet and do well for herself, no matter what. I shouldn't tell you this—it's on the edge of something I don't want any part of, and it's not my business, but you're the one who bought me this drink—but Philip is already worrying about what will happen when you leave the lab."

"Which I'm going to do sooner rather than later. I've already got feelers out. Things look promising."

"Well, from the way he talks about you, it sounds like he thinks the whole project is going to fall apart when you're gone. And I doubt he talks about me that way, or anyone else in the lab, for that matter."

"If he doesn't, that doesn't have anything to do with your talent, Carson." Alicia looked directly at him when she said this, though Carson got the distinct impression that she'd rather have looked anywhere else.

"I don't mean to turn this into a pity party for me," Carson said. "I'm sure this is the basic self-doubt that any young scientist deals with, at one time or another."

"This is true," Alicia said, though Carson thought that what Alicia was thinking was at sharp odds with what she was saying. He was sure that Alicia had never doubted herself in her life, that she had never thought of herself as young in any way, much less a young scientist. Alicia had probably snapped her own umbilical cord and walked out of the delivery room on her own two feet.

"But that doesn't mean I'm not having that self-doubt. Especially now, when it'll soon be too late for me to choose another path in life. You know—when you look back on your life, you want it to have the shape of a good story, where each year is better than the one before. You don't want your story to be one where you hit a plateau and tread water for the rest of your life, and you tell yourself you're happy because you're getting by. And I'm not sure the life I'm leading now is one that I'll be happy with, years from now."

"Again, I sympathize," Alicia said. "But this is dangerously close to the pity party you feared. I can tell you this: that one of the strategies young scientists use to cope with the constant threat of failure in their field is to tell themselves that leaving the academy would be the biggest failure of all. The part of your mind that tells you that is also wrong. It may well be the case that you could do more for the world, and be a happier person in the bargain, in another life outside academia, rather than inside it. Just as it is highly likely that my skills make me more suitable for a life in academia than anywhere else. But you have to decide that for yourself."

"Are you saying that I might not be cut out for this?"

"You're not hearing what I'm saying. But you will if, and when, it matters."

Alicia took another drink of her whiskey. "I feel we're not getting to the root of the matter here, though. This stuff you're talking about is just an academic's garden-variety malaise: there's nothing special about it. It's not the kind of thing that'd make you think it was a good idea to willfully damage a piece of computer hardware. I am a perceptive person, and I can see that something else is going on that you don't yet want to talk about. So: more alcohol. Drink the rest of that bourbon—drink it all down, right now; there's more where that came from—and then you will tell me what the real problem is."

"I don't know," Carson said uneasily, reaching for his glass. "It's a personal thing, and you and I don't really talk about . . . you know, personal stuff much. Things seem to go better at work if we stick to talking about work."

"Carson, I'm very good with people."

"You are?"

"Certainly! And I'm certain you'll find it useful to tell me what's wrong." Alicia pointed at the glass in Carson's hand. "Drink. Talk."

■

"So Kate and I broke things off," Carson said after Alicia placed the second glass of Knob Creek in front of him. Carson looked up and across the bar at the bartender, who subtly smiled and winked—*Good luck, tiger.*

"Oh, I didn't realize we were having celebratory, kicking-out-the-jams drinks instead of consolation, crying-in-your-glass drinks," Alicia said. "Sixteen-year Scotch of some kind is what I *should* be buying you. Congratulations."

"I liked her."

"I didn't."

"You've only met her . . . twice!"

"That was enough. She was so *ordinary.*"

"Alicia. I liked her. And . . . you know, usually when something like this happens, you get a warning, right? She floats a trial balloon or something, even if you don't realize it was a trial balloon until it's too late: she says that maybe you ought to be doing something differently, or mentions things she wants that it's apparent you don't have. But here's what happened: she called me last Sunday afternoon and asked if she could come over, right then. And I was just cleaning the apartment and I said, sure, whatever. So she came over, and I let her in, and she just stood there in the middle of the living room floor, not saying anything. Didn't even take off her jacket. I was sitting on the couch and I said, 'Do you want to sit down?' And she said, 'I'm okay here.' I thought, *Well, okay, then.*

"So we just made small talk for a little bit, which is weird because one, we had kind of gotten past that small-talk phase of things, and two, she's still standing in the middle of the floor in her jacket, and then she blurts out all at once, 'I have something I need to say to you. I don't—we can't see each other anymore. I like you and you're a great guy, but . . . yeah. I don't have a good reason for this. I'm sorry. So yeah. That's it.'

"And I just look at her, and she doesn't say anything.

"And I say, 'Kate, what the fuck?' and she just stands there.

"And I say, 'Do you at least want to talk about this first? Because this is a hell of a way to end things.' And she says, 'I don't really want to talk about it, I don't think.' And she just stands there in her jacket and doesn't say anything else.

"And I say, 'We have mutual friends. Your best friend is my boss's wife! We can't just unfollow each other on social networks and pretend we never met.' And she just stands there, and she does this thing that's kind of like a shrug but not even, just kind of moving her shoulders around.

"And I say, 'Well, do you want to go then? It looks like you want to go. It looks like you've said all you want to. I'd ask you to take off your jacket, but I don't see the point.' I shouldn't have made the crack about the jacket. And she says, 'Yeah, okay then; see you around.' And she lets herself out without another word. And that was that.

"It was awful, Alicia."

"Well, in her defense, and I can't believe I'm actually defending her, she wasn't *completely* cowardly. She could have just sent you an e-mail or a text message or something."

"This isn't about whether she had the guts to do it, though. If someone makes up their mind that they want to call things off, there's nothing you can really do about that. But it didn't make a lot of sense, you know? It was just so sudden and weird, the way she acted. And I like things to make sense. I like it when the facts fit a standard model. So I start thinking about it, and thinking about it—and I'm using the part of my brain for this that's been trained to see patterns in data, the part of my brain that I ought to be using to do science. And I start to see some patterns in all this noise. And I don't like them."

"What do you mean: patterns? Hold it. We need nachos. It's important to keep the proportion of booze to fatty foods in your digestive system carefully balanced at a time like this. I'll go up to the bar. Stay here."

■

Maybe Alicia actually was as understanding and empathetic as she claimed she was. She waited at the bar for the plate to come out from the kitchen, leaving Carson to himself for a little while. A guy next to her started to lean into her personal space, saying something that Carson couldn't hear, probably a backhanded compliment meant to sting the mark into acquiescing to a later request for her digits. Alicia turned to him and spat out five quick syllables in response (though Carson couldn't tell what they were, either). The guy stood, lifted his coat off his chair, and quietly removed to an empty seat at the other end of the bar, leaving his half-full glass of Guinness behind.

A few minutes later Alicia came back to the table, managing to juggle two glasses of water and another shot of bourbon for Carson, along with a heaping plate of tortilla chips covered with mounds of ground beef and diced onions and black olives and shredded lettuce and sour cream and salsa, the whole concoction slathered with gobs of melted cheese. Carson lifted one of the chips and placed it in his mouth, wiping a searing rope of cheddar off his lip. "Good," he said.

He ate a few more nachos while Alicia watched. Then he sighed and said, "So then."

"So then," said Alicia, pointing at the whiskey once again.

"Hey, I'm a little bit drunk," he said.

"Correct. So then."

"So I had some people over for dinner the other night. Philip and his wife, Rebecca, and Kate was there. This was Kate's idea, for me to have Philip and Rebecca over for dinner. She and Rebecca have been friends for . . . years, I guess."

"Mmm-hmm."

"And she—Kate—got really drunk. She wasn't really watching her drinking: her glass was always two-thirds full, and she kept topping it off. And actually, the next morning she told me she didn't remember a whole lot of what happened the night before. And to be honest, I didn't believe her at first. She was kind of out of it toward the end of the night, and she threw up in my bathroom later on, but she didn't seem *blackout* drunk, you know. But then I remembered the couple of times I blacked out from drinking in college, and my friends told me the next day they didn't notice a thing. Though maybe I did something embarrassing and they were just sparing my feelings. Anyway, it's hard to say."

"Continue," Alicia said.

"So I served this barbecue I make. And for this whole meal I went modernist—nothing too traditional. Showing off a little, maybe. So the courses might have seemed unusual to someone who wasn't used to this sort of thing, and the servings were satisfying though not overly generous."

"I want you to make dinner for me," Alicia said. "But continue."

"So when I brought out the barbecue from the kitchen, Kate— she had already had a couple of glasses of wine and a cocktail by then—well, I guess you could say she made fun of it. Lighthearted. But—except—well, I guess the subtext was that this wasn't how *real* black people made barbecue. And she talked about it in this voice that was—well, it was like an imitation of the way you'd think black people talked if you'd never met a black person in real life, just seen them in movies."

"But she said later that she didn't remember any of this."

"Right. And whether people are responsible when they're sober for things they say and do when they're drunk is a different issue. Let's table that."

"Okay: tabled. Continue."

"So when I brought out dessert—and, okay, she was definitely three sheets to the wind by then—she makes this I guess joke about how watermelon would have gone better than what I served."

"Carson, I'll go ahead and say it. In the back of your head—the part of your head that's always looking for patterns in data—you're thinking that a few too many drinks brought out the fact that deep down Kate, this woman you were into, is a little bit racist."

"I guess," Carson said.

■

"But I'm not even sure that's the right word," Carson said after he and Alicia silently finished the plate of nachos. He was not unaware of the favor she was doing for him, keeping him company in this way. She didn't normally eat this kind of food at this time of night, or at all, really, since she claimed it wrecked her times when she went running the next morning. He couldn't help but think that Alicia was acting as his shrink not out of empathy for its own sake, but so he'd get his head straight and get back to work. But still: maybe she *was* good with people, when she wanted to be.

"Why don't you think 'racist' is the right word?" Alicia said. "Because I think it is."

"Because it's not like she was saying that the new science of phrenology had conclusively demonstrated the smaller brain of the Asiatic peoples, or something like that. But . . . and I see what you're saying. Racism usually doesn't do you the favor of making itself plain: you usually aren't *sure* if it's racism or not. Most of the time it's there and gone before you can point at it. And maybe you're just being paranoid, or overly sensitive. Like: maybe you misheard when the date your friend brought to the cocktail party casually mentioned that she envied Jews because they were so good with money. No one else at the party seemed to have noticed anything, right? Surely someone would have called her out if she'd said something so patently offensive in public, right? You must have misheard what she said. Or maybe you misheard the tone: maybe she was making the kind of joke where you say something really offensive in a public place, and it's funny because no one—no one we know—would actually believe such a thing."

"You know what kind of people really like to make jokes like that? Racists."

"I know! But it's not as easy as that. Is it? It's not as easy to distinguish the out-and-out racist from the one who is and thinks she isn't, or the one who actually isn't but sometimes sounds like she is, if you misinterpret her. I mean . . . I don't know. It's really confusing." Carson laughed nervously. "I mean, when she said that watermelon is a good finisher for a meal that has barbecue for a main course, it's not like she's *wrong*."

"I've heard enough," Alicia said. "Now I will render advice. Are you prepared?"

"I am prepared!" said Carson, slapping his open hand on the table.

"Then here it is. Carson: history lives in the gap between the information and the truth. And each of us has no choice but to determine our own history, for ourselves. We don't have perfect information here, because that's not possible—we would have to know what was going on in Kate's head, and whether you yourself are a reliable narrator. So the history is under-determined. There are several possible interpretations.

"Let's consider the set of possible histories in which you behaved honorably, but she nonetheless acted as she did. All but one of these are uninteresting, as far as we're concerned. She is flighty; she is afraid of commitment; she is not in love with you; there is another, more suitable man, or she believes there soon will be; she wishes to die alone. All of these and many others are possible. What she says is not necessarily what she believes; what she believes is not necessarily what is true. But you can't do anything about this. Your best course is to leave the matter alone. Don't speculate on her motives and don't pursue it further. Let it go.

"This leaves the interesting version of events, and when I say 'interesting,' I mean this in an unfortunate way. This is the version where . . . okay, let's not use the word 'racist,' though I do feel it's the right one. Let's say this: she grew up in a certain culture; she developed certain opinions. Even though we live in the twenty-first century, most of us are still children of the twentieth in one way or another, as much as we like to flatter ourselves by thinking otherwise.

"Now, Kate likes to think of herself as a modern woman. But her twenty-first-century mind was trumped by her twentieth-century heart. The dissonance between the two . . . well, it caused problems. One night she said a few things that might have been interpreted as . . . untoward. The motives don't really matter. The next day she felt ashamed and tried to lie her way out of it. Or she truly didn't remember. Same difference, really. The point is: something made it apparent to her that this whole grand adventure wasn't going to work out. Do we agree that this is the . . . interesting scenario? Can we say that this is a scenario that you would rather not believe is the case, but that you suspect is highly likely?"

"That's about right," Carson said, his voice not much more than a whisper.

"So here is the question. Given that the information you have is necessarily imperfect. Given that the history of events is necessarily under-determined. The history that you choose to believe will determine the person that you are. If only in a small way. You will be a person who chose to see the world one way instead of another. And that choice will color the way you see the world, and your future, and your image in a mirror. You will never be able to determine conclusively why she acted as she did. But you can determine what kind of person you want to be.

"I can tell you this. That in the absence of perfect information, I choose to believe in the version of events that would occur in the best of all possible worlds. What that version of events is: that's your decision. That's up to you. I can't decide that for you; I wouldn't try.

"That's all I have to say."

■

"That was a long way around to tell me I'd be happier if I gave her the benefit of the doubt and dropped it," Carson said, after a few moments of silence.

"That's not what I said," Alicia replied.

"And this 'best of all possible worlds' thing. I don't know. I'm all for optimism, but it seems like in some circumstances, thinking like that would be a little naive."

"I've given you my advice," Alicia said. "It might not work for you; you can take or leave it. It looks like they want us to clear out of here. Let me pick up the check."

Carson reached for his wallet and Alicia said firmly, "No." He obediently placed his hand back on the table.

■

It was half past one when they left the bar, and they took a short walk through downtown to let the alcohol clear from their heads. The air was crisp and called for jackets, and the moon hung low in the sky, pale and bright and full. The streets were nearly deserted, though on the sidewalk across from Carson and Alicia, a bar patron who'd been pulled over was trying to plead his way out of a DUI by pointing at the license plate of his autonomous car. "Sir," he said. "Sir. I was not *touching* the wheel of this vehicle. I was not *going* to touch the wheel. This is like—this is like if you pulled over a taxi and handed a DUI to the *passenger*! C'mon: you can't fucking *do* that! It's ridiculous! I didn't mean to say 'fuck,' officer."

"I feel a lot better about the whole thing now," Carson said as they left the groveling driver behind them. "I'm not sure why. But I do."

"It was the whiskey," Alicia said. "And the nachos."

"You're underselling yourself."

"I never do that."

"Seriously—I appreciate you talking to me. Or forcing me to talk to you, I guess I should say."

"Thank you."

Behind them, they heard plaintive protests and the clink of handcuffs. "You gotta be *kidding* me with this shit!" the driver screamed. "Fucking *kidding*!"

"You are one cool lady, Alicia Merrill," Carson said.

"This is true. Did you decide to take my advice?"

"In a sense. You could say that."

"What did you finally decide? About Kate."

"I . . . I think I'd rather keep that to myself."

"That's fair. But whatever you decide: let it go. Or the knowing and the not knowing will eat you up."

"I know. I will."

■

"We didn't talk about you at all this evening," Carson said as they reached their cars. "I did all the talking."

"That's fine. I'm fine with that."

"How are you and Philip doing?" he asked, and immediately felt that he'd made a severe mistake.

For once, Alicia would not meet his gaze. "We're okay."

15

TRUE ENOUGH

There is nothing wrong with a glass of white wine with breakfast: it is one of the world's rare and secret pleasures. Peppery scrambled eggs are nice with a good dry Riesling; Frosted Flakes pair well with Chardonnay. Besides, Rebecca was finding out more often lately that waiting out the clock until noon, the earliest socially permissible time to pour yourself a libation, was . . . well, it was unpleasant. When she woke up in the morning her brain felt half a size too large for her skull, and her head was full of whispers. But with that first sip of wine at twelve sharp she felt great: her mind got quiet and her mood evened out. There was no reason to wait until the sun reached an arbitrary point in the sky to feel normal.

So there was no reason why she would expect Philip to make some sort of remark when she served him black coffee with his eggs and toast, and poured two percent milk for Sean with his half-size serving of same, and then placed the milk carton back in the fridge, retrieved the bottle of Chardonnay, poured herself a healthy glass, and put the bottle back. Philip and Rebecca didn't talk much at breakfast anyway—she wasn't much for morning conversation, because of the headache she usually had on waking (which wasn't a hangover or anything like it, but just the kind of thing that happens to you when you get older), and Philip usually had a tablet in front of him displaying a PDF of an article in some science journal, highlighting significant passages with a fingertip. He glanced up at her, looked at the glass of wine, and looked at her again (and this is when the voice in the back of her head was actually *screaming* at him to, fuck, say *something*, not even in anger—just a slight harrumph of disapproval might have been enough to get her to pour the glass down the drain, to tough out the headache, to turn down the hair of the dog that bit her). Then he went back to his tablet, unnoticing, or having decided that noticing, and the consequent unpredictable conversation, would take too much work at a time when he needed his brain for other, grander purposes.

She drank the glass with breakfast and poured herself another. By the time she'd gotten Sean off to school (second grade) the edges had been taken off her thoughts and the world seemed as it should be: not too real, but real enough.

■

If the marriage into which the two of them had settled was not the most communicative, they both had the projects of their lives to occupy them: Rebecca had their son, and Philip had the causality violation device.

After a couple of years of wandering in the wilderness, spending more time applying for grants to keep himself afloat than he did on research, Philip suspected that he might have finally found a reliable source of funding for his work. They'd reached out to him first—a division of the Department of Defense that had been spun off from DARPA a few years ago and that, even if it wasn't exactly a *secret*, preferred to cultivate a strong aura of secrecy about itself, now that the parent organization once nicknamed "darkest DARPA" had become common knowledge and therefore mundane. In its place, DAPAS began to play the role of the government's all-seeing apparatus that could not itself be seen, as DARPA and the now even less mysterious NSA had before it. (When the DAPAS representative had called Philip on his personal phone—nice touch there—and Philip had asked who he had the pleasure of speaking with, the gravelly voice on the other end had said, after a suitably dramatic pause, "You may refer to me as Mr. Cheever." It turned out that this was because his name actually *was* Mr. Cheever, Mr. Michael Cheever. Born and raised in Baltimore, a die-hard Orioles fan.) Mr. Cheever had, he said, "become aware" of Philip's research (most likely through reading some or all of the published papers he'd authored) and had also found out about his funding difficulties (which wouldn't have been much harder—the community of physicists whose work was related to causality violation was small and tightly knit, and a conversation over a couple of beers with any one of its members would get you the dope on them all). Mr. Cheever gave it to be understood that his superiors (the sort of people who sat behind clean desks in dimly lit rooms, their faces veiled in shadow) felt that the project showed "significant potential," and that they wondered, with a curiosity that possessed the force of command, if Philip would be willing to come down to DC on their dime to make an informal presentation on his work—something with lots of slides that would last about an hour.

Now, by this point in his career, Philip had developed a number of different dog-and-pony shows about his research, with different degrees of granularity in the detail depending on his audience—specialists in the structure of spacetime, or particle physicists, or astrophysicists, or physicists in general, or scientists in general, or nonscientists. But one thing that all those talks had in common was a scrupulousness about their claims. This was especially the case in the presence of nonscientists, who were as likely to misunderstand what he claimed as they were to be deaf to words like "might" and "maybe" and "possibly." When that happened (see, for instance, the tale of Edmund Taligent), things were inclined to go sour: the audience was likely to leave his talk thinking they lived in a science-fictional world that did not yet exist. So the more specialized his audience, the more comfortable he was with slightly stronger statements and slightly more fanciful speculations.

But Philip had no idea what he was getting into here. On the one hand, his conversation with Mr. Cheever indicated that he or his shadowy superiors had knowledge of causality violation that significantly outstripped a layman's; on the other hand, he felt certain that literally everyone in the world who had an understanding of the state of the field that was close to his own was someone he knew personally, and so there had to be at least a little bluffing behind Mr. Cheever's pose of silent omniscience. The only thing for it would be to load up all the slides he had to a thumb drive, try to size up the audience before he began, and decide what to say to them on the fly.

He took the Amtrak Silver Star down to Washington, feeling that this was his last chance. The rejections of his grant proposals were becoming increasingly desultory—he was more likely to get flat, form-letter *no*s instead of being strung along for a little while. He feared that his name was becoming known in a bad way, unfairly associated with the taint of past and future failure. Sure, he had several published papers and more stuff up on arXiv, but the journals in which his work had appeared were neither the sexiest nor the most storied. Worse, he was rarely cited these days, as if the appearance of "P. Steiner" in a bibliography or a footnote was not a mark of a paper's credibility and rigor, but a symptom of infection, a sign that the best response to the article was a quiet intellectual quarantine. If other physicists had been willing to rebut him in public and in print, at least he would have felt like he was still in the game, but in his darker moments these days he believed himself to be the victim of an implicit conspiracy of silence. He'd seen it happen to others: without really talking about it openly, it suddenly became clear to everyone that to speak a certain scientist's name without the necessary ritual expectoration would levy a curse upon your own career. The next you heard of the guy, you found out through the rumor mill that he'd taken a job as a hedge fund analyst. The unemployment rate of physics PhDs was always going to be zero, but Philip felt that a burgeoning bank account would be an inadequate consolation for his failure to convince others of the truths of ideas that were doomed to remain locked in his mind alone.

The meeting took place in a featureless room in an equally featureless building across the river in Arlington. There were nine men seated at a round table about ten feet in diameter: they wore white long-sleeved shirts and dark ties, and most of them sported closely trimmed hairstyles and clunky plastic spectacles. They had the builds of people who felt that physical fitness was a moral and patriotic obligation. The table at which they sat was a neat piece of tech: its entire surface was a screen, and as Philip plugged his USB stick into the laptop they supplied (*I must remember to dispose of that stick as soon as this presentation is over*, he thought) and projected the first of his slides on a wall, the slide duplicated itself in miniature in front of each of the audience members. Several of them produced styluses from shirt pockets and began to make notations, scribbling directly on the table.

Mr. Cheever was seated on Philip's right. "I won't introduce you," he said. "We already know all about you—ha, ha! Just—we're really excited about this. Just begin."

Philip looked across the table at the man seated there, who seemed thirty years older than everyone else, if well preserved—he had a thick white mustache that seemed to be the result of decades of careful grooming, and the frames of his eyeglasses were metal instead of plastic.

As Philip stared directly into the other man's eyes, the older man extended his hands over the table with their palms down and waved them back and forth, the gesture snappy and precise. Eight pieces of paper with messages that Philip couldn't read materialized on the tabletop display; as Philip watched, they folded themselves into a phalanx of origami pigeons, which flapped their wings as they flew across the table to the other people seated there—that is, all the other people besides Philip.

Huh.

Once the paper pigeons reached their destinations, they unfolded themselves, and the audience members read the message from the person who Philip now assumed was their boss. A couple of them chuckled, and Mr. Cheever nodded with approval. "Yes indeed," he said, as if to himself. "Definitely a thing to keep in mind."

They looked like students who couldn't have cared less if the substitute teacher spied them passing notes, and what was worse, they *wanted* Philip to know they didn't care. But this was clearly all theater.

And Philip died a little inside when he thought this, but he realized that if these people were going to open their wallets, then he would have to deliver a little theater in return. Not too much: just a touch. An extra sentence or two would do.

He went through the lecture as intended, opting to take the middle of the road: not so detailed as to bore and confuse, but not so generalized and simplistic as to come off as patronizing. He spent a good deal of time describing the difficulties of performing an experiment of this kind in an environment such as earth's, one that was moving through space at a very high speed—audiences always seemed to find that sort of thing interesting.

He found the conference table an extremely annoying distraction. He could see the others making notes with their styluses on slides that he had carefully designed to have just enough information, no

more, no less. And the table's large display made it more than apparent that there was a second, silent conversation going on while he was
talking. Every once in a while someone would bring up a display of
one of his earlier slides with scribbles all over it and send it gliding
over to another listener with a flick of his finger, as if it were an air
hockey puck. The person receiving it would trap it with his palm,
read the notation, and make further notes. If there was something
they wanted to say, they should have been able to say it to him, he
thought.

Philip saved his theater until the middle of the presentation. After
explaining how the Planck-Wheeler clock worked, and how it would
correct for the movement of the earth through spacetime when
stitching the two ends of the wormhole together, he said, as casually
as he could manage it, "Now would be a good time for me to limit my
claims and tamp down any expectations you might have. It's highly
unlikely that what we're doing will have any sort of technological
application. The end result is going to be the accumulation of knowledge for its own sake."

He could feel his face wanting to twist into a wince.

"It's not like you're going to be able to use this thing to go back in
time and kill Hitler, or anything like that," he said.

That was enough. The assemblage of listeners remained completely poker-faced—maybe one of the eyebrows of the bossman
in the back of the room lifted just a little—but first a message flew
across the table on paper wings, then another, and by the time Philip
had wound up his presentation (and made his other big gamble: leaving no time for questions) the table's display was a blizzard of origami
birds. "That was an *excellent* presentation, Mr. Steiner," Mr. Cheever
said, with the relief of a man whose ass had been on the line. "You'll
be hearing from us with an answer soon. Very soon."

Mr. Cheever escorted Philip out of the conference room (and
Philip could see that the people they were leaving behind couldn't
wait to burst into conversation). The bossman sent Philip on his way
with a barely perceptible nod: Philip guessed that he'd be nearly silent
during the dialogue that followed once the conference room's door
was closed, preserving his status as the taciturn authority figure, but
he'd be the one who went to sleep tonight and dreamed of choking
Hitler to death with his right hand and Stalin with his left.

"I'm not going to lie to you," Mr. Cheever said when he met Philip for breakfast the next morning in the tiny, overpriced café attached to the lobby of Philip's Washington hotel. "A lot of people in that room figured you'd be really smart. But those same people thought you had a good chance of also being bonkers, that maybe you were going on some kind of wild goose chase. Those two states aren't mutually exclusive, you know. And we agree with you that even if you are able to open a wormhole like you say, it isn't likely to have any practical application—certainly nothing defense related. Sure, we made a couple of jokes, but nobody seriously talked about it."

Philip found it interesting that that was something Mr. Cheever felt the need to clarify, but said nothing.

"But it doesn't really matter to us if you actually make your wormhole, or whatever," Mr. Cheever continued. "We feel like your laboratory is one with a lot of intelligence, a lot of enthusiasm, a lot of energy. And some of the most useful inventions in history have been those that came about entirely by accident, when smart, enthusiastic researchers were focused on another task entirely. Plastic wrap. Microwave ovens. Viagra. We feel like even if you don't accomplish the goal you're shooting for, *something's* going to come out of that lab, something really good. Maybe something that will change the world. So we're going to fund you—you're going to get the grant. Probably not as much as you might like—it never is, is it? But enough. And the funding will be steady, and it'll last for a while."

Mr. Cheever offered his hand. "Congratulations."

■

"One more thing," Mr. Cheever said as he finished his coffee. "If anything, you know, unusual, happens with this project—and I mean not garden-variety weird, but *really* bizarre, the kind of stuff we'd be interested in—I want you to call this number." He wrote a telephone number on the back of a napkin and pushed it toward Philip. "Copy that somewhere safe: somewhere analog, not digital. Multiple backups in multiple places: got me?"

Philip nodded.

"It'll only work once: after that we'll have to get you another one, and that'll depend on whether you're judged by my superiors to have wasted the first one. And burning one of those numbers is . . . non-trivial: that phone call entails no small expense. But dial it if something weird happens, and I mean only if it's *really* weird. I won't pick up, but the message will get to me fast.

"I'm guessing you won't need it. But you never know. It's best to be prepared."

■

All things considered, Philip would have preferred a little more faith from his newfound patrons—one couldn't help but find it slightly disheartening to be supported not because your goals were attainable but because your blunders were bound to be interesting. But their money was as green as anyone else's, and far less subject to a private benefactor's caprice. As he said to Rebecca over dinner once he got back from Washington, he expected to be able to purchase the equipment to do the initial modeling, and hire a couple of post-docs, and support the three of them on a salary—himself, Rebecca, and Sean—if they tightened their belts a bit.

Something about the way he said that last thing made it clear to Rebecca that their good fortune, which they would share, entailed certain duties that would be hers alone, at least for the most part. Back then Philip still kept roughly normal hours: out of the house by nine, home by nine at the latest. Later, once he got deep into the project, it would be as if the causality violation device possessed the body clock and blind need of a newborn child, demanding undivided attention at the most inconvenient times: Rebecca would get used to Philip getting home or, worse, leaving the house, at four a.m., even as Sean's sleep patterns settled down.

But that duty, Rebecca repeated to herself, was not unpleasurable. Day by day, she watched her strange boy become more human, as he learned to speak in sentences and figured out how the world worked, enchanted by things as simple as heat and gravity (though Philip, when Rebecca told him this, would pedantically remind her that while these phenomena might be *elemental*, they were not so simple at all). Sean was happy to spend ten minutes watching an ice cube melt, whispering secret incantations to it as if he were seeing a spirit on to the other side; he was happy to stand on a chair with a square of toilet paper in his hand, repeatedly letting it fall to the floor and tracking it with his gaze as it turned end over end. He was endlessly fascinated by the tessellations of bathroom tiles, and the warp and woof of carpet, and the light that danced behind his lids when he turned with closed eyes to face the sun.

At seven Sean was insatiably curious, and he swallowed facts like chocolate. He badgered his parents with questions until Rebecca began to rue the day he'd learned of *how* and *why;* when he found out new things in school, he would repeat them at home with a studied gravity, the idea apparently not occurring to him that his mother and father probably already knew this stuff, since they had been on the planet for decades longer than he had. Once he approached Philip at his desk and said, "Dad. If you want to tell if a number is dividable by threes—"

Philip closed the lid of his laptop. "Divisible."

"Divisible. Here's what you do. No matter how many digits it has, you add up all the digits, and then you divide *that* number by three. And if there's no remainder, then the original number is divisible by three. You don't have to waste your time dividing this super-long number." Sean looked at his father with lidded eyes, as if he was thinking with sadness about other children who did not know what he knew, toiling away at their desks with needless long division.

"That's a cool trick," Philip said, beginning to open his laptop again. "It'll save you a lot of effort. Now I have to—"

"If the last digit of a number is *zero,* or *five,*" Sean continued solemnly, "then the number is divisible by five. That's all you need to know."

Sean was just as curious about colors and shapes and words and motions as he was about numbers, and because of this, Rebecca felt that he had the makings of an artist of some kind. She presented him with a constant supply of crayons and pencils and construction paper, and the things he drew were surprisingly complex for a boy of his age, even in their abstraction and their defiance of basic rules for portraying objects in three-dimensional space. One Father's Day morning Sean entered his parents' bedroom and presented Philip with a portrait that he'd spent a couple of days on, drawing and redrawing, making sketches and throwing them away. Philip took the sheet of paper from him and squinted at it. "This . . . this is very nice, Sean," he said. "Thank you."

"Drawing you was really hard," Sean said. "It was hard to fit every-thing in there that I wanted."

Still looking at the picture, Philip tilted his head and frowned. "What is this . . . on my head?"

"That's a football helmet," Sean said with what Rebecca heard as just the slightest bit of pique, as if the fault here was not in Sean's rendering of the image but in his father's failure to perceive it cor-rectly. "It's also a cowboy hat. And it *can be* an astronaut's helmet, sometimes."

"Huh. And . . . it looks like you spent a lot of time getting my hands just right."

"I did! Your left hand is a pair of handcuffs: that's in case you need to take someone to jail. And your right hand is a knife, for when your enemies don't want to go to jail and they get out of control. When you see your enemies you give them a choice: the handcuffs, or the knife."

Beneath the sheets, Rebecca squeezed Philip's hand. This was a good morning: she was not yet thinking about drinking. The other day she had done a little reading online about alcoholism—she was just curious—and found that its cause wasn't necessarily some kind of existential despair that needed booze for relief, but that it could also be genetic or chemical, the result of a smaller amygdala than the average person, or a skewed balance of neurotransmitters. It seemed unfair that you could have just about everything in life that you wanted and still have a chance of ending up an alcoholic. It seemed unfair that problems of the mind and spirit could arise from weak-nesses of the body. And yet moments like this—seeing her son's naive attempts at self-expression, free of the fear of criticism or embarrass-ment; watching his father, her husband, tentatively working out the best way to demonstrate his love—did provide some kind of relief. It was good to be unexpectedly reminded that merely being human had its pleasures and its beauties, and that they were best seen with clearest eyes.

"One more thing," Philip said. "What's this circle you've drawn above my head? I'm already an astronaut, and a football player, and a cowboy, and a police officer: am I an angel, too?"

"No, that's the circle on the back of your head where you don't have any hair," Sean said. "I was drawing the front of you and didn't have a place to put it, but it's important, so I just drew it up there."

"That is a lovely portrait, Sean," Rebecca said. "It is surprisingly true to life."

Please don't ever draw a picture of me, she thought.

■

Questions, questions, questions, and the boy couldn't just deal in the kinds of inquisitions that could be dispensed with by straight answers: he had to go into counterfactuals and hypotheticals. One evening when the three of them were having dinner together—Thai takeout that Philip had picked up on the way home—Sean put down his fork and knife and announced, "I have a question." Lately he did this almost every time he saw his parents together, as if he meant to set the two of them in competition, and was quietly weighing which of them was capable of providing him with superior truths.

"What's your question?" Rebecca said.

"Why isn't the sky green?"

"Well, I—"

"Because okay look. Plants are green. The energy that makes plants grow comes from the sun. And that energy has to go *through the sky* to get to the plants. So if plants are green, why isn't the sky green, too?"

"I've got this one," Philip said, making a show of cracking his knuckles. At these times, rarer than Rebecca would have liked, a light came back into her husband's eyes that reminded her of when they'd first started dating: once again he was the magpie, flitting among a hundred different subjects, reveling in the pleasure of knowing solely for the sake of knowing.

"So this question is actually a two-parter," Philip began. "Actually, you could break it down into a huge number of smaller parts, but let's call it two. First: why are most plants green? That's because of the pigment chlorophyll, which absorbs the energy from sunlight. Specifically, chlorophyll absorbs light from the blue and red bands of the visible spectrum and converts that light to energy, but it reflects the green light to your eyes. Which raises the question: Why didn't plants evolve to be black instead of green? Wouldn't they grow more quickly if they chose to absorb green light instead of reflecting it? Not to anthropomorphize plants by suggesting that they choose their energy sources, like a diner at an all-you-can-eat buffet. But it's an interesting question. Digressive, though."

"Uh . . . huh," said Sean. He was stroking his chin with his thumb and forefinger, a gesture that Rebecca suspected he had picked up from television: she had noticed that he did it when he was the only child in the company of adults, and wanted to give the impression that he was following the conversation.

"Now, second half," Philip continued. "Why is the sky blue, and not green. And you'll notice that though it's not always blue—it shifts toward red as the sun descends to the horizon—it's never green! This is because of Rayleigh scattering, which is—"

"The sky isn't green because it would look ugly," Rebecca said.

Sean gave his mother a suspicious side-eye: this appeared to be another gesture he'd picked up from TV, or videos on the Internet.

"Think about it," said Rebecca. "You go out to a field on a bright spring day. There's green grass beneath you and a blue sky above you. Maybe throw a cloud or two in there. It's beautiful, right? But imagine what the world would look like if the sky were the color of pea soup. People would never want to go outside because their eyes would get bored. But a blue sky is really nice to look at."

Sean continued to stroke his chin, looking upward. "That is a very good answer," he said at last, and Rebecca beamed.

■

Later that evening, when Philip slipped into bed next to Rebecca and spoke the command to shut off the lamp on the nightstand, he said, "I want to talk about Sean's question."

"Oh, *do* you?" Rebecca turned over to face him. "Still feeling the sting of defeat, are you? It's okay—"

"But all you did was feed him a just-so story! If he's going to grow up to be a scientist, it's best for him to get into the habit of rational thinking as early as possible—"

"Okay. Okay. First of all, your answer, whenever you got around to finishing it, would have been great for someone who *already knew* why the sky was blue, because then they could just agree with how thorough your response was. But Sean is seven. What does a seven-year-old know about Rayleigh scattering, whatever that is?"

"I was going to explain that in terms a child could understand—"

Rebecca placed an extended index finger on Philip's lips. "Shh. Second. I don't know where you got the idea that Sean is going to turn out to be a scientist, because it's clear to anyone with two eyes that our son has the blood of an artist in his veins: he's going to become a great painter, or a filmmaker, or something. Remember that picture he drew of you for Father's Day? You can already see him working on the techniques that will later come to define his middle-period style. And my answer to his question, the *best* answer, was intended to gently ease him into the basics of color theory, which he'll find *quite useful* in the decades to come."

"Dear," Philip said, "at the end of the day, your answer just wasn't true. Wait—that's not right. It wasn't . . . I don't know what it was."

"Honey," Rebecca said, slipping her arms around him, "it was true enough."

16

SPIVEY'S LAMENT

Terence.

Hey Terence!

We haven't even been here ten minutes and you've already got your head buried in that book. I suppose you expect me to sit here at this desk for however many hours, staring at the ceiling and not saying anything until I go crazy or something. Put that book down and help me bullshit!

I got something for you: I got something I want to throw at you. You might not believe this, but I have figured out how time travel works.

Oh, *now* you're putting the book down. Now I've got your attention.

You're thinking: how could a security guard who hasn't seen the inside of a school in who knows how long sit here and solve a question that has continued to stump the minds of the double-degreed geniuses walking in and out of here every day? But I've been thinking, *way* outside the box. I don't even know where the box is: if you want to find it, ask some people who don't know how time travel works, and maybe they can tell you.

Listen.

■

I got the idea when I went down to visit my sister Rita. The doctors finally took her leg off, by the way—I go over there to keep her spirits up. She was sitting on the couch, watching this time travel movie. It was about the time of the civil rights movement: you know, there are these black maids scrubbing floors and cleaning toilets and white women not even noticing they exist, except when they want something from them. You know: Rochester smiles in the mirror as he puts on his tuxedo 'cause he's proud to be a butler for that rich family with a house at the top of the hill, but then a car comes by and splashes mud on him in the street. The kind of movie you watch so you can get good and pissed off and talk to the screen, you know? And that's just what Rita was doing. "Oh, if that white woman talked to *me* like that it'd be her first and *last* time. I'd snatch that apron off and slap her like she'd lost God's love. I'd say: *You come over here and sit still a second so I can slap the taste out of your mouth.*" She was good and mad! See why it's a time travel movie? The time machine isn't *in* the movie, on the screen: it's in your *head*. You watch a movie like that and you get to imagine yourself going back in time so you can trash-talk a bunch of dumbasses. You look at what happened between the time of that movie and now; you think about all those people who put their asses on the line ramming equal rights down America's throat, day after day, 'til it had no choice but to swallow or choke. All so Rita can sit in her air-conditioned house, *in the future*, safe as could be, telling off a bunch of ghosts, acting out some stuff that happened before she was even born. It was the history between then and now that made it easy for her to sit on her couch and say that. For the maid, back then: not so easy. Do you hear me?

■

So this is the thing about time travel that means that anyone with even the slightest bit of common sense would stay away from it. Because if you went back in time, the history that made you what you are would not have happened yet. And you would *revert*. You would become someone else.

You like science fiction, Terence: it's time for some science fiction. Let's imagine there's a scientist, an anthropologist or what have you, and he's got a time machine. And he wants to go back to the dawn of man to look around. He gets in the time machine, pulls a bunch of levers, and gets out again at about three million years BC. Then he turns around and, shit. Where'd the time machine go? It was here just a minute ago! Thing is, the history that made a time machine possible hasn't *happened* yet, so how can there be a time machine there? This guy turns around and where he expected to see a time machine, there's just a pile of metal. He's in trouble now.

By the way, you would think that if, in the future, people ever made time machines, we would know about it, because they would have come back in time to visit us, right? This is why we've never seen them: because going back in time is a one-way trip. You get out of the time machine, and then it turns into a pile of rocks, or a covered wagon, or a washer-dryer combo, and that's your ass. And no one is going to believe you if you point at, like, a *stove*, and say it used to be a time machine up until about a minute ago.

So this guy, this scientist, he's stuck in three million BC and he figures he may as well make the best of it. He doesn't have any paper—he had a notebook in his pocket, but it turned into a hunk of wood—but maybe he can find a way to chisel some messages into some stones so his buddies can pick them up in the future, three-million-odd years later. He goes around watching these apes do what they do, and after a couple of days he notices he's got a little more hair on his knuckles than he used to, and after a couple more days he notices he's not as quick a thinker as he used to be, and after a couple more days he reaches up to feel his head and he finds out his skull is changing shape. Then he realizes. The history that made apes into humans hasn't happened yet. He is turning into an ape.

It takes a couple of weeks. At first he's scared shitless, and he gets really desperate, and he even takes that pile of metal chunks and halfway thinks about trying to build a time machine out of it. But he never knew exactly how the thing worked in the first place, just like *you* don't really know how a phone or a computer works: you just follow the instructions and use it.

And he's getting dumber every day: he's going backward. Then he just says *Hell with it* and gives up and joins the apes, and they take him in as one of their own. There are nights when he's in a cave with about fifty other apes, huddled there with his ape girlfriend to stay warm, and when he goes to sleep he has dreams about what it used to be like to be human: these dreams where he's using a socket wrench, or putting on a rubber, or looking something up on Google. But when he wakes up the dreams don't make any sense to him, and after a while he doesn't have them anymore. He's just an ape now, like all the other apes.

■

This is why anyone with common sense would stay the hell away from time travel! Because history makes you what you are. And if you traveled back in time you wouldn't get to be you anymore. You would have a different history, and you would become someone else. Do you really *want* to become someone else?

Going back to that movie. We live in the future now. And white people will look at that movie and trash-talk it just like Rita. *Oh, goodness, it's just so self-evidently wrong how those people treated their domestics. It shows an absolute lack of empathy. Why, I'm completely appalled.* You know. But put a white woman in a time machine, and hell, throw a black woman in there with her too. They go back to the South in the 1960s, they get out of the time machine, they turn around and see it's turned into an AMC Rambler with a busted transmission. You give them a while to live there in the past, day after day, without that constant reassurance from other people that it's safe and okay to think the way they do. Nine out of ten white people would go from thinking the idea of equal rights for everybody was as obvious as the nose on your face to saying, *Well, goodness, we'd be perfectly happy to make at least a few concessions to the Negroes if they'd just stop making so much noise!* I've got one more for you that's worse: nine out of ten black people would drop to their knees without even a peep, scrubbing toilets and proud to be Rochester. *These people marching around with signs and trying to get served in restaurants are gonna get sprayed with fire hoses and jumped on by dogs—God bless 'em, but I ain't getting mixed up in that.*

Isn't that the fantasy? If I go back in time, knowing what people back then didn't know, then I can *change history*! But history made you what you are. And it's bigger than any one man. It takes a lot of people working together for years to change things even a little! And you're gonna make the world different all by yourself, you and no one else, because you think you know a little something. You must be joking.

You might be able to change history a *little*. A *tiny* little bit. But if you went back in time I know one thing for certain: history would damn sure change you.

Do you hear me?

Do you feel me?

17

SAFETY FOAM

Later, when the time came to assign the blame, Rebecca's father would tell her something he believed but was too afraid to say in the pulpit: that the true enemy of humanity was not Evil, an abstract idea personified by some sort of crimson-faced creature dancing in flames, but Chance, that smoky million-handed monster forever fitting its tiny fingers into the fissures of your life, working to tear it apart, loosening the fatal screw, turning that first cell cancerous, sending lightning to strike the tree that you chose for shelter from the storm. The version of Satan that embodied every ill of human life had been patched onto the Judeo-Christian tradition because the early God that Moses knew was too tough and terrible for worshippers to want to deal with. The fear that Moses had of Yahweh was as much of His caprice as of His power—He was just as likely to force the Hebrews to wander in the wilderness as He was to rescue them from the Egyptians. In short, He was not the embodiment of good, but of chance: neither good nor evil, but inscrutable and unavoidable.

Seen this way, Woody believed, the relentless catalog of God's commands that makes up much of the early books of the Bible seems less arbitrary: the actions of humans that are most likely to "please God" are also those that allow humans to act collectively to mitigate the negative effects of chance on individual lives. It is why there is such an emphasis in the Torah on attempting to return lost things to their original owners instead of keeping them for yourself, or why the greatest of sins is failure to offer hospitality to a random stranger in distress. If God created humans with the ability to dictate the direction of history (by imagining future states of the universe and steering its path toward one version or another), then humanity's duty to God was to direct history toward the best of all possible worlds.

Once Satan was invented, though, once it became possible for humans to convince themselves that they might be able to cleanly separate good from evil, the idea was lost that those actions that are morally good are also those that allow humans to remain vigilant against chance. And when something grievous happened to us that we could never have seen coming, our first and worst impulse was to try to discover what unknown person had done the clear evil that started the chain of events that led to our tragedy, or to wonder whether that person was, inadvertently, ourselves.

"What I'm saying," Woody said as he, Marianne, and Rebecca sat on a couch together, his daughter laying her head on her mother's lap and sobbing so hard that pain shot down the center of her chest, "is that what happened yesterday isn't the result of you being evil. It was greatly *unfortunate*. And I dearly wish that it had never happened. But to say that it was *evil*: that is to simplify a complex matter, and to take a burden upon yourself that you cannot bear if, in the long, distant future, you are to have any chance of happiness.

"As callous as this might seem, Rebecca: you have to grieve, and understand, and make it a part of you. And then you have to stop asking questions: you have to let it go."

■

What led to the tragedy was this:

Rebecca got a call on her cell at three o'clock in the afternoon, smack in the middle of her private time, the time during which she had the quiet drink or two that would let her deal with being in her own head for the rest of the day. She would have let it go to voicemail, but it was Sean's school. Probably last-minute permission needed for a forgotten field trip, or some other overly cautious pedantry meant to cater to helicopter parents. She answered: the ice in her second gin and tonic (okay, third today) was already starting to melt.

"Rebecca Steiner?"

"Rebecca Wright."

"I'm sorry. I didn't know you weren't married."

"I *am* married."

"I'm so sorry. I didn't—"

"This conversation isn't going well. Let's begin again. Who are you?"

"I'm Mrs. Baldridge: I'm here at Stratton Elementary. I need to let you know that your son was . . . in an altercation during the lunch period today. And we're keeping him after school, as a measure of discipline."

Well, I hope you're springing for a cab, Rebecca thought but didn't say.

"No, we're most certainly *not* 'springing for a cab.' You, or your partner, will have to come here to pick him up, or make some other arrangements."

Oops. But also: *so* fucking angry right now. Not at Sean, but at this *woman*. Keeping him after class to inconvenience the mother, too: punish her for her bad parenting. She had to be getting her jollies off this: she'd go home tonight to her empty apartment and her nightly frozen dinner, and while she dug into a microwaved chicken pot pie with a chunk of ice still in the middle she'd think about how, oooh, she *kept a kid after school*, oooh oh God yes she *made his mother come to pick him up.*

"What time should I be there, Mrs. Baldridge?"

"Four thirty will be perfectly fine, after an hour's detention." *It will be perfectly fine for you to drive out here during rush hour.*

"That's fine. I'll see you then."

■

So, two and a half hours—plenty of time to enjoy this drink in peace, and maybe knock back one more to fortify herself so she could deal with Mrs. Baldridge without biting out her throat. They'd just bought a second car, this one autonomous, and Philip had taken the old manual car to work that day. The new car was a better driver than Rebecca could ever be, even when stone sober, and the cops *never* pulled over cars with green plates because, why would you? And Rebecca was super skilled at looking straight when she was schnock-ered: she always had been. Lately she'd been lit like a Christmas tree in front of teetotaler Philip almost every time she saw him, and he hadn't said a word.

Though maybe Philip could pick him up? She dialed him.

"Why are you calling me, Rebecca," he said, not even bothering to disguise his exasperation.

"I . . . I'm picking Sean up from school," she said.

"Isn't the bus running?"

"He got in trouble," she said, feeling as if she was admitting her own failure. "He's in detention."

"So one of us has to collect the boy when he's badly behaved? Is that how it works?"

"Yeah." *Ask me if I'm good to drive. I fucking dare you. Please please ask. I'm begging you.*

"Well, you'll have to do it, then. I'm deep in work here."

"That's what I *said* I was going to do! Why do you always—"

"You don't need to yell, Rebecca. I need to get back to work. Goodbye."

Click.

■

Philip wasn't one of the first people to buy self-driving cars once they were widely available—he'd reined in his early adopter's impulse until the prices dropped a couple of times—but the vehicles with their swooping, bullet-like shapes and bright green license plates still drew occasional stares from drivers who had to keep their hands on their steering wheels. The first models hadn't been all that different from conventional cars, but as their designs evolved, they began to incorporate a philosophy of relaxation and inattention. The interiors of third-generation self-driving cars were more womblike: they were dark and comforting, letting your mind go somewhere else while the computer at the wheel piloted your body to the place you wanted it to be. The driver and passenger seats in Rebecca's car reclined fully, and would have made suitable beds if one were to take an overnight trip down an interstate highway; the front windshield had an emissive film applied to its surface, so that a video projector mounted above the backseat could display a transparent image on the inside of the windshield, through which you could still see the road.

Rebecca lay back in the driver's seat and lazily swirled the ice in her fourth G&T. She'd brought up the afternoon news on the windshield. It looked as if the federal government was finally admitting that the United States no longer fully held the Dakota Territories, that they'd been, in part, taken over by a ragtag, nameless assemblage of survivalists, hardcore libertarians, Luddites, sovereign citizens, black militants, and white supremacists, who seemed to have formed an uneasy, chaotic alliance that presumably would hold for only as long as it would take for them to win the right to lawfully secede.

On the windshield screen was their leader, or one of their leaders. His appearance was apparently meant to befuddle facial recognition technology, with one side of his face bearded and the other clean-shaven, and his forehead dotted with flecks of reflective foil. "We only want to escape from American surveillance," he was saying, his voice heavily distorted by electronic manipulation. "We are fighting against the reduction of flesh to data. We are fighting for the privacy that is our natural right: we want to not be observed and tracked, by drones and phone cameras and RFID chips. We are not a violent people. We merely wish to pursue the secession that is our God-given right. But if we have to fight, we will fight."

The official word from the government was that this was a "conflict," and a few truckloads of National Guardsmen were being sent in for show. But the whole war was likely to be conducted electronically, with military drones piloted by acne-prone kids who'd been racking up kills in first-person shooters since the age of five. Poor bastards didn't stand a chance.

Rebecca drained her glass and chased the dregs of her drink with a breath mint. Things could be worse: at least she didn't have tinfoil glued all over her face, huddled in some damp, cold bunker along with members of splinter groups from the Klan and the Black Internationale, waiting for the gas or the bomb. All she had to do was retrieve her son from Mrs. Baldridge.

■

It wasn't until Rebecca got Sean in the car and talked to him alone that she was able to piece together the whole story. There was this kid named Brian who'd been held back from third grade and therefore towered over all the other boys in his class, a Cro-Magnon holy terror. And Sean, with his short stature and reedy frame, with his open face and perpetually wide-eyed stare, became the target of Brian's ire. Brian tormented Sean like it was his job: at least once a week the boy came home from school with telltale salt tracks on his cheeks, claiming that nothing was wrong.

Today things had finally come to a head. Last week all the kids in second grade had taken a test—these days the students had to take tests of one kind or another every few weeks, and report cards had grown from simple two-column records of scholarship and conduct to multiple-page spreadsheets adorned with the presidential seal. These multiple-choice exams were in Sean's wheelhouse—if he could ever find a job that consisted solely of finding the next number in a series, Rebecca was certain his future would be secure.

Naturally, he killed it on the test, and since it was one of those federal things, everyone in the top quintile got a voucher for a free ice cream sandwich at lunch. Which, in the fishbowl world of a second grader, was a huge deal. To hear Sean tell it, the school lunches were just as bad as they were in Rebecca's day, except that instead of limp French fries and rectangular slices of pizza, they were made up of things intended to be *healthy:* mealy apples, and clumps of undercooked brown rice, and string beans that had been boiled until their color was nearer to gray than green. Most of the food went in the garbage, day after day: kids who didn't pack their own lunch came home starving. In such an environment an ice cream sandwich in the middle of the day would taste like ambrosia.

The problem was that the teacher had handed out the coupons in front of everyone at the beginning of the school day ("I want the smartest children in the class to *get their recognition,*" she had said, once again demonstrating her utter failure to understand the dog-eat-dog nature of second-grade society), and Sean had had to hold on to the coupon from then until lunchtime (with its drawing of a chocolate ice cream sandwich emerging from a golden explosion on the front, and a portrait of the President on the back, beaming a benevolent attaboy smile). Three hours was an eternity, one that would afford his nemesis Brian plenty of opportunities for ambush and assault.

From there the narrative got a little murky: Rebecca had to piece things together from what Sean told her, from what his face told her he was unwilling to admit, and from Mrs. Baldridge's version of events, which was in turn gathered from the testimonies of other excitable second-grade witnesses, and thus was undoubtedly embroidered.

Apparently Sean got jumped when he was coming back from recess. Brian threw him to the floor on his back, straddled him, and popped him in the face with a quick, stinging backhand. "Give it."

"I'm not," Sean said.

Brian slapped him again. "Give it, I said."

"*No!*" Sean shouted.

"But I'm *hungry*," said Brian, roughly squeezing Sean's cheeks with one hand while he rummaged in the pockets of his jeans with the other. Sean's bucking and writhing did no good: Brian had fifteen pounds on him, and the boy was pinned. "Where is it. Where *is* it."

"Help," Sean squealed.

"There it is," Brian said, extracting the slip of paper from Sean's pocket. Some bespectacled do-gooder had run to get help—he'd be next on Brian's list, but that meant Brian only had fifteen seconds tops to do some serious damage. He'd never get away with actually *redeeming* the coupon; slapping the kid around wasn't that much fun. What was called for here was something that'd cause nightmares, something that'd grant Sean an unforgettable reminder of his powerlessness. Yes.

"I'm *so* hungry," Brian said, and then he crumpled the coupon into a tiny ball, popped it into his mouth, and swallowed it.

"Geez," said an awed bystander.

Still straddling Sean, Brian lifted his head and rolled his eyes back in his head in mock ecstasy. "Oh, it tastes *just like* the best ice cream I've *ever had*—aw *crap!*"

Sean had turned his head and buried his teeth into Brian's hand, biting as hard as he could. If the world wanted him to act like an animal, fine. He'd forget the facts and the colors and be an animal.

Brian leapt off of Sean and started crying, just as Mrs. Baldridge showed up, on cue. "That kid *bit* me," he said, displaying the dotted line of red that ran in an arc along his palm. "See? He *bit* me! He's *crazy!* I bet he's got *rabies!* He's *crazy!*"

"My word. My word! It's okay," Mrs. Baldridge said, taking Brian's tender hand in hers and looking at it closely, as if she was looking for signs of viral infection that could be seen with the naked eye. "It's okay. We'll take you to the nurse's office; we'll get that bandaged up."

Meanwhile, Mr. Davis who taught fourth grade had hoisted Sean up and, rather unnecessarily, locked him in a half nelson. "I'm going to put you in jail!" Sean screamed, his legs kicking fruitlessly in the air, his eyes squeezed shut. "I'm going to put all of you in jail!"

■

Rebecca and Sean ended up getting stuck in Route 1's notorious traffic on the way back, the car speeding up as it came within six inches of the bumper in front of it and then suddenly decelerating, then speeding up again, merging into the next lane with less than a foot to spare. The damn thing drove like a daredevil: it was beautiful.

In the passenger seat, Sean was curled up in silence. Rebecca had brought up what used to be one of his favorite cartoons and projected it on the windshield, an episode from a long-running series about two armies of giant robots that were forever at war, good fighting with evil over the possession of one glowing MacGuffin or another. But the boy wasn't paying attention.

The nerve of that woman. "In addition to talking to several of the students who saw this regrettable contretemps—and who were quite troubled by witnessing such violence, I should add—I spoke to Sean's teacher, just to get a different perspective on the situation," Mrs. Baldridge had said. "And after collating our notes I want to present you with some constructive feedback on your son's behavioral issues." Then she'd handed Rebecca a pamphlet entitled "The Cycle of Violence: Warning Signs." It featured a table divided into three columns: yellow (caution), orange (beware), and red (danger!). "As you can see here," Mrs. Baldridge had said, "today Sean exhibited two of the behaviors in the yellow column—rebellion against authority, and verbal threats—and one in the *orange* column, physical violence requiring minor medical attention. The *orange* column, Mrs. Steiner! We don't see ten orange-column incidents in a *year* in this school. This is a well-behaved school, Mrs. Steiner. This is a peaceful school. You should take that pamphlet home and share it with your family: it's something you really need to think about before things get worse." The red column was full of things like "brings a gun to school" and "pleasures oneself in public": real psycho stuff. Whereas to Rebecca, half of the behaviors in the yellow column seemed less like signs of potential violence than excess common sense.

"Thank you for telling me the whole story, Sean," Rebecca said, looking through transparent images of robot warfare at the highway ahead of them.

Sean turned to face her, his eyes bloodshot. "I tried to tell her the story too! I tried to tell her but when I started telling her she said be quiet."

"I'm really sorry this happened today, Sean."

"I'm sorry, too!" Sean said.

One of the lights on the dashboard in front of Rebecca changed color from green to yellow and began to blink.

"Life is unfair," Rebecca said. "Mostly, that's the fault of the people whose job is to make it fair for you. I wish you could have waited a little while longer to learn that, but here we are. Don't tell Mrs. Baldridge I told you that."

"I won't," Sean said.

"You didn't want that ice cream anyway," Rebecca said. "The ice cream in school cafeterias tastes terrible. Do you know what it's made out of?"

"No, what?"

"Packing material! It's made out of little Styrofoam peanuts, and wood shavings. And also: mealworms. They grind all that stuff up in a blender and freeze it, and it looks just like ice cream, but it isn't."

"No way!"

"Way! You may not have realized it at the time, but you avoided a terrible fate today, Sean."

It felt good to hear him laugh.

"I'll tell you what," Rebecca said. "I'm really proud of you, because you were smart and you stood up for yourself"—this was probably bad parenting, but the thought of that other kid sitting in class with a halo floating over his head made her think *Fuck it*—"and I'm going to get you an ice cream sandwich, right now. Not a cafeteria one, but a real one, with ice cream made from milk and sugar instead of chemicals and bugs. Would you like that?"

"That'd be cool," Sean said.

"Alert," the dashboard announced in a brusquely masculine voice, and Rebecca turned to look at the road.

■

Later, Rebecca would only remember what happened as a series of snapshots or fragments of sounds, as if her memory of the event had chosen to tear itself to shreds out of tender mercy.

First:

Projected on the windshield, a humanoid robot that was half the size of a skyscraper stared at Rebecca with red pinpoint eyes that glimmered beneath the darkness of a metal cowl.

Through the image of the robot she could see a car. It was a cute little forest-green convertible with its top down, and instead of having all four of its wheels on the ground it was somehow standing on its front bumper, its rear pointed in the air. Its driver was a woman dressed in business attire—simple white blouse and binding pencil skirt—whose head was obscured by a cloud of wayward strawberry-blond hair.

Then:

"Alert," the car said calmly. "Trouble ahead."

Then:

The woman's body somehow freed itself from the seatbelt of the convertible and began to fly over the lanes of the highway, arms windmilling, legs asprawl, a single black high-heeled shoe chasing behind. From somewhere ahead there was a wrong kind of light: something was on fire.

Then:

"This is an emergency," the car said. "I will pull off of the road as soon as is safely possible." On the windshield, the cartoon suddenly disappeared.

Then:

"Uh-oh," said Sean.

"If you wish to assume control of your vehicle, please touch the steering wheel with both hands," the car said.

Then:

I ought to do something, Rebecca thought, looking at her son. *I have to do something.* She wanted to wrap her arms around Sean and take flight; she wanted to rewind time. But her head felt full of sludge, and her nerves were screaming, and her arms, as they lifted themselves toward the wheel, were made of lead.

"Don't," Sean said, looking at his mother.

Then:

Behind her—was it behind her?—she heard the muted bang of one car colliding with another as, in front of her, the falling woman collided with the roof of an SUV two lanes over, one of her legs bending unnaturally. The cars ahead of her began to drift, pointing in unorthodox directions.

Then:

"You are now assuming control of your vehicle," the car said.

Then:

Rebecca felt a blast of heat against the side of her face from somewhere. Acting purely on instinct now, she whipped the wheel to her right, turning it hand over hand. (And when the time came to mete out blame in her mind, she would think: *Left*. If she was going to take the wheel in the first place, she should have steered left.)

Then:

"Alert," the car said, its voice still placid.

Then:

Noises. Horns and screams and curses.

Then:

Rebecca's neck jolted with a sharp snap as another car rammed into hers from the other side, from the passenger side, oh no, oh God. As she felt her own vehicle lift from the road she looked over at Sean and oh no, oh God.

Then:

"Catastrophic collision," the car said, raising its voice slightly. "Safety foam is coming: close your eyes and mouth. Breathe normally."

Then:

She shut her eyes as the car's interior suddenly filled with sticky, creamy lather, muting the sounds from outside. Her face somehow felt both numb and stinging: later, she would find that it had sustained first-degree burns from the safety foam's impact. But she was secure, swaddled in the quickly solidified glop as her center of gravity bounced in her gut: she could feel the foam between each of her fingers, and down her shirt, and in her ears.

Then:

Another jolt, surprisingly slight, as her overturned car struck the asphalt and skidded until it came to a stop.

Then:

Nothing is as it should be; everything is upside down. That is what Rebecca Wright thought. She hung there in darkness, her seat-belt chafing her shoulder and pinching her breast, her field of view entirely filled by the dimly lit yellow foam that was just in front of her eyes, pressing against her face, reducing each of her breaths to a rasp.

Then:

"Sean?" she shouted. "I want you to yell as loud as you can. Tell me you're okay."

No answer.

Oh God. Oh no.

Then:

Grating, scraping sounds as the Jaws of Life tore the door on her side open, and hands began to claw away chunks of the foam. More sound; more light.

Then:

Hands removed her from the totaled car: it felt like a dozen of them, all over her, clutching and pulling.

Then:

The blanket draped around her, more valuable for its signal of anonymous care than for its warmth. Someone handed her black coffee in a Styrofoam cup and disappeared. In a daze she plucked bits of foam from her ears and the sounds of the world returned, the noises of machines and human wails.

Then:

She watched as paramedics chiseled a large block of foam from the other side of the car, placed it on a stretcher, and carted it away, its custard color shot through with thin red streaks of blood. A small hand stuck out from it, unmoving.

Oh no.

Oh God.

Sean.

■

Later, when the time came to portion out the blame, the insurance agent told Rebecca and Philip that bad luck favored complex systems. "The thing you have to understand is that the mass introduction of self-driving cars onto highways made auto liability cases insanely complicated," he said to them in his small office with its thin walls through which Rebecca could hear the sounds of a woman weeping, a man cursing. "In the twentieth century," the agent continued evenly, as if these noises were nothing to be concerned with, or as if they were so common that he'd learned to tune them out, "assigning fault to one actor or another in an accident was a fairly straightforward process. But with autonomous cars it's more difficult. Because unlike brakes or pistons, the actions of artificial intelligence routines aren't entirely predictable *by design*. They make thousands of decisions based on the contexts in which they find themselves, and it's impossible to know what those contexts will be. And if they make decisions that perhaps lead to tragedy, is the owner of the vehicle to blame? Is the manufacturer of the computer software? Or someone else entirely? Who can say for sure? New Jersey's a no-fault state, which makes things a little less complicated in some ways, but in many states this still isn't even completely settled law. Which is why when you purchase an autonomous vehicle, you sign one title for its hardware, and a second, separate license for its software, which, unfortunately, has the effect of limiting the extent of the manufacturer's liabilities in the case of . . ." He sighed, and it was a practiced sigh that Rebecca was sure he'd made a hundred times before. "An incident," he finished.

He paused to let that settle in, and then continued. "This isn't legal advice: I'm just speaking from experience. You're going to want to go after the manufacturer. And what they're going to do is pull the data your vehicle sent back to home base, the same data I've got right here. And . . . look. You took the wheel, right? When all this happened."

"Of *course* I did!" Rebecca said. Then, with a plaintive squeak: "It *asked*!"

"I understand. But there's this clause in your software license. Basically, when you take control of the vehicle in circumstances like this, you relieve the manufacturer of liability from the consequences of any actions that the software took immediately prior to your assumption of control. In plain English, the manufacturer is going to argue that you can't blame the software for getting you into a mess if you then tried to get yourself out of it. Because how do we know the driver, by taking the wheel, didn't make the situation worse?

"I know, I know. It's bullshit. But just eyeballing this, there are so many possible complicating factors here that . . . assigning blame? In a manner that would hold up in a court of law? You could try, but . . . look at who they are, and look at who you are.

"As for knowing how and why it happened: honestly, I don't think you ever will, not with any certainty. My advice—and as a father of two I know how you feel—is: just accept that it happened, and find a way to move on from here.

"I'm sorry."

■

That was not a satisfactory answer for Philip, though, and so, with the dogged persistence of a physicist used to spending years on projects with little chance of success, he did his research. But he didn't get very far. The corporate functionaries he could manage to get on the phone had their tongues tied by considerations of liability, and the company documents he got his hands on dissolved into jargon when they threatened to touch on the truths he needed. By lurking in less reputable areas of the Internet he was able to acquire schematics for a few makes of autonomous vehicles, as well as various versions of the AI routines that powered them, and with that he was able to propose a conjecture of what might have happened that day. But it would forever sting him that conjecture would be his only consolation.

What might have happened, Philip thought, was this:

Most autonomous vehicles had three methods of performing the crucially important task of confirming their own position in spacetime, as well as the spacetime positions of other nearby cars. They had an average of a dozen cameras mounted on their exteriors; they regularly broadcast their positions to each other via Wi-Fi nodes; and they sent their positions to satellites that also relayed those positions to other cars in turn, as well as to other interested parties (automobile manufacturers; insurance agencies; companies who'd paid to place innocuous personalized advertisements in the corners of windshields; the NSA). The three methods were intended to provide a high degree of redundancy, since knowing exactly where a self-driving car is and how fast it's moving is of utmost importance.

However, one particular carmaker, not the manufacturer of Rebecca's and Philip's car, had announced their intention on the day of the incident to push a firmware update that, in the patch notes, only vaguely said that it was designed to "improve functionality." Somehow, autonomous-car aficionados had gotten hold of the update in advance and found out that it in fact *decreased* functionality: specifically, it cut off access to an extremely popular, remarkably addictive video game that millions of commuters played on their windshields each morning on the way to work. So when the predictable instructions circulated on social media for how to use USB sticks and a homebrewed mod to uninstall the upgrade and revert to the prior version of the firmware, while still telling the manufacturer that the firmware was up to date, at least a few car owners took advantage.

The problem with this was that the new version of this particular car model's AI routine *did* have some specific advantages, among which was a decreased latency in the constant transmission of the vehicle's location in spacetime. However, those cars that had been hacked to run the prior version of the firmware, with its greater latency, could still communicate with the rest of the system, which in turn assumed that those hacked vehicles were actually running the most up-to-date version with the lesser latency.

So because of this, the three methods that vehicles had of confirming each other's positions—camera; satellite; Wi-Fi—could no longer agree in the cases of those cars still running the firmware's prior version. The difference in the transmission latency was only fifty milliseconds, but that is long enough for a car traveling at sixty miles per hour to move four feet. Vehicles in the close proximity of those that were covertly running the obsolete firmware became confused: the location signals they were receiving from Wi-Fi and satellite agreed with each other, but not with what their electronic eyes told them, and they were unsure which to trust. In most places, such as the rural highways that stretch across the Midwest, this didn't matter; on crowded roads where the cars traveled fast and stuck close, that four-foot discrepancy was incredibly important.

Different makes and models of autonomous cars dealt with the perception of this discrepancy in different ways, depending on the rigors of their programming. The smartest ones played it safe, assuming that the cars running the obsolete firmware were both in the places indicated by the cameras and the places indicated by their Wi-Fi and satellite signals, receding from them accordingly. Other cars, among which was Rebecca's, detected the discrepancy in the information sources but had no real idea how to process the error: in a circumstance like this the best course of action was to pull off to the side of the road, hand control over to the driver, and refuse to reactivate the autonomous systems until a mechanic had performed a diagnostic. Had Rebecca's car been in the right lane at the time of the incident, things might have turned out relatively fine for her and Sean. Such little things only become important after the fact.

But Rebecca's car was in the middle lane and barred from escape, which put it at the mercy of those few cars that had the poorest programming, those that, when detecting the discrepancy between the spaces where the erroneous signals said the cars were and the spaces where their own cameras said they were, assumed that the cars only occupied the positions where both those spaces overlapped. In their electric eyes the vehicles shrunk to the size of motorcycles, leaving four feet of empty space to accelerate into, to get their passengers to their destinations just a little more efficiently, just a little faster. Suddenly—and Philip discovered that several accidents with similar causes happened within minutes of each other on the same day on the country's most crowded roads, in Los Angeles and Tampa and Washington, DC—the badly programmed cars accelerated and rammed those in front of them at a life-threatening speed, the momentum transferring between the closely spaced vehicles and sending them ricocheting crazily against each other like billiard balls just after the break. Most roads saw no trouble at all that day, but those few where circumstances met the necessary unfortunate conditions descended into chaos.

■

And finally, when the blame was all shared out and it came time for Rebecca to swallow her spoonful, her mother was there beside her.

"When it came down to it," Rebecca said, "the car was a *coward*."

She and Marianne were back on the couch when she'd laid her head on her mother's lap the night before and wept. "The car was totally fine with taking you to get groceries or going on a Sunday joyride, but when the situation got tough it *chickened out*. And the thing is that when I could have let it decide what to do anyway, *I* took the wheel. My hands just jerked up like I was a puppet on strings and I did it before I even thought. And then the car was like, *Well, good luck to you then*."

"You did that because you're a mother and a human being," Marianne said. She had a drink in her hand: sparkling water in the glass tumbler that usually held her vodka and cranberry. Most of the time when she and Rebecca had these mother-daughter chats, she mixed vodka and cran for the both of them without asking, and even though Rebecca hadn't told her mother about the drinks she'd had before getting into the car that day—the drinks were what one might call an unacknowledged complicating factor—she had read her mother's offer of Pellegrino in the place of Absolut as an acknowledgment of a certain possibility, and of a silent signal.

"Because you're human," Marianne continued, "you couldn't do anything other than what you did. When the people you love are in danger, you act on instinct." Looking at the floor, she slipped into a short reverie: "I remember when I was a new mother. With you. And I was learning how to read all those noises you were making: your giggles and your whimpers and your cries. You cried a *lot*. And it didn't take me long to interpret those cries even if I was in another room, you know? One was like, *She needs her diaper changed*, and another one would make me think, *That's something she's going to have to get over, because it'll only get worse from here*. But there was one. And I can't really describe it, and I only heard it out of you two or three times. But when I heard it, it was like I got this haze in my head, I dropped whatever I was doing and I *ran* to you. I was drawn to you like you were a magnet and I was an iron filing. You know?"

Slowly, not looking at her mother, Rebecca nodded.

"Same thing with you and Sean," Marianne said. "You're flesh and blood, and you saw your son in danger and did what flesh and blood instinctively does to save its own. And imagine what would have happened if you *hadn't*: if you'd just sat on your hands and let a calculator take care of things. You realize that thing doesn't have magic powers, right? You see that at that point there was no way to stop things from turning out any way other than the way they did, right?"

"Yes," Rebecca lied.

"You and I would still be sitting here on the couch, just the same. Except you'd be saying to yourself that you failed because you didn't even try. But because you were human, you had no choice but to try, and you did the best you could do."

Marianne embraced her daughter. "Now," she said. "Have you talked to Philip: I mean *really* talked to him about this?"

"I . . . he's keeping it bottled up. I try to talk to him and he won't talk back. He tried to figure out why it happened and he couldn't figure it out.

"I . . . I don't know what's going to happen, Mom. I really don't know."

■

—Philip. Philip? I'm home.

—Rebecca.

—Philip. It's dark in here.

—I want it dark. Rebecca.

—Philip, why don't I just turn on—

—Please don't. Sit down. Rebecca.

—Philip.

—I need to ask you something.

— . . .

— . . .

—Well, what?

—I need to ask you if you were drinking in the car. If you'd been drinking before you got in the car.

—Ohhhhhaaaaaah Philip.

—Because—

—Aaaaaaah. Aaaaaaaaaaaah.

—Because if—

—Out of all the questions you could ask. You ask that question. That question.

—I need to ask you if you had a drink before you got in the car.

—I'm not sitting here asking who thought it was a good idea to buy a car that was driven by a fucking computer.

—That's not the same.

—It is the same it is. This is about blame and nothing else.

— . . .

— . . .

—You're not answering me. I'm concerned that you're not answering me.

— . . .

— . . .

— . . .

—Rebecca.

—I didn't, okay? I can't believe you're asking me this. And I doubly can't believe I'm answering. How much must I hate myself. How much.

— . . .

— . . .

— . . .

—Oh what you don't believe me? Is that what you're going to say next? Say it.

— . . .

— . . .

— . . .

—Philip.

—I . . . I choose to believe you.

—Well, I'm glad you're choosing to believe what's true. That's mighty big of you.

—But Rebecca.

—After what happened the only thing you care about is evidence and proof. I cannot believe this.

—Rebecca.

—You realize there was nothing I could have done, right? Do you think I wouldn't give everything I could if I could get things to turn out another way?

—But Rebecca. You have to stop. I really can't . . . I don't want to see you drinking again. I wish I had said something earlier.

— . . .

—If I tell you I believe you, then you have to stop drinking.

—Are we making some kind of a bargain? Are we going to decide what the truth is based on a bargain now?

—No, this isn't a bargain.

— . . .

—I believe you. But you have to stop drinking. Or . . . I don't know.

— . . .

— . . .

— . . .

—We can get through this. But Rebecca, I don't want to see you drinking again. I can't find that you've taken another drink, ever again. Or I don't know.

— . . .

—Rebecca.

—Okay. I will.

—If you need help, you need to go somewhere and get some help.

—I don't need help. I'll stop.

—Okay.

— . . .

— . . .

—You really believe me, right?

—I believe you.

—Oh God I'm so sorry.

—Come here.

18

NO DIGGITY

Quitting drinking meant that you had to live with your memories. Not all the time. But every once in a while, you'd wake up to see that your mind's projectionist had discovered a fresh print of one of the most luridly crimson episodes of your past, and was displaying it against the featureless white of the ceiling above you. And you had to lie there in bed, and look at it while you listened to your husband grunt his way through his morning push-ups (though perhaps he saw his own memories projected on the carpet beneath him as it bobbed closer and farther away from his head). And without recourse to alcohol's anesthesia, you had to live with what you saw there.

Philip stood and looked down at Rebecca. "Fifty-eight," he said, breathing heavily. "Fifty-eight. A record."

Rebecca blinked away the vision before her (the convertible with its hind end tipped into the air; the woman beginning to fall) and turned on her side to face him. "That's excellent, dear."

"I bet I could do a hundred." He rolled his sore shoulders. "I'm going to do a hundred someday."

Philip cocked his head in consideration of the woman before him (and this was one of the things that Rebecca would remember later, when she combed through her memories: that quizzical tilt of the head before he spoke). "What are you up to today?" he said.

"A shift at Lovability from ten to one. Then shopping for a dress. Did I tell you? We're invited to a party in New York, you and I. By one of my old girlfriends, from back in the day. Britt. I don't think you've seen her since the wedding, but she's getting the band back together. Mostly so she can show off her perfect life, I think. So I need a new dress. I have to look good. And so do you: we'll worry about that later. You're going, by the way: no's not an answer."

"Shopping for clothing seems so tedious for women," Philip said, wiping sweat off his face with the hem of his shirt. Rebecca noticed (and would later remember herself noticing) that Philip's stomach was, if not quite a six-pack, rock hard. Maybe doing all those push-ups hadn't been such a bad idea after all.

She playfully reached out and slid a fingertip down the thin line of hair that began at his navel and disappeared beneath the band of his boxer shorts. The Philip Steiner of years past might have caught the hint and climbed back into bed, but this morning his mind seemed elsewhere.

"It's bullshit," she said. "Bodies have so many different shapes, and the sizes on the clothing tags are all flattery and lies. I never know if I'm a twelve or a double-O, or a four up top and a ten down below. It's going to take *all day*. Even if I'm lucky, I won't be back home until evening. Takeout?"

"I'll pick up Mexican on the way back from the lab," Philip said, turning away from her and leaving the room.

The way he turned, with an unspoken urgency, his feet on his way out the door while his eyes were still on her. Strange.

■

After Philip left for the lab, Rebecca pulled herself out of bed, show-ered, dressed, and had breakfast (generic-brand frosted flakes in two percent milk; a slice of buttered raisin bread; no mimosa. She had come to terms with the fact that all her breakfasts from here on out would be flavored with the desire for mimosas. A glass of orange juice just reminded her that it was missing something effervescent and vital. No mimosas; no Bloody Marys; no simple glasses of white wine). Then she donned her monitor shades, hit the treadmill, and began her Lovability shift.

"Lova-*bil*-ity, this is Re-*bec*-ca," she sang. "How may I *help* you?"

"Hello?" the voice on the other end called, its vowels clipped by a bad connection. "Hello? My name is. Yes. I need help." The profile associated with the caller was trying to load on Rebecca's monitor shades: a twirling circle hovered before her eyes, meant to pacify the impatient with the illusion of progress.

"How may I help you?" she said again.

A pause. "Well, here's the thing. I'm not exactly sure. I just opened this account. And I'm on the Silver Plan. And I filled out the profile: I uploaded the photos; I entered all the demographic data; I answered all your questions about my likes and my dislikes. And I looked at the profile—and this is going to sound, like, crazy—but *it isn't me*."

The spinning circle was replaced by an angrily red triangle with an exclamation point floating inside. A failure; a warning.

"And I don't know if something went wrong with the servers on your end, or if the profile is a lie I made up, or if *I'm* a lie. Or maybe I'm true, and the rest of the world is a lie. Do you understand?"

YES YES YES, Rebecca wanted to shout, but the algorithms that monitored her speech would hear the spike in volume and flag it as screaming at a client. "Please continue," she said. "I'm here to listen."

"Your voice doesn't sound right to me," the caller said. "I've never spoken to you before—have I spoken to you? I haven't. But I know your voice doesn't sound like it should. Just like my own voice doesn't sound right to me, in my own head. This is a serious problem!"

"I certainly agree with this."

"Can you help me?"

The voice monitors would definitely red-flag her if they picked her up saying the word "no." (Rumor was, you could get dismissed for that automatically without someone from HR even looking at the case: the whole procedure would be handled by AI routines in seconds.) "I will do what I can to assure you that your profile has been properly uploaded to our servers." No chance of upselling this guy to the Gold Plan: you had to pick your battles.

"Your name is Rebecca, yes?"

"Yes, that's me. If you wish to speak to my—"

"Are you *sure*? Has it always been?"

"Well, I've gone by Becca sometimes, but I'm quite certain I've always been Rebecca. On a birth certificate, somewhere."

"You don't understand! You don't understand. Rebecca. This world

is a dream. This world is a house on fire, and all of us must find a way
to escape."

He hung up.

■

And so Rebecca finished her Lovability shift (six marks upsold: still
a pretty good haul in the end), ate a quick lunch (catch-as-catch-can
college student fare: three-minute ramen noodles that she sprinkled
with a few frozen peas; a candy-like "nutrition bar" from a box that
featured a fresh-faced blond woman in hiking gear; not an ice-cold
bottle of Corona Extra), hopped in the car, and drove to the shopping mall in Bridgewater, a half hour or so up Route 206. Years ago
that road would have been hell to drive on at this time of day, but the
computers that piloted autonomous cars tended to take 206 only as
a last resort, opting for highways with more lanes and higher speed
limits: with the raised limits for green-plated cars it was sometimes
possible for them to get you to a destination faster by taking a longer
route. So if you drove an old jalopy, or were a Luddite, or preferred
the feel of a stick shift's knob in the hand, then 206 was a paradise,
its traffic pleasantly light, the red plates on its cars seeming less like
scarlet letters. Besides, Bridgewater's mall would suit Rebecca's purpose better than any of the shopping centers on Route 1: the Bridgewater mall was a place of extravagant luxuries rather than necessities,
and for this party Rebecca wanted to give the impression that she and
Philip were people who worried about wants instead of needs.

She hadn't seen Britt and Victor in a while, or any of the gang of
girls that she'd run with in her twenties; she didn't even know what
they were up to. She'd kept up with their Facebook feeds for a while
after they all began to live their own separate lives, but just as people
had drifted away from Myspace, and few in the United States even
remembered Friendster and Orkut, there soon came a time when most
of Rebecca's social networking contacts all simultaneously seemed to
find something better to do with their time than check Facebook
incessantly, and with other things on her mind (Philip; Sean; okay,
booze) Rebecca had somehow failed to join the exodus to whichever
network had offered the slight but necessary change in function or
design that had made Facebook yesterday's news. Facebook was still

around, of course, but except for the retirement home residents who still used it out of habit, it had largely become an electronic wasteland, its profiles either time capsules that documented the teenage fashions and slang of past decades, or creations of AI-managed bots that persistently soldiered on in their duties despite having been forgotten by their creators, clicking "like" on each other's posts and blindly spamming each other with endorsements for products unavailable for sale.

So if Rebecca wanted to hear the news about someone, she either had to e-mail them (which was only a little less weirdly formal these days than mailing a handwritten letter) or call them (which was far too intimate) or text them (and a text from someone you hadn't kept in touch with regularly had a good chance of going ignored—people got too many texts to respond to them all). And all of these involved remembering that someone existed whom you hadn't thought of in a while, an ability that had atrophied in the minds of people who could not remember a time without social networking, just as people near the end of the twentieth century had lost the ability to remember the long and semi-random strings of digits that made up phone numbers once cellphones began to do that for them. Why bother to try to recall the people you had once known and would like to know again, if a computer was happy to handle those duties by pushing status updates at you (and quietly deciding by means of its own secret algorithms which updates were more important than others)?

Which is why the e-mail from Britt was such a sweet surprise (even though it nauseated Rebecca slightly to see that its domain of origin was actually brictor.net). The party, which Britt was billing as "just a little celebration of happiness and life!!!," was in three weeks. That would give Rebecca plenty of time to drop a pound or two, time enough to make an appointment at a hair salon, and let the new 'do grow in a little so she wouldn't look like she'd gotten it just for the party. Time enough to pick up a nice new dress.

She was not looking forward to having to tell her old friends and their significant others about what had happened to Sean, potentially over and over again. (And she couldn't imagine having had to relay that kind of tragedy on a social networking site: having to perform her own grief for an audience in some kind of blog post, and having to read a comment trail full of the public performances of sympathy from near strangers.) But maybe everybody already knew. Maybe

they'd done the due-diligence Googling that had become increasingly socially acceptable in recent years—these days you just got
used to people knowing things about you that you'd never actually
told them. If they didn't know, she could just tell Britt, and with her
mouth everybody at the party would know within ninety minutes.

But if she was going to have to stand in a damned impromptu
condolence line, listening to boilerplate expressions of sorrow, then
at least she was going to look good. If it worked for the heroines of
chick-lit novels, it would work for her: she was going to purchase a
dress, to boost her self-confidence, in any color but black.

■

The Bridgewater mall was a cathedral of white light and open spaces,
its dozens of stores sparsely populated with objects of presumably
inestimable worth. Rebecca walked past one electronics store that
was dark and completely barren, except for a single blacklight that
shone down on a man who wore jeans, a tight-fitting black T-shirt
that showed off hard-won gym muscles, and a pair of wraparound
sunglasses. He stood as still as a guard at Buckingham Palace, and
in his outstretched hand he held a package that appeared to contain
a pair of audio cables. There was no checkout counter in the back of
the store, or even a sign to be found that advertised what the cables
were for or how much they cost; you got the impression that if you
asked the man holding the cables about them, he wouldn't answer,
and if you tried to take them out of his hand you'd end up with a
shoulder bone slipped out of a socket.

Another store was as brightly lit as the electronics store had been
dark, and its sole furnishings were three-yard-high Lucite pedestals,
each of which held a single left high-heeled shoe. A slim, fey propri-
etor in a pinstriped suit stood beside the shoes, scowling with impressive imperiousness at any passersby who slowed down and seemed to
consider entering. Perhaps his death glare was an attempt at reverse
psychology: out of pure spite, you'd spend the money on the shoes to
prove to the guy that people of *your* station in life didn't *get* looks like
that from the help.

Even Conrad's, the "anchor" store that in Rebecca's teenage years
would have been packed with rack after rack of clothes in a cacoph-

ony of colors, was more or less empty. Four mannequins behind plate-glass windows guarded the arched entrance to the store, two on either side—they were on horseback, and their steeds were of different colors: red, white, black, and a fourth horse whose body was transparent, its glass skin revealing a skeleton of steel rods and spinning gears beneath. The mannequins that sat astride the horses and held their reins were naked, with matching blond bobs, and sculpted cheekbones, and slender noses, and swollen lips, and ivory bodies, and small nipple-less breasts; their eyes were oddly alive and human, though, and Rebecca could have sworn that their gazes followed her as she crossed the store's threshold, looking her up and down.

There were more mannequins hanging by cables from the cavernous ceiling of the store's main hall, two stories up. They looked just like the ones at the entrance, except that they held long, slim, brass trumpets to their mouths, and had four wings of tissue paper affixed between their shoulder blades that gently flapped back and forth by means of unseen mechanisms. They made Rebecca a little nervous.

Deeper into the store was a row of a dozen extraordinarily tall women who faced the entrance—they all must have cleared six feet. They were dressed in matching navy-blue pantsuits, and each of them cradled a tablet in her arms; every once in a while, one of them would consult her tablet, peel off from the row, stride authoritatively toward a customer wandering through the store's capacious space as if she had recognized her from afar, greet her, and slip into the easy patter of a sales pitch. After a couple of minutes, the saleswoman would casually slip her arm around the waist of the customer with presumptive familiarity, leading her over to an area of the floor that appeared to be just as featureless as any other part of the floor. The customer would tap a few buttons on her phone and wave it in front of a device that the saleswoman wore on a holster at her side; about a minute later, a hatch would open up in the floor and a platform would rise out of it that held some sort of cardboard box or shopping bag. The customer would take the package, smile, and be on her way.

Where was the *shopping* happening here? The browsing through the clearance rack, the giggling that went on in the fitting rooms?

Rebecca wandered a little farther into the store, and sure enough, one of the saleswomen left the line to approach her. "HelloI'mCla ricewelcometoConrad's," she said, running all the words together through force of habit: Lovability's AI voice monitors would have hit her with a yellow card for that. "What are you looking for today?"

Couldn't she, you know, just *look*? There didn't seem to be a single article of clothing on display here: even the mannequins were nude. "I'm going to a party," Rebecca said. "I need a sort of a going-out party dress. You know."

"We have *just* the thing for you," Clarice the saleswoman said, flipping back her tablet's cover and quickly tapping her way through a few menus. Three dresses appeared, each being modeled by the same woman (and, in fact, in each image she had the same facial expression, as if her head had been photographed once and repeatedly cut and pasted). One was a black, form-fitting, knee-length, V-neck thing with leather bands that crisscrossed at the bosom and made the whole outfit look vaguely S-and-M-ish (ugh: also, black); the second was a skimpy little red affair that flared at the bottom and featured a bust covered in sequins (argh: no no no no *no*); the last was a simple, shoulder-baring dress in deep indigo, that looked as if it might shimmer a little in the right light (yes, actually: yes. Maybe).

"You like the blue one," Clarice said. The pronouncement sounded half like a statement, half like a command. "Blue suits you. Come on and we'll set you up."

Feeling a little rushed—she was not expecting mere department-store shopping to involve the sort of hardcore hustle you got when buying a used car—Rebecca said, "I think, I *think* I like the one in blue, but . . . could I see it? You know, to try it on?"

Clarice took a step back. "Oh, you've never *shopped* at Conrad's before."

Rebecca shook her head slowly. "Not for years."

"Well, last year we retrenched in order to be able to better compete in the modern marketplace. Our biggest change was the introduction of the Conrad's Magic Matching Fit System. Which is amazing, and which no online service can provide. You don't need to try things on here. They just fit."

"Magic Matching Fit System," Rebecca said suspiciously—having worked for Lovability for a while or, as some of the more hysterical privacy advocates might have said, having "carried water for Big Data," she knew the habit corporations had of giving the software being used for invading your privacy the most cheerful name possible.

"See those mannequins?" Clarice indicated the angels in flight above them, and the sentries on horseback at the entrance. "Cameras in the eyes. We film you from several angles when you enter, and analyze your clothing and gait to determine your body type. Facial recognition, too: we correlate that with any publicly available information online to see how your appearance has changed over time, what styles of clothing you've chosen to wear in certain situations in the past, and so on. It's amazingly, *amazingly* accurate. Our average customer is in and out of here in eight minutes; our rate of return on items is less than one-half of one percent."

"I don't recall consenting to any sort of . . . measurement," Rebecca said, knowing full well what Clarice's response would be.

"I'm sure you remember consenting by the act of entering those doors," Clarice replied, gesturing at the entrance. "I'm sure you read the agreement mounted on the plaque at the entrance, or the duplicate copy that was sent to your phone."

"Oh, yes, I did notice those," Rebecca lied easily.

"Well, okay then!" Clarice suddenly became congenial again, and Rebecca, to her own surprise, felt a little relieved.

Rebecca felt Clarice's arm creep around her waist, and she stared up into the saleswoman's eyes. Deep in her brain she felt the instinctive reflex of compliance. She could actually see the hustle working— they'd probably even shown her those two crappy dresses just to make the third one look more desirable—and she still couldn't resist. The minions that lived beneath the floor of the department store had probably already pulled the box with her cocktail dress off a shelf, and placed it on the conveyor belt that would carry it to that mysterious hatch in the floor.

"Come with me," Clarice said, gently nudging Rebecca along, "and we'll get you fixed up."

■

The dress was, to be fair, cheaper than she expected—if Conrad's was sending almost all of its customers in and out in eight minutes like Clarice the saleswoman had said, instead of having to deal with the twentieth-century custom of women coming in to try things on but not to buy, then they were doing so much volume that they could afford to take a haircut on the price. To be fairer—and this is what bugged Rebecca a little, though not nearly as much as it would have ten years ago—she was sure that the dress would fit, and that the fitting rooms in Conrad's had been boarded up because they weren't necessary. She was sure that when she put the dress on, she would absolutely love it (even if in the back of her head she might think that it was a little too loose in the bust, or a bit too binding in the waist, or that it would look better in another color).

If Big Tobacco's cunning had once involved dosing brands of cigarettes with particular chemical cocktails so that you'd quickly come to prefer them above all others, and Big Pharma's talent was convincing people that what they thought of as minor inconveniences or unfortunate quirks of character were in fact problems that required regular medication, then Big Data's gift, the way it kept itself growing stronger, was in its ability to persuade the majority of people that the unique collection of physical and personality characteristics that they naively referred to as the "self" was in fact made up of a complex matrix of statistical values, too complicated for humans to process but not so hard for computers to comprehend. Whether this was true, or whether it may as well have been true because everyone believed it was, was hard to say—the line between the two possibilities had blurred too much.

And yet Rebecca felt that it was hard to tell whether the secret algorithms of Big Data did not so much reveal you to yourself as they tried to dictate to you what you were to be. To accept that the machines knew you better than you knew yourself involved a kind of silent assent: you liked the things Big Data told you you were likely to like, and you loved the people it said you were likely to love. To believe entirely in the data entailed a slight diminishment of the self, small but crucial and, perhaps, irreversible.

But Rebecca was, as she had to remind herself, thirty-eight, and though she was still young in some ways, she was old in others, and the fact that she'd been born before the advent of Google practically made her as ancient as Methuselah. These concerns about the self, and privacy, and the aggregation of data, were an old person's worries. Women in their early twenties who walked into Conrad's probably knew, in some vague sense, that they were being scanned by the mannequins that hung from the ceiling and stood sentry at its entrance, and that wire-frame models of their naked bodies and lists of their measurements appeared on computer monitors within seconds after crossing the store's threshold. They probably knew this and didn't care; if they ever thought about it, they probably looked back with pity on women of earlier decades who could spend four hours searching for a flattering pair of jeans and return home with nothing to show for it. And Rebecca had saved a lot of time. In life you made your little negotiations and you struck your little bargains, and while Rebecca had woken up this morning thinking that she'd have to spend all day going from store to store, the Conrad's Magic Matching Fit System had granted her a few hours of life back. Getting back home at three instead of six or seven: today, in spite of that ever-so-slight misgiving about Conrad's business practice, Rebecca felt lucky. She felt like she'd won.

■

When Rebecca got back to the house, she had to park in the street because there were two cars in the driveway—one was Philip's manually driven Ford, the other a vintage silver Volkswagen Beetle, its compact body made of simple, appealing curves, its condition scrupulously maintained (though it wore green license plates, marking it as retrofitted and autonomous). Later, Rebecca would note that that was when she just stopped thinking, for a little while. She was clearly absorbing information—she remembered the second car, and remembered thinking that she had no reason to expect a vehicle in the place in the driveway where hers belonged—but she was not interpreting that information, or considering its implications. She was not wondering whose car it was, or why it was there, or why in fact Philip's car was there when he'd said this morning that he'd be at the lab all day. It wasn't that these weren't questions that were worth asking. But somehow, even though she hadn't articulated them to herself, she instinctively realized that when she knew their answers her life would become terrible.

The party dress she'd bought was in the passenger seat next to her, in its minimalist, off-white, plastic-sealed cardboard box with the widely kerned C O N R A D ' S logo stretched across its middle. She would enter the house, go into the bedroom, *don't enter the bedroom,*

this is the place that holds answers to questions, she would enter the bedroom and try on the dress. She hadn't been able to try on the dress
in the store, but as she'd checked out the saleswoman in Conrad's
had shown her a computer-generated depiction of what she'd look
like in it, its rendering of her face sourced from the dozens of photographs taken by the mannequins of the Magic Matching Fit System.
In the image she'd had a beaming smile and a slight redness to her
cheeks: despite the fact that it wasn't real, it convinced her and struck
her as a picture of the way she imagined herself at her best. Rebecca
wouldn't be surprised if, in a year or two, Conrad's began mailing
actual physical catalogs to its most loyal customers, printed on glossy
stock; you'd open them up to find that all of the models inside were
happy and beautiful versions of you.

She took the box off the passenger seat, got out of the car, and
locked the doors. She entered the house, whose door she found to
be left unlocked when she tried the handle, *don't ask why the door
is unlocked, do not ask why you have the strange feeling that you should
have rung the doorbell before entering your own home.* She put down her
purse. She would head to the bedroom to reveal the mystery inside
the Conrad's box. She would try on the dress that had probably never
been touched by human hands, that had probably been stitched by
robotic seamsters in a factory in Detroit. She would slip on the dress
that had come in contact with no other skin but her own, and she
would look into the bedroom mirror, *what are you doing, Rebecca, do
not go into the bedroom,* she would look into the full-length bedroom
mirror, and the version of herself that was built out of data would
stare back at her from the other side of the glass, imaginary, perfect,
and true.

Music was playing in the house at a low volume. It was coming
from the television: some video that looked as if it had been shot in
the nineties, with a row of women in cheerleader-ish outfits engaged
in a dance that seemed to be derived from calisthenics. The music
was half rap, half R-and-B warbling, the kind of stuff Rebecca knew
drove Philip up the wall, with his preference for the raspy voices and
oddball time signatures of seventies prog-rock. "I like the way you
work it," a crooner in dark sunglasses sang as he sinuously threaded
his way through a crowded bar, the patrons around him dancing in
slow motion. "No diggity: I got to bag it up."

Rebecca slowly made her way down the hall to the bedroom, from which she heard, or chose not to hear quite yet, sounds of exertion and delight. She left the loops of R and B behind her, the calling card of an intruder, *do not think about the music, do not think about the noises coming from the bedroom, you still have a few seconds of ignorance remaining to you, treasure each and every one.*

She entered the bedroom. The sheets of the bed within had been thrown back, and lay piled on the floor. On the mattress was an unexpected monster, singing to itself with two mouths. This is the last moment of contentment untainted by sorrow, when the brain hesitates before delivering the message to the heart that it knows it must. The topologically bizarre horror that Rebecca saw at first was preferable to the truth she knew was coming, and she felt a surprising regret as the image before her resolved itself: not beastly, but human; not one being, but two. One was Philip, lying on his back, his feet pointed toward her, his legs unceremoniously tangled in his boxer shorts; the other, sitting astride him and facing Rebecca, rocking back and forth, was Alicia Merrill. "Because maybe I don't want to see your face," Alicia was saying to Rebecca's husband. "Because maybe I don't want you to see my face. We don't have to be so lovey-dovey all the time."

Then Alicia focused on Rebecca, and before Rebecca could quite parse what was going on, Alicia leapt off the bed, off of her husband (and Philip lifted his head and looked at the two women in dazed confusion as his stupid cock sprang and twitched), retrieved a copy of *Marie Claire* from the nearby nightstand, rolled it up, ran over to Rebecca, and began fiercely beating her about the head and shoulders with it, still unembarrassedly bare-ass naked. "Don't you have any *decency?*" Alicia yelled at Rebecca. "Do you just barge in on people while they're screwing? Are you out of your mind?" Rebecca dropped the box from Conrad's and held her forearms in front of her face to shield herself from the blows of the magazine. "I'm *sorry?*" she said, more of a question than a comment, not quite sure what the proper response was here, strangely detached from it all. "You need to get out of here!" Alicia shouted. "You'd better get out of this room right now." Which sounded, right then, like a good idea, a way to move forward, a way for Rebecca to give herself a chance to try to make sense of things. "Oh, okay, I'm sorry," Rebecca said again, the payload of bad news not yet fully delivered—it would be a few seconds more until she thought to herself *my husband has been cheating on me with Alicia Merrill*—and for now an apology seemed to be the best way to bring an end to all this noisy surprise. She bent to pick up the Conrad's box as the tiny woman delivered a quick backhanded *thwack* with the magazine to the top of her head; then she quickly retreated, closing the bedroom door, and drifted back down the hall as she heard Alicia saying, "You'd better talk to her. You'd better sit her down and talk to her." "Okay, okay, I'm sorry, okay," she heard Philip say: at least he felt the need to apologize, too.

My husband has been cheating on me with Alicia Merrill, Rebecca thought.

She walked through the living room and into the kitchen (on the television was some other old R-and-B tune about the fun of a house party on a Friday night, with more of that aerobic dancing, performed by men in leather vests and baggy black pants. The tune's refrain repeatedly announced that "this is how we do it!"). Sean was not in the living room when she passed through; he was not hiding behind the couch, peeking over the back of it in abject terror. Rebecca went into the kitchen, sat down at the table there, placed the box with the dress in front of her, clasped her hands in her lap, and waited, with patience, for the crying to start.

■

Later—how much later? Hard to tell. In times of tragedy clocks will trick you—Philip stood in the kitchen doorway. "I'm going to the lab," he said to Rebecca.

Rebecca said nothing.

"I packed a suitcase," he said. "After I check in at the lab, I'm going to a hotel or something."

Rebecca looked at Philip, and then looked down at the table.

"I'll have my laptop, and my phone. If you want to call me or e-mail me, you can. I'll get right back to you."

Rebecca said nothing.

"Or I can call you, or e-mail you, if you want," Philip said. "I'm not sure if I should call you, or if you should call me, if you want to talk. I kind of don't know what to do here."

Rebecca closed her eyes and put her head down on the table.

Philip stepped into the kitchen. "I don't understand this," he said. "I don't know why it . . . I don't know how it could be true that I . . . that I love you and that . . . this other thing could also be true. Both of these things are true. It doesn't make sense."

Philip took another step into the kitchen.

"It's hard to have an intellectual connection with someone else that's that intense," he said. "When you have this really powerful idea in your head that's almost fully formed and about to come into the world, and there is one other person that shares it with you, then that intellectual relationship . . . it can express itself in ways that I guess don't make a lot of sense to everyone.

"It's not so much about . . . I mean, it means a lot to a person, to feel understood."

Rebecca lifted her head and looked at Philip. Then she squeezed her eyes shut and put her head back down.

"I didn't tell you about what was happening," Philip said. "Because I didn't think it was something you wanted to know."

Rebecca kept her head on the table.

"I'm going to the lab," Philip said. "I have some routines running that I need to check. I need to check on the routines."

The shivers of Rebecca's back were barely visible: one might have thought she had fallen asleep.

Philip withdrew from the kitchen. Some time later, Rebecca heard the front door shut, and she knew then that she was alone.

■

She was really tired. She wanted to sleep for a while, but she didn't want to sleep in the bedroom, did not want to imagine herself dumping the dirty sheets in the laundry bin and replacing them with new ones, did not want to put herself through any further ignominy. She decided to sleep on the couch, in the living room.

So she went into the living room and stretched out on the couch, but she couldn't sleep a wink—all she could do was stare at the ceiling while nasty thoughts marched around in her head on parade. So she got up and went back into the kitchen, and Philip was sitting at the kitchen table, wearing jeans and a wrinkled polo shirt and sporting a day's growth of beard. Rebecca sat down across the table from Philip.

Philip had a bottle of Jim Beam in front of him and a shot glass. He upended the bottle and poured whiskey into the glass, carelessly sloshing the liquid over its edges, and drained the whole thing in one long gulp. "You have to admit," he said, slamming the glass down and refilling it, "that she's perfect. Smart as a whip, and that gorgeous face, and that knockout tight little body. Whereas you: yeah, okay, sure, you're alright, but you're not the same. Not so brainy; not so self-confident; not so toned and young. Hold it."

Philip opened his mouth as if to yawn, as wide as it could go, and in the darkness behind his tonsils Rebecca could have sworn she saw the reflections off two little eyes, a matched pair of tiny glinting lights.

"Hate can build up in any marriage," Philip said after he closed his mouth. "Left unexpressed it takes physical form. Left unspoken it must be vomited up. My aunt and uncle were married for seventy-six years. They died within weeks of each other. Their coroners found families of field mice nesting in their stomachs. Hold it." He opened his mouth again, so wide that Rebecca feared he might unhinge his jaw, and out of it sprang four garter snakes, striped black and gold and coated with phlegm and blood, their eyes pale blue, with the lids and lashes of a human's. They fell to the table where they thrashed around in wild confusion; then, in unison, they fell into a parallel formation, zipped off the table, and slithered across the kitchen floor where they disappeared beneath the oven.

"Oh geez I feel *so* much better now," Philip said, wiping his mouth with the back of his hand. "Rebecca, honey, you have to do this. You have to give this a try. Just close your eyes, and find the thing inside that's poisoning you, and let it out. And it'll be like it was when we first met. All those shining possible futures will be ahead of us once again. Hold on a second." A large, translucent, nine-legged spider the size of a tennis ball launched itself out of his throat, its belly rupturing as it splattered against the table, spilling forth a hundred baby spiders that refracted the kitchen's fluorescent light like little glass beads. "See?" Philip said, swigging back another shot of bourbon as the tiny insects scurried mindlessly over the tabletop, their dead mother's body going limp like a deflating balloon. "Give it a try, Rebecca! You can do it!"

Philip stretched his hand across the table to grasp Rebecca's, and she took it and closed her eyes, feeling the faint tickle of dozens of little spiders swarming across her forearm. She concentrated, and felt the wordless hate that she'd been too polite to express given shape, felt what seemed like some sort of centipede-like thing choking her, felt its myriad legs scrabbling for purchase on the inside of her throat as it climbed. "That's it!" Philip said enthusiastically. "Attagirl! Keep it up!" Rebecca opened her mouth, hung her head, and gagged a little as the whatever-it-was thrashed its way past her tongue to drop to the tabletop. Then she opened her eyes to see what had come out of her.

It was, in fact, a centipede, a large one, but the thing was . . . well, it was kind of cute. It looked like a five-year-old's drawing of a centipede: it was made up of a dozen spherical pea-green segments and its eyes were ovoid and iris-less like Little Orphan Annie's, and each of its tiny little feet was clad in a tiny little Chuck Taylor sneaker. "Hey guys!" it said, looking up eagerly at Rebecca and Philip, its smile a perfect half circle. "I'm Charlie the Centipede! Whatcha guys up to?" "Rebecca, you've never been able to do anything right," said Philip as he snatched his hand away, and then she woke up on the couch, and it was morning.

■

She sat up and looked around her. It didn't seem like Philip had snuck back into the house while she slept: everything looked the same except for the change in the light.

She took a moment to clear her head. It was hard to know what to do. It was hard to know what direction to take when you suddenly found yourself in a future different from the one you'd expected to be in the day before. The first thing, Rebecca decided, would be to do some little kind thing for herself, to remind herself that she was a good person, that she was someone who merited kindness. Still in her clothes from yesterday, she stood, deciding that this was what she needed, a single indulgence, to begin the day, to get her in the state of mind where she'd be able to figure out what to do next.

Scallops and bacon for breakfast. Yes. The meal of kings and champions, served at an illicit time of the day. There were still some scallops in the freezer left over from the party she'd thrown for

Philip and his colleagues a few months back. And bacon was always around! She went back into the kitchen, which was good because it did not involve going back into the bedroom, the place of her humiliation, she had actually apologized to her, the word "sorry" had just come out of her mouth like that was the right thing to say, while the woman was hitting her with a magazine. She went back into the kitchen. The plastic-sealed box from Conrad's was still there on the table. She pulled the bag of scallops out of the freezer, dumped them into a large glass mixing bowl, filled the bowl with water, and put it in the microwave to defrost. She would prepare the scallops and bacon carefully, ritualistically, to give her mind and her hands something to do. She retrieved the bowl from the microwave, fished each scallop out of the bowl, wrapped it in a paper towel and patted it dry, and placed it on a plate. She got a box of wooden toothpicks out of a drawer next to the oven; there was not a garter snake waiting in the drawer to wind itself around her wrist. She got a package of bacon out of the fridge. Each strip of bacon wrapped around a scallop and speared with a toothpick, two, three, a dozen, she would eat a dozen slices of bacon this morning, Alicia Merrill had probably never eaten bacon in her life, oooh if I eat this greasy fatty bacon it'll mess up my marathon running times, poor, pitiful thing. Place the tray of a dozen scallops into the oven, each one nested in its own comfy pork blanket, and broil them for fifteen minutes, during which you are forced to be with your own thoughts, to recount the sighting of the beast, the unforced apology, the humiliation. The bacon smells good now. Put on an oven mitt and pull out the tray, the scallops sizzling in a pool of their own grease. No need for a plate: she is alone now, and there is no one to judge her manners. Pick a scallop up by the toothpick and plop the morsel into your mouth, devouring it in a single bite, yes, delicious, this is good. Another, another. She should be logging on for her shift at Lovability soon, but today the lovelorn can look out for their own damned selves. Another, another, another. Rebecca is eating scallops and bacon, the best meal on God's green earth. She is not drinking a bottle of Killian's Irish Red; she is not nursing a glass of sparkling white wine; she is not chasing each scallop with a swallow of single-malt scotch; she is not chugging a bottle of mouthwash; she is not grabbing a handle of cheap rum and getting good and fucked up—

■

"Kate?"

"Rebecca! You sound awful."

"Sorry to call you at work." Sorry, sorry, sorry: all apologies.

"No no no! Don't be. What's up?"

"It's . . . I."

". . . Becca! What's going on?"

"I mean . . . I guess Philip and I broke up. Or that's not the right word. Because we're married. But I don't know. I came home early and I walked in on him."

"Becca. Start over, okay? What do you mean you walked in on him? Doing what?"

"I went shopping yesterday. And I came home before I was supposed to. And he wasn't supposed to be there and he was there, and there was another woman there. It was that post-doc. It was Alicia. And I walked into the bedroom and."

"Oh my. Oh m—ohhh Rebecca."

"And they were."

"Rebecca."

"I don't know where he is."

"I'm so sorry."

"I don't want to be alone right now."

"I'll come right over. I just need to take care of one thing and I'll be right there."

"Kate?"

"What?"

"I really need a drink right now."

Please don't say what I want you to say.

"Definitely," said Kate. "The bars open at eleven thirty. And it's five o'clock somewhere."

■

They met just before noon in a bar attached to a hotel in the heart of downtown Stratton, sure that there they'd have some peace and quiet. They sat across from each other in a darkened booth, the only two people in the place except for the bartender. Kate bought the first round, an ultra-hoppy craft beer served in a brandy snifter.

When Rebecca took the first sip, after two years without a drink, she expected it to taste bitter, flavored with failure, and giving up, and the admission of her own weakness in the face of adversity. But— and for a short moment between the first and the second drink, she thought this was even worse—it tasted *good*. That first swig after a couple of years away from the bottle: there's nothing like it, the way it tingles on your tongue, the way it promises a loosening of your limbs and a lifting of your cares. Between the second sip and the third— that third was more of a gulp, really—she knew that calling Kate instead of, say, her father, had been the right decision. Her father would have dropped what he was doing just like Kate, and given that he'd had his reservations about Philip that it had taken him years to stifle, he would have been more than empathetic. But all of his consolations would have been laced with his peculiar, skeptical, cynical brand of Christianity, his reminders that we see the world as through a glass, darkly, that our journey through this world takes us through a vale of tears, full of sorrow and doubt and confusion. Sometimes you didn't want to hear all that shit.

And he wouldn't have offered her a drink. Though her parents had never openly mentioned the fact that Rebecca had quit drinking, and she'd never discussed it with anyone else but Philip, and then only briefly and painfully, Woody couldn't have failed to notice. In the past couple of years he'd seen her push away the wine list at a restaurant too many times to think it was just a whim. So if she called him up at ten thirty in the morning, saying that she'd found out in the worst way that her husband was cheating on her and she could really go for a daddy-daughter libation, he would have picked her up and brought her home and poured them both a glass of orange juice, and kept an eye on her until the urge for a drink had passed. She didn't really want to deal with that do-gooder good-for-you stuff right this second, either.

No circle of friends was complete without a guiltless enabler, and Kate, dear Kate, had always been that for Rebecca. If you wanted to cut loose, or if you wanted a shoulder to cry on, or both at the same time, she'd be there for you. Maybe she had her flaws, but her heart was in the right place, and you always knew that if you really wanted to get away from yourself, if you really wanted to throw down, then Kate would grant you permission. She'd do it without judging you, and she'd keep you company for as long as you needed. That kind of friendship was rare, and priceless.

Kate brought the second round before Rebecca finished her first glass. "I took the rest of the day off," she said. "You and I are going to get trashed. And don't even think about opening your wallet today. Don't even touch it. I wish this had been on a better occasion, but it's been too long since we got ripped together. Years. *Years!* Drink up, buttercup. Drink and we'll talk it out."

■

Kate and Rebecca hung out in secluded corners of Stratton bars for the rest of the day, maintaining a decent buzz, in undeclared communion with all those whose lives had made it possible, through good fortune or ill, to have the time and the desire for a beer or two in a bar on a weekday afternoon. Rebecca did most of the talking, and Kate listened. That was another good thing about Kate: she was a good listener. She kept the drinks flowing at good intervals, making sure the two of them stayed tipsy but not quite smashed.

In the late afternoon, when they were both on their fifth beer, Rebecca said, "The hell of the thing is, the worst thing is, what he said was, 'Oh, yeah, I didn't tell you because I didn't think you wanted to know.' I mean what is that. Because when you think about it, it's obvious, it's *obvious*, that *everybody* knew, and nobody said a goddamn thing. When the four of us were having dinner, you and me and Philip and Carson, Carson knew. And he didn't say a thing. When that whole bunch of physicists came over to watch that thing on TV, *including Alicia*, all of them knew. Every single one. And none of them said a word: they just kept their mouths shut and let me serve them tortilla chips and beer. I'm so embarrassed."

"Well, you can't blame them for not speaking up," Kate said. "It's not like they were, you know, *colluding*. Not like they'd gotten together to decide to keep you in the dark. Each of them probably just decided it wasn't their business—"

"Bunch of fucking bystanders—"

"—and Philip was their boss? You're not going to just stroll up to the boss's wife and tell her that—"

"Did you know?"

Kate paused. "Did I what?"

"Did you know. Because you were seeing Carson while this was going on. And *he* knew. He had to know, it was obvious to everyone, if you didn't have blinders on like I did, it was plain as the nose on your face. Did he tell you? After a couple of drinks or something? Pillow talk? Did he tell you and did you not tell me, Kate? Because—"

"Rebecca! I—"

"Because it was something *you* didn't think I wanted to know? Because—"

"Rebecca. Rebecca." Kate gently took Rebecca's hand off the glass of Brooklyn Lager she was holding and clasped it in her own. "We're best friends, since like forever. You know I wouldn't do that to you. If I'd heard anything like that was going on, I would have been on the phone to you like *that*. You have to believe that."

Not meeting Kate's gaze, Rebecca nodded. She tried to pull her hand away, but Kate tightened her hold and wouldn't let go. "Becca. Look at me."

Rebecca looked up at Kate, tears brimming on the edges of her eyelids.

"Do you believe me?" Kate said.

Rebecca tried to pull her hand back again. Kate gripped it harder still.

"You really believe me, right?" Kate said.

"I believe you," said Rebecca.

"Okay," said Kate, letting her go.

■

Around dinnertime Kate and Rebecca climbed into Kate's self-driving car, and Kate commanded with mock hauteur, "Jeeves! Take us somewhere extra fancy!" The car obediently conveyed them to a steakhouse in Cranbury that had once been the main-street residence of a twentieth-century local bigwig, and the two women ordered up a pair of rib eyes drenched in peppercorn sauce, along with a couple of Grimbergen Blondes. Rebecca, who hadn't exactly been eating right today, only got halfway through hers; Kate polished hers off easily and used the fries on the side to sop up the rest of the sauce.

Kate did all the talking during dinner, and this was another good thing about her: she knew that shriving and catharsis involved letting you be silent for a while, and not just spilling your guts without

end. She was circumspect, too, even as she became more garrulous
and the mischievous college girl who still lived inside her after close
to twenty years came to the surface. Usually when Kate got like this
she wanted to talk, ad nauseam, about "boys," said "boys" being more
likely to have bum knees or developing bald spots than they used to.
(And Rebecca was sure she was seeing a new guy, post-Carson: given
her skills with online dating, and the fact that she was rarely without a boyfriend, it would have been weird if she wasn't.) But in these
circumstances, chatter about the petty dramas of budding romances
would have been highly inappropriate. And so Kate filled the air
with discussions about the comical things that had happened at her
job, and movies she'd seen, and anecdotes about her teenage years.
When the check came, Kate smacked Rebecca's hand away from it
and slipped her credit card inside the folder. "Whaddaya wanna do
next?" she said.

"I don't know," Rebecca said, trying to respond in kind, letting
herself be taken along for the ride, not yet really wanting to go back
to her house. "What do you want to do?"

"I have an awesome idea. I know an awesome place we can go.
Because it's night, and the stars are out. Let's go look at the stars."

■

They picked up a couple of bottles of cheap wine from a liquor store
on Route 1. Then, as they both sat in the backseat, Kate's car drove
them to a golf course in Princeton Junction, which they snuck onto:
granted there was not much sneaking required, since it was well past
ten o'clock at this point and the place was deserted, but there was a
sign forbidding entry after dusk that the two of them walked past,
and that made them feel naughty enough.

They plopped down on the closely shorn green of the fourth
hole, screwed off the caps of their wine bottles, and took long pulls
straight from the neck. ("This is so *ghetto*," Kate said.) This far out
from nearby towns, the view of the sky was relatively free of light
pollution, and the stars above seemed as if they'd been strewn reck-
lessly across the sky in handfuls, solely so that they could shine down
on the gently sloping hills and valleys of this perfectly manicured,
mathematically dictated landscape.

"I don't want to leave here," Rebecca said, after they had each drunk about a third of their bottles in companionable quiet. "I don't want to have to go back to the house, and figure out what to do next. I just want to stop time and stay here, right now, looking at the stars and drinking with a good friend. You know?"

"Yeah. Except for the whole thing with your husband cheating on you, this moment right now is pretty much perfect."

"Yeah," Rebecca said quietly.

They watched the blinking red light of a night flight out of the Newark airport as it cut across the sky.

"You know this isn't really about him and whatsername, don't you?" said Kate.

"What do you mean?"

"I mean that when he was making his excuses to you, sure, he was being an asshole, but he wasn't *wrong*. And sure, it's more than luck that he didn't happen to have this fantastically profound intellectual connection with some hairy beary dude too fat to see his own dick when he looks down. But it's not about her with him. It's about the *machine*. Not to be crass, you know that crassness is unlike me, but if he could have fucked it instead, he would have. Now laugh."

Rebecca obeyed, with not as much guilt as she would have liked to feel.

"But I'm serious. What he was saying sounded cruel to you, but in his own head he was just telling the truth. That's why he didn't ask for forgiveness or anything like that. I'm not saying it isn't messed up; I'm just saying he was just telling you how it is."

"It doesn't make me feel much better to think he was cheating on me with a woman as a proxy for cheating on me with . . ." She trailed off into silence.

"With a fucking *broken time machine*," Kate shouted, her voice carrying across the darkened fairway. "Come on, we're drunk, he's not around, we can call it a ridiculous busted not-working time machine instead of a causality whosywhatsitz, and he'll never know. I'm not saying I told you so, I'm honestly really not, but fact is, he's been thinking about this thing day in, day out for how long, years now, and he's too full of himself to know when he's failed, so every time someone tries to tell him he has it just makes him double down. And it's obsessed him and it's totally taken over his life."

"Kate, what are you getting at?"

"I'm saying that what you need is *closure*. You're not going to be comfortable going back to your house, and maybe changing the locks and lawyering up, until you get a little bit of closure. And he hasn't called you—has he?"

Rebecca checked her phone. "No."

"So unless you want to call him, which I say hell no to that, you can't get closure from him. But it doesn't matter. And you can't get closure from that other chick: I guess you could get yourself a cross-bow and hunt her down, but that'd just be stupid. But that doesn't matter, either.

"Because in order to be satisfied and put a final period on this whole thing, you don't need to face him down, and you don't need to face her down. You need to face down the machine."

■

"Look," said Kate, "here's the thing. It doesn't matter if that thing is the love of his life. It's a *failure*. And you're *not* a failure. You're a *sur-vivor*. I mean, that car accident you were in? Something that would've made hash out of a lot of people just made you *stronger*. You're stronger than that thing. It doesn't matter what he thinks: that thing is a bunch of junk. And you're not going to be able to shake this—you won't stop asking yourself if this whole thing is somehow your fault, because you didn't measure up—until you really realize that, in your bones. That this didn't happen because you were imperfect enough to drive him to find someone better, but because he threw his life away on a mistake.

"So here's what we're going to do, right now. We're going to hang out here and drink a little more of this wine. Then Jeeves is going to take us over to that lab. You're going to go in, and you're going to size up that machine and look it right in the eye. Then you'll have your closure. Because you'll know, you'll *remember*, that you're stronger than it."

"Kate, that's crazy!"

"If by crazy you mean *awesome*, then yes. Listen. That one time I went to the lab, I saw it. I saw this pile of wires and metal that doesn't even do anything, and Philip had run such a game on these guys working on it that they were treating this piece of junk like it was a holy relic, and acting like they were the priests in charge of it. Oooh, it's such a big deal: building a time machine is so hard, you wouldn't understand. You know what whatsername said when I took even one step toward it? 'Physicists touch. Tourists look.' Well, la-de-fucking-da.

"Listen. How great would it be if Philip comes back to the lab, and he goes into his time machine chamber, and he sees scrawled on the inside, 'REBECCA WAS HERE.' I'm telling you, he'd feel just like you did when you found him in bed with whositz. He'd feel even worse."

"That sounds like the kind of behavior that would land me in a lot of trouble down the line, and I'm not really seeing what this gets me—"

"Come on come on come on. Look: it'll be easy. You've got a card that'll let you in the lab, right? That's what Carson told me: spouses of people in the lab get cards. So we don't have to pull any secret agent stuff."

"I have one in my wallet somewhere, I guess, but I've used it like twice."

"Well, now will be the third time. Here's how we'll play it. You and I will go in together, and I'll create a diversion. I'll just hang out by the security desk while you go in. There's a guard there who was totally looking me up and down the last time I went in there: if we're lucky he'll be on shift again."

"And what am I supposed to do in the meantime? Sabotage?"

"No no no! You let yourself in the lab—you're going to get something, or something like that; we'll figure it out on the way—and you go up to the machine, and you see that it's not such a big deal, that you're bigger than it is. You don't even have to leave evidence or anything: let's forget about the whole graffiti thing. You just have to give it the finger and I guarantee you, you will feel so much better. *So* much better."

"There might be other people there," Rebecca said, feeling her hold on this situation slip away. "Philip might be there. Alicia might be there."

"It's after midnight. There's not going to be anybody there! Come on."

"Physicists work weird hours, you know."

"Well we'll just swing by the place and if we see too many cars in the parking lot then we'll call it off. Easy. Come on. I'm ready. Take another swig of liquid courage and let's go. Let's go!"

■

"Terence. Hey Terence. Put down that book."

Terence closed the book. "What."

"Look," said Spivey. "Someone's here."

Terence turned to see the two women through the glass doors of the building's entrance; the taller one of the two had pulled a wallet out of her purse and was fumbling through it. "Do they look a little drunk to you?"

"*Yes*," said Spivey, as the woman picked a keycard out of her wallet and waved it in front of the door's reader. With a heavy, hydraulic sigh, the door swung open.

"I don't recognize them right off the bat."

"One is that girl who showed up with my man Carlton a while back. The other: I don't know."

"Well, she's got a card to the lab, whoever she is," said Terence. "Shh-shh-shh."

The two women approached the security desk, and it did seem to Terence as if they were on the tail end of a long, *long* night on the town, one that by all appearances must have started that afternoon. "Hey, guys," the shorter one of the two said, and yeah, that was definitely the lady who'd come in with Carson to get the tour of the lab. "It's nice to *see* you again," she said, making eyes at *Spivey* of all people, but damned if Spivey's face didn't light up like he was a kid finding a PlayStation 5 under the tree on Christmas morning.

"This is Rebecca," said the woman—Kathryn? Katie? No: Kate. "Philip Steiner's wife."

Rebecca, the other one, was doing that thing drunk people do when they're trying to sell themselves as sober to someone with a badge: standing up super straight, talking like she was on the radio. "Philip is under the weather," she said, "and I am coming in to check on something in his absence. I'm reading the causality violation accuracy index. It'll just take a couple of minutes." She brandished the keycard before her.

Something about this was a little off. Spivey, who was closer, plucked the card from Rebecca's hand and squinted at it; then he ran it through the scanner at his desk. It came up legit: sure, it was an old card, and she'd only been in twice, and for some reason the data encoded in the card's magnetic strip identified her as Rebecca Steiner instead of Rebecca Wright, as was written on the card's face. But everything else checked out: no red alerts or anything.

"So you're checking the causality violation index?" Spivey said, still holding the card.

"The causality violation *accuracy* index," Rebecca said. "Philip wrote down the instructions for me, for how to do it." She patted her purse. "I'll be in and out in five minutes." She held out her hand peremptorily: *now give it back.*

What else to do? At the end of the day she was still the boss's wife. "Don't get up to too much trouble in there," Spivey said with a wariness that he passed off as a joke, handing back the card. "And *her*," he continued, pointing at Kate, "she's got no clearance, and you aren't authorized to bring in anyone else with you, so she'll have to stay here and wait for you. I told you we didn't want to see you around here anymore," he said, his voice suddenly shifting to that of a man who'd only consider a freshly picked carnation for the buttonhole of his jacket.

"Oh, I don't mind," Kate said. "I'll be happy keeping company with you guys. You'll be alright, Rebecca?"

"Sure, Kate," Rebecca said, heading toward the doors to the lab. "Back in a few."

Rebecca disappeared down the hallway beyond, leaving Kate alone with the two guards.

Spivey pulled his chair closer to Kate, looking up at her conspiratorially. "You saw what they were building in there, didn't you?"

"Yeah, I saw it," Kate said. "Ridiculous, the things people spend their time and money on."

"Maybe, maybe not," Spivey said. "But one thing's for certain: they haven't gotten it to work yet, and they won't unless they figure out how time travel works. They don't know." Spivey tapped his forehead with an index finger. "But *I* know. I sat here, watching these people go in and out, listening to what they say to each other, and I figured it out."

"No *way!*" Kate cooed.

"Do you wanna hear how time travel works? I'll warn you: it's gonna blow your mind. I haven't even told any of the geniuses working on that thing yet, because I don't think they're ready to handle it. But are *you* ready?"

"Sure!"

"Okay. Then listen."

■

Were those guys at the desk watching Rebecca through some sort of camera mounted on the ceiling? It was hard to say, but Rebecca figured it would be a good idea to leave the lights in the lab down just in case—the streetlamps that illuminated the parking lot outside were bright enough to let her see, once her eyes adjusted. Just in case they were keeping an eye on her, she turned on one desk lamp next to a computer and hit a keyboard's space bar to wake up a monitor, feeling all spy-like.

The central cylindrical chamber of the causality violation device rose above Rebecca. But the hair on her arms did not stand on end; she did not experience any strange instances of déjà vu; she did not see the ghosts of future selves shimmering before her, shouting stock picks back through time.

It should have all been better; it should have all been great. She thought back to the first time she had entered this room eight years ago, at the establishment of Point Zero. There had been so much promise in the air then. Her husband had been ambitious, and she'd been certain that ambition would pay off; she'd held a child in her arms that she was sure would grow into someone wonderful. Not everyone had believed in Philip at the time, but back then, that didn't matter. She could see the brightly lit path that led to the best of all imaginable outcomes, not thinking about the infinity of dimly lit byways that led to futures full of mediocrity or, worse, catastrophe.

She stood before the dead column of metal in the darkness, and she realized, perhaps too late, that the reason people so often condemn reckless ambition is out of a sense of self-preservation.

Ambitious people who fail at their great endeavors destroy not just themselves, but those unwise enough to love them. The ambitious failure either becomes a shell of what he once was, having fallen victim to the peculiar and powerful brand of self-doubt known only to those whose slightly too-long reach had exceeded their not-quite-long-enough grasp; or, as Philip had, he retreats into himself and constructs a personal version of history in which, despite mounting evidence to the contrary, he is the one who is headed toward success, while all others who disagree with him will eventually fail. If you chose to love a person like that, it meant accepting, and believing in, their causes and their dreams; if those dreams caused the world to break them, then the world would break you as well.

Rebecca approached the causality violation chamber (too grand a name for such a faulty thing), placed her hand against its door, and closed her eyes, much as Philip had during its christening, years ago. There was no response from the machine; no prophecy; no apology; no advice. It did not relay the news from other, brighter timelines. It did not tell her what would have transpired had she returned from yesterday's shopping trip a few hours later, or had she turned the steering wheel left instead of right two years ago, or had she not taken that first drink, or had she turned down any one of the thousands of drinks that had followed, or had she chosen not to respond to Philip's insistent and perhaps deliberately oblivious messages during the early days of their online courtship, or had her parents or her grandparents or her great-grandparents never met. The machine's obstinate silence was all it had to offer; the message of that silence was that she had made her choices in life, and her choices had made her in return.

Even with her head full of boozy fog and the depression of the past thirty-six hours weighing her down, she was glad, in the end, that Kate had suggested she come in here, though not for the reason that Kate suggested. Sure, she could flip the bird to the machine, or deface it, or whisper obscenities to it, but those would be empty gestures, signs of a futile attempt to struggle against fate. And she was so tired, too tired for that, and the right symbolic action to take at this moment was completely plain to see.

She slid her hand across the touchscreen next to the chamber's entrance, and the door swung open (the chamber's interior some-how blacker than black, a trick of the lab's dim light). She stepped inside, and the door shut behind her, and she sank to the floor, and she interred herself, for a short time, in her husband's dark monument to his own grand failure.

PART II

THE SHADOW
BROUGHT BACKWARD

19

LATE RETURN

When thinking back on it later, Rebecca wouldn't be able to recall exactly how long she had spent in the causality violation chamber. It had to have been . . . not even a minute. Less than that. She clearly remembered thinking that she could feel the darkness inside clinging to her hair, and her skin, and the surfaces of her eyeballs. She wanted to leave as soon as she entered. She couldn't have been in there for more than thirty seconds.

But she felt a lot better after she left, as if a great weight had been lifted off her. Her decision to enter the chamber had only been a symbolic gesture, but history showed that gestures actually mattered to people. Whether or not it was because of some kind of placebo effect, the fact was that she'd gone into the lab feeling like a wad of chewed-up gum stuck to the sole of the world's shoe—dirty, used, and stretched—and just the act of entering the machine that Philip had built had made that dark mood disappear. She didn't exactly feel like a princess or a heavyweight champ, but her spirit was lighter, as if she'd shed a dead skin while huddling in the chamber's darker-than-darkness: in fact, it was the first time in a while that she'd felt anything even close to optimism.

The chamber's door shut behind her as she climbed out. She quietly made her way out of the lab, turning off the desk lamp she'd turned on when she entered, and putting the computer she'd fiddled with back to sleep.

Kathryn was still waiting at the security desk when Rebecca exited the lab. It looked like she'd gotten into some kind of debate with one of the security guards. "But that's not how it'd work at *all*; that *can't* be how it'd work," Kathryn was saying, while the guard repeatedly spoke over her: "I'm telling you. I'm *telling* you."

"What are you two having it out about?" Rebecca asked, approaching the security desk.

"I'm trying to explain to this woman how time travel works," the guard said, "but she doesn't want to hear it! She is having trouble coping with the truth."

"Because it's *not* the truth: that's not how it would work! If I went back in time, I'd still be *me*, because I would have my experiences and my memories and *that's* what makes you what you are: not history. And I'd use what I learned from my experiences and my memories to make things better for people: I wouldn't become a *worse* person, or a *dumber* person, or an *animal*, just because I went back in time."

"Oh, sure, that's what *all* the badass big-timing wannabe time travelers say, everybody who thinks going back in time is such a *great* idea. You read a couple of books in school and now you're the queen of history: leave it to you, you'll make everything better for everybody."

"Well, thinking that way is better than thinking that everyone who jumps into a time machine turns into an ape or an asshole!"

"Not that you asked me, but the way I see it from over here," said the other guard, who was leaning backward in his chair with its back propped against the wall, "is that both of you know roughly the same amount about time travel, which is nothing. You're *both* just speculating."

"I'm telling you I'm right," the first guard said sulkily, looking away from them both.

"Hey," said Rebecca to Kathryn, "if you guys are through with the stoner arguments, can we go?"

■

Terence waited until the two women left and then asked Spivey, "Look. Don't you think it's weird that Dr. Steiner's wife came in this evening? Doesn't that seem really weird to you?"

"She still had a card, and the card still checked out," Spivey said. "I don't know why she still had the card: it's not my business. But I wasn't about to catch hell by getting mixed up in it. If her card had scanned red, sure, we would've stopped her. But the card scanned green, so my name's Bennett and I ain't in it."

"Well okay. But don't you think we ought to mention it to the boss, just as a CYA, even if it's after the fact?"

Spivey thought about it. "Yeah. We probably ought to."

"All I'm saying," said Terence, "is that we should just flag that entry in the log, so the boss'll see it the next time she checks it, if she ever looks at the thing."

"Yeah," Spivey said. "Just as a CYA."

■

Kathryn and Rebecca got into the backseat of Kathryn's car; she told it to drop Rebecca off at her place first, and then to head home. "How do you feel?" she asked.

"It sounds crazy, but I feel a lot better," Rebecca said. "I mean, we'll see how I feel tomorrow." She laughed a little. "But for now: pretty good. Going in there to see the machine: you were right. It helped."

"I knew it would," Kathryn said.

Their car merged seamlessly onto Route 1, whose traffic at this time of night was mostly made up of autonomous tractor trailers delivering the groceries and fashions that late-night stock boys would place on shelves in time for tomorrow morning's opening. The giant AI-piloted trucks in adjacent lanes towered over Kathryn's tiny vehicle, casting long shadows and shutting out the streetlamps and starlight.

"This was a hell of a day," Kathryn said.

"It surely was."

"We needed this."

"Yeah."

"*You* needed this." Kathryn reached over and patted Rebecca's hand.

"Yeah: I guess I did."

Kathryn slouched in her seat and sighed. "I haven't cut loose like this in years. And it might be the last time for years more. I am going to be hung the hell over tomorrow. I don't bounce back from drinking like I used to."

"Me either," Rebecca said.

Kathryn pulled her phone out of her purse and checked her messages. "And Carson's worried sick. Three messages tonight, while I haven't been paying a bit of attention to this thing. He's probably called the cops by now."

Rebecca looked out the window of the car at the trailer rising above them, its side displaying an enormous stylized drawing of a woman whose body was all short-skirted legs and whose face was all lips and lashes.

"Becca," Kathryn said, reaching out and grasping Rebecca's hand. "Remember what I said. You're a survivor. It's true."

Still looking out the window, Rebecca gave Kathryn's hand a slight, tentative squeeze. "Thanks," she said. "I know."

■

When Kathryn's car pulled up to Rebecca's house, the lights in the living room were on, and Rebecca could see the silhouette of a person moving around behind the drawn curtains.

"You'll get in touch?" Kathryn said as Rebecca unlatched her car door. "Coffee or something in a couple of days?"

"Sounds good." Rebecca got out of the car and hesitated, holding its door half open. "Or what about brunch, maybe? Sunday."

"If we don't sleep in," Kathryn said, in a slightly distant way that implied that she was already planning to sleep in. "Play it by ear?"

"Will do," said Rebecca. She shut the car door and the vehicle pulled away, sharply accelerating as soon as it left the driveway, its engine barely audible.

Rebecca turned to head up the walk to her front door. Her throat felt raw from the day's drinking; she suddenly became aware of how desperately she wanted to sleep. But she felt okay. She knew she'd wake up in the morning and feel better still. Even if it wasn't full of promise, the future before her at least looked manageable.

The front door of her house banged open before she had gotten even halfway up the walk, and out of it ran her strange and beautiful boy, his father's eyes staring out of his mother's face. His babysitter, a nineteen-year-old girl who'd done up her blond hair in a pair of pigtails, followed just behind. She stopped in the doorframe, full of concern; it was then that Rebecca saw the smear of blood on her son's mouth, and knew that this was yet another sitter with whom she wouldn't be doing repeat business.

Rebecca bent as Sean feverishly clasped his arms around her neck. "You're *late*," he accused her. "I thought you were *never* coming back."

"I'm sorry I'm late. But here I am." She felt the warmth of his embrace and buried her nose in the crook of his neck, taking in the slightly sour smell of a child in need of a bath.

"I was supposed to see my boyfriend at ten thirty," the sitter said, still standing in the door. "I was supposed to leave here at nine, and see my boyfriend at ten thirty, and now it's after twelve. Overtime is time and a half."

"You're late," Sean said again.

"I tried to put him to bed at nine," the sitter said, "but—"

"But I told her I wasn't going to sleep until you came back home. I told her that if I bit my tongue hard you'd know about it and you'd come back. You'd *run* back. And now you're here."

"I was always going to come back," Rebecca said tenderly. "I'm just a little late. Biting your tongue didn't help, and you didn't need to do it. Please don't do it again."

"Overtime is time and a half," the babysitter said again, tapping the place on her wrist where a watch would have been in an earlier century. "Three hours: time and a half."

"But you're *here*," Sean said, still believing in his own boundless power to steer the path of the world.

"Yes," Rebecca said, not inclined to argue the point right now when all she wanted to do was pay off the sitter, get out of her clothes, climb into bed, and sleep for days. "Yes, Sean. I'm here."

20

MORNING ROUTINE

Rebecca snapped awake and rolled over to look at the alarm clock, its amber digits glowing in the darkness. Four fifty-five: way too early. It was times like these, when she'd have an hour of lying fruitlessly in bed waiting for the alarm to ring, too tired to move but too alert to drift easily back to sleep, that she'd remember she hadn't had a good solid eight hours' slumber in who knew how long: years, probably. Even a couple of nights ago, when she'd come back from her impromptu trip to the lab, dead on her feet after a marathon of drinking, she'd woken up at four fifteen, been unable to get back to sleep, and drifted through the rest of her day with constant fantasies of feather mattresses.

But who, in these modern times, slept well? If you didn't have a kid waking you at all hours, and you weren't so stressed with life that you were constantly wired from adrenaline, then you were probably drinking a lot—a lot of people drank a lot these days—and alcohol was notorious for screwing with your sleep cycles. But one of the nice things about living in the future was that, even though it was a lot more difficult to separate your work life from your personal life thanks to always-on connections, it was also a lot easier to carve out places in the day for catnaps: half of the people that Rebecca saw in their autonomous cars on the morning commute to Manhattan were asleep, the men in suits and ties with their mouths hanging crudely open or their heads jerking back and forth on their necks as they nodded off, the women serene and still as if they knew they were being watched as they slept, their faces naked as they left their makeup until the last minute, just before their arrival in New York. And at least a few of Rebecca's coworkers used their lunch breaks for sleeping instead of eating: there was a great over-the-counter sleeping pill called Siestalert that sent you right into stage-two sleep, kept you there for a quick twenty-minute snooze, and then woke you up and dosed you with a little caffeine so that you felt bright-eyed when you returned to the office (though Rebecca suspected that it wouldn't be on the market for much longer: the latest moral panic on cable news channels involved teenagers who'd take them in groups and keep each other awake, fighting the effect of the drug. Apparently if you did this, you'd start to trip, having dreamlike hallucinations with the alertness of one who was fully conscious, and these kids were using the drug to participate in some kind of secular analog of a Navajo peyote ceremony. As pharmacological adventures went, it seemed pretty harmless, but this was a country in which you still had to sign a form and show ID to get allergy medicine that actually worked, so regulation was probably due any day now).

And so though the feeling of being truly well rested and alert was but a memory for Rebecca, this wasn't *really* a problem. Not worth cutting down on the booze, anyway. Everyone needs at least one vice to keep them human.

After a half hour of meditation, she heard Sean in the kitchen, precociously self-motivating: he was probably already making his breakfast, and at age nine he could manage the construction and packing of a lunch PB&J, a nutrition bar, and a juice box. Dressing was a little tougher, but once she restricted his wardrobe to clothing that was guaranteed to match no matter what—all solid-colored shirts; all jeans and khakis—that problem solved itself. Still, though, she was awake, and it was always nice to see him off each morning.

She rolled off the bed—even after two years, she slept on what she thought of as her side of the bed, the half of the mattress beneath her sagging with age while the other side stayed firm. She dropped to the floor and knocked out twenty quick push-ups to get the blood flowing: not girly ones that used bent knees for a fulcrum point, but real ones. Then three quick chin-ups on the bar she'd mounted above the bedroom door a year ago. That was the habit—three chin-ups whenever she entered or left the bedroom, a gentle self-imposed toll for sleeping and waking. The results added up. At thirty-eight she had an upper body she was proud of: arms that said she was not to be messed with, rack still perky, taut stomach proudly bearing the faint autographs of post-Sean stretch marks. She took care of herself. It was easy to take care of your body if you worked it into a daily routine, if you had one vice instead of many. After a while, once you got strong, living in your body and using it became a pleasure, rather than a constant struggle. No excuse for getting soft around the edges with age.

She showered and dressed, opting for a charcoal pencil skirt, matching hose, and an off-white blouse. She went into the kitchen shoeless: Sean was sitting at the table with a bowl of Raisin Bran in front of him, a tablet propped up on a stand to his right, and a phone on his left. The phone had an app open that tracked the location of his school bus as it made its way through the neighborhood and gave him an ETA: he had a few minutes yet, which was good, because he was an excruciatingly slow and fastidious eater of cereal. Instead of pouring the milk into the bowl with the Raisin Bran and wolfing it all down, Sean's habit was to pour the milk into its own glass, pour a couple of tablespoons' worth of milk from the glass into the bowl, dig around in the bottom of the bowl until he'd gotten a spoonful that was appropriately moist without being soggy, and place it into his mouth, chewing it slowly, as if the taste of Raisin Bran varied enough to deserve a connoisseur's consideration from mouthful to mouthful. Soggy cereal was the worst, though, and a bad way to end a meal: Rebecca saw the sense of it.

She cracked open an egg into a cast-iron pan and began to whisk it. "Morning, Sean: what's on tap at school today?"

"Part 4-G of the Federal Education Standard," Sean said, his voice oddly businesslike: he was at that age when his language was a mix of childlike expressions he'd invented and adult ones that he'd overheard and appropriated for himself, like a DJ sampling beats. Or maybe this was how teachers actually talked to elementary school students now. "Area of a right triangle; surface area of a cube. That's in the morning. Then we have to study informational texts in the afternoon: we're learning how to figure out the central idea of an argument."

"Sounds like heavy going," Rebecca said. *Especially for a fourth-grader,* she thought, but then again, there was more to know now than there had been when she was in elementary school, and so it made sense that if you were going to condense all that information into twelve school years, you'd learn some things earlier. These days you probably got quantum physics in your sophomore year of high school.

"We have to get by 4-N by the end of the marking period," Sean said, after another thoughtful mouthful of cereal. "I don't see how we're going to do it. A lot of the kids in class are slow." His homework assignment, left until the last minute, was on his tablet, a series of multiple-choice questions that he somehow was answering even as he ate breakfast and talked with his mother, his fingers dancing nimbly across the glass. (It was amazing what he could do with that thing, Rebecca thought: she'd seen him drawing pictures on it, and he was more dexterous with the tablet than Rebecca had ever been with a pencil.)

"Well, if you ever need help with your homework, let me know," Rebecca said.

"I won't need help," said Sean, sounding like his father. His phone chimed. "Bus is coming." He'd timed it so that he finished his cereal at the last possible second, of course.

He grabbed his tablet and phone as Rebecca put on slippers and walked him outside. The bus pulled up as Sean gave her a quick peck on the cheek and ran down the walk to meet it. Rebecca felt the reluctance in the kiss and knew that the boys on the bus were staring at Sean through the windows: that ritual didn't have much life left in it. The driver waved cheerfully at Rebecca. Since the bus was autonomous, her only duties were discipline and waving at parents, and it looked like she handled both of them well enough.

As the bus's door slid shut and it pulled off, Rebecca went back into the house, and in the kitchen she slid the scrambled eggs (slightly overcooked now, and a little rubbery) onto a plate that seemed to have slight remains of egg from a few days ago (the housekeeper would need a gentle talking-to). She poured herself a helping of Pinot Grigio in a goblet, seasoned the eggs heavily with cayenne pepper, and took her breakfast into the living room on a tray to eat it off her lap in front of the TV. The channel she landed on was showing the last hour of a morning news program that began when every sensible person was still in bed. During the first hour or two its demeanor was deadly serious, each bit of news delivered in gravity by newscasters who spoke in dulcet, melodic baritones as they stared straight into the camera, but by the fourth hour the all-business anchormen were switched out with a pair of middle-aged women who reported on events of the day with glasses of wine in plain sight on the desks in front of them. The whole thing was supposed to be relaxed and comical: you could see that the women had kicked off their heels beneath the desk, and they played the whole thing broadly, talking while making grand motions with their hands, giggling at each other's jokes, chiding each other for lack of decorum. But Rebecca figured the whole thing was a performance to get ratings, and that their wine glasses were filled with grape juice or colored water. She guessed that real alcoholics wouldn't act like that: they'd do their drinking before they went on the set, not so much that they got silly in front of the cameras, but just enough to maintain a buzz. The guy who reported financial news at five in the morning was far more likely to be a hardcore drinker than these two.

■

Later, in her autonomous Audi on the way to work, Rebecca checked her messages: one voicemail and one e-mail. The voicemail was from Alicia Merrill, and, well, that was expected, after her mischief of a few nights ago. Her voice played over the car's speakers, curt and officious. "Becca. Alicia. Two things. First, I'd like to come by tonight: there's something we need to talk about. I'm sure you have half an idea what it is, but probably only half. Second. If you don't have any plans for Saturday morning or afternoon, I think you and I should go for a run together on the towpath. The weather ought to be nice that day. I've mapped out a route: ten miles round trip, and we'll end up at a restaurant with staff that won't turn their noses up at us if we come in wearing exercise gear. A relatively light run, but perhaps you'll want to prepare. Send me a text to confirm one or both. See you soon. Bye."

Rebecca reasoned that if Alicia wanted to go running on Saturday, she wasn't as pissed as she could have been, even though, as usual, her social graces on the surface left something to be desired. She quickly texted back Hey A.: yes and yes. Tonight's conversation would be a little awkward (and what did she mean, "probably only half"?), but not too bad, and she had it coming.

The second message had been sent from Lovability late last night: the dossier for the romantic avatar she'd be piloting at . . . oh, great, one o'clock this afternoon, thanks for the heads-up. Too little time to prepare, and she was short of sleep to boot. The demographic profile for "Marcus" scrolled up the car's windshield, along with links to the Wikipedia entries that described his special interests: music by Ella Fitzgerald and Nina Simone; the life of Paul Robeson; books by Barack Obama.

There wasn't much time to bone up, but she checked the Wikipedia entries just in case. As expected, they were useless for her needs: the pages had clearly been curated by pedants more interested in completeness than in synthesis or comprehension, and so while you could find out how many hairs were in one of Fitzgerald's eyebrows, you wouldn't know where to begin if you knew nothing about her and wanted to learn the basics. Best to wing it. She tapped the dashboard's touchscreen and said, "Hey, play me some Ella Fitzgerald. Whatever."

After a couple of seconds of searching, the car cued up some live video on the windshield from . . . 1957, it said. The singer stood in front of a microphone stand in an elegant black dress, an orchestra full of men in tuxedos behind her. Rebecca realized that the music would have once been considered beautiful. But her ears had trouble tracking the melody, as the musicians involved all seemed to be dancing coyly around the notes the song's writer had actually wanted them to play and sing. And Rebecca couldn't remember the last time she'd heard a singing voice that hadn't been processed by auto-tuning, so Fitzgerald's voice, though she guessed it was on pitch, still sounded imperfect, in need of subtle correction. ("Marcus," she thought, would not think that way. She'd have to remember that.) The lyrics, which scrolled up the windshield beside the video, were slightly disquieting, full of contradiction and regret, all out of sync with the gentle mood of the song itself. She didn't quite get it. She'd have to stick to just mentioning Ella during the conversation like she was on a first-name basis with her, nodding knowingly: odds were against her getting called out.

Rebecca yawned widely: her sleep deprivation was catching up with her, and she was being soothed into slumber by Ella's singing and the gentle hum of her car's motor. "Need I say that my love's misspent?" Ella asked, and that, Rebecca understood. "Hell, *some-*

one's got to say it," Rebecca replied to the empty car as she reclined in her seat. After another verse Rebecca dropped off, as Ella continued to sing to her and her automobile joined the throng of bumper-to-bumper vehicles moving at a steady seventy-five miles an hour, down the asphalt artery that led to the heart of Manhattan.

21

THERAPY BUTTERFLY

Sean's class convened in an auditorium that seated four hundred. The school's building was a repurposed shopping mall that had gone defunct about a decade ago, after the multiplex and the bookstore that had anchored its ends went under. The movie theaters were great for elementary classes, though: sometimes they showed you films about hygiene and good manners, and every once in a while the President would appear and say hi to everybody, his head five times as large as Sean was tall, offering words of wisdom or encouragement in one's studies. If you were doing really well in school, like if you came in first place in the state Math League tournament, sometimes he'd call you out by name: whenever that happened, the kid he mentioned would be a celebrity for weeks.

Sean found his assigned seat, with his name taped to the back of the one in front of it. Down at the front of the theater, the teacher looked out at all the kids. Next to her stood a guard in camouflage gear, the clothes decorated in a pattern of green and brown splotches that made him the most visible person in the place. He was portly, bearded, and wore big clunky eyeglasses, and he had a rifle strapped across his back. It wasn't really clear to Sean what the guard was there for, but there he was anyway. Sometimes the teacher would let him tell the kids stories about the hunting trips he went on during the weekends, and those were pretty cool (though one of the stories he'd told about a pack of wolves seemed made up).

Sean's tablet logged in to the Wi-Fi network, registered his attendance, and cued up the app that would run him through his Daily Pre-School-Day Diagnostic. Every kid had to do this each morning, though the diagnostic activity each kid had to do was different, and it changed from one day to the next. The app displayed a minimalist, stylized forest in primary colors with a bunch of cartoonish talking animals bouncing around in it; eventually one of the animals would break away from the pack and approach you, looking out of the tablet's screen as if it were a window onto your world. If you got the rabbit that was dressed in a track suit (its fur powder blue) you had to do exercises for ten minutes, lifting the tablet over your head while you sat in your seat, or standing up and doing squats: the tablet's accelerometer made sure you weren't cheating on reps. If you got the owl with pince-nez glasses on its beak, you had to do a few quick math problems; the turtle (which ambled over to you while awkwardly balancing on its hind legs) made you read a paragraph and answer a couple of questions about it. Every once in a rare while, if you were totally acing all your classes and you were really well behaved, you got the phoenix, the bird materializing out of nowhere, each of the red feathers of its tail trailing a brilliant flame behind it, and if the phoenix showed up you just played games. This was a big deal: the phoenix only showed up on a tablet somewhere in the four-hundred-strong homeroom a couple of times a week, and the kid who got it always started jumping up and down and cheering while the others around him came over to look.

You could tell the app was rigged, and that the animals that assigned your tasks each morning weren't truly random, but were partly dictated by the profile the teachers had worked up for you. Kids who were doing badly in math got the owl: Sean was doing well in all his math classes, and he saw the owl once every couple of months at the most. Fat kids got the rabbit half the time, and when they stood up to do their squats you could see the shame on their faces as all the skinny kids stayed in their seats. If you weren't white, then sometimes you saw this thing come out of the forest that Sean guessed was supposed to be an alien—it had a bulbous body encircled by purple and green stripes, and large milky blue eyes, and a bobbling pair of antennae. The alien told you little stories about how it was okay to be different from everyone else, and it talked a lot about "diversity" and "heritage."

Sean pretty regularly got the butterfly, which came around to visit kids who . . . had issues. For two years Sean had been drawing the butterfly in the diagnostic at least once a week, while some kids never saw it at all (or hid their tablets from everyone else if they did). Though he'd also gotten the phoenix three times this year, at least one more time than anyone else in the class, so maybe you could say things evened out.

The butterfly showed up this morning, hovering in the middle of the screen, lava-lamp patterns swirling in its gigantic red and yellow wings. "Hey there, Sean," it said in its reedy voice. "I just wanted to check up on how you were feeling today." A dial appeared on the screen beside the butterfly, with notches marked from one to ten. "On this dial, could you just tell me how happy you are? Where one is down in the dumps, and ten is the happiest boy in the world. Go ahead! Tell me!" The dial was set at one, and in the pastoral landscape behind the butterfly, it began to rain heavily as the other animals began to scurry for cover. As Sean turned the dial, the rain slowed and stopped, and a yellow sun with rays shooting out of it began to emerge from behind a cloud.

He stopped the dial at eight, even though he was in a really good mood today. A couple of years ago, when the butterfly had first started showing up in the diagnostic, like *every day*, he tried turning the happiness dial to ten again and again just to get it to shut up and go away. Instead what happened was that Mom got this e-mail from school. Mom came into the kitchen one morning while he was eating breakfast. "I got this e-mail from your school that suggested I should ask you a question. It had to've been sent by a computer: it's not the kind of thing a person would say." She sighed. "It's kind of ridiculous."

Sean looked at his mother and shrugged.

"The e-mail says that I'm supposed to preface this question-asking by saying this is a serious question, not a joke. I'm doing that now."

"Gotcha."

"Sean, have you been taking MDMA? Colloquially, it is known as 'ecstasy' in its street pill form, or 'molly' in the purer, crystalline form. That's what this computer-generated e-mail says."

"I know a girl named Molly, but I don't hang out with her. Why would school e-mail you about her?"

"That's a good enough answer, Sean. You might not be aware of something: if anyone asks you how happy you are, and you always say that you're as happy as you can be, they think you're lying or you're crazy. So if you're really in a good mood, don't, you know, advertise it. Keep it a secret."

"Okay, Mom."

From then on he'd always turned the happiness dial to seven or eight, leaving a single cloud to half obscure the face of the sun, and the butterfly had eased up on him. Mom figured that by the end of this school year the red flag would probably expire from his profile, and he'd get other stuff like the turtle and the owl (though probably not the rabbit: he was as thin as a rail).

"Hey!" said the butterfly. "I'm glad you're feeling pretty good. It can be hard sometimes to have a family that doesn't have as many people as other families. But if you're feeling lonely, there's always someone to talk to. Your teacher is up at the front of the class, and she's ready to listen. Or you can speak to a counselor at any time by loading this app and touching the butterfly symbol in the dock at the bottom of the screen."

"Thanks," Sean said. The butterfly waved its wings goodbye, their roiling patterns briefly resolving into a pair of smiling faces. Then it turned and flew away to gambol amid the trees with the rest of the animals.

The butterfly didn't understand: it was just an AI routine that Sean had gotten good at gaming. The teacher didn't understand either: Sean had never even been close enough to her to be able to recognize her on the street. No one understood, and Sean was wise enough not to tell them: he was never lonely, because he was never alone.

■

The accident happened two years ago. Sean had gotten in detention for something that wasn't even his fault: all that had happened was that he'd been attacked and he'd fought back. But Ms. Baldridge didn't understand what happened and she put him in detention. It wasn't fair.

And Sean had had to sit there in front of Ms. Baldridge's desk while she called his mother and told her she had to come to pick him up. It was awful. But at least on the way home he'd be able to explain what happened to Mom, and Mom would understand, and then Sean would feel at least a little better.

But what happened instead was that Dad showed up. He came into Ms. Baldridge's classroom looking distracted, the way he did when his mind was really on equations and he couldn't even bother to hide it from you. Ms. Baldridge told him what happened, which wasn't what *really* happened: it left some stuff out, and it got some other stuff wrong.

Dad just said "uh-huh, uh-huh" while Ms. Baldridge talked, because he was moving numbers around in his head. Ms. Baldridge gave him a pamphlet to read: it was a pamphlet for parents of kids who have issues. Dad looked at it, and he said "uh-huh," and he folded it up and put it in his pocket. Then Sean and Dad got in the car to go home.

Dad had the old car, not the cool new car: if Mom had come, with the new car, Sean would have been able to talk to Mom, and Mom would have let him watch cartoons on the windshield. Mom would have taken his side and cheered him up. But Dad just stared out at the road in front of him and didn't say a word. When Sean said, "Where's Mom?" Dad didn't say anything at first, and then he said, real quiet, "She couldn't make it. So I'm here."

Then Dad said to Sean, "Whatever you did at school today, don't do it again. I can't afford to take extra time out of my day to pick you up just because you've been bad." It made Sean so angry, with anger he couldn't even do anything about: it just had to sit there in his stomach like a hot ball of lead.

They were both quiet then. Dad drove while he thought about numbers and Sean stayed angry. Then something amazing happened. Sean heard a loud noise down the road: it seemed like it came from way ahead of them. He looked up at Dad, who had that look on his face that people get in movies when they see something beautiful: eyes wide and mouth half open. Sean looked out the window to see what Dad was looking at, and ahead of them there was a car that was standing up on its front bumper, like a dog performing a trick. The car didn't have a top, and Sean could see the woman who was driving it. She had long red hair and it was flying all over the place.

"Sean!" Dad said, suddenly here in the world, suddenly excited.

"Sean! Watch the math!" Those were the next-to-last words he ever said.

It hadn't made sense to Sean what Dad meant at first, not for a while, not for months. He thought that Dad had told him he should be *afraid* of math, that numbers could hurt you and kill you. But then after thinking about it he realized that Dad had wanted him to *look at* the math: that the reason that Dad thought about numbers and formulas all the time was that they gave the world its shape and told it how to move. If you could see the math, you could find the beauty in things, and you could tell the future.

The red-haired woman flew out of her car, and the world got strange and noisy. No one cared about the lines on the road anymore. Dad was looking all around him, out the window and over his shoulder and in the mirrors, looking at the math that was moving the cars.

Then Dad got scared. "Sean!" he shouted. "Close your eyes! Hello—"

Sean shut his eyes as Dad began to spin the steering wheel to the left, quickly turning it hand over hand.

There was a really loud noise: *bang!*

Sean felt his skeleton try to leap out of his body. Glass cut up his face.

■

Four days later Mom sat down in front of Sean. He had been out of the hospital for a day already and hadn't seen Dad: Mom had come to visit, but Dad hadn't. For the past few days people had been telling him how lucky he was, but the looks on their faces made him think that what they *really* thought was that he wasn't that lucky at all. His face had a lot of little nicks on it from the glass, and he felt bruised all over.

Mom looked at Sean. Her face was made out of wax. "Do you remember anything about what happened?" she said. "When you were in the car with Dad."

"Dad said *Close your eyes*—"

"Oh God—"

"—and then he turned the wheel." Sean mimicked the quick hand-over-hand movement his father had made. "Then . . ." He frowned.

"Then I was in bed here, and I had a thing around my wrist with my name on it. I had a bruise here—" He pointed beneath his eye, where a contusion still bloomed, purplish and angry. "And here," he said, indicating his knee. "What's Dad doing?"

"Jesus, Sean," Mom said. "I don't even know how to say this."

■

For the rest of that school year and into the next, the other kids in school treated Sean like he was a walking urban legend. *Look at what happens when you're bad in school. Look at what happens when you get detention.* When he came back to school after a few weeks some things had changed. Brian, the kid who had taken his coupon for the free ice cream sandwich, had transferred to another school in the same district, but across town. Ms. Baldridge had taken an extended leave, and a substitute teacher taught in her place. But Ms. Baldridge never returned, and soon all the kids in school forgot about her.

In the Daily Pre-School-Day Diagnostic, the butterfly began to visit Sean every day, asking him to "self-monitor his mood" and nagging him to go to an adult if he was ever feeling like life wasn't worth living. But here is the thing you couldn't understand if you were just an AI routine that was programmed to pretend it was empathetic, or if you were a guidance counselor who flagged a student's profile as "psychologically traumatized" without ever looking the kid in the eye. The last lesson his father had taught him in the car was that beneath the things of the world lay ideas, and those ideas lived not in the world, but in the mind. Everything was made of numbers and formulas; formulas and numbers were ideas. And his father had done so much thinking about math that he was basically made out of it. And if his father had been made of math, and math was an idea that lived in the mind, then there was no reason that his father could not live on in Sean's mind, after the accident.

His father's last word, which Sean had never told anyone, not even his mother, hadn't been *goodbye:* it had been *hello.* He hadn't died; he'd been set free from the constraints of history and flesh. And while the fathers of the other children could only be the people they were, and were forced to live the lives they'd made for themselves, the Philip Steiner of his son's daydreams was all the possible versions of himself that Sean could imagine. He was always near, always ready to listen, always offering solace. He was all the possible fathers. He was a dragonslayer and a titan of industry; he was a cunning detective and a grizzled gunfighter; he was an astronaut and a priest and a jailer of thieves. He lived in the shadows, and he filled his son's world with light.

22

GAIA WILLIAMS

Marcus was the fifth romantic avatar that Felix Scott and his team had designed for Rebecca, and Felix thought he was one of the best they'd ever made. He was a dark-skinned African American, thirty-four, his smile wide and bright, his head cleanly shaven and shining. "There's a lot of late-nineties Taye Diggs in his face," Felix said as Rebecca seated herself in front of the array of electronic equipment that constituted the avatar modeler. Felix was fastening a skullcap to her head that was studded with motion sensors, while his assistant painted the tiny white dots on her face that would allow the modeler's camera to track her expressions for duplication. "There's a little bit of young Laurence Fishburne in there, too. We pulled reference images from *Apocalypse Now* and *King of New York*."

Marcus wore a charcoal pinstriped suit with deep purple accoutrements: the neatly folded handkerchief in the suit pocket matched the shirt and tie. The outfit looked to Rebecca like something a Wall Street financial analyst would have worn in the 1980s. "A handsome guy, right?" Felix said. "Let's try the voice now: let's get some levels."

"Call me Ishmael," Rebecca said into her headset mike. "It was the best of times, it was the worst of times." In her ear her own words came back to her in a stentorian bass after a slight delay: the dissonance was startling. "Can I have this voice for the rest of my life?" she said. "Surgery's not off the table."

"You know who that is?" Felix could barely contain his glee.

"No idea."

"Avery Brooks! More precisely, Avery Brooks as Captain Benjamin Sisko, the commanding officer of Federation station Deep Space Nine. Get this. We actually tried to legitimately license his voice for this, like we usually do for these things, but . . . well, when his people heard what we were going to use it for, that wasn't on. But I'm like, Marcus is totally Ultimate Black Man—he's *got* to sound like Sisko! No one else will do. So here's what we figure out. All we need is some recordings of phonemes, right? There are forty phonemes in North American English—our speech synthesizer works by stitching those phonemes together. And *DS9* ran for 176 episodes. So I sit down with a sound engineer and a box set of Blu-rays, and we go through pulling—not even a full word of Sisko's dialogue from each episode! Just *part* of a word: the *buh* sound that starts 'Bajoran'; the long *o* from 'Odo'; stuff like that. Completely covered by fair use doctrine. We got three to five instances of each phoneme, cleaned them up, and looked at similarities in the waveforms to generate a bunch of variants. Then we fed those into the speech synthesizer. Sounds great, doesn't it? Though our lawyers keep fretting that we're gonna get sued anyway. Audio's good, Rebecca: let's check video."

In the image on one of the three monitors on the desk in front of Rebecca, Marcus looked trim and muscular, seated in an office chair as he stared into a webcam. Behind him was an image of a well-appointed living room with cream-colored walls and plush leather couches, and a fireplace burning in the background. "Too warm for that," Rebecca said, pointing.

"Oh yeah," said Felix, and tapped a few keys: the flames blinked away.

"He doesn't look alive," Rebecca said.

"Still loading some of the idle animations," Felix replied, and as he spoke the avatar began to blink at random times as his chest started to rise and fall. With that he leapt to the other side of the uncanny valley: he probably wouldn't fool anybody for more than ten minutes, but that would be long enough.

"Looks good, doesn't he? I'd date that guy," said Felix, and then Marcus barfed up his tongue as his entire head turned inside out, his eyes staring inward at his own brain, his teeth hovering in front of his inverted lips. "What in the holy hell," Rebecca said, and Felix apologized as he opened up a terminal window on another monitor and hammered in some commands, his vintage Model M keyboard going *clickety-clack*. Marcus's head disappeared, leaving a neck with a void of unrendered geometry in its middle; then it snapped back into existence, smiling gently as if nothing had gone awry.

"He's not going to pull that shit while we're on the call, is he?" Rebecca said.

"He won't! He won't! He's under control."

"It's one o'clock. The call's coming in."

■

Rebecca had been piloting romantic avatars for about six months now. For all the advanced tech the project used, it was still a small one in the company, housed in a single room of the offices that Lovability occupied in an Eighth Avenue skyscraper. The project was funded with a trickle of R&D money diverted from another division of the enormous marketing, advertising, and social media conglomerate of which Lovability was the tiniest part. (Felix said he'd heard that the software was actually repurposed from another unknown project within the conglomerate that had been funded by DAPAS, the defense organization that, in the fever dreams of conspiracy theorists, was always pouring money into oddball research projects for its own unimaginably nefarious ends. But Felix was apt to say that sort of thing: for him, the spaces between words in front-page newspaper articles spoke of a web of connections between DAPAS and the Dakotan insurgents and the Davos World Economic Forum and the Bilderberg Group and the Illuminati, links that were plainly obvious to those with eyes to see.)

She had come to work at Lovability full-time soon after the accident: before then she'd just been handling customer-service calls from home, but suddenly she'd needed more than pin money to get by, and so she'd applied for an opening handling calls in-house, five days a week. It was monotonous work, but she was great at it: she upsold so many customers from Silver Plans to Gold and Platinum and Diamond that the gift certificates for restaurants that she got as regular rewards paid for dinner out for herself and Sean several nights a week, and the seasonal cash bonuses came close to covering the cost of Sean's school clothes and tablet upgrades. Finally, after about a year, she received an e-mail one morning summoning her directly to the office of Gaia Williams, the CEO of Lovability and the company's public face. It was Gaia who had (supposedly) used a combination of sociological studies and dark arts to design the matrix containing the twenty-six axes of compatibility that powered the mind of the company's electronic matchmaker.

Rebecca had shown up at Gaia's office at one thirty sharp that afternoon, only to be kept waiting. The atrium before the closed office door was dead quiet; the only other person there was a young female assistant who brought Rebecca a slim, tall glass of water wrapped in a neatly folded paper napkin, three perfectly formed spheres of ice floating inside. It was too early in the day for the assistant to look as completely shell-shocked as she did; Rebecca figured that Williams must be tough to work for.

After fifteen minutes on the dot, the door to Gaia's office swung open and there she was, looking just like she did in the commercials: deep blue blouse, black pencil skirt, and slightly naughty stiletto heels; legs for days. "Re-*bec*-ca," she sang, as if greeting a long-lost friend. "So sorry to keep you waiting: I was on a call that ran over. Come in. Come in! Come come come."

Rebecca followed her into her office. She guessed that Gaia Williams was probably black, though it was hard to say. She was either well tanned or naturally dark-skinned; her hair was black and straight and cropped in a flattering pixie cut, but that could mean anything or nothing. Her eyes were such a dark brown that it was difficult to distinguish between her pupil and her iris: Rebecca found Gaia's gaze slightly unsettling.

Latino, maybe? No: Latin*a*. Maybe.

Gaia's mahogany desk had nothing on its surface but an ultra-slim computer monitor and a keyboard. The single chair that faced the desk was a little low, even for Rebecca: if you were a six-foot-tall man, then scrunching into it with your knees halfway up to your chin probably made you feel awkward and goofy, and Rebecca sensed that, like being left to cool her heels while Gaia "finished up her call," this was deliberate. Gaia's chair, meanwhile, was upholstered in leather and heavily padded, loudly advertising its own comfort. Gaia took a seat, wheeled her chair forward so that she could rest her elbows on the desk, and pointed a long, delicate, neatly manicured finger at

Rebecca. "I've seen your numbers. Your volume and your upselling. They're very good. *You're* very good."

"Thank you—"

"Gaia!" *I grant you this largesse, to speak with me familiarly.*

"—Gaia."

"And they're good enough for me to want to spend some time chatting with you about a little project we're putting together at Lovability, something I'd like to tap you for. It's still in the research stages. A small thing, but very exciting, with a lot of potential. Would you like to hear about it?"

"Yes, I would," Rebecca said, hoping she'd successfully hidden her confusion behind her smile.

"Then let me cut to the chase. Or not, actually: if I cut to the chase you'll probably run out of here screaming and call the cops and the newspapers or something, ha-ha! Let's start from the beginning."

■

"Rebecca," Gaia said. "Think about what Lovability does, and what it is. From the point of view of the client, we provide a matchmaking service. People join up—they can even join for free with a Bronze Plan if they want—and they fill out a profile, and we use our algorithms to find them a suitable mate more easily than they could find one on their own by leaving the house. That's what they think, based on what they can see of our systems and on how we present ourselves in press and advertisements. And that's perfectly fair. It's not false.

"But here, in this room, we have a different and more informed point of view. We know that Lovability's—well, not its true value, but its most important value, is not as a matchmaking service, but as a collector and repository of self reported data. And the longer an account stays open, and the more data the account's holder adds to it, the more valuable the access to that account becomes to the corporations we sell those profiles to, and who are our primary source of revenue. The few extra dollars a month that we collect when we convince someone to upgrade to a Gold account or whatever: that's just gravy. What's more important to us is that Gold account holders stick around a whole lot longer than Bronze account holders, because with the payment of a fee comes a psychological commitment. They're much more likely to link Lovability to their other social networks; they're much more likely to click on several different profiles each time they visit; they're much more likely to participate in our daily love quizzes and our market research questionnaires.

"So from our perspective we want to have as many genuine accounts as possible, but more importantly, we also want many of these accounts to be as persistent as possible. When we go to other companies with our rates, we charge roughly eight times the amount for access to a Platinum account holder as we do for Bronze account holders. And this is a bargain! Because the higher-level account holders have provided much more information about themselves, which makes them easier to target.

"Do you see the problem here?"

"Sure," Rebecca said, recalling something that Philip had told her on their first date, when they'd met at the sculpture garden and he'd introduced himself by launching into a breathless, esoteric lecture. "Every time we do our job we cripple our own business."

"That's right," said Gaia. "Whenever Lovability makes a match with an ideal long-term romantic partner, the repository of data that represents Lovability's true worth declines in value, because the account holder loses interest in the site—even if they do log on now and again, it's out of idle curiosity, and they pretty much stop providing us with additional information altogether. We need at least a few people to find true love or whatever on a regular basis, so that we can point to those success stories as evidence that Lovability actually works. But if everybody actually found their soulmate as soon as they logged on, it'd finish us!

"So from our point of view, the people who log on for a few weeks and meet the perfect guy and then leave, or who just nose around on the site for a little while and give up but leave their accounts open—they're basically freeloaders. And we need some freeloaders to populate the system—we want to be able to say we have hundreds of thousands of members without buying profiles from defunct Russian social networking sites or something like that. But there are two general categories of people who are most likely to be our bread and butter.

"The first are serial daters with demographic profiles that make them highly in demand: you know, the guy who's six foot two and clears six figures, who's got a corporate job with a wordy title. Every time he logs on he's got a full Smilebag; he spends *hours* each night sending out *dozens* of messages, each one hand-tailored to the recipient. He basically treats Lovability like a second job. This guy goes out on dates with different women a few times a week; some weekend days he doubles up, with a lunch date with one woman and dinner with another. He's good for us and he's easy to manage, because he's going to get hit with choice overload: he's always going to have in the back of his head that there could be someone better out there for him. And if he's highly desirable demographically we can use his profile in the targeted ads we place on other sites to draw people in.

"But the second category—and really, these people are more valuable to us than the serial daters—are people who rarely if ever get dates through our site, but who stick around anyway. The disabled; the morbidly obese; the man or woman who will never take a good photo in her life. Middle-aged women; divorcées; women with a couple of kids. Black women. Look at our numbers: you can look at the numbers for any dating site and see that black women are more likely to send messages than women in any other demographic, and are most selective with the men they choose to message, sticking primarily to messaging black men. And yet they *still* get the lowest rate of return from the men they *do* message. And once they hit forty, forget it. And they're highly desirable for marketers to reach, too, especially if they're middle class and have a fair amount of disposable income. I'll tell you, I'd trade a half dozen pretty blondes for one forty-three-year-old black woman with a white-collar job, career driven and childless, if she'd stick around on Lovability for a year or two—"

"Um, Ms. Williams?"

"Gaia, I said! Call me Gaia." Her voice reminded Rebecca of wind chimes in spring.

"Gaia, this conversation is going in . . . a weird direction? I don't know that—"

"Oh goodness. I can see that you're a little bothered by this. I can see the wheels spinning in your head right now: *I can't believe she's saying such racist things!* This is why we're having this meeting in person: otherwise it would be easy for you to misunderstand me. I don't think I need to say that Lovability is not a racist organization. I don't think I need to say that Lovability has a deep commitment to diversity."

"Of course," Rebecca said. (Maybe Gaia was Hawaiian or something? What did Hawaiians look like? Sort of Asian, but not really? Polynesian. Maybe?)

"It is extremely important in this business," Gaia said, "to keep in mind the difference between a *person* and the *data* generated by a person as she moves through life. This is a distinction that is easy to forget. Information is not a person, and a person is made up of more than information. A person has beliefs and feelings and a will and a soul: information does not. You have to remember this because we do not want to dehumanize our clients by speaking of them in terms of numbers, but you must also remember that while it is possible to have a moral or ethical obligation to a *person*, it is impossible to have such an obligation toward *data*. The very idea is nonsensical. What would it mean to talk about being fair to . . . bits? How would you talk about treating bits with respect?

"And so because our language isn't set up to express that distinction neatly, the distinction between the person and the data that person manufactures, we fall back on using the language in its old traditional way, and trust that between us the distinction is understood. I could have said, for instance, *Messages that are sent from profiles whose gender is set to 'female,' and whose race is set to 'black,' and whose age is set to a numerical value greater than forty, are less likely to receive responses than those whose race is set to a value other than 'black' or whose age is set to a numerical value lower than forty.* But if we had to spin out these long torturous sentences every time we wanted to refer to a phenomenon exhibited by the Lovability database, we'd never get anything done. So among ourselves, here in the office, we speak in an efficient short-hand, and trust each other to remember that our concern here is not with a person, but merely with the data that is actively and passively generated by that person. It's possible to make sexist or racist or otherwise derogatory statements about a person, or a group of people, because people are sentient, and have individual identities, and can reason and feel. And to make such statements about people is despicable. But we are concerned not with people, but with information, and information has none of the traits that make humans what they are—it is not sentient, not even corporeal. To speak of having sexist or racist sentiments toward information would be the same as having sexist or racist sentiments toward a chair, or a table, or an abstract concept like grace or evil. It just doesn't make sense.

"Do you understand, Rebecca? Do you agree with me?"

"I . . . I guess?" Rebecca paused. "I mean, I wasn't expecting a metaphysical argument when I came in here," she said. "I need to think about it. But I think I agree. People are more than just numbers: sure. And numbers aren't people. All that's obvious."

"Good," Gaia said. "Then we can move on. Where were we? Oh yes. Black women are going to have a really tough time finding love on our site, especially if they're old. And so these people tend not to remain at Lovability. *Except* that when people from undesirable demographics are contacted, even once, even if that contact does not lead to a face-to-face meeting, then they're much more likely to stick around. And we offer mediated communications with varying degrees of intimacy: there are Smilebag Smiles, and messages, and then the People Peeks, the video chats that customers can request that have a ten-minute time limit. Ever since we've instituted the video chats last year, they've been astronomically successful! A black female who engages in even one People Peek is highly likely to upgrade her account status, and highly likely to stay on Lovability for several months more. If only more black women, or severely overweight men, or other people from demographics that are considered desirable by marketers but undesirable by our dating pool, could have more People Peeks. Our data repository would be so much richer, so much more robust.

"This is where our romantic avatars come in."

■

"Goodness, you look *just* like your picture," the woman on the other end of the connection said as she stared into her webcam.

"Oh, I wouldn't say I look *just* like that picture," Rebecca replied, her voice in her own ear full of melodious gravitas. "It was taken about a year ago: I've gotten a little older. But I do appreciate the compliment."

The two women shared a deep, long laugh.

Then silence descended as the woman on the other end fished around for something to say. Rebecca usually found it safest to wait out the mark on the other end. She looked over her profile on another monitor: her handle vrksasanalady, her real name Sara Ross. Forty-one, with a seven-year-old girl from a previous marriage. Her profile photo showed her in loosely fitting yoga gear, standing on one leg with her foot tucked in against her inner thigh and her hands extended in the air: she had looks that would make a man turn his head if she walked up behind him unannounced. It was baffling that she'd even need a site like this, but then Rebecca saw what she'd filled out as a career: adjunct prof in the history departments of two different universities; yoga teaching on the side. No wonder: with the kid she'd rarely have a free minute. The salary from one of the adjunct jobs probably went entirely to day care.

On the screen Marcus continued to go through his idle animations. Finally vrksasanalady said, "So it says here you're into Ella!"

"Oh, yeah, Lady Ella!" Rebecca said. "I *love* that old stuff. There's just something pure about it: something beautiful about a voice that hasn't been overproduced and processed with computers, like all music is these days. Her voice just rings out, you know? She can take any standard and just fill it with surprises. You know 'Angel Eyes'?"

"Absolutely. Ella took that song. That's *her* song."

It turned out that vrksasanalady was an expert in twentieth-century jazz. (Not Sara, Rebecca reminded herself. vrksasanalady was an electronic golem, a construct of pixels and signals made by Sara, one that resembled her and spoke with her voice: there's a difference; it's important.) She burned three minutes of the ten-minute chat time with what Rebecca assumed was a learned disquisition on the changes rung on "Angel Eyes" by various musicians: Nat King Cole; Pat Metheny; Shirley Bassey. ("I feel a touch guilty about loving Dame Shirley so much—I think I've got a dozen of her albums, and she never met a tune she couldn't belt—but you can't help it!" "No need to feel guilty at *all*," Rebecca said.)

"In fact," vrksasanalady said, "I know a place. A little place in Greenwich Village, a club where you can get in for next to nothing late at night. Not crowded and noisy, like a lot of New York clubs. Going into this place is like going back in time. A lot of musicians just drop in unannounced when they've finished up a gig somewhere else in the city, just to jam for a little while—you'll see a guy stride up on stage when the band is in the middle of a tune, pull a sax out of a case, and start blowing like he was there all along. I'm thinking maybe I could drop the little rug rat off at my sister's for an evening and you and I could, you know, go there sometime?"

"That sounds *great*," Rebecca replied. "That sounds really inter-

esting. Here is the thing." She paused. "My secretary: she keeps track
of my schedule for me, and without her I'm a mess. No idea if I'm
coming or going, where I'm supposed to be, who I'm on the phone
with: hell, who I even am sometimes."

"I hear you!"

"So how about this. I'll talk to her and see where the blank spaces
are in my calendar, and then I'll send you some dates and times. How
about it?"

"Sounds like a plan. I am—it was really great to meet you, Marcus.
I'm looking forward to seeing you again."

"It was great to meet you, too, finally," Rebecca said. "I'll send you
a message soon." Then the clock in the corner of the chat window
ticked down to zero and the line disconnected, vrksasanalady's feed
replaced with the Lovability logo next to a caricature of Gaia Williams's smiling face.

■

"You were laying it on a little thick there with the bit about the secretary, don't you think?" Felix said as Rebecca removed her headset
and wiped the motion-tracking dots off her face with a handkerchief.

"It was the first thing I thought of! Listen, it's hard enough playing
the guys, and when the women get aggressive and go off-script it's
even harder to think through it. But it was okay. Look: we'll wait a
couple of days and then message her—say someone special came back
into his life unexpectedly, and it wouldn't be fair to his old flame to
continue communicating with her. Say he's sure she'll find someone.
Be a total gentleman about it. She'll be fine. She'll even switch up to
the Gold or the Platinum: watch."

Rebecca stood up and rubbed her eyes: even ten minutes as an
avatar made it weird for her to hear her own voice coming out of her
chest. She liked to talk aloud for a couple of minutes after a session
to get rid of the sense of disorientation. "Marcus is good," she said.
"Better than Helen, even, in the visuals." (Helen was the avatar that
Rebecca liked to play as a conspiracy theorist: there were a lot of
conspiracy-theory types on Lovability. She had the strong chin, wide
brown eyes, and dark-haired bob of a young Ayn Rand, and she was a
hell of a lot of fun to pilot: Rebecca would go to town for ten minutes

with the *craziest* monologues, not even letting the guy on the other end get a word in edgewise. The trick was mixing the language of skeptic rationalists with a bit of the "everything is connected" stuff that Felix liked to go on about, along with a small dose of batshit insanity: "I'm just throwing the question out there—remember, it's still okay to ask questions in America—but I just have to say it's really *curious* that the media has completely failed to report on the clear evidence that this persistent insurgency in the Dakotas is a false-flag op perpetrated by our own government. You've seen plenty of evidence in favor of that hypothesis, but none *against* it, have you? Yeah let's get coffee somewhere sometime: I'll send you an e-mail, but we'll have to figure out a way to do this with a one-time pad cipher. You send an unencrypted message these days and you've as good as called up the Feds and whispered it right into their ears.")

"I'm getting better at the avatar visuals," Felix said. "Every time we get a software upgrade I can get a little fancier, more subtle, with the animation. Marcus's skin has *layers*, like a real human's does, and when the software renders his image it actually computes the way light moves through them differently. In real time! Really sophisticated stuff. And do you know how many profiles of African American women I looked at to work up that avatar? Hundreds. Thousands!"

■

On the way out of Gaia's office after their first meeting, Rebecca had paused. "Gaia?"

"Rebecca."

"I just wanted to ask: you have a beautiful voice. Where are you from?"

"The San Francisco area. My parents met there—they were working at competing tech startups. Very Romeo and Juliet, but without all the murders at the end."

Rebecca smiled and turned to leave, then felt her body swiveling back, her mouth opening. "I meant—"

"Goodbye," Gaia said, "Ms. Wright."

23

FILE MANAGEMENT

When Rebecca clocked out and left the tower that housed Lovability, her car was waiting for her in the autonomous-vehicle holding area out front. Forty-five minutes before, it had roused itself in the garage in Jersey City where it parked itself after dropping her off at work each morning; then it had driven itself out to Manhattan in time to pick her up. (The fuel expenditure was wasteful, sure, but the avoidance of New York City's exorbitant parking fees made up for the extra tank of gas every few days.) Rebecca got inside, kicked off her heels, pulled her flask of bourbon out of the glove compartment, and poured two fingers' worth into the plastic tumbler she kept in the cup holder next to the driver's seat. Her father would have blanched at her choice of glassware, but it's not like she was drinking top-shelf stuff: merely Jim Beam, a booze with no pretensions, a decent enough sipping whiskey to celebrate the day's end. She reclined the seat, punched a button on the dashboard's touchscreen, and settled back for the hour-long ride home.

She preferred to spend her evening commute in relative silence—no satellite radio or windshield video; nothing but the barely audible whine of the car's hybrid engine and the sounds of traffic from outside. She liked to take the time to let her thoughts drift; she liked to hear the sound of her self. The injunction that Gaia Williams had given her, not to confuse the data with the people who generated the data: that cut both ways. You could look at a bunch of numbers in a spreadsheet and make the mistake of thinking you were dealing with something other than, or more than, numbers. Or you could look at a person and think that he was a creature made out of digits, and fail to see the singular self that lay behind his eyes. And so Rebecca liked to sit and think for a while after work with a drink in her hand, to get her mind back in the space where a name identified a person and not a profile stored on a server.

Take Kathryn and Carson, for instance—they were getting on now like a house on fire, at least from what Rebecca could tell. Carson was all Kathryn could talk about, to the point where it got tiresome— after just a few months, she hadn't just uttered the dreaded *l*-word that she'd sworn in youth would never pass her lips, but also seemed to be dancing around the *m*-word as well. But Kathryn and Carson had actually tried dating twice: once when they'd met online, and a second time after they'd run into each other again at a party that Rebecca had hosted for Alicia Merrill when a cable newstainment show had run a story on the causality violation device. (Alicia hadn't wanted to get mixed up in it at all, fearing the way that journalistic reportage on physics often turned out sounding like science fiction, but Rebecca had talked her into it. In the end Alicia's fears had been unjustified, for the segment was surprisingly tasteful, if perhaps a bit mawkish: they'd covered Philip's career up to the accident, and used a bit of deft editing to portray Alicia as a bright and confident young upstart who'd taken over the lab once her mentor had passed away, swearing to realize his ambitious vision in his absence. Rebecca had teared up a little, watching it; big bearish Dennis, the lab's resident code monkey, had bawled like a baby.)

Rebecca hadn't been fully privy to the reasons why Kathryn and Carson had broken up the first time, but she had her guesses. For a while, Kathryn had been a notorious love-'em-and-leave-'em serial dater. She was good at online dating—she was slim and cute with a face that promised mischief, and behind a keyboard she had a snappy way with words that made her fun to flirt with. It got to the point where when she went out in small-town Stratton to shop for groceries or browse in the local indie bookstore, she figured she had a one-in-three chance of coming across an ex. Finally, Rebecca had a sit-down woman-to-woman talk with her—more accurately, Rebecca staged an intervention, mostly because she'd gotten tired of hearing Kathryn diss Boyfriend #268 because he always had beads of sweat clinging to his upper lip, and Boyfriend #269 because when she went out for sushi with him he used a fork instead of chopsticks. "Look," she'd said. "I know how this works. You're looking for quality, but these profiles you're sifting through are more likely to show you quantities than qualities: you get me? The stuff that makes you who you are can't make it through the wires: even the most exciting person in the world will end up bland and standardized by the time he answers all those questionnaires and fits himself into our templates. And when you finally meet up with these people you don't really *see* them: you're looking at them, but you're seeing the shadow versions of them that you corresponded with online. And you're always thinking in the back of your head that you can find someone better, because the site's rigged to make you think that way. Which is why you complain about being lonely even though you've got dates three nights a week. My two cents."

Rebecca wasn't sure at first that she hadn't crossed a line with Kathryn after that talking-to—Kathryn had sulked at the time, and Rebecca hadn't heard from her for a couple of weeks afterward. But Rebecca got the impression that Kathryn had been dating a little less, if she hadn't quit entirely. And when she'd met Carson again at the party for Alicia, they'd hit it off as if they'd never even met before.

And perhaps it wasn't entirely wrong to say that in a sense, they *hadn't* met before, until then. Maybe their second meeting felt so much like a first because it hadn't taken place through the inadvertent distancing of electronic mediation, and enough time—a couple of years—had passed to let the memory of that earlier meeting fade and be forgotten (and there was something to be said for forgetting, whether willful or not).

Rebecca knew that Lovability's algorithms attempted to predict the probability that two given people who contacted each other would go on to have a romantic relationship with any degree of seriousness. Even Lovability's developers would admit, after a couple of beers, that the methodology was sort of ham-fisted. Rebecca expected that in Kathryn and Carson's case, Lovability would have made a negative prognosis with a high degree of certainty, considering the difference in their race and the extreme difference in their educational level. And yet here they were, happy as could be, because while Lovability's servers could take a decent stab at guessing the chances for harmony between a white female with a bachelor's degree in theater and a black male with an astrophysics PhD, it had no way of predicting the probability of romance between Kathryn and Carson, two people whose most significant commonality with all other humans was their lack of perfect precedence in history, two people who had their own memories, and secrets, and dreams, and interior lives.

As Rebecca's car neared home it occurred to her, as it regularly did, that her job might be, in a trivial way, morally unconscionable. But there were far worse sins perpetrated each day than those of the employees of Lovability. And it did, in all honesty, help a great many people find true love. There was an LED display mounted over the reception desk in the company's main office that showed the number of marriages that had come about as a result of Lovability's match-making services. The counter ticked up once or twice a day, and whenever it did, a recording of wedding bells would play through speakers mounted on ceilings throughout the company's offices—in response, all the employees would drop what they were doing, come to their feet, and applaud, even if they were in rooms alone. Sure, it was one of those practices intended to inculcate corporate spirit, but you couldn't deny that it genuinely felt good.

■

By the time Rebecca got home, Sean had already been in the house for a couple of hours. In the days of Rebecca's own childhood that would have made him a latchkey kid, a matter about which she felt some slight guilt, but if there was a benefit to this always-on surveillance culture, it meant that you didn't have to worry nearly as much about stranger danger. (At the last PTA meeting she'd managed to attend, Rebecca had ended up talking to a husband-and-wife pair of electronic engineers who'd had a subcutaneous RFID transmitter implanted in the sole of their daughter's right foot when she was born. "It's not really invasive, like in a privacy sense," the father had said, showing Rebecca the app on his phone that displayed his daughter's location, blood pressure, and heart rate. "It just gives us enough information to let us know that she's okay, without infringing on her rights. And of course she's got the option to have it removed when she turns thirteen." "Though we do hope she'll keep it," the mother had chimed in. Rebecca wasn't crazy enough to do that to Sean, but technological advances had enabled helicopter parents to a greater degree than ever before, and there were enough of them around to act as a deterrent for everyone, so Rebecca felt little fear that Sean would be harmed by some mischief.)

Sean was sitting on the couch in the living room, playing some sort of game on his tablet. "What's that about?" Rebecca asked, putting down her purse and slipping off her shoes.

"Hey, Mom," Sean said. "This game is *old:* older than me. You have to . . . you have to obtain the facade used to overcome life's hardships." Rebecca looked at the tablet's screen, which showed a bunch of kids in Japanese school uniforms running around some sort of laboratory laid out like a maze, the sort of thing a Bond villain would build.

"Well, I guess it's better than killing someone."

"Way better!" Sean said. "This is like the best game ever."

"What's for dinner?"

"Indian delivery. I ordered lamb brrr-yonney for me, and the stuff with the chickpeas for you. Can I use your credit card? I already used your credit card. I got some samosas too."

"For food, any time," Rebecca said. "But not for those games on your tablet. And it's biryani: *beer*-yonney, like—" She made a motion with her hand that mimed tipping back a bottle to her lips. "Speaking of." She went into the kitchen.

Alicia showed up just as they were finishing dinner. Sean opened the door when the bell rang and greeted her with his usual "Hey, Aunt Alicia" that seemed an oddly precocious mix of mockery and sweetness. Rebecca offered Alicia a tall can of Six Point Sweet Action as she popped open a second for herself; Alicia silently waved it away. Sean, sensing his cue, cleaned up his dishes. "I'm gonna go in my bedroom now," he announced. "You two can talk about whatever."

"Thanks for your permission," Rebecca said. "Get some homework done. Try not to spend too much time on your . . . public face, what was it?"

"The facade used to overcome life's hardships," Sean said, with the exact same intonation as before. He fidgeted in the middle of the living room, the odd one out in age and gender.

"Have fun inside the Midnight Channel, and remember that the fog comes after several days of rain," Alicia said, and Sean relaxed visibly. Alicia was good with Sean. Even Rebecca found herself having to actively ignore his strange affect sometimes when she spoke to him, so that he wouldn't feel so alien. But Alicia had this effortless way of getting on his wavelength and speaking the code words of his private world, letting him know that there was someone else who saw and understood things the way he did.

"I know I know I know I have to rescue Naoto from his Shadow now!" Sean said, and he would clearly have gone on for another hour with Alicia about whatever it was if he'd had the chance. Instead he looked at Alicia shyly, turned, and scampered to the back of the house, clutching his tablet to his chest.

■

Alicia wasn't really one for small talk with adults, on the other hand: she could manage it for short periods, but her idle conversation had the feel of being spoken in a second language. It was a sign of their close friendship that Rebecca didn't find it odd when Alicia got quickly to the point. "We had to deactivate your ID card," she said. "You can keep it. Or you can cut it up: it won't work anymore."

"Gotcha," Rebecca said quietly, after a pull at her beer.

"Why did you do it? We looked at the feed from the night-vision cameras: you may not have known they were there. They showed that you entered the causality violation chamber. Why did you do that?"

"It's hard to explain."

"You should try."

Rebecca took a good long swig. "Alicia—you don't know what it's like to be I guess widowed, I guess that's the word I'm looking for, it's what people say I am, you don't know what it's like to be widowed at thirty-six. At thirty-six! Like, if I had to fill out a Lovability profile, I'd have to tell the matrix of twenty-six axes of compatibility that I was *widowed*, and then it would pair that with my age and it wouldn't know what the hell to do.

"You know what I went through, Alicia," she continued, "and you helped me get through that, and I really appreciate it. But the thing is that you never get over something like this. You maybe learn to live with it having happened to you, but you never ever get over it.

"This is getting heavy."

"I expected it would," said Alicia. "Go on."

Rebecca sighed, and pressed on. "The thing that's hard about it—the thing that makes it so hard when the person you love has been taken from you, not by something evil that you could have seen coming, but by pure random chance—is that you find yourself suddenly living through a history other than the one you expected to live, through no fault of your own. I feel . . . it's hard to describe, but I feel weirdly outside of time. Ever since the accident I've had these moments when I felt like a visiting guest in this world, not a permanent resident. Like sometimes I look in a mirror and I feel like I can almost see through the version of me on the other side of the glass. And sometimes I feel like I can see the history I used to be in more clearly than the history I'm in now—the real history is one where Philip and Sean and I are all together, being a family and doing whatever family things people do, and this one's like . . . like a *fake* version of events that I've just been *yanked* into, where everything's gone wrong.

"But I know this is the real world, and not a fake or a dream. I know you only get one chance at life, as much as it'd be great if things were otherwise. I don't have any delusions on that score."

"That's probably wise," Alicia said. "But I still don't understand why you did it. I don't see why you snuck into the lab in the middle of the night to see the machine."

Rebecca paused for a full minute, her arms folded, and Alicia let her think. Then Rebecca said, "Okay. Sometimes . . . it gets dark in my head. You know. You don't know. But. Anyway. I woke up early the morning of the day I did this, just wide awake at four a.m., and I felt *so* fucking lonely, so lonely I hope you don't ever understand how lonely I felt. And I just kind of drifted around the house, and eventually I called Kathryn at work and I was like, I kind of need to spend some time with someone today, this is the worst it's ever been, this is the worst it's been since I actually found out about the accident. And she took the day off work to hang out with me. She's the kind of woman who would do that for a friend. And . . . well, we spent the day out at the bars like we were a couple of not-giving-a-shit college girls again, with all the time in the world and nothing to do. And Kathryn listened to me while I just poured *all* this stuff out, stuff

I'd been carrying around with me for over two years and never told anyone, not even you.

"So Kathryn listened to all this stuff, and then she gave me some advice. Because sometimes you can give advice to someone even if you don't really understand what they've been through. She said, Look. The thing is that you want closure, and you didn't get it. But here's the thing that was great about Philip. He was a brilliant physicist; he was almost literally a man of ideas. And really ambitious ones, too! And his ideas were what he valued most about himself! Even if he's gone, he left this great idea behind that the people following behind him are going to make better. And how many people in the world are able to leave something behind that will make strangers think about them even five minutes after they're dead? Just about nobody.

"So here's what we're going to do. We're going to the lab, tonight, and you're going to go look at the causality violation chamber. And you're going to touch it, and you're going to remind yourself that it's here and it's real, in the world with us. Because all that a grave will do is remind you that he's dead. But that machine he made is your reminder that in a way, in the most important way, he's still alive. And as long as people are working with that machine and thinking of how to build on the ideas that brought that machine into existence, he always will be.

"So we went to the lab and we went straight up to the security desk and . . . pretty much told the guards how it was. I said that I was the widow of Philip Steiner and I had come to view my husband's work. And to be honest the guards looked like they wanted to stop me, but I handed them my ID card, and they ran it, and it checked out. So while Kathryn stayed there and talked to them, I went into the room that held the causality violation device.

"And okay—I did go inside. I don't know how long I was in there, but I didn't go in there intending to, you know, mess anything up, and I was only in there for maybe a minute. But just being in there for a minute made me feel a lot better. This is going to sound a little weird to you, but . . . being inside it was like being inside his mind, you know? Like there was this part of him that was always a little walled off, a little inscrutable, even though I was married to him, and here it was. That part of his mind that had always been a secret to me was made real. And once I realized this—once I saw the machine again, and touched it with my hands and knew this in my bones—it was like I'd had these shackles on my ankles and someone had finally cut them off and set me free.

"I mean, I'm always going to have this shadow on me, I think—what happened to me is a part of my life now. But though it seems strange, I wouldn't have it any other way. I've really come to terms with it. It hurt, it hurt a lot, it still does sometimes, it always will at least a little, but at least I know now that I wouldn't want to *forget* what happened, or trade this life for another one that didn't have Philip in it. Because in the end, I was lucky. I was lucky that Philip came into my life. I was lucky to have gotten to spend the time with—lucky to have been loved by—such a wonderful, brilliant man. And I have a kind of happiness now, a kind of satisfaction, the best I think I'll be able to come up with.

"Do you understand? Does that make sense to you?"

Alicia looked at Rebecca for a little while as she thought about it. "I would not have done this, if I were you," she said eventually. "But I think I can see why you did it. You wanted to be close to the thing that was the physical incarnation of the idea. The way I see it, the ideas that Philip had don't need things to make them real—the causality violation device is the result of an idea and the potential proof of its truth, not the idea itself. But that's just me. I think I see why you acted as you did."

"Thank you," said Rebecca, who knew Alicia well enough by now to take her statement as an expression of her genuine sympathy.

■

"Okay," said Alicia. "Enough of that. Second order of business. I have a problem at work. And I'm hoping you can help."

"I'm all ears. Hey, you sure you don't want a beer?"

"I don't," Alicia said, "but feel free to get another for yourself."

Rebecca got another.

When she sat back down, popped the top, and took a gulp, Alicia began. "Here's the problem. I have had to admit to myself, since I've taken over the Steiner lab, that this project is a mess, and in deep danger of failure. Even DAPAS with its bottomless pockets is starting to get impatient: they want to see some results. And the worst thing is that it's not a problem with the ideas. We still believe the ideas are solid: it's just a matter of producing the evidence that will get everyone else in the field to agree with us. The worst thing, for me, is that it's a problem of lab management. It was incipient in the lab when Philip was running it, but he did his best to stay on top of it. But when I took over the lab I didn't. I let it go, and it got worse, and now it's coming back to bite me on the ass.

"The difficulty has to do with version control of the software we developed that drives the causality violation device. Needless to say, it's quite complex—over a million lines of code by now, written by dozens of people over several years. And with code that complex you can't just have one person signing it out, working on it, and signing it back in. You want several people to be able to work on it at once—it's so complicated by now that anyone who's an expert in one section will find another section she won't be able to make sense out of at all. So to avoid forking—that is, the development of multiple versions of the software being developed independently that diverge from each other in content over time—you institute a version control protocol. And you use an additional piece of software to track changes between versions.

"There are a couple of ways to do this. The most practical, and the one we should have stuck with, is called *copy-modify-merge*. Two programmers check out copies of the software, make their changes independently, and then check the software back in. A version control system checks both copies for changes, and creates a new version of the program that incorporates the changes from both programmers. If both programmers work on the same section of code, which is highly unlikely, the version control protocol throws up a conflict flag. Then the programmers compare code, decide which of their revisions was best, and pick that one. It sounds chaotic, but it works well in practice.

"So that's the version control protocol we used in the lab for several years. But when we accepted funding from DAPAS, it came with some conditions. We had a guy come up from DC—his name was Michael Cheever—to 'streamline our process.' And it was clear that Cheever would keep his hands off our science, but if we didn't take his advice on process, further funds might not be forthcoming. And his heart was in the right place—he was genuinely enthusiastic about what we were doing, and he and Philip got along well. But one of the things that Cheever absolutely insisted on is that we shift from a 'copy-merge-modify' protocol to a 'lock-modify-unlock' protocol. He wanted one person at a time to check out the entire code for the CVD, make revisions, and check it back in: while one person had signed it out, no one else could make changes to it.

"A moment's thought will show what a bad idea that was. But at the end of the day Cheever was a bureaucrat, and though he understands the science and he cares about it, he has to report to people who don't understand the science at all and have to be convinced to care. And in his report it looks better if he can say the CVD software went through a number of distinct iterations in a given time period, while with the copy-merge-modify protocol the numbers don't look quite as solid. So, because we weren't idealists, we did what he said.

"The result was disastrous. We all copied the CVD software to memory sticks to work on it on our own, because the new version control protocol was too restrictive to let us get anything done. And even though we tried to keep track of it off the books, the code's development forked every which way. I called a meeting yesterday and we finally admitted, all of us, that we don't know what the hell we're doing anymore: we're driving in fog and our headlights are out. The code is a pile of spaghetti.

"But if this cloud has a silver lining, it's that there's hope, a huge hope, that the problem isn't with Philip's theories, but with the code. So we're fixing the code, generating a definitive version, getting everything straight. And that's in part a management problem, so now I'm managing. Dennis is probably our most gifted programmer, but I chewed him out last week, right after that lab meeting, and I'll tell you why. He would come up with these gorgeously elegant solutions to problems—something you'd expect would take a hundred lines, he'd do in sixty-five—but he wouldn't write comment code if you put a gun to his head. Comment code is meant for humans to read, not compilers, and it's marked as such—it explains in plain English how the software works so future programmers will know what it's doing and how. But Dennis could never be bothered to write that stuff—I don't know if it was out of laziness, or arrogance, or a combination of the two. Time and again if I did find one of his comments, it'd say 'purpose and method of the above is self-evident.' And 'the above' might as well have been a Zen koan for the sense I could make out of it. If it was a couple of years old Dennis himself couldn't figure out the code he'd actually written—and I gave him a little test: I showed him five samples of his own uncommented code and he could only recognize the functions of *two* of them!

"Philip, on the other hand, was great at commenting: highly scrupulous about it. He'd write ten lines followed by a whole paragraph, in grammatically perfect English, telling you what they did. Dennis would even complain about Philip's coding behind his back, saying he couldn't read it because all the comments got in the way! So in order to unscramble this mess, we're trying to find every scrap of code that Philip laid his eyes on and marked up. And because the development forked so much, I need to entertain the possibility that Philip had a private version of the CVD driver that none of us saw, one that might help us dig out of this.

"Which leads me to ask you: do you have a laptop of his that's still around? And can I take a look at it, for a little bit?"

■

After a few minutes of rummaging through Philip's office, Rebecca found the laptop—there were three stacked on each other, but the one on the top had been his favorite, its case fashioned from titanium, its body so thin that it looked like you could cut yourself on it if its lid was closed.

Back in the living room, Alicia slid a memory stick into a slot on the side of Philip's laptop, plugged it in, and turned it on. "It wants a password," she said. "Any ideas?"

"Rebecca?"

"Too easy. Not secure at all." Without consulting her further, Alicia hammered out some keystrokes and got a foghorn of rejection. A second attempt got her in, though, and she smiled and laughed. Probably some kind of physics in-joke.

A few minutes later Alicia's face lit up. "This is good. This is good! Look at this, Rebecca: look!" She spun the computer around on her lap to face Rebecca. On the screen was a program that, for the most part, was completely unintelligible to her, but nestled amid the lines of computer instructions were glosses in Philip's precise English:

If the subroutine above returns a value outside the range of ±2 * 10^-3, the routine that computes galaxial drift should be run again. # There must be a better way than this to decrease latency: minimizing lag is of the utmost importance. Return to this with a clear head. And so on.

"This'll help," Alicia said as she copied files to her memory stick. "This'll help a whole lot. Thanks, Rebecca: I'll save our asses with this. Watch."

■

In his bedroom, Sean played video games for a while on his tablet while his mom talked with Aunt Alicia. He had homework but that could wait until tomorrow morning—the game was more important. If Mom had watched the game for more than five seconds she would have flipped and taken it from him because it was for people older than him. It was about a bunch of kids who ran through mazes made out of the strange things of adulthood: old decrepit castles; and places full of sweat and steam; and other places with neon lights and curtains that were decorated with pictures of women who were all lips and butts and boobs. None of the kids wanted to be in the mazes—every time you told them they had to go they'd get sad and look down at the floor—but they had to rescue their friends from school who had been kidnapped and taken there, where they were guarded by demons. Sean thought he was old enough to play the game even though he wasn't as old as the kids in the mazes: they were fifteen and sixteen. The game made it look like being that age meant that the world started dumping things on you whether you were ready for them or not. Sean felt like he could understand that.

After a while he placed the tablet aside, changed into his pajamas, got under the sheets, and turned off the lamp on his nightstand. Tonight would not be a night when Mom tucked him in: he would have to tuck himself in. After Aunt Alicia left, Mom would have another beer. Maybe she would come in super late when he was already asleep, and wake him up with a smeary beery smooch and a tender good night whisper. It was annoying when that happened, because he was already asleep and then he woke up and then he had to get back to sleep again.

As he drifted off, his father came to visit him, clothed in all his possible shapes. He wore an astronaut's black latex spacesuit with six slits in the back, from which three pairs of idly flapping angel's wings emerged. On top of the spacesuit's helmet was a tall black stovepipe hat that was also a rakishly skewed fedora and a wizard's pointy cap. In one hand he held a king's scepter; in the other, a policeman's baton. His feet were clad in roller skates that had switchblades in their toes in case he needed to kick someone.

"Hello, my son," Sean's father said. "I am busy being a hero. But now it is time to tuck you in for bed: good night."

"Hey, Dad," Sean said, keeping his voice down. "Whatcha doin'?"

"I am climbing high mountains; I am making all the sciences; I am putting all the thieves in jail where they'll die." His wings shivered.

"Thanks, Dad."

"Do you need help with your homework?"

"Nah: I'm gonna do it tomorrow before school."

Dad chuckled heartily. "This is what you *should* do, because you are as smart as I am! Tonight, the other kids are looking at their homework and saying dirty words. They say *I don't understand this,* and then they say the *f*-word."

"I know! I don't know what their problem is."

"It's because they don't pay attention! They just sit there in class like *duh*." Hovering in midair, Dad twirled in a tight circle. "Sean! I have to go save the princess from the tiger now: it's already eaten off her foot! But remember: you are my one and only. Call me and I will forget the princess, and I will forget the mermaid, and I will forget God. I will be here as fast as I can! I will put all your enemies in jail!"

"Thanks, Dad."

"Goodbye, my son; good night, good night," Sean's father said, and disappeared.

24

LEVITICUS TATTOO

It sometimes seemed as if Rebecca's father, Woody, might have taken Philip's passing almost as badly as Rebecca herself. Though the irregular conversations he'd scheduled with Philip on abstract philosophical matters were his not-so-covert way of keeping an eye on the unknown quantity who'd somehow managed to snare the love of his only daughter, over time those discussions had grown into something rich and vital and perhaps inexplicable.

Woody had, in fact, gotten a tattoo in Philip's memory, at what he himself admitted was "well past the age when a man should think about getting inked up." It was on his forearm, and read, in a font that looked lifted from a twentieth-century schoolbook, "Leviticus 19:28." It got him dirty looks sometimes: the sight of it would inspire occasional atheistic hisses and comments about why he'd want to memorialize a book of the Bible so strongly opposed to basic human rights and the consumption of shellfish, but then he'd point out that that particular verse, in the KJV, read, "Ye shall not make any cuttings in your flesh for the dead, nor print any marks upon you: I am the LORD." This brought people up short: sometimes, if he was lucky, Woody would get to have a good debate about the fallibility of texts, or the presence of comedy and irony in the Bible, or some other subject, right there in line at the hardware store or the local coffee shop.

"My faith is at its strongest when it sits on its weakest foundation," Woody had said, once, evasively, when Rebecca had come across him with a glass of Scotch in his hand and gotten him to talk about his decision to get the tattoo: she'd known better than to ask him who or what he placed his faith in, since that always resulted in some kind of cryptic question meant to make her meditate on the ineffable or some such. But Woody had delivered Philip's eulogy, and in it Rebecca thought there might have been more of a clue of what he was thinking. "The man we lay to rest today was my son-in-law; he was a physicist at the cutting edge of his field; and though he did not attend my church, like at least a few members of my congregation, he was an atheist who believed in the necessity of evidence to verify claims made about the world in which we live. And though I disagreed with him on that last point, I wouldn't have had him any other way.

"When he first asked for my daughter's hand in marriage, I set a condition: that he engage with me in conversation on matters of theology and metaphysics, areas in which I have to say I initially found his knowledge lacking, as smart as he might have been in other respects. We kept these meetings up for years, and I'm happy to say that he regularly proved me wrong, disturbing preconceptions I had about the world even as I tried to shake his own. I must admit that I entertained a faint hope of converting him, or at least getting him to acknowledge that if atheism was a valid way of relating to the world, it was not the *only* way. I imagined myself finally winning our long argument in my old age, and regarding it as one of my greatest achievements as a man of the cloth. Now I realize that if I had ever won that argument, I don't know what I would have done. I never wanted to have the last word in our decade-long debate. Especially not this way. Especially not now.

"Philip Steiner was a man who believed in the sanctity of evidence, in that which could be observed and verified. Well, death is the last brute fact. For some of you this is the first time you've been in a room with the dead; for most of you it won't be your last. I have delivered eulogies at dozens of memorial services, and I've never gotten used to it. I always find myself wanting to shrink away from the bare fact of another person's mortality, and with it, the reminder of my own. And as much as I hate this forced knowledge, I cannot imagine what it is like for my grandson, deprived by his father's passing of decades of innocence that should have been his by right.

"You get used to seeing the dead. But you don't get over it.

"So you use humanity's most precious talent, the gift of language, to try to cheat the reaper, to keep the best part of yourself alive past the day your body drops. You speak to those you love and you try to copy your thoughts into the minds of others. You write things down in the hope that your words will come before the eyes of strangers. You try to be the first to uncover a new truth about the world, so that when others repeat that truth it carries your name along behind it. But at the end of it all you have to face that last brute fact: not even the most cunning of us can negotiate with a stopped heart. And to be reminded of this, to see the bare evidence of it in front of us, is to remind us that we have so little time, and there is so much in the world to see and know, and that even if we use that time as best we can, even the most fortunate of us will see and know so little. Not even a neuron of God's mind. Not even a drop of the great ocean.

"But despite this, despite this confrontation with our own certain and inevitable failure, we keep trying. And sometimes we succeed, a little, and ensure that those who follow us will succeed a little more.

"In 1834 Ralph Waldo Emerson wrote in his journal that 'to distrust the deity of truth, its invincible beauty,' is 'to do God a high dishonor.' And I believe him. And I hope that Philip Steiner would not be offended if he heard me say that I also believed that through doing science he was honoring God, in his own way."

■

Woody and Marianne Wright had a reception at their home after the funeral, and at Rebecca's recommendation they had it catered by a Mexican restaurant nearby: there were foil trays full of enchiladas in neat rows and coolers full of craft beer in tallboy cans, and the physicists tucked into the food in reverent silence. Rebecca herself didn't have much of an appetite—she mostly sat on the couch in the living room and received condolences, though at this point she'd rather have taken all these expressions of sympathy for granted: the performance of bereavement was tiring.

If such performance was bad for her, it had to be worse for Sean, who could not be entirely certain what had happened, or what he was doing, or how he should think. She felt protective of him: she knew that there was a certain kind of well-meaning person who saw a child's grief as pure in a way that an adult's could not be, and who might offer him a treacly kind of insistent sympathy that would end up provoking him to public tears. So far he'd been holding up well, with occasional twitches of the lip during the service: Rebecca had held his icy hand throughout. But his reserves of composure had to be coming to an end. After he'd eaten a little she asked him if he wanted to go back to his grandparents' bedroom to play video games on his tablet, and as he left the reception, his eyes already beginning to glisten, he seemed grateful to be relieved of duty.

In addition to the grief was the awkwardness that resulted from people who would not have been in a room together except for another person who was irrevocably absent. Rebecca's parents had not seen Philip's parents since Rebecca and Philip's wedding, years ago: Rebecca saw the four of them in one corner of the living room, standing there in communal silence, unsure of what to say. Despite his stooped shoulders, and his hair that had gone fine and white, Philip's father resembled Philip enough for Rebecca to have a slight jolt of mistaken recognition when she caught him in her peripheral vision. It was his eyes that were nearly identical, though age had turned Mr. Steiner's to crystal. They would twinkle in better times.

Philip's colleagues approached her one at a time, shy and strangely shameful. Most of them just offered quick consolations and retreated, as if she had something catching, though Dennis favored Rebecca with a lengthy monologue on the status of work in the lab and how they were planning to pick up where he'd left off. Rebecca only understood about a third of what he was talking about—he seemed to assume that she knew as much about his research as he did—but she figured that this was his own way of memorializing Philip, and she genuinely appreciated it.

Alicia Merrill spoke to her last. This was after most of the guests had already left, though a few diehards had decided to stick it out for a while, and Rebecca's parents thought it'd be rude to ask them to leave. Someone had gotten some more beers from a nearby liquor store, and a few people had taken it upon themselves to reheat some of the leftover Mexican food in the microwave for a second meal. There was laughter in the living room now, light and forgetful. But Rebecca retired to the kitchen, cleaning dishes by hand even though there was a dishwasher right next to her. She wanted to give her hands something to do; she wanted to give her face a chance to wear whatever expression it wanted.

Alicia appeared in the kitchen doorway. "Hello," she said.

"Hi," said Rebecca, her syllable half sigh. Truth be told, she'd never really liked Alicia: she seemed to have a kind of arrogance that was more attributable to malice than obliviousness, and Rebecca had halfway suspected she had a crush on Philip that he had either not picked up on or been too circumspect to mention to his wife. Though Rebecca felt sure it wasn't the kind of thing he'd ever have acted on—he wouldn't have endangered the completion of his great work for a frivolous dalliance with an academic underling, and he was a better person than that anyway.

Not was: had been. Had been a better person.

Alicia stepped into the kitchen. "I'm very sorry," she said, looking up at Rebecca, small and unblinking.

"I appreciate it," Rebecca said, which was the response she'd settled on: *Thank you* seemed somehow inapt, and *Well, how do you think I feel* sounded ungrateful.

"There was one thing I didn't like," Alicia said. "During the eulogy I didn't like the God talk. We didn't need that."

"Hm."

"You don't need God to explain these things. That's the point. He did what he did because of the person he was. He was a good person. You don't need to explain that."

"Oh, wow," Rebecca said before she thought, then turned her attention back to the dishes in the sudsy kitchen sink, scrubbing off stubborn strings of hardened cheese with a sponge.

But Alicia still stood there silently, and when Rebecca turned to face her again, she drew near her and gave her a full and unexpectedly intimate embrace, standing on tiptoes and fitting her whole body against Rebecca's. She had a faint smell of vanilla.

"I was inappropriate," Alicia blurted. "I'm sure your father meant well. I'm sure he was describing things as he saw them."

"It's okay," Rebecca said, marveling that she herself had the spiritual resources to console another.

Alicia clutched Rebecca for a few moments longer, then abruptly stepped away. "Okay then," she said, smoothing her blouse and flicking away a stray soap sud. "Okay."

"Okay," Rebecca said, smiling slightly.

Alicia continued to stare up at her owlishly. "I have an idea," she said. "This is what I wanted to tell you. You and I. You and I . . . we could go running together. Let's go running together, on the towpath. We'll do it a couple of times, and if it works out well we can make it a regular thing. It'll get you into great shape. I'll go a little more slowly than I usually do so you won't tire out."

"I'd . . . I'd like that," Rebecca said, surprised at herself for saying so.

"You should be able to carry on a conversation while running: if you can't do that you're going too fast for your fitness level. So we'll have to talk while we run. To make sure I'm not pushing you too hard."

Rebecca nodded. "I understand."

25

BRICTOR'S PARTY

At last the dreaded day finally arrived, the Saturday night of Britt and Victor's party in New York City, and wouldn't you know it: the dress that Rebecca had bought from Conrad's, the one that had been selected just for her by the benevolently invasive Magic Matching Fit System, didn't actually fit. It looked *okay*, but it hung on her like she'd borrowed it from a friend: shapeless in the waist, baggy in the butt. It was stupid of her not to have tried the dress on as soon as she'd gotten home, she thought. But Sean had been home when she'd returned from the mall, and he'd been bullied *again* at school and was lying on the couch, sniffling. So as soon as she'd seen him, she'd just plunked the Conrad's box down in the bedroom and left it in its sealed shrink-wrap, taking most of the rest of the evening to talk it through and settle him down. And she hadn't opened the box until today. She should have known better than to have that foolish faith that Big Data knew you better than you knew yourself. Still, though, the color was nice: she'd deal.

(Note to self, Rebecca thought: karate classes for the boy. Even if they wouldn't actually teach him to whip someone's ass, they'd make him *think* he could, and the bullies would sniff his self-confidence and back away. At least one hoped. Anyway, mere mothering wasn't cutting it.)

Then it turned out that her car was down: apparently it had started downloading an automatic firmware update at three a.m. last night, and the installation process had frozen with the progress bar a few

pixels short of completion. A call to customer service got her nothing but a synthesized voice that somehow still seemed exasperated,
saying that the car's manufacturer was "aware of an issue" and that
technicians were "working to resolve it as quickly and as safely as
possible." Little good that did, and without the complete firmware
update the car was basically bricked: she couldn't even boot it up to
drive it manually. She'd have to ride the train.

A taxi ferried her to the Princeton Junction station, arriving just
in time for her to board a double-decker New Jersey Transit car that
took the express route into the city: the next stop was New Brunswick, and then it sped through a bunch of smaller towns to stop at the
Newark airport, the junction at Secaucus, and the city. (Strange how
all New Jerseyans still referred to New York City as "the city," as if
it were some kind of Platonic ideal and New Jersey's own attempts at
metropolitan areas were pale, unworthy imitations.)

She had failed to charge her monitor shades the night before, since
she rarely used them, and without a book or an e-reader she was
forced to resort to her own thoughts to pass the time. She seemed to
be the only person in the car without some sort of gadget to keep her
company, except for a mother and five-year-old son in the seats opposite her. They looked, she thought with a slight twinge of shame,
poor, and after considering her own visceral reaction she realized
that it wasn't because they were Hispanic, or because they were both
a little overweight (the mother more so than the son), or because
the boy was pulling a burger with a machine-milled patty out of a
greasy paper bag, or because if they were already on the train when
she boarded, that probably meant they lived in near-dystopian Trenton. The impression she got of their poverty was because neither
of them had electronic distractions for eyes or ears, and in a public
place that marked you as hard up as surely as if you were dressed in a
black plastic garbage bag. Rebecca, realizing this, suddenly became
self-conscious, and sat up straight in her seat, as she imagined she
would if she'd learned her manners from parents with old money.
(Though then she thought that if almost all the people on the train
were ensconced in their own private electronic spaces, she was essentially invisible, so her appearance didn't actually matter.)

So it was just her and the mother and son, here in what Rebecca
would have once thought of as the "silent world." Most other people

on the train were quiet, staring at whatever video image or website was being projected on their monitor shades, but two passengers in the car were shouting into the air at random times: a woman who, Rebecca gathered, was having an argument with her husband concerning some drama with the extended family ("I *am* relaxed. It's just that Irene's coming and I wasn't *expecting* Irene to actually *accept* my invitation. . . . I just made it out of politeness, she should have *known* that. . . . If I'd figured Irene would actually come I wouldn't have asked Bill to come too. He's going to throw a fit. . . . Yes he will, and Irene knows full well we're loyal to Bill, not her.") and an adolescent boy who sounded like he was playing a video game online with a group of people scattered across the world, one of those first-person shooters in which men scavenged blasted hellscapes littered with weaponry, piercing each other with bullets and blades while their scores ticked upward with each kill. Rebecca looked over the back of her seat at him: his thumbs adroitly manipulated a pair of wireless controllers in his hands while explosions bloomed on the insides of his shades' lenses. "Come on would you *pop* that motherfucker?" he screamed. "The fifty-cal spawns right there! Grab it! Split his head open."

Britt would be the one to answer the door, Rebecca thought, and the first thing she'd want to know is why her RSVP, sent a month ago, had been minus the expected plus one. She could already hear Britt saying, "But where is your *husband*," in the tone of voice a teacher would use to reprimand a delinquent student who'd forgotten his homework, expecting to hear an excuse involving foreign travel, or separation at the very worst. If she left things vague at first then she'd only be letting herself in for later inquisition once the drinks started flowing, but if she unloaded all the details then and there, then she'd come off as vindictive, as if her sole reason for showing up had been to cast a shadow on another's grace. No: better to be inexplicit at first, to relay the basics without the backstory. More circumspect; more considerate.

"I told you I *am* relaxed, Gary. . . . You're my husband and if there's one person in the world I ought to be able to talk to however I want, it's the man I chose to spend the rest of my life with. Out of all people you ought to understand this. Out of all people you should be the one to cut me a little bit of slack."

"Guys, we're fighting a bunch of niggers this round. You can tell 'cause as soon as they respawn they run straight for the nine-millimeter, like they're gonna get you with a gat, holding it sideways and shit. A sniper rifle is a white man's weapon. Let's grab 'em, head for the high ground, and rain death on these niggers from above."

Past New Brunswick the train picked up speed, gravity's hand gently pressing Rebecca back in her seat as the scenery outside turned to a smear of gray skies and graffiti-covered warehouses.

Maybe they already knew, all of them: the details were easy to find online, though since she hadn't shared social media connections with the rest of the gang for years, they would have had to remember that she existed in order to decide to Google her. Rebecca expected that at least some party guests would sneak off to the bathroom to surreptitiously retrieve her vital stats from a phone, sparing themselves the trouble of pretending they hadn't forgotten her. Though sometimes people would run a search on you while you watched these days: that wasn't as rude as it used to be.

Britt had probably Googled her already, actually: it'd be like her to Google everybody on the invite list. Maybe that would make things easier.

"I told you, Gary, that it's a bad idea to do business with family. Didn't I say that. Keep business and family separate, I said, especially if you're talking about a *loan*. But you said I needed to be an adult. . . . *Yes that is exactly what you said.* . . . How are we all going to look Irene in the eye with Bill standing right there?"

"Thanks for the friendly fire! Fucking faggot."

In the seat across from Rebecca, the mother reached over, a beat too late, to cover her son's ears. She scowled over the back of the seat at the teenager a few rows behind.

There were times, and this was one of them, when Rebecca quietly yearned for twentieth-century definitions of civility, when commonly shared air was meant to be filled with words generally agreed to be suitable for all. But in the years after Rebecca's travels through the silent world, the exodus of its former citizens was nearly complete—the only people who remained were the ones who could not afford to leave. Each person now lived in his own handpicked society with its own rules for behavior, and so the world they left behind had no rules at all. If you entered a public space without the electronic means to escape elsewhere while machines ferried your body from one place to another, then you knew what you were getting into.

Maybe she wouldn't stick around at the party for long. It was kind of a shame to take this long trip into the city only to turn around after ninety minutes and head back home, but that would be enough time to do what she wanted: put in an appearance, look good (though not as good as she'd have looked if the Magic Matching Fit System had served its purpose), and leave them while still wreathed in mystery, that rarest of information-age commodities. She'd found this Bulgarian woman on Craigslist to babysit Sean overnight. Maybe after the party she could hit a bar before catching the two a.m. drunk train back to Jersey: she could spend some time in one of those well-appointed lounges in the hotels along Central Park South. Maybe she could try her hand at being smiley and leggy and getting a guy to buy her a martini. Though maybe there'd be an interesting guy at the party, some guy who'd also failed to complete his homework assignment of bringing a life partner.

God, why was she even going to this? What reward was there in revisiting one's past?

"Well okay then. . . . Well *okay*. At the party you take Bill aside, and I'll take Irene aside, and you talk to him man to man and I'll talk to her woman to woman. But this is your fault. I just wanted to have a few good friends over for drinks and snackies without all this *drama* for once in my life."

"Where the fuck are you people *going*? Why the fuck are you dropping out when we're six kills ahead? Are you leaving me alone here to get shot up by these niggers? Guys I'm gonna get raped right in the ass—"

The teenager threw his hands up in the air, tossing his controllers away as his monitor shades were yanked off his face. He stared up at the woman who looked down at him, breathing heavily with wordless rage. "I'm not racist!" he yelped.

In the woman's fist the featherlight frames bent, and broke.

■

"Welcome to our humble abode," Britt said as she waved Rebecca into the apartment with a grandiose sweep of the arm intended to scotch any attempt to read that greeting without irony. New Yorkers, even the transplants, took such pride in the bits of light and space they'd carved out for themselves in this cramped and darkened metropolis. Rebecca's house in Stratton was twice the size of this apartment, with its own backyard, but in its context this smaller place, with its low ceilings and rooms that were shaped and fit together like Tetris blocks, still seemed somehow much more opulent. And it had to have been ridiculously expensive as well: Victor had some sort of three- or four-word title at his pharmaceutical corporation—"chief" and "director" and "executive" were all in there somewhere—and pharma money had brought them an expansive view of Central Park uninterrupted by the buildings in between. "The developers bought their airspace," Britt said as Rebecca drifted to the window. "It cost a pretty penny: we barely make ends meet." There was no need for that last little lie: Britt's mouth twisted unprettily as she said it.

She looked good. Her face was a little rounder, and each strand of her hair was the same flat gold shade instead of the natural mix of brown and blond she'd had in her twenties. But she'd taken care of herself. Victor had gone stone Daddy Warbucks bald, and also slightly jowly: perhaps the shape of his body had changed to complement his job. He didn't quite seem to make the matched pair with Britt that he used to. She doubted they chatted about each other constantly when they were apart; she doubted they still dealt in feverish public nuzzling. Such behavior would not be suitable for an Executive Chief Director, a Chief Director Executive.

Kathryn and Carson were already here, seated on a plush, leather-upholstered couch that looked like it was meant for people who had the money to purchase it but not the time to sit on it. Rebecca could see Victor cutting his eyes over to it nervously—he was probably calculating the social cost of suggesting that everyone make themselves at home on the floor, and weighing that against the expense of shipping a couch polluted with sweat and skin oil back to its Austrian makers so it could be cleaned by the only people who'd know how to do it properly. His desire to avoid embarrassment was barely winning out.

Kathryn was conversing with a guy who seemed like he was probably one of Victor's underlings at his job—they even looked a little alike, though the guy's suit was a touch threadbare, and his scalp was wavering on its commitment to baldness instead of going all in. Carson was sitting awkwardly between Kathryn and the larval-Victor, who were talking over him; he seemed perfectly at home with his own thoughts (and the expression on his face reminded Rebecca briefly of Philip's, at times when he'd been at social gatherings and hadn't been able to conceal his feeling that he'd rather be in the lab instead). Kathryn had placed her hand on Carson's knee with the ease of familiarity and habit, their touch the sign of a second silent conversation they carried on as she talked about whatever it was with the Victor-in-training. That was good to see.

"Can I offer you a drink?" Britt said as she drew Rebecca farther into the room, then: "Listen to me: *a* drink. Can I offer you a *lot* of drinks?" Whenever someone made an unprompted joke about knocking back a lot of booze like that, it made Rebecca paranoid. It made her wonder if she *looked* like an alcoholic, sallow-faced and sagging. If this dress had fit, if the Magic Matching Fit System hadn't taken it upon itself to serve up a practical *muumuu*, then Britt wouldn't have cracked that joke: she might have passively-aggressively offered her some water with no sparkle and a stick of celery on the side.

"Let me show you what we've got at the *bar*," Britt said as she slipped her arm into Rebecca's and steered her toward a table draped with a simple white cloth. The man standing behind the table was not more than twenty-four: he stood at military ease with his hands clasped behind his back, his white shirt still showing the creases it had acquired in its cellophane package, his bow tie comically dwarfed by his tree trunk of a neck. Before him were rows of bottles of red and white wine; some beers and canned sodas in a plastic bucket with ice; some decent gin and vodka; and, off by its lonesome, a bottle of one of the Scotches that Rebecca's father preferred on special occasions: Glenrothes, the squat spheroid bottle of dark amber begging to be cradled in the palm. "I'll have a glass of that, neat," Rebecca said, and the young bartender smiled with approval: gin- and vodka-drinking women of a certain age were likely to get suspicious looks, but a woman with a taste for good bourbon or single-malt Scotch could enjoy the pleasures of eighty-proof liquor while maintaining an air of mystery and class. The bartender broke the seal on the bottle, uncorked it, and favored her with what had to be somewhere between a double and a triple shot.

"Oh, goodness, that's more than Victor would pour for *himself* at home *alone*," Britt said, the melody of her voice failing to mask the miserly nature of her reprimand. "But does it matter? We're here to have *fun*, right?

"Let me introduce you around, now that more people are showing up," Britt said to Rebecca (and Rebecca shared a conspiratorial glance with the bartender as she turned away: the next time she came to the bar she'd pass him a palmed Reagan and ensure she got generous pours for the rest of the night). Then Britt leaned over and hissed in her ear, "I heard about poor Philip. I am *so* sorry."

She "heard." As if this were seventy years ago, when the news of the day passed between gossiping housewives over back fences.

■

After a couple more drinks (one of which gave Rebecca the chance to prove her bona fides to the bartender by slipping him the twenty and saying this particular vintage was pleasantly peaty), the party reached its maximum of around thirty guests: not so crowded that it was hard to move, but a little close. Despite the implication of the invitation that Rebecca had received from Britt—that this would be an intimate "getting the band back together" sort of thing—the gathering seemed to be dominated by Victor's executive-level colleagues, most of whom had wives with them who looked decidedly younger. (Several probably actually were, but Rebecca had heard about a few people who'd gone through this extraordinarily expensive treatment that involved getting nanobots injected into your skin beneath the epidermis, where the microscopic, spiderlike machines went about the business of reconstructing your face at the cellular level, lightening dark spots and smoothing out wrinkles. It gave better results than plastic surgery hands down, but supposedly it itched like mad, twenty-four/seven, and antihistamines offered no relief: you had to learn to ignore it.)

Rebecca found herself feeling wallflowerish, wondering again why she'd come. Kathryn and Carson had withdrawn to a corner by themselves, her hand reaching up to gently cup his shoulder (the public performance of her affection subtle but continuous). Britt was flitting from person to person, playing the hostess, too busy to talk: you never had fun at your own party.

But: across the room, here at the party by herself apparently, munching a handful of Chex Mix, was Jen. She seemed . . . long? Not tall, but long. Her face had gotten longer, as if Time's hands had grabbed her hairline and her chin and pulled. There was an odd dampness to her too: not as if she'd just stepped out of the shower, but as if a cartoon raincloud hung over her, constantly sprinkling her with a light mist.

Jen had never exactly been one to cripple you with laughter, but any company was better than none right now. Rebecca angled through the gathering, holding her drink out ahead of her, trying to remember how to summon the music in her voice that signaled unexpected recognition. "Jen?" Yes. There it was. "So good to *see* you." Now the lie. "You haven't aged a *day.*"

"I'm quite sure I have. But it's good to see you, too. Chex Mix?" Jen proffered the bowl, but Rebecca waved it away.

"I know how you feel," Jen said. "If they could shell out for a college-boy bartender, you'd think they'd have those guys who come around with little doodads on trays. Like those little hot dogs that are wrapped in croissants."

"You'd think." Rebecca already felt trapped. Her glass of Glenrothes still held a healthy serving—unless she drank it faster than alcohol of this quality ought to be drunk, she wouldn't have an excuse to return to the bar for another forty-five minutes. Well, the gods of whisky would have to forgive this little indiscretion. She belted back a big swallow, trying to hide a grimace.

Jen's eyes suddenly lit up, like a child's who had just caught the first glimpse of the gift that lay beneath the glittering wrapping paper. "I heard about your *husband!* That must have been *awful.*" She leaned forward expectantly.

"I still miss him," Rebecca said. "And how have *you* been?"

Jen's face fell slightly. "I came here alone, if you're wondering. I was married for a little while, but then I got divorced. I didn't have any kids, so there's that. Now I cook all the time—I have a blog where I talk about my recipes; you should check it out—and I raise my basset hounds. I've got five in the house right now. The dog smell gets in everything, but I don't mind. I like it. I hope I don't smell too much like dog for you."

"I'm going to get another drink," Rebecca said. "Do you want one?"

■

Well. After that another drink was *certainly* called for. That would be her: third? Second? Third. But the level in the bottle was lower than Rebecca would have expected: clearly someone else around here was hitting the good stuff as well.

She could see what the immediate future held: the fuzz that adhered to the edge of her thoughts indicated that she was past the point when she'd stop drinking this evening. Her third would turn into a fourth as people with other evening obligations (kids or spouses or other parties) drifted out; then the diehards would be left behind as the hosts began to gently hint they ought to go. Maybe the old gang would be the last to leave, and they could put a period on the evening with some pleasantly drunken reminiscences.

Rebecca turned to see Kathryn looking up at her—she'd finally pulled herself away from Carson (and she saw him in the middle of the room, surrounded by a group of young men in suits, talking a lot with his hands: his bystanders sometimes found themselves dodging his expansive gestures). "He's explaining the causality violation device to those guys," Kathryn said. "But I've heard his spiel before. How're you doing?"

"I'm okay. I don't really know anyone here. Britt's busy being Britt, and Jen's, well . . . still the same."

"I *know*! She's so gloomy that I practically had to *run* from her: she harshed my buzz so hard it felt like a punch in the stomach. She said she was sorry if she'd forgotten how to, you know, *chat*: she sometimes goes for days without talking to anyone but her dogs, and they're not good at small talk. Jesus! She *always* got this kick out of bumming people out: I never understood why we didn't just boot her out of the core group. Just sat her down and said, Look, you're not pulling your weight here, the written warnings haven't helped, and we're going to have to let you go. Here's a cardboard box for your personal belongings; a security guard will escort you out."

"Core Group Incorporated."

"Ha!" Kathryn sighed. "Listen to us. We're so mean."

Rebecca looked around at the partygoers and the way they performed their laughter for each other, the women covering their mouths and looking away, the men tossing back their heads and letting loose with sequences of merrily bassoonish honks. "Everyone looks so happy," she said.

"I *know*, right?" said Kathryn. "Okay, you figure these people maybe just see each other online, where they've been keeping up appearances: like, you only post videos of your baby when he's smiling and giggling, not when he's bawling and crapping all over the place. You figure everyone censors the bad stuff because *you* do it! But then you meet in person and you think, maybe things actually *are* okay for everyone. I mean, I'm actually happy in my life right now, so it's not impossible that everyone else is, too. You know?

"Hey, Becca, can I tell you something that I guess I should have told you already?"

"You sound like you're about to tell me I'm adopted."

"No! I . . . I wanted to say I'm glad you set me up with Carson. I mean, I guess you didn't *actually* set me up with him, so much as put us in a room together and let things happen."

Kathryn edged closer to Rebecca and dropped her voice as she slid a stray lock of hair back behind her ear. "You remember, you gave me this fussy talking-to about guys, like a year and a half ago, and I was like, *Where does she get off?* But I guess I got over it."

She drew her arms around herself and looked at the floor. "Honestly it scares me that he might be *the guy*, you know? I've never met *the guy.* And he's not what I thought *the guy* would be, when I think back on what I thought my wedding would be like at thirteen. But that's the thing, right? You have to realize that if you don't find your dream guy like the one in the movies, that's not settling—that's just being real. You know?

"So thanks."

Kathryn pulled a mockingly dour face. "Okay: that's enough *unburdening.* I'm killing the mood. I'm gonna go rescue Carson from those pharma guys—or maybe rescue those guys from him, it looks like. Wanna come with?"

"I'm gonna get another drink," Rebecca said. "I'll join you in a sec."

■

But by the time she got back to the bartender (after a side trip to the restroom, which involved waiting in line behind a couple of guys) the bottle of Glenrothes was almost cashed out. "Sorry about this, ma'am," the bartender said as he poured the dregs of Scotch into her glass and tossed it away. "Everybody's going to have to move to the cheap stuff soon: either that or start tripping on Siestalerts, if you got 'em." "Don't *ma'am* me," Rebecca replied in a tone intended to be a little flirtatious, but the expression on the bartender's face indicated that she hadn't pulled it off. Well, too bad.

Suddenly she just felt, geez, *tired*. Not full-on, passing-out tired: just enough to want to sit down for a bit. There was that nice cushiony leather couch that she had yet to try out, with an empty space right in the middle that was just asking for her butt to plop down on it, and the couch was placed so that it granted a great view of the windows through which you could see the high-rises on the opposite side of Central Park. It would be nice to sit there and watch, and just chill out for a little bit.

The couples on either side of her shifted over to the ends of the couch to make room—they both seemed like they'd met at the party, and while the guy on her left made a big show of ignoring her in order to lavish attention on the woman who was beginning to find herself pinned against the arm of the couch, the guy on her right (to the slight dismay of the woman he was sitting next to) greeted her with a firm, businesslike handshake. "I'm Bruce," he said. It was that guy that Kathryn had been talking to when Rebecca arrived at the party, the Victor version two. He had a glass in his hand like Rebecca's. So that's where the good Scotch had been going: some of it, anyway. "How do you know these guys?" He waved his free hand as the woman on the other side of him aggressively nestled closer to him.

"Britt and I used to hang out together back in the day. Me and Jen and Kathryn and her." Rebecca thought she'd made some kind of grammar mistake, something really embarrassing, and was aware, even as her perception of time began to alter and her eyelids got a little heavier, that that kind of extreme self-consciousness meant that she was on the edge of a drinking blackout, fighting against it, losing. Her hand brought her glass to her lips and tipped it back; she swallowed.

"Jen and Kathryn and Britt and *I*, I should have said." Was her head bobbing around or something? Did she look funny? The chick who was with this guy was looking at her funny.

"Oh gotcha—what was your name?"

"Rebecca."

"Nice to meet you. I'm Bruce! I'm one of Victor's work buddies, though I guess what I should say is that I *report* to him. A lot of us here are in pharma. You must feel lonely." He moved a little closer to Rebecca, a millimeter or so: Rebecca could hear the squeak of the couch's leather as he shifted.

"Not really," Rebecca replied, though in other circumstances she might have been a little friendlier: the woman (who the guy was slightly pulling away from, and probably not consciously doing so) had placed her hand on Bruce's leg about halfway up his thigh, and was sliding it toward the inside, in a gesture meant to be seen. If you have to pull that stunt you've already lost, Rebecca thought; the guy would sense the move as an admission of failure, and it'd blow up his ego beyond repair to have women on either side of him, having their quiet little war.

Bruce moved another millimeter closer; the couch's leather cried again. "Let me tell you something. My official title is . . . what is it. It's Vice Chief Executive Director. I report to Victor, the Chief Director . . . Executive . . . Cheevector Directrix."

Rebecca tried to edge away from Bruce as he continued, but didn't want to come too close to the guy on her other side, who was now leaning over and whispering intently into his potential inamorata's ear. "I report to Victor, who reports to a guy who reports to the CEO!" Bruce continued. "Our CEO has written a very popular book about getting ahead in business. His *secretary* has even written a book, that's not as popular but is still pretty popular, about being a woman and, you know, being powerful, in business, being in the proximity of power. It's like, ladies can be badasses in the workplace but also they can be ladies too. It's like, each chapter in the book gives you good business advice, and the chapters all start with pictures of bras: like there's a sports bra, and a lacy thing, and a *boostie-ay*." Bruce held his hands in front of his chest and mimed lifting invisible breasts upward. "It's like, you don't just wear a bra for *support*, but for *identity*. It's like the bra you choose is the role you choose to play. But you can have plenty of different bras! And beneath your business suit you can wear *any bra you want*. It's *your choice*."

"That's . . . very affirming," Rebecca said.

The woman's hand crept slightly farther into Bruce's lap.

But Bruce kept talking. And Rebecca soon realized that this wasn't an attempt to pick her up by tossing around his job title and playing the sensitive feminist: he really found workplace politics legitimately interesting. "Let me tell you about the world at the *executive* level," Bruce said, and then dropped into a monologue riddled with business-speak: nominalized verbs, and verbalized nouns, and sentences like "So *finally* we settled on this list of action items, right?" Rebecca caught the other woman's gaze and they shared a covert eye roll. Good: she'd know Rebecca had no aspirations here.

The point of Bruce's story appeared to be that Victor was an incompetent poseur. "He's got the *look*," Bruce said. "But anybody can get the look: I'm halfway there myself. When he got hired into that position he didn't look like that. Beanpole thin; full head of hair. People are like, who's the kid in the suit too big for him, got an office all by himself. I'm telling you he went bald as a *pure act of will*. To look the part. Ate steaks drowned in butter and gained six inches in the waist. If you asked him what goes *on*? Like in the company, right under his nose? He'd bullshit you with a bunch of bullshit, but he wouldn't know. But *I* know."

Suddenly Bruce slipped his arm around Rebecca's shoulders (no!) and leaned in to speak to her *sotto voce* (no! bad!). The other woman lifted her eyebrows as Rebecca tried to pull away.

"I see you're drinking his Scotch, too," Bruce said.

"Hey," the other woman said, patting Bruce's leg.

"It's okay," Rebecca said. "Hey look I'm gonna get another—"

"I don't even *like* Scotch. I think it tastes like *soil*. But I've been drinking the most expensive stuff in the house because I hate the man, he's a fucking fraud, I want to hit him where it hurts however I can, I can't wait for the day when he gets caught out and shows his ass in front of God and everyone."

Bruce withdrew from Rebecca, breathing a little heavily. "Then *I* will be the Chief Executive Director," he said, stabbing his chest with his thumb. "Everyone'll be like: yeeeah."

"Hey," the woman on Bruce's other side said, squeezing his leg. "Let's go have a cigarette."

"I don't smoke," Bruce said, confused and bleary-eyed.

"Then now's a good time to try it: you'll like it." She stood, taking Bruce's hand. "Come on: let's go outside. Get some air."

Bruce rose, a little unsteady, and looked down at Rebecca. "Okay," he said. "I'm going to . . . *have a cigarette*, I guess."

"It was nice to meet you," Rebecca said, not getting up, speaking to Bruce but keeping her eyes on the woman.

"Nice to meet you, too," Bruce said, and then the woman fairly pulled him away, into the dissipating crowd.

Well. Let love bloom where it might. Or a good lay, anyway. Though likely not that good.

But that was over. What had Rebecca come to sit on this couch to do? Oh yes: chill out, and check out the skyline, and try to enjoy the pleasure of being alone in a crowd.

But it was not two minutes before some other dude with gin on his breath sat down next to her and said, "Listen: I don't know you, but I've seen you here at this party all night, and I just want to talk to you for a little while. Just . . . I have things, in my head. Just want to talk."

■

This guy (and Rebecca had already forgotten his name, just as she was already failing to remember whatever—what's-his-name . . . Bruce? Bruce—whatever Bruce had said about whatever it was) wanted to talk, at some length, about a taco truck that he visited on his lunch break, almost every day. "There's this taco truck, it's out front of the building around lunch time: a *real* taco truck that's all dirty and sketched out, not one of those big clean shiny fake ones that's run by some corporation. And the girl who works in the taco truck is some kind of art-school chick with pink hair and a little piercing in her nose. And the thing is—I'm married, but I totally want to marry this art-school chick. Not bang, but marry. I look at her as she leans over to hand me this greasy taco that might have a little bit of rat meat in it for all I know, and I feel like a *vampire*, I want to just jump up and latch my teeth into her neck and give her that bite, you know, just freeze her as a second-year art student who's selling tacos part-time to cover the rent. 'Cause what's going to happen is: she's going to finish art school, she won't be able to get a job, she'll let her piercing close up and dye her hair brown and go legit, she'll end up at some kind of soul-killing job in a cubicle, she'll marry another dead soul, then one day she'll come out to the taco truck that is the *sad highlight of her day*, eating this rat-meat soft taco instead of charging a forty-dollar pizzetta to the corporate account is the *only act of subversion available to her*, and she'll see some wiry scruffy dude serving up tacos and think, *I want to marry that guy*. And it won't be some kind of, you know, escapist fantasy. The thought will *hurt*. Like getting slapped hurts."

Rebecca was too drunk, but at least she was aware of it—she knew that she was comprehending but forgetting, and knew that words were merely passing through the mesh of her mind instead of sticking there. She wanted to respond: clearly he'd poured his heart out over whatever it was, and some acknowledgment of that was the least she could do. But the subtleties of reliably coherent speech were well beyond her capabilities at this point—any idea she had would fall out of her mouth in a slurred tangle of syllables, and she would be *so* embarrassed, she would have to deal with that look someone gives you when they're trying to pretend you haven't done something extremely embarrassing, that way they look away and say *Aaaaany-way*. So she settled for arched eyebrows and the slightest of nods, playing the silent sage.

It worked! The guy smiled. "I shouldn't have told you all that," he said. "But I just . . . it just came out of me. Stupid story. Cheesy little story."

"S'okay," Rebecca said, trying to ignore the way the guy's face was blurring as the room rocked back and forth. Her brain and stomach were beginning tense diplomatic negotiations.

The guy stood. "Well: see ya."

Rebecca lifted a hand in a desultory wave as he backed away, but soon someone else slid into his vacated spot on the couch, a woman, the one from the beginning of the party who Rebecca thought had had that nanotech skin-resurfacing procedure done. "Excuse me?" she said. "I . . . I just wanted to tell you that you have this look about you. Like, a glow. Can I just . . . *be here*, to talk with you for a second?"

Rebecca felt glass sliding against her fingertips: she looked down to see that as the woman spoke she was extracting the empty glass from Rebecca's grip and replacing it with another, this one full of something clear and strong.

She looked up from her seat to see that there were a half-dozen more people standing around her, making a show of looking away, but still waiting, with the fidgety nature of those unused to needing patience. Was that . . . were these people actually in a *line?*

■

Many of those who remained at the party at this point, close to one a.m., had seen their fortieth birthdays, and so if their memories of the world before the advent of the Internet seemed almost ancestral to them, passed on through blood instead of having been obtained by firsthand experience, at least they had a dim idea of a past world in which you could remember what you wanted to remember, and forget what you needed to forget, a world that existed before fear of the permanence of information changed each and every utterance into a self-conscious performance. In the new world a woman who was blackout drunk was the rarest of beauties: how often could you have the pleasure of speaking to someone while being dead certain that they would never remember what you said? Who would pass up the chance to write history on water?

And so each of the last guests sat down next to Rebecca, one at a time, to toss their confessions into the bottomless pool of her alcohol-addled mind. *I shouldn't tell you this,* but I've been cheating on my husband. It's not out of revenge—it's not like he deserves it or anything—but just out of boredom. Also, his face has changed. It looks . . . I don't know. Like dough. Like he eats nothing but cake, morning, noon, and night. The guy I'm cheating with still has cheekbones. *I shouldn't tell you this,* but sometimes in stores I get a little light-fingered: I have for decades. I toss the trinkets in a dumpster as soon as I get outside—it's just the rush, you know? Beating the guards; beating the cameras. Knowing something that the cameras don't know. Having a secret. *I shouldn't tell you this,* but last night for dinner I just ate an entire jar of candy sprinkles, the kind you put on cupcakes. I looked in the mirror and my teeth had turned eight different colors. I brushed them until my gums bled. *I shouldn't tell you this,* but I have no idea what I'm doing at my job and I'm supposed to be in line to run this company. Basically I say things like *This is a high-stakes endeavor, guys* and *If we reclaim the buzzwords, we reclaim the market* and everything just kind of works out. I mean, if I can get by at this level knowing as little as I do, the guy at the top may not know a goddamn thing. *I shouldn't tell you this*, but I just bought this toy. It's got one knob here, and another knob here. *I shouldn't tell you this*, but I have this kid now, it's eighteen months old, and—listen to me. *It's*. I've been drinking. I have to remember. I have this kid and *he's* eighteen months old and when I look at it in its crib I don't feel anything. Not love or hate or anything. I literally feel more affection for the purse I got on sale last week. And I meet all the other mothers for afternoon coffee and they've all parked their strollers at the coffee shop entrance like they're Harley hogs, and I listen to them billing and cooing, baby this and baby that, mine's crawling, is yours talking, baby baby baby, and I feel like such a fucking fake. I can't remember the last time I sat down in a chair for an hour to read a book in peace and quiet. *I shouldn't tell you this*, but there are times at work when I've been staring at the same spreadsheet for two straight hours and I'll just quietly reach into my pants and stroke myself a little: not going all the way and bringing myself off, I'm not crazy, just getting kind of halfway there. Because I need to remind myself that if I can do that, if I can get a hard-on even while I'm looking at this spreadsheet, then I'm still an animal, and that means I'm still human. But I have this fantasy where I get hauled in front of the head of HR and he says, I hear you were pitching a tent while looking at the April sales forecasts. And then I get promoted. *I shouldn't tell you this*, but whenever I see one of those Muslim women in public with her head covered by a scarf, I think about just reaching over and ripping it off and running my fingers through her long dark hair, right in front of everybody. I think about the look on her face when I do it. *I shouldn't tell you this*, but I love it when my husband's away because at night I get an entire queen-size bed to myself. I sleep sprawled on my back like a child making a snow angel, and as soon as my head hits the pillow I'm out for a solid nine hours. Bliss. *I shouldn't tell you this*, but sometimes when I'm alone in the house I hang bedsheets over all the mirrors: it just makes things easier. *I shouldn't tell you this*, but I've been having these weird dreams like every single night for three weeks now, where I'm being *contacted*. Not by ghosts, exactly, but people from other histories, where things turned out differently than they did here. And they're all envious. And they all say: *You are so lucky. You live in the best of all possible worlds. And you don't even know it.*

■

What—

What the—

Where? What's that?

Neet neet neet neet. Alarm.

Not fire: clock. Not danger: alertness.

But the light isn't right and the world is at the wrong angle.

In front of Rebecca—no, beneath her: she was hanging off the edge of a bed—was a carpet, industrial, the pattern one of navy and burgundy triangles. On the carpet was a dark brown pool of: ugh. It was a few hours old. There were chunks of undigested food in it: the sight of them as the stink of the puke hit her face made her dry-heave, her stomach muscles twisting themselves in pain as a rope of yellow bile dangled from her lip. She spat it away.

Next to the puddle of vomit was a trash can, which presumably she'd aimed for in the middle of the night and missed. She slid over and looked inside—ungh, she'd left a gift there, too.

Where the hell was she? The alarm was still buzzing insistently. Oh. Yes. Hotel. New York City hotel room, as the sun's persistent rays shone down between skyscrapers and peeked around the edges of privacy curtains. The alarm clock sat on the nightstand: like hotel room alarm clocks generally were, it was crazily complicated, but a couple of blind slaps at the top silenced it, at least for a little while.

What time was it?

Eleven *forty*?

Shit!

She pulled herself up to a sitting position, leaning back against the headboard. In a hotel room. Checkout time at noon, probably. But how did she get here?

Then she saw that propped against the lamp on the nightstand was a little cream-colored envelope, with a single word embossed across it in dark blue foil:

brictor!

Oh. Oh no.

With shaking hands (half from DTs; half from terror) she took the envelope from the nightstand, opened it, and pulled out the matching piece of stationery inside. The message was handwritten, the letters loopy and childlike. Britt.

Hey, Becca—

I don't know how much you remember about last night. (I bet not much: things got a little crazy!) We decided to put you in a hotel so you could sleep off the fun times. (Don't worry about it: it's on us. We passed the hat and everybody chipped in a couple of bucks. It was the LEAST we could do.) I called your place, too—your sitter said she'd stay with Sean until you get back, but she's charging time and a half and she sounded pretty pissed off on the phone. We can't do anything about that, though! So don't hang around: if you catch the 12:30 train out, which you can if you check out by noon—oh by the way you're at 33rd and 7th, near Penn Station—you can get back to Stratton by a little after 2:00.

It was so, SO good to see you. We all had SO MUCH FUN. It was just like old times, in more ways than one hehe. Let's not wait forever to do it again!

Britt

P.S. Srsly: don't WORRY about this. We're your FRIENDS. *FORGET* about it.

■

Eleven forty-four now. Checkout in sixteen minutes. There were a lot of unanswered questions here.

Had she made such an unimaginable ass of herself last night that Victor (or, worse, Britt) had decided she was not welcome to sleep it off at their place, but that she was too drunk to dump on the street without feeling guilty about it?

But then Britt wouldn't have left such a nice note. And that postscript: what was that about? Was that like, *We've all been there, so no worries?*

The last thing she remembered, she thought as she pulled herself out of the bed—her clothes were still on, including her shoes; really, she could just grab her purse and go—was sitting on that couch and talking to what's-his-name, who was it . . . Bruce. Bruce had said something about his job, and he had this girl on his arm he'd just met there that he was . . . that he must have been really into. Rebecca remembered them leaving so they could go get it on, and then . . . not much after that. There was some talking to someone or something. But the party as a whole had been kind of subdued and adult, with many of the people there being Victor's coworkers: it wasn't the kind of party where someone would paint a pentagram in the middle of the floor and try to summon Astaroth. It was unlikely that it got too out of control.

Rebecca shuffled into the bathroom, which looked awful—the toilet was unspeakable, with vomit coating the inside of the bowl and spattered on the outside; more puke painted the floor next to the shower. But surely the cleaning ladies of this hotel had seen worse.

Eleven forty-eight: no time to linger. She pulled down one of the plush white towels from the rack mounted over the toilet and wiped down the stains as best she could. She wanted to at least give the impression that she'd made an effort.

God, Sean must be losing his mind right now: he hated when people didn't stick to their promised schedules. She'd pay the sitter beyond the call of duty: time and a half was asking too little. Between the expenditure for bonus babysitting and the Reagan she tossed on the bed on the way out in mute apology, this was getting to be an unexpectedly expensive outing.

She took the elevator downstairs and hurried out of the hotel, tossing the keycard at the front desk without waiting to see if the woman behind it picked it up. Ten minutes of purposeful striding (each click of her high heels keeping time with an icepick stabbing at the back of her eyes) got her to the bowels of Penn Station, and though she really could have stood to find a toilet stall somewhere to sit and be nauseous, even a grotty Penn Station toilet stall, the place where Despair made its home, there was no time—the train she needed to board had issued its final call, and she scooted on board the double-decker, getting a seat alone up top, in a rear car, before the train got under way.

She leaned her head against the window with her eyes closed and her hand on her chin, trying to look as if she was not ill, so much as deep in thought. Boarding the upper floor of the double-decker may have been a mistake—the swaying motion of the train car up here was jostling her delicate stomach around inside her, and she was really longing for a nice clean sparkling toilet right now, just imagining leaning over and gagging and spewing up the rest of what was in her, thinking about that good, good feeling you have after you've gotten poison out of your system, the spiritual relief that comes from your body's involuntary confession.

She must have made an absolute fool of herself: not just some penny-ante acting out, but something completely deplorable. And the worst thing was that she could be sure that Britt would never, ever tell her. That was the bargain that drunken friends made: whatever you did during a blackout dropped out of history. If she called Britt up and sheepishly said, "Hey, did I do anything crazy last night?" then Britt would be guaranteed to reply, "Oh, nothing at all, nothing at all, we didn't even notice anything wrong, just forget it," no matter what happened—

—oh God. As her stomach muscles clenched without warning, she felt bile burble between her pursed lips, felt it collecting in the palm of her hand, felt it running down her arm to pool in her lap. This was what it was like to feel pure unalloyed shame, though even this was probably not the shame she'd feel now if her actions last night, whatever they were, hadn't been stricken from the record. She furtively looked around her: no one was paying attention. There was a teenager watching some kind of action movie on a tablet; there was a guy with monitor shades who was shouting that you couldn't *possibly* realize who you were fucking with if *that* was the deal you had the nerve to bring to the table; there was a young woman wearing a clunky pair of pink headphones, bobbing her head in time to a secret syncopation. No one noticed the quietly retching woman in the seat near them, or everyone pretended not to notice. Which, in the end, was much the same.

26

GRAND PROTECTORATE

It was Carson's love of science fiction that awoke within him the desire to become a scientist, though the chain of events that led from one to the other was not what one might have expected. As an adolescent Carson had spent one long summer devouring the classics of golden-age SF that took up dusty racks in the back of the local public library, checking out a seemingly endless series of smelly, coffee-stained omnibuses with yellowed paper and loose bindings, their detached signatures Scotch-taped back in. He was too young then to be annoyed by the workmanlike quality of sentences more notable for their concepts than their felicity, but he liked thinking about what he would later learn is called "worldbuilding" by science-fiction writers: he liked to consider the invention from whole cloth of cultures and languages that only vaguely recalled those with which one might be familiar.

Through junior high school, and into college, Carson built a world in a stack of fourteen thick spiral notebooks. It was not so much a narrative as a travelogue of an imaginary place. The time was the year 141,015 AD, otherwise known as the 562nd year of the Founding of the Grand Protectorate. The setting was Jupiter, along with sixteen of the largest moons that orbit the gas giant. Each one of the moons was home to a different species that had evolved from humans over the past 140,000 years: the Pa'Thrawn from Ganymede were cat-like creatures who excelled at hand-to-hand combat; the mysterious beings known only as the Kin lived on Io, and were telepathically linked so that any one of the Kin was involuntarily privy to the thoughts of all; the Zik-Zik of Amalthea possessed space-folding technology that would allow them to instantaneously teleport from one place to another; and so on. Each of the emperors of the sixteen moons of the Grand Protectorate held a key to an indestructible strongbox kept at the heart of the planet Jupiter itself; the strongbox contained an object whose true identity had been lost to history. It was known only as the Gift. But the millennia-old ancient scrolls that had been passed down to the monks of the Grand Protectorate implied that whoever obtains the Gift would acquire ultimate power: eternal life, omniscience, and all sorts of other good stuff. But even if you could manage to extract the strongbox containing the Gift from the planet's core, the box required all sixteen of its keys to open. And so the members of the Grand Protectorate were perpetually at war with each other in an attempt to collect the keys and gain ultimate power for themselves.

The best you could say about the idea of the Protectorate was that it was obsessively detailed: by the time Carson reached college each of its species had its own elaborate history as well as a somewhat rudimentary philosophy to match. He kept his major undeclared for as long as he could: he was a decent student in the history classes he took, and equally decent in the low-level chemistry and physics courses he signed up for to fulfill requirements. But he couldn't decide which way to jump: science promised better job prospects after graduation, while the humanities courses had the greater share of women, a benefit not to be underestimated.

In the spring semester of his sophomore year, he took a creative writing class as an elective from a guy who'd only started teaching there a year ago. He insisted that students refer to him by his first name, Corey. "I want you guys to just feel loose and free and experimental and unpretentious," he said on the first day. "No fake Hawthornes up in here! No, like, Raymond Carvers!" Carson could not have been more excited. This was a guy who didn't have a prejudice about which tales were worth telling and which were not. At last those notebooks would have a use beyond solitary pleasure: the world within them was realized well enough by now to support a few short stories. He envisioned a linked cycle to begin with, something like Bradbury's *Martian Chronicles*, and saw a future in which Volume

Four of the Saga of the Grand Protectorate reached the top of the best-seller list, the first three volumes having staked out more or less permanent positions a few slots below.

But as the semester progressed, Carson began to suspect that Corey's protestations of literary tolerance were not backed up by his true beliefs. He wasn't too hot on workshopping—"true genius isn't the result of a committee," he said a couple of times—but he'd pick a different story out of the submissions each week and photocopy it for the class so that he could tell them what he thought was good about it. Six weeks in he still hadn't gotten around to Carson's work, though Carson was pretty sure that in terms of pure quality he was miles ahead of everybody else in the class. The other students were just turning in wish-fulfillment fantasies! Lynn, who was attending college on a golf scholarship, wrote a story about a woman in the LPGA who was on the green of the eighteenth hole and attempting to make a game-winning putt; eventually she cleared her mind of all distractions (her family, who didn't think her career was worthwhile; her boyfriend, who wanted her to spend less time on the links and more with him) and sank the ball. Anne, the secretary of the Inter-varsity Christian Fellowship, had a story about Jane, an objectively gorgeous woman who attends her first fraternity party; a handsome senior hits on her but she turns him down because he's just trying to carve another notch on his bedpost, and she feels good about herself in church the next day.

It was all so on the nose. Meanwhile the short stories that Carson was turning in, which he was planning to polish up at the end of the semester to send out to science-fiction magazines, were being returned with no comments save an irritatingly noncommittal "B+/A-" at the top of the front page. Occasionally there would be a single exclamation like "Crazy!!" along with it, but none of the comments on style or character or plotting that the other students seemed to be getting. He was not naive enough to imagine that his writing was perfect—if anything, the wishy-washy grading said otherwise. There was nothing for it but to go to Corey's office hours.

"Carson, my man, come in, come in, pull up a chair, have a seat," Corey said when Carson knocked on his door. The office was a tiny room, and Corey kept it dim: a single lamp on the desk lit the professor's face from below, giving him the unintentional appearance of an interrogator. Behind him hung a poster of Jimi Hendrix in tie-dyed tones, smoke blooming from between the guitarist's parted lips. Next to that was a blowup of a black-and-white photo of Miles Davis in what looked like a glittering gold tank top, cradling his trumpet with his eyes closed as if in meditation.

"I guess I'm wondering what you think of my writing," Carson said. "Other than, you know, A-minus, B-plus."

"Well!" Corey said. "I'm glad you came in. I was *hoping* you'd come in on your own at some point, actually—I would have extended the invitation myself for you to come to my office hours, but when you write *See me* at the top of a paper, students come in thinking they're doing something disastrously wrong! Ha-ha.

"Anyway . . . this is some crazy stuff you're writing here! Really, really out there. No one else in the class is doing anything like this. Like, that one story, about these people who live on the planet Europa—"

"Europa's a moon."

"Yeah! They live on Europa, and they've been gene-tweaked—"

"Gene-spliced."

"Gene-spliced! It turns out that like thousands of years ago their ancestors were gene-spliced with turtles, so they can grow their own body armor for combat. That is an idea I would not have thought of!"

"Thank you," said Carson.

"Okay!" said Corey.

They sat there quietly for a moment, the professor looking at Carson and Carson looking over the professor's shoulder at heavy-lidded Hendrix. "Okay!" Corey said again, a little more loudly, making Carson jump in his seat. "Before we move on to the next part of this conversation, the critique, as it were, we need to acknowledge the elephant in the room: we need to look at that elephant and say, okay, I see you, now move on over there out of the way. Here we are in this room, you and me, and it is hard to escape the fact of our races. It is hard to avoid the fact that American history has granted my race certain advantages that it has not bestowed on yours. And I'm aware that I have this 'invisible knapsack,' so to speak, that grants me certain social privileges. But please understand that I'm *aware* of the unequal power dynamic between us, I can examine my privilege, I've got that *awareness*, and I'll do whatever I can to mitigate it.

"Now. That dirty business is out of the way. This science-fiction stuff, it's okay. But I really feel like you could be tapping a richer vein here. There is an American rage that is your birthright, handed down to you from many generations! That's your history! And if you were to let a little bit of that out on the page instead of, you know, keeping it bottled up, I think that you would find your work to be much richer as a result. But this stuff—and I'm going to be frank here, and I apologize for that in advance—it's thin gruel. This is denying your birthright. Is this the best you can do? I don't think it is!"

It was about then that Carson figured that going into a science major would involve dealing with a lot less day-to-day bullshit. The message was clear: that while the work of Corey's white students would be taken at face value, whatever Carson turned in was doomed to be read through the lens of his race. If the story was not explicitly about race, then the tale would instead be of his reluctance to speak on the one subject that, surely, must occupy all his waking thoughts.

The fact of the matter was that Carson did tend to avoid talking about race: not because he was afraid to confront certain nebulously defined truths about himself, but because he found the subject to be excruciatingly uninteresting. He felt that race was not a characteristic that was a part of his identity, but one that was projected upon him by the gaze of others who looked on him; as such it was ephemeral, there and gone as soon as the gaze was broken. And yet other people, most other people, seemed not to think that way at all: they seemed to insist that race was a thing as real as flesh.

A career doing science would be a way around all that. No one would look at a published scientific article and comment with a sorrowful shake of the head about its author's reluctance to confront issues of identity. The author would merely relay the results obtained from the data; the data, which knew neither race nor gender nor any other demographic, would be free to speak for itself. A community that thought in that way would be a good one to join. They'd understand what really mattered. What a relief that would be, to gain entry to a place filled with those in love with fact and not belief.

Carson declared a physics major near the end of his sophomore year. He continued to submit more Tales of the Grand Protectorate to his creative writing professor, who gave him the same vaguely noncommittal grades in return, refusing to discuss his work with the rest of the class (though, years later, when he dug those stories out and reread them, Carson wondered whether that might not have been a tender mercy). But something of the pleasure of writing those stories had been taken away.

His final grade in the class was a B+. On his final paper, a thirty-page epic about the formation and subsequent fracturing of the alliance between the Protectorate members that inhabited Jupiter's four largest moons, the professor wrote, "I really liked having you in my class. I know you'll do good things eventually!" Carson never wrote another word of fiction again.

∎

And so Carson had one of the qualities that would go on to help him thrive as a young physicist: a willingness to spend as much time in the lab as possible, away from people. If he did not have the monomaniacal love of science that seemed to be typical of the most successful in the field, he did have a love for the company of the people he thought of as his own, and for being alone when the lab cleared out late at night. He rarely, if ever, thought about the fact that black physicists were so uncommon, or why that might be; he could go to a three-day conference and easily not notice that he was the only African American in attendance. As a professional you learned to focus only on what was interesting. Here was a place where one was judged on the quality of one's ideas, not on irrelevant social externalities.

But Carson could not live every second of his life out among scientists. In particular, there was this one guy who sometimes manned the security desk at the entrance to the Merrill lab who really got under his skin. His name was Spivey. The guards worked in pairs that were constantly being changed up according to some apparently randomized schedule, and most of the time, when Spivey was with that Brazilian woman, or that guy with the buzz cut who had the gone-to-seed build of an ex-military man, then he'd leave Carson alone. But when that other guy Terence was there, then Spivey would have himself a grand old time, heckling Carson as he entered the building and went into the lab. "Hey! Hey, Carlton! Why don't you come over here and talk to us a second! I don't *bite*. In such a hurry! You guys are building a time machine in there, right? I'd think the point of that is so you don't *have* to be in a hurry. Fine—get on in there, Carlton."

Just race, race, race, all the time with this guy. And whenever Spivey shouted at him like that Carson felt a certain unwelcome pressure to behave in a certain way, as Spivey thought a black person should, or shouldn't, in order to be judged "authentic," whatever that might mean. It was bad enough to have a white person try to press those obligations on you, but to have a black person do it was even worse. The whole idea was so depressing.

And yet Spivey got to him, even though Carson kept his interactions with him down to a curt hello at the most. The man's voice got into Carson's head, and during times that should have been tranquil—doing science; spending time with Kathryn—it spoke up, and needled him, and ruined everything.

■

Carson's love life was a little complicated right now. He was seeing Kathryn, whom he'd met, or re-met, at a party thrown by Rebecca, the widow (what a weird word for someone so young) of his former boss who'd died in a car accident. But he was also occasionally, or maybe not so occasionally, sleeping with he guessed was the phrase, sleeping with Alicia Merrill, the former post-doc who'd stepped into Philip Steiner's place in the lab after his death. But that, the sleeping with, took place off the books, outside of time. That would be hard to explain to Kathryn. She would be unlikely to understand.

Kathryn was confusing. Even someone like Carson, who was not the savviest at picking up signals, could see that she was into him. She never failed to slip her hand into his when they walked side by side down the street; she called him on the phone sometimes just to talk; mornings in bed she preferred to linger. But . . . well, it was hard for Carson to explain it, really, but Kathryn found race really interesting, to a point that was, well, a little weird.

It was probably too strong a claim to say that Kathryn was racist: there was the obvious reason that that didn't really make any sense, and after all, she was given to make unprompted statements like "I really feel we've reached a point where race doesn't matter to people anymore." But in the lab, or at a conference, no one would ever actually *say* that: they'd take it for granted, and get on with the science. And Kathryn had . . . well, a curiosity, about people not like herself. But there was nothing wrong with being curious, right? There was that time when she'd wanted to go to the Bridgewater mall for an afternoon of browsing followed by dinner at one of the swanky restaurants there. There was one store that seemed to deal exclusively in preppy college-boy gear—khaki slacks, and floppy baseball caps, and long-sleeve shirts in washed-out colors—and yet standing at the entrance were a pair of leggy mannequins who were dressed in slim-fitting jeans, black stilettos, and blood-red T-shirts featuring silk-screened images of a young Angela Davis, her name helpfully stenciled in block letters beneath her portrait. The mannequins each had their right arms extended, holding black-gloved fists in the air. Their eyes followed Carson and Kathryn as they passed by, and Carson could faintly hear the whirring of the motors that drove their cameras. "I wonder what it's like to have a 'fro?" Kathryn said, looking at the mannequins' shirts. "Like, this big thing on your head that *grows out* of it. I bet you have people coming up to you all the time to ask if they can touch your hair. You go to sleep and wake up and your hair's got this crazy shape, I bet." It wasn't like she'd suggested that black women were ugly or stupid, was it? Just because she found race interesting in a way that Carson did not didn't make her a racist, did it?

Spivey, or at least the embodiment of doubt that had lodged itself in Carson's mind and taken on Spivey's voice, had different opinions. "Listen, Carlton. You have to understand something about white people. Not *all* of them, but a *lot* of them. A lot of white people *love* the twentieth century! They *love* it! And they are doing the best they can to tow the corpse of the twentieth century behind them into the twenty-first. Because they want to convince *you* that you are still in the twentieth century, when *they* were on top. And they will do every sly little tricky thing they can to get you to go backward in your mind, to back then."

But Carson was sure, or thought he was, that there was no malice in Kathryn; he was certain that what existed between them was some form of love, and that what they were engaged in was the mutual making of pleasant memories. She comes over to his place a couple of times a week now, and as they sit on the couch talking, she has an occasional impish habit of whipping off her top without warning, as a means of announcing that the time for conversation is over. She crosses her arms, grasps the hem of her shirt, and quickly lifts it over her head, but sometimes the neck of the shirt catches on the tip of her nose, and there she is, hands above her head, her face obscured save for a smile graced by a dimple on either side. She's wearing a bra that Carson hasn't seen before, and her lifted breasts invite themselves to be cupped by his hands. She shakes herself free of the shirt, tosses it to the floor, throws her arms around his neck, gently pulls at his earlobe with her teeth, and whispers: "Now then." A memory like that will keep a man warm in a cold time.

But then that doubting voice intrudes. "Aw, come on, Carlton, get out of here with that. You know what she's thinking right now, 'cause you know she's got that twentieth-century heart. You don't have to shy away from the truth. You don't have to be shy." And the memory wilts.

■

It wasn't like what Carson was doing with Alicia was cheating, or anything like that. Sure, Kathryn didn't know about it, and Carson was perhaps not telling her something that she would prefer not to know. Besides, it was hard to explain.

The work that was going on in the Merrill lab was intense. And Alicia felt like they were really close to a major breakthrough. Once she'd taken over the lab she'd adopted Philip's work habits, and she'd always been something of a workaholic to begin with. Carson had stepped up his time in the lab as well—sometimes he'd spend fourteen-hour days there—and so the two of them were there together a lot, batting ideas back and forth. Sometimes they'd get so deep into the work that they'd forget to eat: suddenly, one or the other would say "I'm *starving*," and they'd head to a bar with a late-night pub menu, get a couple of beers and a plate of nachos, and head back to the lab for another hour or two. It was exciting, in the way that you hope science will be exciting when you enter the field, and it so rarely is.

Carson had found Alicia a little off-putting at first, a little snappish and cocksure, but over time he'd decided that she was actually really cool. She was smart and self-confident, and on the occasions when she and Carson talked about something besides causality violation, she had a quick wit about her. Once you got used to her she was really great to be around. And, yes, she also had a certain effortless beauty.

It was hard to say which one of them came on to the other—they probably both remembered it differently. But one evening, around midnight, after they'd gone on a late-night trip to the bar and had their usual nachos and beer—and Alicia had pressed an eye-watering shot of single-barrel bourbon on Carson in addition to the beer this time, since she'd been in a particularly good mood—they were deep in discussion about the CVD that loomed over them in the center of the room, and they'd both felt as close to solving the central problem of getting the device to work as they'd ever been. Carson remembered thinking to himself that he'd wanted that moment to stretch out forever—feeling like they were just on the edge of discovery, the two of them sharing this incipient idea with no one else, the future full of potential. This, right here, was the most exciting that science got—after this, either you failed and went back to the drawing board, or, if your results survived the withering gaze of skeptics, you got your accolades and it was over. If you could just stay right here forever, just on the edge.

The next thing either of them knew they were rolling over and over on the floor together, trying to swallow each other and push their hands through each other's flesh. Unlike the times he'd slept with Kathryn, several of which he could remember in fine detail, there was something about this particular encounter that would not let it stick in the memory: he could remember that it happened, and its aftermath (Alicia's flat "That was quite pleasant"), but nothing more than that.

Soon after, the whatever-it-was became, if not a regular thing, then something more than a one-off event, at random times of the day. Alicia would note that she was leaving the lab for a few hours, and a half hour or so after that Carson would also leave: he'd drive over to her apartment, they'd spend some time in bed together, and then he'd return to the office. Alicia would come back a half hour later. It was hard to imagine that no one in the lab noticed that Alicia's and Carson's absences tended to coincide, trained as they were to search for patterns in data, but no one ever mentioned it. It wasn't their business, after all.

Carson never thought about Alicia when he was with Kathryn, since he had gotten into the habit of never talking about his work with her, and Carson only saw Alicia when he was at work. Sometimes he thought about Kathryn when driving back to the office after an impromptu visit to Alicia's apartment, and it was only then that he indulged in comparison: how Kathryn's disrobing was usually accompanied by a self-deprecating remark, even though Carson was by now intimately acquainted with her shape and appearance, while Alicia stripped with an efficient indifference born of self-confidence; how Kathryn's lovemaking was warm and languorous and communicative, while Alicia's was fierce and mechanical. Sometimes a few minutes after sex she would roll out of bed, open her laptop, and send an e-mail.

Kathryn didn't know about Carson's sort-of, affair he guessed you'd call it, with Alicia, though when he'd brought Kathryn to the lab, before he and Alicia had started sleeping together or whatever, it seemed that Alicia had perhaps gone out of her way to be curt toward her. Kathryn just plain didn't like her: after her visit to the lab she'd said, "I get that she's trying to be, like, a strong woman, but that doesn't mean she has to be *mean*. She's so *mean*. I don't see how you put up with her every day." Alicia knew about Kathryn, but she and Carson never talked about her. And presumably, Alicia didn't much care.

■

One night Carson was the last person still in the lab, after even Alicia had gone home: the time was half past midnight. He hadn't wanted to leave: Alicia had shown him some of the comment code from Philip's private versions of the software driver for the CVD, and it had given him some ideas about making a routine run a bit more efficiently. And there was that feeling of being close: in the air, all the time now. Everyone felt it, but nobody really wanted to talk about it, out of fear of a jinx.

The knock on the door didn't register in Carson's mind as such until he heard it twice: he said, "Come in," and Terence entered.

"Just making the rounds," Terence said. "You doing okay?"

"Sure," Carson said. "No . . . thieves, or anything."

"That's good," Terence said. But instead of leaving he edged farther into the room, almost shyly. "How's the time machine coming?"

"No idea," Carson said. "Maybe we'll be done any second now; maybe not."

"You guys are really busting your behinds on this thing." By now Terence was looking over Carson's shoulder at his desk.

"No other choice, really," Carson said.

Terence stood there for a moment longer and said, "I got a story for you. You want to hear it?"

Carson turned to look up at Terence. "Sure," he said. Alicia would have said the word in a way that made it clear that she resented the interruption, but Carson didn't have the heart.

"It's a good story," Terence said. "It won't take much of your time.

"Okay. My daughter Harlie is in fourth grade. And this is about the age where kids start to hear little bits and pieces about what it's like to be an adult, but they don't have the whole picture yet. So they come home repeating things they heard, that they don't really understand. And whenever Harlie says, 'Dad, I heard something at school,' I get this pit in my stomach, because instead of kicking back and relaxing, I might have to have some kind of a talk, about what happens when two men or two women love each other, or a guy thinks he should have been born into a woman's body, or who knows what else.

"So I'm talking to Harlie—this is last Saturday afternoon. And she says, 'I heard a joke at school. Do you want to hear it?'

"And I said, 'Sure.'

"And she said, 'Okay, here goes. Why do black people like watermelon?'

"And I thought, *Oh no, here it comes.* But before I get into it I at least want her to finish the joke. So I said, trying to keep my voice even, you know, like there's nothing wrong, 'I don't know, Harlie. Why do black people like watermelon?'

"And she gets this big smile on her face and says, 'Because it has a good flavor and it'll cool you off on a hot summer day!'

"And she looks at me confused, and then she laughs—*ha-ha*—to let me know she said the punch line, so now it's time for me to laugh, too.

"And I look at her. And I say, 'Harlie. Be honest now. Do you even understand that joke you just told? Do you even get why that's a joke?'

"And she kind of cocks her head sideways, and she says, 'No?'

"And I have to tell you. Maybe I shouldn't have been. But I was so relieved."

27

WEAKNESS LEAVING

Sundays in Rebecca's and Sean's household tended to be days of indulgence. First there'd be breakfast of Belgian waffles and strawberries, perhaps with a little scoop of vanilla ice cream on the side. Then in the early afternoon Rebecca would drop Sean off at the multiplex for a double-feature matinee, while she got four or five hours of alone time. Sean selected the films himself, though Rebecca forbade him to see anything with too much sex or violence. Still, though, he picked movies that someone his age should have had zero interest in—comedies about rich, lonely old men having their lives redeemed by perky, quirky women half their age; turgid tales of couples who lived in improbably spacious Brooklyn brownstones and who were forced to come to terms with their inherently adulterous natures. When Rebecca asked him about it she found that his choices were largely determined by the picture's director of photography: it seemed that he was purely interested in the interplay of color and light, finding performance and narrative irrelevant to his pleasure. (And indeed, on a few nights, Rebecca had entered his bedroom to find that he'd fallen asleep while a clip from a late-period Terrence Malick movie looped on his tablet, the screen showing a woman in a long cotton dress spinning in a wheat field like some kind of midwestern whirling dervish.)

He liked to sneak into movies, too: he'd time his picks so that he could leave at the end of one movie in time to get to the next before it started. It was a quaint, twentieth-century crime, and Rebecca opted to let it go: at least he was paying to get into the first movie, and he knew he was stealing something of value, rather than indiscriminately pirating flicks by the hundreds, hoarding them on a hard drive, and making specious arguments about how information wanted to be free. He'd grow out of it.

And so on this particular Sunday, Rebecca dropped her son off at the theater, returned home, and had a light lunch (a prepackaged dish of mattar paneer from Trader Joe's along with a bottle of Rolling Rock: taking it easy with the booze for a little while). Then she changed into her running clothes and drove down to the towpath in nearby Princeton to meet Alicia: she'd agreed to go on a run with her when they'd talked a few days ago. Alicia had suggested an "easy" six miles, but once she got out on the road she had a habit of willfully underestimating distances, so eight or ten was more likely. Rebecca was not looking forward to it: two days after her out-of-control binge in New York she was still feeling the effects, and though she hoped that some vigorous exercise would help her sweat the last remnants of the toxins out of her body, she had a feeling that if she didn't perform up to her usual standard, Alicia would sense her weakness and quietly—or perhaps not so quietly—judge her.

Alicia was lazily jogging in place when Rebecca pulled into the makeshift gravel-covered parking lot that let onto the towpath: her bike was locked up in a nearby rack. (Alicia's apartment was about four miles away: the ride over must have been her warm-up.) "Come on," she said with an odd impatience as soon as Rebecca got out of the car. "I already stretched. You stretch; let's go."

A few minutes later they were running beside each other down the towpath that ran alongside the Delaware and Raritan Canal, looking down on nuclear families in dingy life jackets who were attempting to steer canoes that insisted on fishtailing. A storm-felled tree jutted out from the shore into the water, and several turtles with tufts of moss on their shells had climbed out onto it to take in the early-morning heat. A portly, shirtless middle-aged man whose chest had been fried lobster-red by the sun sat in a kayak that drifted down the river, pulling at a joint as he thumbed out a message on the phone in his other hand.

Rebecca was already beginning to feel the ghost of a stitch in her side: a bad sign, this early on. And she felt like Goofus to Alicia's

Gallant: Alicia was setting pace as she chattered away, and the four strides that Rebecca generally needed to match five of Alicia's did not offer much of an advantage. But Alicia seemed like she had a lot on her mind and was happy to talk: perhaps she wouldn't notice that Rebecca was already flagging, ever so slightly. (It seemed to Rebecca that Alicia saw these regular towpath endeavors as opportunities for long, uninterrupted conversation. Alicia wasn't the kind of person who'd just sit and chat for a while. She was happy to talk if talking could take place during some other ostensibly self-improving endeavor, or she'd go out for coffee with a colleague to, as she said, "acquire social capital," but booking a spot on her calendar solely to shoot the shit with a girlfriend over a couple of beers was, in Alicia's view, not the best use of her time. Rebecca had tried to get her to be a partner in crime on a girls' night out—cute skirts and dinner and drinks in strange colors—but her proposal had been greeted with a flat exasperated *no*.)

"I went to this junior high school in Hopewell to give a talk the other day," Alicia said. "The general science teacher had asked someone from our lab to come out and talk to the kids about our work, to get them interested in science. And I have the best social skills out of anyone in the lab, so the duty fell to me. By the way, it helps a lot if you change the modulation of your voice when you talk to children that age. Not singsongy baby talk—they find that patronizing—but something subtler. Their ears perk up when they hear voices that aren't just a monotone. I bet you could do an interesting study about whether teachers whose voices vary significantly in pitch produce students with superior understanding and information retention. Interesting, but off-topic. I prepared an accessible talk for these kids about how gravity and time are related: nothing too complicated. And here's what ticks me off. After the talk I left some time for questions. And a bunch of hands shot up, which is what you'd expect. But all boys! Every one! And they were really eager, too. They weren't asking questions that were going to advance the field—even the smartest one of them was still just thirteen—but they were the kinds of questions that showed they were thinking about what I said and considering its potential implications. The kinds of questions that lead to doing good science. But the girls are not saying a thing! I'm answering questions from these boys left and right—and their hands keep shooting up, and they're almost about to jump out of their chairs—and the girls are just *sitting* there. Hands in their laps, looking at the floor. So finally when the Q-and-A dies down there are a couple of minutes left, and the teacher says"—here Alicia's usually smoky voice went high and mincing and full of up-speak—"*Maybe you could talk for a little bit about what it's like to be a woman in science? For the girls?* And I just got so sad. What the hell am I supposed to say? When I'm doing science my gender isn't interesting to me; the science I'm doing is interesting. And okay. There was a past when women in science were anomalies, but that was a dark and ridiculous time. We live in the future now! Can we just agree that I can talk about gravitation without having to point out the existence of my vagina before I begin? It's all so *trivial*. I halfway feel like I wasted my time going out there. I could have spent that time in the lab. We could have sent the possessor of a *penis* out there to handle the PR while I got some serious work done."

"I'm sure everyone involved meant well," Rebecca said. "It's not like the teacher wasn't on your side. She was trying to help."

"Everyone *always* means well!" said Alicia. "Everyone's *always* on my side!"

■

They jogged on in silence for a mile or more, Rebecca finding it increasingly difficult to stifle her rasps. "Can I give you some advice?" Alicia said.

"S—sure," Rebecca replied, wincing as she wheezed.

"A smoothie," Alicia said, "about thirty to forty-five minutes before a run. An insect smoothie. Not too heavy. A cricket powder base, for the protein. Add banana; mango; papaya; coconut water, or almond milk in a pinch. Throw all that in a blender with some ice. Drink it and you're good to go."

"Sounds good, but, see . . . crickets. No. I know they're ground into powder or whatever, but . . . not eating anything with six legs."

"You need to get over that," Alicia said. "Crickets are a fantastic food. Sustainable; inexpensive; full of vitamins and amino acids. The chicken of the entomophagy world: tasty and versatile. This is far enough: let's turn around here."

Rebecca's relief that more of the run was now behind them than ahead of them was muted by the slow realization that there was a slight upgrade all the way from this point on the towpath back to the car.

"I have something to tell you," Alicia said as the second half of the run began. "About that software I copied from Philip's laptop. This will matter to you. Listen."

Rebecca listened.

"Philip always wrote a lot of comment code, which is why I wanted to look at the versions of the CVD software he'd stored privately. But when I examined it I wasn't prepared for how much comment code there would be: several paragraphs of commentary following a single line of code, sometimes. And I wasn't expecting the comment code to . . . digress, in the way that it does. Not all of his comments are about the code they follow. In some versions of the software, almost none of them are."

"What do you mean?"

"The reason that some versions of the software were absent from our central repository was because Philip had been using them as a kind of private diary. In the comments he talks about himself. He talks about the past, spending a significant amount of time addressing events that occurred in the year 1996. He talks about feelings he experienced and actions that he took. He mentions you. He says a number of things about you."

"Alicia!" A sudden jolt of adrenaline gave Rebecca a second wind.

"After thinking about it, I decided that it was right, and necessary, to share all of this with you. I'll e-mail you the material in a couple of days. I want to extract the comment code from the rest of the program to make it readable for you, so that paragraphs of English aren't interrupted by blocks of Python."

"Alicia, I really appreciate you letting me know about this. And . . . I . . . I guess I'm really curious to know what he said. I mean, he wasn't the kind of person who'd openly talk about his feelings. You just kind of had to infer them. I . . . what I guess you'd call his silence on certain matters is something I had to learn to accept."

Alicia took a few moments to weigh her words carefully. "I'm not editing it," she said, "other than taking out the code. That was what I had to decide: either to give you all of what he said or none of it.

It wasn't an easy choice. Don't read it at a time when you're feeling fragile. You'll want to prepare."

■

"Come on, Rebecca, get it in gear," Alicia said a little later as she began to pull ahead. "Pain is weakness leaving the body. I've got to bike back to my place after this run while your car ferries you home! You can do this. I've been sleeping with Carson, on and off, the guy your friend is dating. What's-her-name. Katie? Kathryn."

How weirdly calculated and yet inexplicable that last disclosure was, following so soon after Alicia's previous revelation: Alicia's attempt to make it sound offhanded was so clumsy that it unwittingly came off as charming. Why now and why to her? Surely Alicia must have been at least half aware that Rebecca and Kathryn were lifelong friends, and that by speaking she therefore ran the risk of her declaration making its way to Kathryn's ears in one form or another. Was this some test of loyalty: was the information that Alicia had in hand the kind of thing that would make Rebecca beholden to her? Or was Alicia secretly *hoping* that Rebecca would tell Kathryn, because that would surely cause Kathryn and Carson to break up? Or maybe this wasn't a wheels-within-wheels, soap-opera kind of thing: maybe Alicia just wanted to share, and wasn't considering the consequences. Maybe she didn't think whatever she had to say was interesting enough to merit repetition out of her earshot.

Or maybe whatever was in Philip's comment code, which Alicia had seen and Rebecca had not, had given Alicia the impression that she and Rebecca were bonded in some elemental way.

"The whole thing is nonsexual," Alicia said.

Each drawn breath made razor blades bounce around inside Rebecca's lungs. "Wait: are you just lying in bed next to each other? Taking naps?"

"We take naps sometimes after sex. But it's all nonsexual. I'm aware of how that may sound to you. But it's true. Working on this project for years together we've developed an intense but entirely intellectual connection, and it turns out that sex is the best way to express that. But the sex doesn't mean what sex usually means to most people. It's hard to explain."

"What does Kathryn think about it? Have you or—"

"Well obviously I don't *know* what Kathryn thinks about it because I haven't *told* her about it: that's not my business. It's Carson who's dating her and if he wants to tell her about it that's his job. But I'd hope she'd understand that what we're doing shouldn't mean anything to her. Or at least she'd accept it if she didn't understand it. I'd understand it if I were in her position, knowing what I know."

Was Alicia picking up the pace a little? Yes: she was, even if it wasn't a conscious decision to do so. Rebecca, despite her best efforts, began to fall farther behind.

"It shouldn't mean anything and it doesn't matter at all," Alicia said, and Rebecca thought that if Alicia ran so fast that Rebecca was too winded to speak, then Alicia would leave herself free to interpret her silence as consent.

As if reading her mind, Alicia sped up again: now she was nearly sprinting. "I said you need to *get it in gear*!" she hollered over her shoulder; then she turned from Rebecca and obstinately drove herself up the towpath's grade, breathing heavily, stretching out the distance.

28

UNEXPECTED CALLOUT

At work the following day, still sore all over from the punishing run that Alicia had led her on, Rebecca was a little off her game as a pilot of Lovability's romantic avatars. None of the marks tipped to the idea that they were communicating with fictional constructs—the People Peeks were fixed at ten minutes, Felix's skills as an animator were getting better every day, and, unlike photographs, which people had learned to distrust, moving images still tended to be accepted as conveyors of unvarnished truth.

But Rebecca was not inhabiting her performances in the way she did when she was fully invested in the work: though the facial expressions of the avatars signaled engagement and interest, their voices seemed a bit distracted, and the conversations that Rebecca had with the marks regularly trailed off into confused silence, the two of them staring at their cameras until the clock ran down. Halfway through the day Felix had asked her if she was okay, and she'd said she just hadn't gotten any sleep the night before. But if Felix could pick up that something was wrong, then who knew what these eager suitors were thinking, inclined as they were to read the gravest import into every twitch and sigh and eyeblink.

Why was she not particularly eager to find out what Philip had written in the comment code: why was she, in fact, a little afraid? First of all, there was Alicia's troublesome warning that she'd "want to prepare." And presumably Philip had made those notes for himself alone, and had never expected Rebecca to read them. So it wasn't quite right to call this a "message from beyond the grave": such a label implied intent that wasn't there. But to find a lingering unread missive from someone no longer living, and someone whose life had been so deeply entwined with one's own, raised the possibility that the past could never be a fully settled matter. It meant that your own past could be altered without your action or consent, that the story of your self that you continually told back to yourself could be revised by force, making you into another person who you would, perhaps, prefer not to become.

■

". . . but I have to say, I really have to say, that Sidney Poitier really has gotten a bad rap from history. If you go back and really *look* at those movies where he was pretty much the only black actor in Hollywood: sure, he had to play tokens and magical Negroes because those were the only parts he could *get*. But really *look* at those movies: at the way he walks and talks. You can see this kind of smoldering rage against the role that's been forced on him: behind his eyes you can see this *subversiveness*—"

"Marcus."

Rebecca suddenly realized she didn't actually remember what she'd been saying for the past thirty seconds: she'd just been babbling on autopilot, riffing off the Wikipedia entries that Felix had been pulling up on one of her monitors. She wasn't sure she'd even ever seen a Sidney Poitier movie. What was the name of this woman she was talking to? Something lilting, what was it, think fast—

"Catalina."

"Marcus. I mean this in the nicest possible way: please cut the bullshit. We have had three of these People Peeks now, and you have gone on and on about Sidney Poitier and Lucille Clifton and Wu-Tang Clan, and you *must* have done enough peeking by now to know whether you actually want to see me or not. What's the holdup?"

Rebecca looked offscreen to try to catch Felix's eye, but got pulled back when Catalina said, with a playful hint of menace, "I'm over *here*."

"I really need to have my secretary schedule something for us, yes—" Rebecca stammered.

"What, you're so manly that you aren't even allowed to keep your own appointment book? You have to ask your secretary for permission to go on a lunch date?"

"It's unfortunate, but I have a very busy—"

"You need to straighten her out. You need to tell her she works for you, not the other way around."

"Ha—I—" This was rapidly going south.

"Unless you're chicken. A lot of people are chicken these days: shy as a mouse, but can talk a good game if you put them behind a keyboard. Look at you. With your gleaming clean head and your neck about to bust out of that shirt collar, and you're just as chicken as anybody."

"I'm not chicken!" Rebecca squeaked to her own surprised embarrassment, and Marcus's bass tones rose in tandem.

Catalina tucked her fists into her armpits, flapping her elbows in a mimicry of vestigial wings. "Buck-buck-ba-*kaw!*" she cried, and then began to guffaw so heartily and shamelessly that she had to wipe away a tear.

As Rebecca sat and fidgeted and Marcus looked on with a half smile as if he hadn't actually been insulted, Catalina caught her breath and said, "Okay. We have a minute left. Time to be serious now. I like you, Marcus, you seem like a nice guy, but don't waste my time. If you don't want to go out with me, just say so, and I can spend the ten minutes I'd've spent with you chatting with some other man. But if you do want to, then you need to get out from in front of that camera and let me see your face. Do you hear me?"

"I hear you," Rebecca said.

"Well, alright then. I guess we're done for now. But I'm telling you, you'd better—"

Mercifully, the call ended.

■

Rebecca waited until after she returned home to check her e-mail. The expected message from Alicia was already in her inbox, with a sizable PDF attached. Even when she saw it, she left opening the file until after she'd made dinner for Sean (sausages and mashed potatoes: easy and English, and he was looking a little thin anyway), talked with him about his homework (really, the only thing in the way of him skipping a grade was that he'd be even more certain to come off as the runt in the class), and looked in on the video game he was still playing (the endless labyrinth that the schoolkids were running through had now taken on the ghoulish appearance of a back-alley crime scene, with garbage-strewn pathways and barriers made from strands of yellow police tape). She put him to bed (and she had the distinct impression that he was slightly peeved at the unusual amount of parental attention) and then, with nothing else to delay her, she sat back down in front of the computer in the living room.

For a long moment she thought about deleting the e-mail without opening it, and never mentioning it to Alicia again. Though never a day went by when she didn't miss her husband dearly, she thought it might be wise to let the past stay in the past. Reading this was like digging the man out of the ground and cutting his skull open to look inside it, wasn't it? Wasn't it sacrilege, of a kind? Wouldn't it just be best to—

Unless you're chicken. A lot of people are chicken these days. Look at you.

She had poured herself a double shot of Woodford Reserve before she sat down, but maybe that wasn't the right choice. She went back into the kitchen with the glass, pulled the bottle of bourbon off the shelf, uncorked it, and poured the contents of the glass back in. If she had determined to read this thing, and deal with whatever it said, then she was going to let herself get hit by the full force of whatever secrets might be contained within those pages, her emotions unblunted by booze.

She returned to the living room (her glass now empty; her mouth suddenly dry), seated herself before the computer again, and opened the file, to see what she would see.

■

Father arrived just as Sean was drifting off to sleep, wearing the clothes of a hundred heroes. Eighty silver medals of honor hung from the front and back of his purple toga; twenty more dangled from the wide brim of his sombrero, jingling as he walked. As a smoldering cigar shifted from one side of his mouth to the other, his machine gun transformed back into his super-strong robotic hand.

"Hey, Dad," Sean said. "What've you been doing?"

"There was a tiger and a shark and I was fighting them both. Both of them were snapping their jaws at me! So I ripped off the tiger's head and stuffed it in the shark's mouth and made him choke on it and then I said, *Now how do you like that: you should have let me put you in jail when I gave you the chance.* Now guess what I'm going to do."

"What?"

"I'm going to change the shape of the world now. I'm going to take the whole world in my hands and I'm going to *squeeze*."

29

PATHOLOGICAL SCIENCE

My name is Philip Steiner, and if you're reading this

But you wouldn't be reading this unless you're me. If you are in fact someone else, looking through these notes embedded in my private version of the software that drives the causality violation device, then two possibilities suggest themselves. Either the CVD has been a success, my reputation as a physicist has been secured, and you are a historian of science who is looking through these documents, which, in retrospect, have been deemed to be of great import. Or spacetime behaves differently than I initially expected, and through the invention of the device I have perhaps made the single worst mistake that any human has made in the history of the world.

But that second possibility is absurdly unlikely. If you are reading this then you are probably Philip Steiner. A future version of myself. The ax head and handle changed but somehow still the same.

If I could only pass a message back in time. That's the fantasy. Not even going back yourself, just sending a message. You could warn your stupid past self of future pitfalls.

But think about it the other way. As you move
through time you forget what you once were. Ax head
and handle change. But you can send a message to
remind your future self of what you once were. What
you avoided becoming. What you might still become.

My name is Philip Steiner. I attempted to commit
suicide nineteen years ago, when I was a graduate
student at Nicolls College in New Jersey. My adviser
there was Peter DeWitt. He has since passed away. I
was invited to a conference in his honor on his 80th
birthday, but chose not to attend.

I cannot blame him for my suicide attempt. But
I feel safe in hypothesizing that he was a causal
factor.

Now I've gotten that out of the way.

■

Though let me flatter myself. Let me imagine that
these words will in fact be read by someone else,
one of those historians of science who are persistent
interlopers among our tribe. Let me tell you of a now-
forgotten research cul-de-sac I found myself in nearly
twenty years before I make these notes, and of how I
came to be there.

As a graduate student coming into the physics
department at Nicolls, I was attracted to the DeWitt
lab because I thought the work he was doing was
elegant and difficult, and I wanted to do elegant,
difficult science. Peter DeWitt was attempting to
directly detect gravitational waves. Theories need
these waves to exist in order to explain why planets
do not spin out of their orbits instead of sticking to
predictable paths around their suns. But these same
theories also say that gravitational waves must be
extremely faint, because these waves are the result of

a conversion of mass to energy. If gravitational waves
were not extremely weak, we would be able to infer
their existence merely from the continuous loss of
mass of all objects, including the sun, and the earth,
and our own bodies. It is easy to see the apple fall
from the tree, but the force that pulls the apple to
earth is nearly impossible to see.

Physicists had been attempting to directly observe
gravitational waves since the 1960s. The founder of
the field of gravitational wave research, Joseph
Weber, devised the earliest detector, a bar of
aluminum alloy studded with piezoelectric crystals
that was designed to be sensitive enough to pick up
the tiniest of trembles as an exceptionally strong
gravity wave passed through it, a wave resulting from
some powerful one-time astrophysical event like a
supernova. But even a strong gravitational wave would
still be extremely weak. And in order to be effective,
the bar of aluminum alloy would also have to filter
out the background noise of the world. It would have
to be deaf to both seismic tremors and footsteps in
a nearby hallway, and it would have to pick out one
particular wave from the many, many other varieties of
energy that constantly buffeted it.

This proved to be quite difficult. Weber's claims
that he directly detected gravitational waves with
his bar did not survive the scrutiny of the physics
community. They had doubts about the validity of
the data he produced, and the way he processed and
interpreted it. Over time Weber's claims became
stronger and more insistent: the skepticism of his
colleagues only served to embolden him. Eventually the
community as a whole decided that Weber was observing
things that weren't there, that his bar had in fact
detected nothing but the constant background noise
of the universe, and that he'd convinced himself that
this noise exhibited patterns that he, and only he,
could see. In the corridors outside of conference

halls, Weber was quietly accused of practicing
"pathological science," what the physicist Irving
Langmuir once called "the science of things that
aren't so."

And so the physics community quietly and
collectively decided not just that Joseph Weber was
wrong, but that he was uninteresting. When he could
find a home for his papers, they were no longer cited,
and a paper that is not cited may as well have never
been written. In his late career he became a forgotten
figure, with those who did remember him more likely
to recall the controversy that surrounded him, not
the science that he did. But nonetheless, the field he
founded lived.

■

The physicists who followed in Weber's wake refined
his technology. When I began my graduate studies,
there were two descendants of Weber's bar that were in
competition with each other for funding and attention.

The first, which was the variety of detector that
Peter DeWitt used in his lab, was a cryogenic bar.
The idea behind it was that Weber's original design
for a bar that worked at room temperature could be
significantly improved upon by cooling it to near
absolute zero, making it more sensitive still as its
molecules stopped dancing, and more likely to be able
to distinguish the one true voice it sought amid all
the noise of the world.

The other kind of detector was an interferometer.
Its basic concept was that it would be far easier
to observe the jostle of a beam of light as a
gravitational wave passed through it than it would be
to observe the tremble of a Weber-type bar.

The important distinction here is that while
cryogenic bars were small science, interferometers
were big science. While a cryogenic bar could

be funded with hundreds of thousands of dollars, interferometry at the scale necessary to observe gravitational waves required hundreds of millions. While a cryogenic bar could be kept in one room, an interferometer required the building of a structure that could house two laser beams that would be fired at right angles to each other, and whose paths would both be four kilometers long. Big science makes a lot of money for a lot of people. Small science usually does not.

I was naive at twenty-three, and unaware. I did not know that in the halls where science policy is dictated, the fate of the cryogenic bar with which I would soon have hands-on experience had already been determined. Interferometers were new, and sexy, and very, very expensive, while cryogenic bars were old hat, and their direct lineage from Weber's original work meant that they carried some of the taint of Weber's past failure. Purses opened and shut, and one technology began to suck money from the other. In science cash is lifeblood.

Champions of interferometry back then would have dismissed cryogenic bar research as "undead science." That is, it was science that continued to thrive in its own small corner of the culture, even though the community as a whole decided to pretend that it didn't exist. Cryogenic bar research was an edge case, but there are examples of undead science that are more blatant. At least one automobile company continued to fund cold fusion research into the mid-1990s, even though the idea had been widely discredited in 1989. Even august Princeton University had hosted a laboratory dedicated to paranormal research as late as 2007. Next to that DeWitt's research wasn't embarrassing at all. It had merely acquired the arguably unearned whiff of the faintly dubious, mostly in circles populated by those who had a likelihood of indirectly profiting if it failed.

I did not grasp all this at twenty-three. If some elder statesman of the field had told me all this to my face, I would have warmed myself under his cold gaze by the light of my ideals, and assumed with certainty that I would succeed where all those before me had failed.

■

Still other things were lost on me in my idealistic youth.

I was not aware of the extent to which, when one gets to the cutting edges of the field, problems of physics become intertwined with problems of sociology. It is not enough to see the truth. You must also convince others that you have seen it, which becomes increasingly difficult as science gets farther away from direct observation of phenomena. Modern physics involves looking at data and making a series of inferences about it, and those inferences tell us things about the nature of the world that the naked eye cannot.

In the matter of gravitational waves, agreeing on the validity of the chain of inferences that connected the data to the claim was no light thing. This is the case in any subfield of modern physics to some degree. Our areas of expertise have become so highly specialized, and those who are even just slightly out of our subdiscipline, not to mention the distant controllers of purse strings, have little idea how to evaluate the quality of the inferences that experts make. They rely on intangibles and externalities. They ask around about a given scientist's reputation, or decide if he's a "good guy," or they "go with their gut." So presentation matters. The data can't make its own case, and only a fool believes otherwise.

I tell the post-docs and grad students who spend their days with the CVD that though they have chosen

to work on an extremely difficult project, they are,
in a sense, quite lucky. When we get positive results,
it won't be a matter of convincing others that we've
picked up a barely detectable signal. The results will
be quite clear, as clear as an apple falling or a
match bursting into flame.

Unless

The last and most important thing I discovered at
twenty-three, and as obvious as it is I still need
to remind myself of it daily, is that science is done
by human beings, who abhor failure above almost all
things. But Science depends on the constant failure of
its practitioners in order to thrive: the wrong paths
that some scientists take in their careers indicate
the correct paths for others.

Science does not have an ego. Scientists do,
though, and in the backs of their minds, they are
all well aware of the high likelihood of failure in
their chosen profession. If even a raft of positive
results sometimes earns a researcher little more
than a few lines in an article or a citation in a
footnote, then negative or null results, even if
they advance the field, are almost certain to be
forgotten.

Put these two things together, then. Consider the
need not just to see the truth, but to be recognized
by others as seeing it. Consider the tendency to view
only positive statements in science as valuable. It
is easy for someone to conclude, perhaps not even
consciously, that if a scientist's career does well
when he produces positive results that are verified by
others, then Science as a whole progresses when those
who practice it are recognized by others to produce
positive results. A statement that is both true and
wrong.

■

I was attending the physics department's open house at Nicolls College. I was twenty-three, and a vessel waiting to be filled.

The open house is when graduate students meet their potential advisers. On the one hand, faculty want to attract the very best students to their labs, since they have limited financial and intellectual resources and don't want to waste them on second-stringers. On the other hand, if they attract few or no students at all, their grant money dries up as the holders of purses begin to suspect that it's time to prune one of Science's dying branches. Meanwhile the students attempt, based on what little they know, to size up their competition, to measure their own potential worth to the department and the field. It does you no good to land in the lab of a storied professor if you can never catch his eye once you're there. You will have a better chance in the long term if you settle for someone distinctly second tier who will listen when you speak.

DeWitt must have seen me as an easy mark. Back then I had this idea of the scientist as an iconoclast who forged his own path. While the other grad students at the open house dressed and groomed themselves in ways that were vaguely reminiscent of the portraits of physicists that were taken during the 1950s, with starched button-down shirts and tweed jackets and even the occasional buzzcuts and horn-rimmed glasses, I'd taken my fashion cues from Apple Computer's new CEO: jeans and a black turtleneck.

DeWitt's gaze lit upon me as I wandered the crowded conference room, with the faculty members standing against the walls as if they were coyly waiting to fill their dance cards. He was, I remember, brazen. He stretched out his arm toward me, curled his fingers, and pulled his hand back to himself, as if he held an invisible rope that was tied to my heart. And I turned and I came to him, easy as that.

He wasn't dressed like the other guys. If you had given the fifteen-year-old version of me a pencil and told me to draw a scientist I would have drawn him. Not a geek in a lab coat with Coke-bottle glasses, but someone at ease with himself, who gave the studied impression that he was only tapping a tenth of the coolness he kept in reserve. He had a mane of silver hair and a salt-and-pepper beard to match. No glasses to obscure his sky-blue eyes. Lanky and rangy, with stringy muscles that suggested regular fifty-mile bike rides. Faded jeans, Chuck Taylor hi-tops, and a Pink Floyd tour shirt that still looked new even though the show it advertised was five years back.

"I don't take you for a Floyd fan. I take you for a Rush fan, you have that look," he said, and maybe he focused on the way my eyes lit up instead of the studied, neutral response I gave. "Yeah."

He slipped into a parody of Geddy Lee's wheedling voice. "No his mind is not for rent. To any god or government." I saw the tease for what it was.

It wasn't long after that before he escorted me away from the open house that was still in full swing and down to his lab. In the middle of the lab was the machine, a capsule about twenty feet long and twelve feet tall, shaped like a vitamin pill for a giant, painted an unfortunate chartreuse. I already knew something of the technical specs. Six layers of insulation, each at a lower temperature than the one before, until you reached the center, where one of the coldest things in the universe lay, trying to hear that long-sought, elusive message of gravity that emanated from the galactic center. Frost-coated pipes snaked from the machine's top. Thick cables dangled from its side, tangled together, and led to consoles. I counted four colors of duct tape holding the thing together. It was amazing.

"You see that?" DeWitt said, pointing at it, his other hand on my shoulder. "Science is going on in

that thing, right here, right now. What's going on
out there in that conference room, the glad-handing
and the butt-sniffing, that isn't science. This is.
I'm taking you away from that nonsense for a moment
because I want to remind you of what really, truly
matters. Because as you go through your career a
lot of people who will look like they have your best
interests at heart will try to make you forget. People
come and go in this business. And it absolutely is a
business. But Science will always be there for you.
Remember that. No matter what happens from here on
out. Whether you end up with me as your adviser, or
someone else."

He talked a good game. And the device before me
looked like something I couldn't wait to get my hands
on. I was ready to coax it into yielding up new and
spectacular truths. I was sold.

Years later, at a conference in Irvine, I ended up
in a hallway conversation between sessions with an
astrophysicist who told me of a saying that she in
turn had heard among the community of science-fiction
readers, who call it "Smullin's Principle."

It is: Science fiction is a fantasy in which science
always works.

■

Only two of my cohort went to the DeWitt lab that
year. I am not sure whether the department as a whole
considered us the dregs of the barrel, but DeWitt, at
least to me, gave me the impression that I had become
his advisee because I was destined to be one of the
elite. I can't say the same for the other grad student
who signed up for his lab.

Her name was Claudia Pierson. She was a geek, in
the days before geekdom became a badge of honor and
then a marketing category. She was very much into Star

Trek: The Next Generation, even though, if I remember
correctly, the series had finished its run by then
except for the occasional feature film. She had strong
opinions about the superiority of Tom Baker over all
other actors who'd played the lead role in Doctor Who.

I think she cut her own hair, because I remember
her uneven bangs hanging in front of her face, and
the way she was always pushing them away. She had a
different idea of the boundaries of personal space
than everyone else, too, so that when she spoke to you
she'd come so close that the two of you were nearly
nose to nose. I had to fight an urge to step backward,
because if I did, she'd just step forward again with
no consciousness of what was wrong, and so she'd end
up slowly pursuing me, chattering all the while, until
I was backed against a wall.

In our second year in the DeWitt lab he put us
on this project that involved using the cryogenic
bar detector in an attempt to pick up a continuous
wave source. I was more hands-on with the detector,
while Claudia's job was writing the code that used
algorithms to look for patterns in the data the
detector generated, attempting to see signals in the
noise.

The decision to shift to a search for continuous
wave sources instead of one-time events represented
a potentially interesting and fruitful change in
thinking. Historically, gravitational wave detectors
had been employed in the hope of observing
catastrophic events like exploding stars. But
because the signal from such an event could only
be received by a bar once, the signal had to be
detected simultaneously by multiple bars in multiple
laboratories in order to be considered valid. Multiple
bars in multiple labs meant multiple physicists who
had to agree that something interesting had been
observed before they could publish their results.

Consider the faint nature of the phenomena being

sought. Consider that not all detectors were "on air" at the same time. Consider that each detector was fashioned somewhat differently, and that each lab had its own in-house algorithms for data processing. The hurdles to be overcome before you could publish results that could stand up to the scrutiny of your peers were nearly insurmountable. At least that was DeWitt's opinion.

Continuous wave sources were different from one-off events in a number of important ways, though. Think of a pulsar, a spinning neutron star. The gravitational waves it emits will be far weaker than the usual events that operators of detectors usually search for, because pulsars aren't converting dozens of solar masses into energy. But those waves will be periodic, in a narrow frequency band, and highly predictable.

So since you're now attempting to prove that an event occurs every few seconds, rather than trying to get people to take your word that an event happened once that isn't going to happen again, a single detector ought to be able to produce credible results without the need to confirm those results with another lab. Observing continuous wave sources would eliminate some of the need to collaborate, and DeWitt preferred to minimize collaboration whenever possible. Collaboration meant there was a danger of things that were "not science" entering into the scientific process, the things that were a consequence of being human.

DeWitt believed that every hand that touched the information tainted it, making the conclusions yielded from that information a little less believable. The idea he had was that the computer would examine the data without bias. Since it had no ego and no desire for publication or a Nobel Prize, it would not yearn to see patterns where there might be none, and its

judgments of the evidence were bound to be fair. One
might argue that because the computer was fashioned
by humans and given its instructions by other humans,
then its output would be the result of human will,
even if the hands of those humans had been concealed
through indirection. But it can be hard to let go
of ideas like self-determining computers and pools
of data that interpret themselves once they reach
a certain size. If the goal is the appearance of
absolute rationality, whatever that might mean, such
ideas are most appealing.

DeWitt was always looking over Claudia's shoulder,
often literally, as she coded. And DeWitt didn't really
comprehend code that well, not nearly as well as
someone like Claudia, who'd entered college knowing
she was going into physics, and understanding that
because of the direction the field was taking, it
would necessarily require a strong background in
computer science. DeWitt had a general knowledge of
programming that would let him muddle through, and
when he looked at Claudia's code he was something like
a native English speaker reading a French translation
of Macbeth with the help of a dictionary, getting by
not because he understood French but because he knew
the beats of Macbeth's story. And as far as actually
providing criticism, he was like a rich patron of the
arts who took pride in not understanding art, but
knowing what he liked. And what he didn't like was the
absence of positive results that Claudia's algorithms
produced. They looked at the data produced by the
gravity wave detector and saw only random numbers. But
the evidence for the waves had to be there. It had to
be. Claudia just needed to look harder.

After a month of this it became clear that DeWitt
thought the problem lay with Claudia's programming,
and so if she tweaked her code enough the pattern
that was surely lying within the data, waiting to be
discovered, would manifest itself. So there would be

days when she'd come into the lab and sit down at her desk, and he'd pull up a chair next to her and watch her code. For hours. She can't have liked that. It didn't help that he was unaware that he didn't quite get what Claudia was doing. It didn't help that when he saw something he thought he didn't like, he'd comment derisively as soon as she typed the line, not getting that sometimes you need to get the line out of your head and onto the screen to see what's wrong with it.

He wasn't nearly as hands-on with me. He showed his tacit approval of my work by leaving me alone. In fact, the work I did on the gravity wave detector took very little of my days in the lab. I drew a decent salary for turning some knobs and making sure that the detector had enough duct tape on it, more or less, and the rest of the time I worked on my own project, the preliminary research on the relationship between gravity and time that would lead to my development of the causality violation device. It was equally as likely that my clumsiness with managing the interface between the software and the detector was to blame for our failure to pick up a signal as Claudia's coding was. Why did he ride Claudia so much, then?

To this day I think it's too strong a statement to say that DeWitt cooked his data. You might say that he wanted to win an argument against the majority of the scientific community more than he wanted to be right, but even that implies an unjustified suggestion of deliberate duplicity. Perhaps you could say that thirty years in the field had taught him to trust his gut, and so he thought it far more likely that Claudia, the wet-behind-the-ears grad student, was wrong, rather than that he himself could be wrong. Trusting his gut had gotten him very far.

Arrogance. It comes in two flavors. The first is the arrogance of youth. A person new to the field is full of ideas and high on his own promise of disruption, and thinks he will change the world with new thinking and sheer exuberance. But the second is the arrogance of old age, and this is far more dangerous.

The first form of arrogance can be easily routed around. A young person is easily dismissed or told that he is wrong. His arrogance, if he chooses to hold on to it, will most likely endanger only himself. But the arrogance of old age can cloak itself in the authority of past accomplishments, which can serve to confirm the belief that one's arrogance is justly held. It can shield a man from the realization that his beliefs have calcified, that he can no longer assess a situation accurately at first glance, that the world has changed around him and left him behind. Guarded from this knowledge, he remains content.

Thus it does not ruin the life of the old person whose career is established, and whose past laurels will not be revoked no matter what future missteps he makes. But it can, and will, ruin the lives of those younger people who come near him, and fall into his orbit.

Because Claudia had to spend so much time writing and rewriting code under DeWitt's eyes, her personal research began to fail. And sitting next to her, DeWitt would ride her about that, too, telling her that she was "a physicist now. Not a poet, not a philosopher, not a biologist. A physicist." He'd tell her that she needed to be more focused, and there were a lot of things she didn't have time for anymore, like "macramé, or flower arrangements, or knitting a scarf for Doctor Who to wear: you are being socialized into the profession, and the profession is what matters." DeWitt imagined that whatever Claudia was doing when she wasn't in the lab was "not science," and therefore unimportant, unworthy, uninteresting: "Have you noticed that even though I've been doing science for three decades I basically live with this detector? I do that so I can understand it backward and forward and know its little moods. And I'm sure that there's a lot of potential left to be squeezed out of this thing if we just try hard enough—what is that you just typed? That's a bunch of nonsense! Is that the best you can do?"

There may have been other issues.

■

Unbelievably, after many weeks of this we began to see results. We took a run on a month's worth of data and saw what appeared to be evidence that we were picking up a pulsar emitting gravitational waves from the galactic center. There was even a clean, predictable Doppler effect that accounted for the earth's rotation and its orbit around the sun, both of which carried the detector toward and away from the source, increasing or decreasing the apparent frequency of the signal. You couldn't wish for neater data.

When DeWitt was finally sure of what we were seeing, he was in the mood to celebrate. He took us out to a ramen joint in Kingston for dinner, where he ordered a steaming bowl of miso charsiu and said to the server with enthusiasm, "Load it up with pork!" He spiked the Diet Coke the server brought him with a half shot of vodka from a hip flask.

He told us we didn't realize how lucky we were. He said that because we'd shown up at the right time in the right place we were going to get credit on a paper that was going to blow the field wide open, and he talked trash about "those chumps in Louisiana who're spending nine-figure sums on this ridiculous project that's good for nothing more than repeating the Michelson-Morley experiment." Even in his exuberance he was still cautious, or at least wanted to give the

appearance of caution: one month was nice, but he
figured four months' worth of results would be enough
to merit publication. But at this point the work was
practically doing itself. We just had to wait and be
patient.

He liked Claudia, that evening. "You look really
pretty," he said between slurps of his ramen. "You
have a kind of glow. Good for you."

■

Now things get difficult to talk about. This is when
I began to see and not see, when my mind held two
competing truths.

I think it was about two weeks later when Claudia
and I were both in the lab but DeWitt was out. We
liked to beat DeWitt to the lab because if we were
there when he came in, he'd have no idea how long
we'd been there. Maybe we got there at four thirty,
for all he knew. We knew he was getting a root canal
that particular morning and wouldn't be in until
eleven at the earliest. I remember that Claudia and I
both arrived at the lab around nine, and it felt like
a vacation day.

I looked up from my desk to see Claudia standing
near me, not alarmingly close like she usually did,
but a few feet away. She looked like she was in a
hurry. "Can I talk to you?" she said. "About the
data?"

No need to ask what data she was talking about. I
went over to her desk.

She pointed at her monitor. "This is from a day's
worth of data from the detector. I filtered out
the Doppler effect due to movement of the earth
around the sun. So there's just the effect due to
the earth's rotation over the course of a day. So
look. From zero to twelve hours the rotation of the
earth carries the detector away from the galactic

center. Apparent frequency decreases slightly as the detector moves away from the source. Now, at twelve hours, the earth is between the detector and the galactic center. The decreased frequency of the waves here is due to the fact that they have to push through the earth to get picked up by the detector—that's not the Doppler effect. Then, between twelve and twenty-four hours, the earth's rotation carries the detector closer to the galactic center. So the apparent frequency increases. Twenty-four hours later, the detector is back where it was at time zero, and the frequency of the wave is back where it should be."

I said, "Sure."

She said, "You see the problem here, don't you?"

I saw, and felt dread pooling in my stomach, but at the same time I didn't see.

She said, "At the twelve-hour mark."

I said nothing. I looked at the graph and squinted, performing the act of thinking. I may have stroked my chin.

She said, trying to lead me to it by the nose, "Gravitational waves are like neutrinos."

I said, "And?"

She said, "They shouldn't be altered by travel through matter. The earth should be transparent to them. So the frequency of the wave at the twelve-hour mark, when the detector is moving laterally with respect to the galactic center, should be the same as the frequency at time zero. That shift shouldn't be there."

I said nothing. I told myself I didn't see the problem.

She said, "This is a huge mistake. If you look at the literature, you'll see this is the kind of thing that'd get you laughed out of a conference as early as the 1970s."

I said, "You coded these algorithms!"

She said, "I know, I know. I'm just trying to admit what's been in front of me this whole time."

I couldn't find anything to say.

She said, "You saw how he's been on my ass this whole time, right?"

The look in her eyes said, Okay, I've laid it on the line, and now I need you to agree with me.

I wish I had not reacted as I did to what she said: looking back on it, I'm not sure why I did. But I know this now: an effect of being socialized into the profession when you are a young graduate student is that certain rare advisers, the ones who tend to be charismatic and single-minded in their focus, can unintentionally alter their students' values, and their perception of reality. It's easy to see the reason for this. Your adviser controls when you graduate, and he can choose to write letters of recommendation that overflow with praise, or that exhibit the studied neutrality that can be a worse black mark than an outright pan. So it soon becomes uncomfortably apparent that in order to escape into your later career, when you can presumably have a greater latitude for independent thought, no matter what else you do you have to please one particular man, who because of his position is by definition everything you want to become. If your adviser tells you that two and two are five, you may find yourself forced to consider whether this is in fact true, for certain values of two and five.

"Why don't you see what Peter says when he comes in," I said. Not even, "This is interesting. Let's show this to Peter when he gets in, and see what he says." That would have required only a bare minimum of bravery, and I couldn't even muster that. I went back to my own desk and sat down.

One thing I have to say about Claudia is that she

kept her head clear, when I couldn't. The woman kept
her head on straight.

DeWitt came in around eleven thirty. He walked past
both of us without a word, his hand to his chin, a
bottle of painkillers clutched in his other fist. He
entered his office and shut the door.

About an hour later I looked up from my work to
see Claudia staring across the room at me, her
face slightly fallen, her badly trimmed bangs
obscuring one of her eyes. Her gaze posed a silent
question, and when I turned away from it to the
oh-so-important business before me, we were both
aware that this was an equally silent acknowledgment
of my cowardice.

About an hour after that, Claudia printed out a sheaf
of pages, collected them, and approached DeWitt's
office door. She knocked, then opened the door just
wide enough to stick her head in and said, "Can I talk
to you about the data?"
   Then she entered and shut the door behind her.

I think she was in there with him for about forty-five
minutes. Near the end they both began to scream.
   I had important things to do at my desk. I had
tasks that were absolutely mission-critical if Science
was to continue its forward march.
   Claudia came out of DeWitt's office and sat down at
her desk. She didn't look at me. She was breathing
heavily, as if she'd just finished a ten-mile run. She
propped her elbows on her desk and held her face in
her hands.

DeWitt came out a few minutes later, also breathing
heavily. He went over to Claudia's desk and bent over
her. His voice was full of honey. I kept my eyes on my

work. I could feel him watching me as he spoke to her.
I could tell I was meant to pay attention.

He said, "You know, there's really no shame in
admitting to yourself that you're not cut out for this
field. It's a tough field, and even a smart person
might not have the particular kind of fortitude to
thrive in it. No one would judge you if you left. Many
people who start out in physics make their way into
finance, for example. A lot of the work in finance
involves dealing with irrational systems, and that's
the kind of work that I think you'd have a natural
affinity for. Just my two cents."

He went back into his office.

■

A few days later DeWitt came over to my desk. Claudia
hadn't been in for a while.

He said, "Well, Phil, it's just you and me now, on
this thing."

I think that was the first and last time he called
me Phil.

He said, "As your mentor I should clarify something.
What she did, coming into my office and just losing
it like that, that's not science. You can't bring
your feelings into this kind of work. The history of
science is full of people who succeeded by ignoring
dumb instinct. And frankly she may not have had the
capability, the presence of mind, to do that."

He said, "To be honest, and this is just between the
two of us, I had misgivings about taking her on from
the beginning. I always do when I take on a female
grad student. This isn't sexist. I'm just looking at
the data, and the data say that women are far more
likely to drop out of the field. The attrition rate
for women in physics is very high. My job is to train
future scientists who are likely to carry on the
torch. And I'm more likely to get better results in
the long run with someone who's going to be willing

to put in the long hours in the lab over his whole
career, rather than someone who has a light turn on
in her head when she turns twenty-nine and decides she
has to get married and have a couple of kids before
it's too late. It's a waste for me to invest that time
in someone only to see her end up at home, cooking
casseroles and dealing with dirty diapers."

He said, "All we've got to do is focus and do some
science. The science is practically doing itself at
this point. We just need two and a half more months
of data, and then we're golden."

■

My state of mind as it was then seems so strange
to me now, full of contradictions and difficult to
describe. The matter of the frequency shift was small,
in the greater scheme of things, and yet it was also
immense. I knew that the frequency shift was a sign
that our research was flawed. And yet I did not know
about the frequency shift, because I preferred to be
in a world in which I did not know that our research
was flawed, rather than one in which I did.

It would have been clear to a disinterested
observer, and it is clear to me in retrospect, that we
were engaging in pathological science. All the signs
were there: a spectacular result that ran contrary
to the literature, the consensus of the scientific
community, and past experience; the fact that this
contrary result was backed up by claims of great
accuracy; the fact that this remarkable result was
caused by a phenomenon of barely detectable intensity,
such that the data we were generating needed to
be measured and remeasured, interpreted and
reinterpreted, in order to see it; the fact that we
had achieved this amazing result in near solitude,
without collaboration. But it is hard to see such a
thing when you're in the midst of it yourself.

The version of reality that existed in DeWitt's lab,

one in which gravitational waves were altered slightly
by traveling through the body of the earth, was
counterfactual to the version of reality that existed
in the larger world, one in which gravitational waves
were not altered by traveling through the earth's
body, but continued unimpeded as if the earth were
not even there. And yet DeWitt's lab was contained
within the larger world. Physical laws had to be the
same in both places.

Though I did not admit this to myself, I decided
that the way out of what I refused to think of as
my "dilemma" was to reconcile the two versions of
reality, the one in the lab and the one in the world
that contained the lab. The key had to be in the code
that Claudia had left behind, and though I was not as
good a coder as she was, I thought that I had to be
better than DeWitt, though I would never say that to
his face. I would find the mistake that everyone had
missed, and quietly explain the frequency shift away.
I would present DeWitt with the new interpretation of
the data, he would be thrilled, and everything would
work out without anyone having to acknowledge that any
kind of error had been made.

For two months I came into the lab earlier than
DeWitt. I tried to get there by five thirty if I
could. And I would spend the time before DeWitt's
arrival up to my elbows in code. The first problem
was that I just wasn't very good at programming back
then. I did not have Claudia's ingeniousness, and
I undervalued DeWitt's experience. The second and
larger problem was that I could not convince the
data to speak with its own voice. I could see how the
composition of the processing algorithms reflected
the struggle of wills between Claudia and her mentor,
and how she ultimately lost that struggle. I could
see how to revise them such that they gave results
that Claudia would think were best, or that would
please DeWitt. But I could not see how to make those

algorithms transparent to the data, in the way that
the earth was transparent to the gravitational waves
he hoped to observe. I could only see how to impose
my own will on top of theirs, to make the data show
what I wanted to be true, and not what all who looked
at the results would agree was true. And I didn't even
know what I wanted to be true, by that point.

With each day that yielded perfect results from the
data, DeWitt became more overjoyed. He was probably
already beginning to draft our landmark paper's
inappropriately valedictory abstract. Eventually, too
late, long after the time when Claudia could have used
me standing beside her, I took the same trip into his
office that she did, and said roughly the same things
that I imagine she did, about how the frequency
shift posed some serious and potentially embarrassing
problems to our research.

I was probably not as blatantly confrontational as
that makes me sound, or as I imagine Claudia might
have been. I don't recall indulging in the flat
declarations of fact that are the privilege of those
who do science. I may have used some weasel words and
qualifiers. I may have said, "Maybe we should take a
closer look at this?" and cringed inside when I heard
my voice change the statement into a question at the
last moment.

I saw a glint of flame in his eyes for a second, and
steeled myself to receive the cleansing blast of his
invective. But the fire faded as soon as it appeared.
Perhaps an attitude of supplication might have been
the best course, or perhaps I merely had better
social skills than Claudia. Or perhaps DeWitt was more
receptive to the news because it came from someone
with broader shoulders and a deeper voice. Or perhaps
he realized that any version of reality requires two
people to believe in it if it is to have a chance of
becoming real.

Instead he tried on the sweet-voiced paternalism
that I should have been wise enough to beware, more
so than if he'd lost his temper. "Philip. I'm going to
tell you something that the founder of this field told
me. He said, Only dead fish swim with the stream. You
and I, Philip. I'm alive. You're alive. You are alive,
right?"

I nodded.

"And that means you have to swim against the
stream. When you are sure that you hold the truth in
your hands, and you do not act upon it, that is the
worst possible kind of failure. Do you understand?"

I nodded again.

He said, "Now, about this frequency shift. I agree
that it looks unusual. We're going to need some new
physics to account for this. But instead of giving
up, why not look for that new physics? That is what
someone who is alive would do."

I nodded.

He said, "You need to grab your balls and do this
thing. As a scientist you never know when truth may
come to you and you alone, and when it will call on
you to be alive, and brave. This may be one of those
times."

He said, "You need to be brave now, Philip. Do that,
and the rest is easy."

It was then, or perhaps a bit before, that I recall
beginning to think that suicide was a viable option
for me.

■

If I'd even thought about it before, I think I'd
always assumed that if I were to ever consider
harming myself, the impulse would arise from a part
of my personality that I would be able to observe
as malfunctioning, as self-evidently irrational and
therefore not myself. It would be at odds with what

I would think of as my own will, and would feel like
a command from a devilish colonizer of my mind that
would be clearly identifiable as such, and therefore
easily resisted.

But the demon of the suicidal impulse clothes itself
in whatever guise its host will find most pleasing.
In each mind it takes a different shape and makes a
different pledge, and it coaxes you to confuse its
own aims with your greatest desires. To the artist
it promises that the ending of one's life will be
a moment of supreme, ineffable beauty, unachievable
by any other means. To the athlete that same ending
is the final, long-sought victory over one's own
body. And to the scientist it offers a demise that
will be a demonstration to the world of one's own
intellectual brilliance, one that will give you the
final satisfaction of solving a difficult puzzle, or
of writing the last line of a proof that has gone
unsolved for centuries.

I am sure at some subterranean level I was aware
of the horns of my dilemma. If I proceeded with my
research as if the frequency shift did not matter,
or as if it could be accounted for by some nebulous
"new physics," then something would probably happen
that had a good chance of ending my career before it
fairly began. It was increasingly apparent to me that
DeWitt's name was not one a young and savvy student
wanted his own attached to. And yet to insist that
the world worked in a fashion other than the one he
described, even in a small way, would raise the threat
of the withdrawal of his love. Love is not too strong
a word. It seems absurd to think about it, now, but
in not much time at all he came to fill the world of
the person I once was, mostly by making that world so
small that he and I were its only two residents.

For whatever reason, once I got the idea, suicide
seemed not like an escape from this dilemma, but like
an act of genius. Clever. Cunning, even. There was a

clear goal to achieve, and a multitude of possible
paths that would take me there. My adviser would come
in one morning to find my body slumped at my desk,
and he would be impressed by my lateral thinking. At
least this is what my demon gave me to believe.

I am not saying it made sense. Even the man I am
now has trouble empathizing with the man I once was,
though we share the same memories. It doesn't make
sense. It never did. That's the thing. Nonetheless,
I was sure that once I completed the deed, the logic
behind the compulsion would reveal itself to me,
confirming that my instincts were unerring. But only
then.

■

At a certain point the demon moved beyond strong
recommendations of the best course of action, and
began to deal in hypotheticals. Suppose we do this,
and I'm not trying to get you to agree to anything,
just putting this on the table, suppose we do this,
what would be the method, what would be the time.
Morning, noon, or night. Knife or pill or rope or
high window. The hypotheticals were a Trojan horse
for negotiations, and if you accept the legitimacy of
negotiating with the demon you have lost. To negotiate
is only to attempt to dictate the terms of your own
surrender.

I should not have tried to weather this alone. I
should have gotten help from someone else. Picked up
the phone or sent an e-mail. I rarely talked to my
parents even though they were nearby. I'd lost touch
with most of the people I went to college with, and
I didn't really make many new friends in grad school.
All of the grad student activities I got invited to
centered around drinking, and going to the Friday
beer hour and the inevitable nerdy shenanigans that
followed was not science, I thought.

   If I had it to do over again. Just saying what was
going on in my head to someone when it mattered would
have gone a long way toward shutting the demon down.

Eventually the thing that wore me down was the
suggestion, from either the demon, or myself, or the
demon that I was becoming, that it wasn't success
that mattered, so much as making the attempt. But it
was then that the part of me that still realized that
suicide was not an escape began to see another way out.
   I reasoned, if "reasoned" is not too complimentary
a word for the kind of thinking I was doing, that
the preferable suicide method would be the one that
had the highest chance of failure. And evolution
and technology have combined to make human beings
extremely difficult to kill. What seemed like a
potentially intractable problem transformed into an
easy one.
   Lateral thinking. My specialty.

I ended up settling on a box cutter. I researched the
method for weeks, keeping the secret of my intent
to fail from myself, hoping that the demon that sat
in my mind and that had my face and voice would not
overhear my thoughts. With each apparent step toward
my goal, a perusal of a web page, a purchase of an
implement, the demon's insistent commands to quit
fooling around and nut up and get this done would
relent for a while. A few hours. Half a day sometimes.

I spent a week before the event rehearsing the moves
I'd need to make, with the blade of the box cutter
sheathed. Economy of movement would matter. Time would
be of the essence. The first time I went through the
motion of swiping the imaginary blade at my wrist the
demon almost shut up completely. And for a while I
thought that might be enough.
   But of course it wasn't.

                        • • •

Finally, the night came. I did it in the lab, at my
desk. I waited DeWitt out, wanting his last memory of
me to be that I was a good student, putting Science
above all things. On the way out of the office he saw
me processing the detector's data from the day before.
The results were shaping up to be perfect yet again,
consistent with the day before, so perfect that they
seemed fictional.

DeWitt looked at my monitor. "Beautiful. Beautiful."

I said, "Thank you."

He said, "No need for thanks. I should be thanking
you."

Then he left.

Then it was time.

I pulled the necessary materials out of the desk
drawer where I'd stored them. Through my eyes the
demon saw the things I'd purchased, the things in
addition to the box cutter that I'd told it I'd bought
for completely different reasons. It took on a version
of the voice of my adviser, rich and smoky and full
of command. "What are you doing? Can't you see you're
crippling your chances of success before you even get
out of the gate? This is nonsense! Is this the best
you can do?"

I spread the towel out on the desk and lined up the
implements on it, left to right. With a flick of my
thumb I unsheathed the blade of the box cutter. Last-
minute thing, the demon said. Last-minute idea that
I have. Instead of just tracing the blade across your
wrist once, why don't you go up and down with it a few
times. Dig in deep and do it right.

I turned my left wrist upward and, committed to
my well-rehearsed course of action, I lightly, very
lightly, drew the tip of the blade across. It bled.
It bled a lot. I didn't take time to stare. I didn't
panic. For once I was determined to fail. To fail was
to swim against the stream. I slipped on the one-
handed tourniquet that I'd picked up from a military

surplus shop and yanked it tight, watching the flow
of blood from my wrist drop to a merciful trickle. I
wound my wrist in a dozen turns of gauze and applied
a compressed bandage. Then, holding my left arm in
the air, I dialed 911, leaving bloody fingerprints on
the telephone's buttons.

Then I waited, safe in the knowledge that I'd
outsmarted them all. DeWitt. The demon. Science
itself.

■

I don't remember much of what came just after. Some of
what I remember I don't want to write down.

One thing I remember is that in the hospital they
wouldn't let me have dental floss. Confiscation of
shoelaces and belts I could understand. But I couldn't
imagine how you could even begin to kill yourself
with dental floss. You would have to be some kind
of genius to pull that off. And for some reason,
this was probably a day afterward, clean teeth were
very important to me. I tried to cajole the nurse by
mentioning the importance of getting back to daily
rituals. I told her about the checkup I had coming in
a month, and the disappointed look on the face of my
hygienist as she noted the recession of my gumline in
my record.

The nurse laughed right in my face. "Not twenty-four
hours ago you were ready to pour out your own blood
all over the floor, and now you're worried about a
little gingivitis. You're getting better already! Still
ain't getting that dental floss, though. You can do
without for a few days."

That laugh, and that carefree mockery. She probably
could have been fired for it if anyone had overheard,
but it felt good. I hadn't felt so human in a long time.

■

After I left the hospital I returned not to the lab,
but home, to my parents. My withdrawal from Nicolls
seemed to have been presumed by someone, and quietly
taken care of. I don't recall being asked. I may have
signed something.

For the next few months I read fantasy novels, nine-
hundred-page paperbacks that were one of a series
of three or seven or ten, full of invented languages
and imaginary races and shifting alliances between
factions, on continents that were perpetually at war.
Not wasted time. It kept my mind busy and helped
it get strong again. And I spent hundreds of hours
playing video games. Not arcade racers or fighting
games, but the expansive role-playing games that
required making detailed maps of dungeons and forests
and ruined castles, where you were someone else,
somewhere else, and your ascent to godhood was more
or less a matter of time because you could save and
reload after a death, and control the way the world
worked by changing the settings in a menu. That was
good for me, for a while.

Eventually I started to miss Science again. It was the
one thing I was cut out for. It was hard to talk about
with my parents, but I had the calling, and they were
behind me. They were determined not to let me fall
down the rabbit hole again, though, and they insisted
that I only apply to places near enough so that they
could get to me easily by car or train.

My CV had a suspicious barren spot and didn't end
the way it should have. A crucial recommendation
letter was missing. And the field was small. Word got
around. I didn't get into Princeton or Rutgers, but I
did get accepted to Stratton, the university where I
made my home as a graduate student and then a post-
doc and then a tenured professor, unlike the average
physics student, who spends most of his twenties and
thirties bouncing from one place to another. This

place has been good to me. Few physicists could claim
to be as fortunate in their careers.

When I had my first meeting with my new adviser
there, he closed the door to his office and sat down
in the chair next to mine, so that his desk would not
be between us. He said, "I talked to your old adviser
at Nicolls. I happened to run into him. He had nothing
but the highest praise for you."

"Thank you," I said, though that didn't seem like
quite the right response.

"He really wanted you to know that," he said.

I never spoke to Peter DeWitt again.

■

I lost interest in gravitational wave research after
that. DeWitt never managed to produce credible
evidence of direct detection. I don't know if my name,
or Claudia's, is on any of the papers he published
after I left his lab. I didn't bother to look them up,
and I don't care.

The three-hundred-million-dollar interferometer in
Louisiana never picked up any gravity waves either,
at least not during the seven years it ran once it
started. It was shut down and retooled in the second
decade of the twenty-first century, and relaunched in
a more advanced version, ten times as sensitive. The
paper published by the interferometry team a couple
of years ago read as if every word in it had been
argued over at length by a committee—even its title,
"Observation of Gravitational Waves from a Compact
Binary Coalescence," struck a careful balance between
brazenness and bet-hedging—but those with eyes to
see could detect a confidence that was missing from
earlier papers on gravitational waves that had made
bolder claims. The smoke is still clearing, but at
this point few would be surprised if the authors of

that paper picked up a Nobel Prize in a few years for their efforts.

So raise a glass to all the failures who blazed their trail.

I read about Claudia Pierson in the New York Times a couple of years ago. The article was in the Real Estate section. She and her husband were part of a trend piece about people who were buying adjacent apartments in Manhattan high-rises, knocking down walls to make two small spaces into one large one. Claudia was a vice president at a company that scraped data from social media networks and used it to tabulate credit scores. Her husband was a novelist.

I guess DeWitt's advice worked out for her.

I have a little scar on my wrist that's concealed by a wristwatch my wife gave me. Most days I don't even think about it. My mind is in a good place now.

Every morning before work I get up and do push-ups to the point of failure, on the floor next to the bed. If I didn't do them to the point of failure, I'd probably be stronger. But getting stronger isn't the point. The failure is the point.

Every day I think of something DeWitt said to me. He said, "As a scientist you never know when truth may come to you and you alone, and when it will call on you to be alive, and brave."

Halfway there.

30

LOST TIME

The wristwatch that Rebecca gave to me as a gift several years ago is powered by stored kinetic energy instead of a quartz battery, and reliably loses forty-nine seconds each week. I set it the first time I put it on my wrist and then left it alone. I have worn it every day since then. It is now a little over six hours behind.

I am afraid that I may not have been as appreciative as I could have been when she presented me with it. I saw it as an imperfect timepiece, one that valued aesthetics over accuracy. But later I reasoned that although it might be bad at keeping accurate time, it could serve another purpose. If the watch kept time inaccurately, but the degree of that inaccuracy was itself regular and predictable, then I could use the seconds gained or lost to measure the time elapsed since she had given me the watch. Therefore I could carry with me an empirical demonstration of the durability of her love, one that also had the secondary benefit of concealing the faint scar on my wrist that reminded me of a time in my life I perhaps could have done without.

The watch is a little over six hours slow now. When it says it is six a.m., it is time for lunch. This

means it has been roughly 8.5 years since Rebecca gave
me the watch.

We married soon after that. It feels like a long
time ago. The watch will lose seven more seconds
today, the record of our love growing one day older.

Machines do not always serve the purpose well
for which they were intended by their designers,
but sometimes they make themselves useful in some
other unexpected, singular way. The Michelson-Morley
interferometer was built in order to produce evidence
of matter moving through the "luminous aether,"
but ended up being a principal contributor to the
development of special relativity.

The causality violation device may be like that. It
may not be capable of doing that which we intend it to
do, just as the Michelson-Morley experiment could not
detect movement through aether that did not exist.
The causality violation device may be doing something
else. May have already done it. Something wonderful
and terrible.

■

I worry about Rebecca. And I worry about myself
and what I may have done to her, if anything, by
marrying her, wedded as I am to this Great Work. To
agree to a marriage is to consent to a mutual act of
transformation, to promise to ensure that the versions
of yourselves that you will become will always remain
in harmony, though you yourselves can never stay the
same. I may have failed here somewhat. I may not have
admitted the extent to which the Great Work would be
a third partner in our marriage with whom she would
have little in common, and that it would always pull
me away, always change me so that I could change it in
return.

When I look at her over the breakfast table, in
the increasingly rare times when we have breakfast
together, I see the glass of wine in her hand, and

the slow accumulation of regret in her eyes that has
changed their shape, making them liquid and heavy-
lidded where they were once sparkling and bright. I
see her fading and blurring. The way her hand drifts
to the bottle reminds me of my own as it went for the
knife. But I do not speak.

   As my son grows older he becomes more of a puzzle
to me, more so than the causality violation device
that takes up ever more of my life. If I could get my
head clear I might indulge myself in the pleasure of
making sense of him. Rebecca seems to have accepted
that he is different from her, and yet they manage
to communicate in a meaningful way. He shows her
drawings that look to me like abstract scribbles, and
she says she can see the President in them, or the
character of Ophelia from Hamlet, or me, sitting at my
desk.

   I could tell him about causality violation sometime.
But I stay silent. I watch Rebecca pour another
glass, and then another to follow that one, and I
stay silent. The Great Work is always calling. Speech
carries the threat of initiating conversation, and
idle talk means time away from my truest love.

■

I am beginning to consider seriously the possibility
that completion of my task is not possible, though not
because the construction of a functioning causality
violation device would defy the laws of physics
as we understand them. There are two separate but
related tasks that I wish to accomplish. One is
the construction of the device. The other is the
production of evidence that a working device had been
constructed, evidence that would be accepted as valid
by skeptical experts in the scientific community, who
would then assure the outside world of the evidence's
validity in turn.

   It may be the case that accomplishment of the

former must necessarily obviate the possibility of
accomplishing the latter.

■

Consider the scientific method. There is the observer,
and the world. The observer acts in a manner that
is intended to alter the world. He drops a weight or
turns a dial or types a command. He observes what,
if any, change occurs as a result of the act, and
attempts to come to a conclusion about the way the
world functions that is based on the nature of the
observed change.

The scientific method entails two assumptions that
are so basic that, even if you spell them out, they
are still difficult to keep in the mind. First: that
the observer stays the same while the world changes.
Second: that cause precedes effect.

But the very nature of the experiment we are
conducting means that the second of these assumptions
is thrown into doubt. We are deliberately attempting
to engineer an event in which effect chronologically
precedes cause.

If one of these assumptions is under threat, why
not the other?

■

This idea needs to be developed further. But life is
taking me away from my work. I need to pick up my
misbehaving son from school. Rebecca called me on
the phone to tell me this. She says she cannot do it.
There were unexpected long silences between her words
when she spoke, and I had the impression that she was
fighting back tears. Not sure why.

31

VERSION CONTROL

Leaving the phone on the nightstand next to the bed was a mistake. Its light punched through Rebecca's eyelids and woke her as its jittering vibration began to carry it off the tabletop. She rolled over and caught it just before it dropped to the floor. Who was calling at this unearthly hour? Wasn't even light out yet.

What the hell?

She answered. "Alicia. Why are you—"

"Hello!" Alicia said cheerfully, as if it were not six forty-five on a Saturday morning.

"Good morning?"

"I wanted to ask you something. Did you get a chance to read that document yet, that I sent you?"

Philip's notes. "Yeah, a couple of days ago. It was . . . it was hard stuff to deal with, and I'm still thinking about it. Alicia, seriously, it's way too early, can we just—"

"Oh, excellent, that'll make this much easier. I'd really like to buy you breakfast, Rebecca. This morning. Say, in one hour."

But they had just gone running together last week, and had planned to go running together again tomorrow! This was a strange conversation, but Rebecca, who was beginning to feel more awake now, reasoned that Alicia probably knew it was strange because Alicia was the one who was *making* it strange.

"Why don't we meet at that place where we go sometimes after our little jaunts?" Alicia said.

Marian's Diner. That greasy spoon on Route 1. "Sure."

Alicia sounded like she was afraid of someone eavesdropping. Why would she be worried about surveillance?

"A friend of mine you know will be there, too," Alicia said. "A bunch of old friends, having a reunion. A grand old time." Nothing anyone would want to observe. The "friend" had to be Carson: who else?

"Okay," Rebecca said, hoping to God she wasn't about to get drawn into some stupid love triangle thing. "See you in a bit."

■

When Rebecca entered Marian's Diner a little over an hour later, in faded jeans and an old T-shirt, her hair pinned up in a sloppy topknot, Alicia and Carson were waiting for her, sitting next to each other in a booth whose other side was empty. Carson still looked half asleep—he was wearing a button-down shirt whose pattern of wrinkles indicated that he'd pulled it from the bottom of a laundry hamper. Alicia, on the other hand, looked perky and fresh-faced, in a navy-blue baby-doll T-shirt that read STRATTON UNIVERSITY DEPARTMENT OF PHYSICS. The two of them had an easy familiarity about them, though when Carson looked up and saw Rebecca approaching, he slid a few inches away from Alicia, probably unaware that he was doing so.

At this time of morning the diner was nearly empty, save for a couple of truckers at the counter and a portly character whose three-piece suit with its shiny elbows fit him like a sausage casing. He was speaking loudly into one of those old mobile phones, the kind that flipped open and had a keypad. "I don't think you know who I *am*," he said. "I don't think you realize that you are wasting the time of a *very important man*. My time is the greatest gift I can give."

A waitress sauntered over with a coffeepot and three mugs soon after Rebecca seated herself, taking the desire for caffeine as a given. Rebecca got steak and eggs; Carson opted for French toast with a side of hash browns; Alicia ordered the cricket cinnamon pancakes. "No syrup, please," she said. Rebecca involuntarily frowned.

"Gotcha," the waitress said over her shoulder as she left the table. Alicia then reached into her pocket and pulled out some kind of electronic device that was about the size and shape of a USB stick. "I picked this up in London while I was there for a conference last year. Makes moviegoing heaven." She flicked a slider on the side of the stick with her thumb, and a blue light began to flash at its tip. The Very Important Gentleman at the nearby table took his phone from his ear, squinted at its tiny screen with a frown, and flipped it shut.

"Now," Alicia said, "we can begin. Rebecca. A question. When you entered the causality violation device. Did you—"

"Oh, come *on*. I've already apologized for that, I've already explained, you've already deactivated my keycard. How many times are you going to go back to that—"

"This isn't about that. Well, it is. But not in that way. Think back. Remember when you went inside. Did you observe anything interesting?"

"It was . . . dark? Pitch black, like you'd expect it to be: it doesn't have any windows, and the lab was pretty dim anyway. I didn't see anything out of the ordinary. And I was only in there for a few seconds, anyway. Maybe thirty seconds. I mean, the machine doesn't work, right?"

Alicia and Carson said nothing and merely looked at each other and back to Rebecca, as if one of them wanted the other to speak. Rebecca sat back in her booth, looking at the two of them incredulously. "The machine doesn't work," she said again. "Right?"

"Keep your voice down," said Alicia, looking over at the Very Important Gentleman, who in turn was staring at the three of them.

"I'd better explain," said Carson.

"Explain *what*?" Rebecca hissed.

Carson smiled weakly. "How time travel works," he said, and though Rebecca got the impression that this was intended to be funny, she also had the feeling that not much of this was funny at all.

■

"Okay," Carson said. "Let's look at this this way. There's what I guess you'd call a traditional time travel story, that everybody hears as a kid in one form or another. Ray Bradbury wrote one of these, originally. I forget how it goes exactly, but it's like: It's the future. And there's a big game hunter who's killed one of everything that's interesting, so he goes back in time to whatever-it-is BC to kill a dinosaur. But while he's back there he steps on—a butterfly, isn't it?—and—"

"And when he gets back to the future it's turned into some god-awful police state," Rebecca finished. "I had to read that story in school."

"And it's never really explained how that happened," Carson continued, "but the implication is that without that butterfly doing whatever it did, there would never have been a Declaration of Independence, or the Allies wouldn't have won World War II, or some other thing like that. But the explanation isn't important. You don't need that for the story to work. What's important is that when the time traveler comes back to that terrible future, he remembers the original future he came from, compares it to the one in which he now exists, sees that this new future is much worse than the old one, and realizes that it's his own fault. That a bit of carelessness in the past, one that would have been trivial if it were not for time travel, has had some catastrophic consequences.

"But look at it this way. Imagine a time traveler who lives in a fantastic future—replication technology has eliminated scarcity; chocolate candy falls from the sky at four o'clock each afternoon. He goes back in time and he steps on the butterfly. That changes history so that this good future never happened. The time traveler returns not to the good future, but the bad one. Smoke-filled skies blot out the sun; the brains of the poor are being harvested to feed to the rich. But if the good future never happened, how would the time traveler be able to remember it? Because it didn't happen, right?

"If the future changed, and the time traveler we're talking about was from that future, and was the product of events that created that future, why wouldn't the time traveler also change when those events changed?"

"There's one way around it," Alicia said, taking over from Carson as their orders came out. "You could consider the idea of the multiverse, and think of it as something like a tree—that is, the universe we live in is one of an uncountable number of branches of possible universes, created by random chance and the decisions of sentient beings. So, for instance, when I rang you up this morning, there was a possible future universe in which you answered the phone, and another in which you did not, and by answering the phone you put us in one universe and not the other. In that instance the time traveler doesn't just move from the future to the past and back to the future: he moves down one branch of the universe, toward the root that's back at the beginning of time, and back up another branch.

"And you can see a couple of reasons why that's appealing. First, the idea of the multiverse is essentially the fantasy of preserving perfect information. One of the hard things to deal with in life is the fact that you destroy potential information whenever you make a decision. You could even say that's essentially what regret is: a profound problem of incomplete information. If you select one thing on a diner's menu, you can't know what it would have been like to taste other things on it, right then, right there. When you marry one person, you give up the possibility of knowing what it would have been like to have married any number of others. But if the multiverse exists, you can at least imagine there's another version of you who's eating that other thing you thought about ordering, or who's married to that other man you only went on two dates with. Even if you'll never see all the information for yourself, at least you'll be able to tell yourself that it's there.

"The second reason the multiverse seems like such a neat idea is that it gives human beings just an *incredible* amount of agency, which they can exercise with the least effort. Why, Carson here created an entire *alternate universe* when he ordered hash browns on the side with his French toast instead of bacon—"

"Ah, I should have gotten *bacon*, how could I forget," Carson said, and attempted to hail the waitress.

"But the history of science shows that any theory that covertly panders to the human ego like that, that puts humans at the center of things, is very likely to be found out as wrong, given enough time. So, just for the sake of argument, let's assume that there's just this one universe, and we're stuck with it. What happens to our time traveler then?"

■

"Alicia let me see some of Philip's notes," Carson said after the waitress dropped off a fractured coffee saucer with two strips of fatty bacon hanging off its edge. "Not all of them—I understand there's some personal stuff in Philip's comment code that's not my business. But there are some undeveloped ideas in there that we've been kicking around. And we have a theory that fits the facts, and Philip's comments as well."

"I don't like it," Alicia said, "and I think that any sensible person would be well within their rights to dismiss it as crazy, and for reasons that will soon become self-evident, I would really rather it isn't true. But it fits the facts, and we have to consider it."

■

"What we are proposing," Alicia said, "is that the laws of physics are such that causality violation is subject to a form of version control, one that prevents a forking of history. That instead of causality violation creating an alternate universe, one version of history is outright overwritten by another. One past is replaced with another past. Which means one future is replaced with another future. Which means that the memories of the past of the people in that future are replaced with memories of a different past."

Carson interrupted. "Including the memories of any—"

"Purely hypothetical—"

"—time travelers.

"So take our time traveler from the traditional story," Carson continued. "He leaves his utopian future for the past. He kills the butterfly. The Magna Carta is never written. He returns to the dystopian future that his misstep created. But he doesn't see it as a dystopia: he sees it as home, the world he grew up in, the world he left to go back in time. Because he doesn't remember that first future, and has no other world to which he can compare this one. Maybe he even sees it as a utopia. Maybe everyone does. Maybe everyone in this dark place believes that they live in the best of all possible worlds."

Rebecca said nothing, but ripples appeared on the surface of the coffee in her cup as her hand began to tremble.

■

"Here's what we already think or know is true about causality violation," Alicia said. "We know that if it's possible, the circumstances under which it can occur are highly restricted. We can't send an object into the future because we don't have the necessary information—we can't predict with sufficient accuracy where the earth will be in space at a given time. And the law of conservation of mass and energy dictates that an object that undergoes a causality violation must return to the exact point in spacetime from which it departs when the violation begins."

"For instance," Carson continued, "we have this robot, Arachne, that we've been sending into the causality violation chamber for experiments. The idea is that we send it back into the past. But it can't stay there, because the raw materials that constitute Arachne already exist in the past in another form: maybe they haven't been excavated from a quarry yet, or maybe they're in some kid's gaming console, but they're there. The rule is simple: in a closed system, mass cannot be created or destroyed, and the universe is the largest closed system there is. So you can't duplicate a mass by sending it back in time: the law of conservation would be violated. Causality violation is only feasible because it exploits a loophole in the law: it cheats it temporarily, but not permanently."

"For certain contingent values of 'temporarily' and 'permanently,'" Alicia clarified. "By the way, our explanation is going to get a little weird now."

"But the point is that if Arachne returns to the exact point in spacetime that she left, then there's still a contiguous history in which mass is constant, so physics lets us off the hook."

"This would be true not just for an object, but for a person," Alicia said. "And when we talk about that, that's when things will get *really* weird."

"I'm not sure I'm going to enjoy your idea of what 'really weird' is," said Rebecca.

■

"So look at the experiment we're doing," Carson said. "We have this robot. It has a clock attached to it that syncs to the atomic clock in Boulder, Colorado, before it enters the causality violation chamber. If it works as we believe it should, and it never has, it should go back to Point Zero, the place in spacetime from which we measure the relative movement of the chamber through space as it moves forward in time. It should remain there for one hour, then reenter the chamber and return to the present. From the point of view of the observer, all this should occur instantaneously. So when the robot emerges from the chamber, its clock should be one hour behind the clock in Colorado.

"You can think of the robot's clock as analogous to the memory of the time traveler in the traditional version of the time travel story. He carries his old memories with him into the new world, compares the two, and has his evidence that he has traveled through time. Similarly, a one-hour discrepancy between Arachne's clock and the clock in Boulder would be evidence of a successful causality violation.

"But it may be—and we think this is what Philip may have been working his way toward—that this isn't how it would work. The consequence of the causality violation might not be as neatly localized and observable as we expect. It's possible, say, that if we send Arachne into the chamber at four o'clock, and it remains in the past for an hour and then returns to the present, it might return to an altered version of the present in which the robot was sent into the chamber not at four o'clock, but at five o'clock. The robot would not record the discrepancy in its clock; we would not notice it, because this new version of history would have no record of the old one. From our perspective the experiment would appear to have failed. There would be no evidence."

■

"I don't like where this is going," said Rebecca. "Because I went into that chamber. And, to be honest, I was kind of drunk when I did."

"I've been in there, too," Alicia said. "Several times."

"Me, too," said Carson. "And Philip entered it a number of times as well."

"Representatives from that creepy quasi-military organization that funds us—DAPAS—they've been in there. They were footing the bill for the research, so even though they wouldn't know a causality violation device from a *Star Trek* transporter and had no business going near the thing, I wasn't going to keep them out."

"How many times do you think someone's gone inside that

machine?" Rebecca said. "That you're now speculating wouldn't look to you like it would work, even if it did."

"When our measurements said it was operating, even though there was no observable effect?" Carson said. "A few dozen? More?"

"That guy from DAPAS brought his kid along, remember that?" Alicia said. " 'Hey, Oscar, come here. Wanna play in the *time machine*?' I think he was *six*."

■

"Wait a second," Rebecca said.

"I have to repeat that this is all highly, *highly* speculative," Alicia said. "I'm not going to have a clean explanation for all of this. We've only been working on this idea for a few days."

"Well, I've got some questions anyway. Like, a bunch."

"That's reasonable."

"First of all. You're saying that the robot is analogous to the time traveler in the story. In the story, this time traveler makes this horrible future because of something he does in the past. What does the robot do in the past? To make a new future? Surely she's not going to step on a butterfly, or reset her clock, or something."

Alicia and Carson sat there for a moment, and then Carson said, "Maybe the action that creates the new future isn't the one that takes place in the past. Maybe the act of creating the causality violation in the first place by sending the robot back in time is what creates the new future, and the rest of what happens in the past is—"

"Don't you say it!" Alicia interrupted.

"—predestined," Carson finished.

"I told you not to say that! I really do *not* want to go there."

"But we've got a ton of free will problems to deal with anyway," Carson said. "Why not pile more on top?"

■

"So we might as well head in that direction now," Rebecca said. "Because there are some serious issues of free will here. My dad's a minister: his head would explode, thinking about this."

"I told you this would get weird," Alicia said.

"First of all—okay. This conservation of mass thing. If the robot goes back in time it has to return to the same place it left. Fine. Did you try sending it back and telling it to stay back there?"

"Sure we did. Before we figured out the problem, we tried a few runs where we programmed it to go back to Point Zero, move a couple of hundred feet away from the chamber, and shut down, thinking that time's natural course would carry it forward to us in the lab, where we could download its data and see our results. We thought we could send Arachne into the chamber and she'd appear outside it, like a magic trick. But it never worked. The robot just wouldn't leave."

"Of course what we observed—the robot staying in the chamber and not going anywhere—looked exactly like what we're seeing now," Carson said.

"Well, okay," Rebecca said. "But I'm not a robot. I don't need to be programmed; I can make my own decisions. Say this causality violation device worked. And I wanted to go back into the past and stay there: I've decided on it, and that's that. What's to stop me?"

"You have free will—at least that's a statement that you could get some philosophers to agree with you on," Alicia said. "But your mind is a manifestation of your body, your body is composed of matter, and that matter is subject to the laws of physics. If you do push-ups to the point of failure, all the wanting in the world isn't going to let you lift yourself again, because your glycogen's been depleted and the energy source for your muscles just isn't there. Free will has its limits."

"You'd probably *have* to return," Carson said. "There'd be no other way. Maybe after a little while back in the past, you'd inevitably change your mind. And you'd think that change of mind would be your own decision, but that would be an illusion: it would just be physics acting on the matter that composes your body, as it must."

■

"But if I were to go back in the past. Wouldn't I, like, *remember* that? That would be a hell of a thing to forget."

"Here's what we think that might be like," said Alicia. "Have you ever had a drinking blackout?"

"Maybe once or twice," said Rebecca.

"I did once during my freshman year of college. The most embarrassed I've even been, afterward. Not the least bit funny. But we think that if a human were to violate conventional causality—"

"By time traveling—"

"Please, *please* don't call it that. If a human were to violate causality, the experience from her point of view would be similar. You would act while in the past, but not be able to recall your actions later, because that period of time for you would be lost between histories: the old one you left and the new one to which you would return. It would exist outside of the normal course of events. It would be, in a very real sense, lost time."

■

By now Rebecca's untouched steak had gotten tough, and her eggs had gone cold and rubbery. Carson's French toast was covered with a congealed layer of maple-syrup analog. Alicia had, of course, finished off her pancakes.

"So," Rebecca said, rubbing her eyes. "To sum up. Suppose a person were to use this thing to travel back in time. Deliberately."

"To violate causality," Alicia said.

"No, I think we can just go ahead and call this time travel—let's not mince words. I go back to the past. I alter the past, and by doing so I change the future. Then I return to the place I left, because physics basically says I have to."

"Then you would have acted to change history, but you would have replaced one history with another. You would not be able to know what past version of history you would have altered, because that history would never have happened. Nor would you be able to know what you had done in the past, or that you had done anything at all in the past, or that you had even *been* to the past. You would not be able to compare histories in your mind; if you entered the causality violation device knowing this, then you would realize that you would be trading one set of memories for another, and that there would never be any evidence, in your mind or in the world, that you had done this."

"And you're telling me this because I went into the machine. But I'm telling you, I didn't see anything crazy in there. No crazy lights, or the Ghost of Christmas Past, or anything like that. But it's really hard to imagine that if I did end up going a few years back in time, I wouldn't take the opportunity to, you know, look around."

Rebecca pushed her plate away. "This is scaring the hell out of me."

■

"We have no way of knowing what iteration of post–Point Zero history we're in," Carson said. "Everything that happened before the establishment of Point Zero has to have stayed the same. But after that? This might be the only version of events that's ever happened. Or it might be the fifth version, or the seventy-fifth.

"People from the military have been inside that thing. If *I* went back in time, I wouldn't necessarily be thinking *geopolitically*, but maybe they would. That has to be half the reason why they're funding us in the first place. Maybe there were earlier versions of history where Republicans didn't vote to pulp all those Andrew Jackson twenties and replace them with bills that had portraits of Reagan. Maybe in the first version of post–Point Zero history, insurgents in North and South Dakota didn't attempt to secede; maybe we weren't fighting enemies both here and in the Middle East. Or maybe there was a full-on civil war going on in the United States and the current state of affairs is an improvement. We don't know. We *can't* know. And we can't know the extent to which any of us, sitting here at this table, is responsible."

Rebecca said, "But you wanted to tell me this—"

"Because even if we have no hard evidence for this, we thought it was the right thing to do," Alicia said. "We wanted you to be informed."

"I kind of feel like this is something I wish I didn't know."

"Me, too," said Alicia, her voice just above a whisper.

She removed the tiny electronic device from her pocket again and toggled the switch. The blue light at its tip went dark.

She lifted a hand and beckoned to the waitress for the check.

32

CATEGORICAL IMPERATIVE

These days it was hard to even have a conversation without the President butting in. Things had gotten really bad in the Dakotas: a member of one or another secessionist faction had actually assassinated North Dakota's lieutenant governor, which made it a lot harder to pretend that these guys were just a bunch of wackos that could be dismissed as crackpots or handled with drones. The President was stopping short of calling this a civil war—the word "insurgency" still applied—but he was in the process of drumming up support for an inevitable "increased military presence," which meant that more people were going to die. The problem was that a fair percentage of the American public actually appeared to be *in favor* of Dakotan secession: why not use the landlocked territory as a dumping ground for survivalists, tinfoil-hat wearers, bigots, and fringe-libertarians, while the rest of the country got on with its own business? Live-and-let-live native Dakotans might not approve of that, but they could be relocated—it wouldn't be the first time—and if you wanted to make an omelet you had to break some eggs. Let bad people do the best they could in the Badlands.

But the federal government wasn't having that: it couldn't afford to lose that kind of face. So for the past couple of weeks the President had been showing up everywhere, on a major PR offensive. On Sunday night Rebecca had gotten pretty drunk—that stuff Alicia and Carson had laid on her had been pretty heavy, and she still didn't know how to deal with what she had found out from Philip's notes—and she turned on her webcam and rang up her dad, who by coincidence had *also* been drinking: he'd just officiated at the funeral of a member of his congregation who'd died at thirty-two from a cancer that had been spotted too late and spread too quickly, and after something like that he liked to tuck into a bottle of whiskey to let himself be human again, to let himself have his own troubled feelings instead of serenely soothing the feelings of others. So they sat in front of their screens with matching glasses at their sides—Dad with his bourbon, daughter with straight-up citrus-infused vodka she'd poured from a bottle she kept in the freezer. Despite the electronic intermediation and the ever-changing ads that floated beside her father's image, Rebecca found this strangely companionable—she felt her father's pride in raising a daughter that he could drink with.

"Dad," she said. "Question."

"Hit me."

"Do we have a duty to do good?"

"Honey, darling, Jesus—when you said *question* I wasn't expecting it to be about, you know, *deontology*. More, like, how the Phillies look this year in the playoffs."

"Okay. Another question instead. Same but different. Say you had a time machine."

"Are you high right now?"

"Dad! No! Listen! Suppose you had a time machine and you could go back in time to kill Hitler, like back when he was just interested in painting, before all that Third Reich stuff happened. You could, but would you *have* to? Or would it be okay to just never use the time machine at all? Just leave the thing in mothballs and let the past stay in the past?"

"Okay." Woody squinted at the camera and rubbed his eyes. "Come at it this way. Kant's categorical imperative, right? Always act in a way you wish everyone else would act. More or less. To know if something ought to be done, you ask yourself whether it would be cool if there were a universal rule about it or not. So if you're thinking of killing someone, would you be okay with a universal law that says it's okay for people to kill other people, just whenever? If the answer's no, and I'm going to guess that it is because if not we need to have a talk, then you have to leave Hitler be.

"You know who really digs Kant's categorical imperative, by the way? Nerds and cowards. I mean, wouldn't it be nice if you didn't have to make decisions about right and wrong for yourself, on a case-by-case basis. Wouldn't it be nice if you had a good book, and you could just follow the directions in it to the letter and be assured you'd never step on anyone's toes, never piss anyone off, never do anything wrong. But life isn't, you know, neat like that. Common sense: if a guy has a time machine and he doesn't at least take a couple of seconds to *think* about killing Hitler, that makes him kind of an asshole, doesn't it?"

"Can we have a universal rule that says it's okay to kill people named Hitler? And write off poor Steve and Susie Hitler as the cost of doing business?"

"Nice try. But cheating. If you've got to qualify it like that, it's not a universal rule. So you've got your Kantians. Call them the *deontologists*. Now on the other hand you've got your *consequentialists*. They don't care about the goodness of the action, so much as the goodness of the result it gets. So it's not so much about the killing of one man as it is about the millions of lives that murder would save. But the problem with that outlook is, again, the world isn't that neat. If there's a silver lining to World War II, it's that people decided when it was over that they'd do their best to ensure that was the upper limit to the horror that humans could inflict on each other. What if killing Hitler just puts us in a world where the U.S. and Russia fire off all their missiles at each other in the eighties? Is that on you? Or do you get to throw up your hands and say you acted the best you could given the information you had and what you believed the consequences would be, so you're blameless? Honestly, it's a hell of a—"

Not again: Dad's face was suddenly replaced by an image of the presidential seal, followed by the man himself, sitting at his desk in the Oval Office with an appropriately stern look on his face. "Hello, Rebecca. And: Woodrow," the President said. "It sounds like you two are having a little talk about: the nature of good and evil. And a lot of Americans are having that same conversation right now, in their living rooms and at their workplaces and in their churches. I want to show you something that will inform this conversation. I want you to see the true face of evil. I'm sorry for this."

On a blasted prairie dotted with tendrils of smoke drifting upward, three pikes were driven into the earth; each had a severed head atop it, gray and misshapen, wreathed in flies that drifted in slow, lazy orbits. "The lieutenant governor of North Dakota, his wife, and his eleven-year-old daughter," said the President in voiceover. "David and Virginia Lowell had been married for seventeen happy years. Virginia's chicken tetrazzini was famous throughout the city of Bismarck. Their daughter was in sixth grade, and was learning to play the viola."

The President's voice deepened. "This image speaks for itself. Such outright lunacy cannot be tolerated in this nation. A predecessor of mine who loved the Dakota Territory once said, 'Speak softly and carry a big stick.' I have spoken softly, and I have spoken loudly, and now it is time for the stick. I say this as your commander-in-chief." It occurred to Rebecca that she had never heard a president say the words "commander-in-chief" without sounding either sheepish or full of false bravado, as if he'd been installed in the position by accident.

"Both your bills will be credited for this seventy-eight-second interruption," the President said. "Good night, and in these troubled times, may God continue to bless America."

■

A day later, Rebecca lay fully reclined in the driver's seat of her car as it ferried her out of New York City after a Monday at the office. She'd kicked off her heels and kept her arms folded across her chest like an Egyptian queen snug in her sarcophagus, watching the streetlights whip by above as she stared up at them through the car's window.

She closed her eyes, and as had been her habit over these past couple of days, she began to imagine possible past histories and what she might have done to change them into the new one in which she lived, either inadvertently, or out of a misguided attempt to play God and make the world a better place, or, worse, with malice aforethought. Any time she spent in the past would have been clipped out of history, as neatly as if it had never happened, because it hadn't happened.

She hadn't gone back in time. The idea was silly.

Or had she? Had she knocked on the door of her home to see a younger version of herself answer; had there been a mutual shock of recognition (as the younger Rebecca realized that, yes, her husband's work was due to be a success, that he was not wasting his time chasing rainbows and tilting at windmills); had she slipped her arm into that of her past self (feeling a slight electric tingle as skin touched skin and a taste in her mouth as if she'd touched a nine-volt battery to her tongue) and said, *We need to talk*? Had she sat in a coffee shop, conversing with a woman who everyone assumed was related to her in some way—*Oh my god you two are so cute, you're mother and daughter but you look like sisters*? Had she made some kind of idle remark overheard by a man on his way to spend two weeks' vacation in North Dakota; had that comment convinced that man to settle there permanently instead, and to contact those who had political sympathies similar to his own? Had that unknown man then begun the slow process of taking over the state by placing his allies in the local governments if he could? Had that strategy failed, leaving brute force as a regrettable last resort?

If she *had* gone back into the past, armed with the knowledge of an earlier version of history, wouldn't she have done what she could to save her husband's life? It would have been such an easy fix— she would barely have had to lift a finger. She could have told the younger version of herself to keep Sean home from school that day— she wouldn't have even had to explain why, when a single dark look would have sufficed. Or she could have told her earlier self to pick Sean up from school herself instead of getting Philip to do it (and now she was doing what Carson had warned her not to do: she was ignoring the way that chance disguised itself as fate when viewed in hindsight). She remembered having had a few drinks that day, and thinking that she wasn't good to drive. She remembered that for some reason she didn't trust the self-driving car—it still seemed like newfangled technology back then. But now, in years of using autonomous vehicles, she'd never come close to being in an accident. Even with a buzz, maybe she should have taken the trip anyway—the computer might have been able to handle a situation that Philip could not have. Wouldn't she have chosen to tell the past version of herself this crucial information?

How could she not have saved him? Even if she had not been prepared to go backward in time when entering the causality violation device—who would be?—how could she have utterly failed to do enough, when there was so little that needed to be done, and the action that needed to be taken was so easy to see?

33

PRESIDENTIAL AUDIENCE

When Rebecca left the office that night, Felix waved to her, said, "See you tomorrow," and went back to gazing at his monitor. He was working late. As a matter of fact, he'd been putting in late hours for the past month, on a project that he wasn't allowed to say much about, including the fact that he was working on it. He'd needed to get real live government security clearance for it, which was pretty awesome, and elevated him a notch in the circle of his white-hat hacker friends.

He was also being quite well compensated for the work, in ways both tangible and intangible. For the past three weeks, Lovability, or, more accurately, its parent company, had put him up at a pretty swank hotel near Lincoln Center, and told him they'd cover room service in addition to his regular bill. That was an especially generous offer, considering that there was a club on the hotel's roof. Two or three nights a week he'd call up some friends—an assistant professor in computer science at Columbia; a couple of grad students at FIT; this guy who played marimba in a band doing a residency in Midtown, who Felix was casually trying to prise away from a boyfriend in Chicago. They'd go up to the roof, settle down in a booth, and Felix would order up bottle service. The kohl-eyed girl whose black bra strap artfully peeked from beneath her too-tight tank top always appeared just as the tune playing on the club's speakers was about to hit its first big bass drop. There'd be that anticipatory ramping up of tempo, and then the server would set down the bottle of vodka in the center of the table with a sparkler fizzing away in its neck, and then you'd suddenly feel that subwoofer's *boom* rattle your chest cavity, followed by an autotuned chorus that told you what a good time you were having.

Each bottle of vodka tacked on three hundred dollars to Felix's tab. Felix figured that the materials needed to make the liquor cost less than the bottle that contained it. He could have picked up the same bottle for forty bucks in a wine-and-spirits shop on 67th and gotten drunk in his room, but it was the principle of the thing. The money was there, it wasn't his, and it asked to be wasted.

Felix was also getting a crazy amount of overtime pay, on top of bonus after bonus—so much money was pouring into his bank account that he didn't mind working what had now become a fourteen-hour day. Truth be told, he would have worked on this for free. His second shift involved really challenging work, the kind of stuff that gave you a sense of real satisfaction: not just grunt coding. And every night he got to hang out with the President of the United States.

■

Around seven thirty, after everyone else had left the office, Felix shut down his computer and headed toward the entrance to the service elevator at the rear of the building. As usual, Gaia Williams was waiting for him there—even with this hotshot clearance rating there were still some places he wasn't allowed to be by himself. Gaia always looked as she did in videos online: she seemed immune to the tiny degradations of appearance that were the usual side effect of a day's office labor. Standing next to her at this late time of day Felix felt a little unhandsome, wishing he could shave his five o'clock shadow, embarrassed by the turmeric stain on his cuff left by the chicken tikka masala he'd had for lunch.

Felix and Gaia entered the service elevator, and as its door lumbered shut Gaia pulled at a slender golden chain that hung around her neck and disappeared beneath her blouse. When she lifted the chain over her head, Felix could see that attached to it was a thin brass rod, about four inches long. It looked like something you'd use for lock picking, but there was definitely some crazy tech going on in it: Felix had watched her do her thing with it a dozen times and never figured out how it worked.

From her tiny little purse Gaia pulled a plastic pill sorter, each of its seven compartments labeled with the first letter of one of the days of the week. "What day is it?"

"Monday," Felix said.

Gaia opened the compartment labeled *M*. "The days blend together for me," she said. "You'd better be right. If it's Wednesday you're getting my doctor's bill. Joke." In the compartment was a white pill, the size and texture of a jellybean; Gaia popped it into her mouth, chewed vigorously (the only time during the day she ever looked unladylike, Felix thought), and swallowed. Then she held the brass rod on its chain in front of her face, pursed her lips, and blew on it.

After a couple of seconds the rod began to quiver and change its shape, extruding an irregular series of notches, becoming a key. Nanotech that reacted to molecules carried along on her breath? Plain magic? Who knew?

She slid the key into a slot on the elevator's panel, wiggled it a little to settle it in the lock's tumblers, and turned it. Gaia and Felix began to descend.

∎

Gaia usually liked to talk as the service elevator made its slow creaking trip downward. Felix thought it best just to listen. After work, during the second shift, she went into what Felix thought of as her "O'Brien the Party Leader" mode, and someone who felt comfortable doing that was probably someone who could utterly screw up your life on a whim, even if she presented during the day as nothing more than the CEO of a company that ran a dating site. Plus there was that weird key, and the indifferent ease she had with it, both of which implied rarefied social circles and badass friends.

"I've been thinking," Gaia said, in a manner that implied that she was about to tell you what you yourself should also think, if you knew what was good for you. "The greatest corporate coup of the twentieth century was not the decision of the federal government to treat corporations as persons, but the success of corporations in convincing the people to confuse their real identities with the shadow personalities that exist on our servers, the versions of their selves that we control. That slight abdication of individual selfhood had an immense benefit to humanity as a whole, at little cost. The acknowledgment of corporate personhood will, by future historians, be seen as an acknowledgment of the ultimate trajectory of human evolution."

From her purse she took an energy bar, nuts and grains glued together with sugar; unwrapping it, she took a thoughtful bite. "That whole self-reliance, great-man, one-person-can-change-history thinking: that made sense in a time when you could go out into the wilderness and not see anyone for days if you didn't want to. But now? There are just too many people on earth. There is not enough will to power to go around to allow everyone to have a full share. But that's not a catastrophe! That's not a bad thing! We have the technological tools necessary to allow the people to consolidate and aggregate their selves, to act with a will to power greater than any one person could ever have alone. The trade for that is the designers of these tools can use them to shape the public's perception of the world. Our cameras replace their eyes; our screens replace their windows.

"And that's a fair trade. Eminently fair."

The elevator's car came to a jolting halt, and its door trundled open.

■

In this central underground chamber, always a little cold, always a little damp, hundreds of people sat before computer consoles, wearing motion-tracking helmets that were stuffed with electronics, all their collective voices changed into a single man's polyphony as they worked together to dream the President into being. They wore turtleneck sweaters to insulate themselves against the chill. They worked six-hour shifts, reading the missives that came before them that were written either by humans or by artificial intelligences: one could never be sure. Felix had been told that this chamber was one of twelve that were scattered throughout the United States, each placed in an area where its online connection would have the lowest latency, which meant that in addition to the AI routines that handled basic scripted conversations, close to two thousand people were performing the President at any given time, day or night.

No one who worked on Lovability's romantic avatars ever seemed to wonder why a mere dating service would have access to such cutting-edge technology; Felix supposed they told themselves that online matchmaking was so important and profitable that such expenditures were merited and deserved. But Lovability's parent company had partnered with DAPAS years ago to develop that technology: the devices that Felix and Rebecca used upside were basically discarded prototypes. The best programmer wouldn't be able to create an avatar with them that could withstand close scrutiny for more than twenty minutes. But down here they were using next-next-gen stuff: rumor had it that even the flesh-and-blood man who sat in the Oval Office had mistaken a recording of a presidential avatar for one of his own past public appearances.

When he had time, Felix liked to wander among the desks and listen to the performers, their voices, male or female, high or low, clear as a bell or tinged with a smoker's rasp, all transformed into the President's peculiar sonorous cadence, their motions of face and hands mapped onto his computer-generated body. He appeared to every state and city and person; to each he was the man they wished to see, and spoke the words they wished to hear. *The opening of this warehouse will bring three hundred jobs to the great state of Wisconsin. I like just a little bit of caramel added to my hot chocolate myself: that makes it into a real treat. If the spirit of the ruler rise up against thee, leave not thy place; for yielding pacifieth great offenses. Within five years, a decrease in capital gains taxes will sharply increase revenue in the great state of California. Before you go through with this abortion, and it's certainly your right to do so, I want to ask if you've considered bringing the child to term and giving him up for adoption: I know of a family who is seeking a child with a genetic profile similar to that of your unborn son. Within five years, an increase in capital gains taxes will sharply increase revenue in the great state of Vermont. One of the secrets to a happy marriage is a regular date night: hire a babysitter and hit the town for dinner and a movie. It's good for you, and it's good for the economy. I have some excellent news for you: I've spoken to your loan officer and he's agreed to lower the interest rate on your mortgage by a quarter percent. It was the least I could do.*

■

But with Gaia Williams in the lead, there was no opportunity to linger and eavesdrop, to listen to the true voice of America: she strode past row after row of desks, munching on her energy bar, while Felix tried to keep up without breaking into a jog. "The irrational twentieth-century fear of the hive mind, of our thoughts and behaviors being assisted and augmented by artificial intelligence—that's something Americans have largely gotten over now, except for the crazies. Think about it, Felix. If you'd told my grandmother that the duties of what we now call the President of the United States are largely performed by computers, she would have wrung her hands and bemoaned the decline of the nation, the shirking of our civic duties, etcetera. But we implemented exactly that, step by step, and no one cares. And it's not like people don't *know:* common sense should tell you that the leader of the free world has better things to do with his time than join a ribbon-cutting ceremony for a strip mall's Chinese buffet via webcam. People know, but they don't *care*, because it's nothing to worry about. AI helps. The President can now have a personal presence in the day-to-day life of the average American that he could never have had fifty years ago. And bills that have grown to thousands of pages of impenetrable legalese are now being read and analyzed by AI routines that make recommendations on whether to vote for or against, based on the preferences of a given congressman's constituency. Politicians are professional chair-warmers at this point." She laughed: a quick harsh bark.

With that strange, special key she unlocked the door to a conference room and ushered Felix inside. "He's late," Gaia said, with the pique that came from realizing that the person they were due to meet was one whose lateness would have to be tolerated. The room was empty except for a long cherrywood table that could seat about twenty. Some minion had left a tray that held a crystal pitcher of ice water and three glasses, along with a platter of four slightly stinky sandwiches: Felix smelled tuna and mayonnaise.

Gaia sat down. "Why don't you pour yourself a drink," she commanded, and as Felix poured her a drink she continued, "We are now well on our way to becoming a classless society. These will be the classes in the classless society. There will be the very small group of people like us, here at this table, who control the screens and the tablets and the phones and the monitor shades that people use to view and manipulate their world. Then there will be the normals, everyone else, who've ceded a fragment of their will to power to us in order to serve the greater good, who have volunteered to see themselves in terms of the data they generate because it is in their best interest. And if you are one of the normals who has a problem with that—well, you can go into the woods and sing a song of yourself, if you can find any woods—"

The conference room's door swung open, to Felix's relief: he was not looking forward to more of that. "Sorry I'm late," the man said as he entered. "I had next week's key pills with me instead of this week's: stupid mistake. Had to get a cab to take me back to the hotel so I could switch them out."

Gaia rose and turned to greet the newcomer. "Mr. Cheever," she said warmly, clasping his hand.

■

Mr. Cheever seemed a little struck this time by the people performing the President in the hall outside, even though he had seen them several times before—had been the person who'd first shown them to Felix, in fact. "Yesterday was—would have been—my aunt Lucy's birthday," he said, seating himself as Gaia motioned to Felix with a desultory flick of a finger; repressing a sigh, Felix got up to pour another glass of ice water. "She was Army," Mr. Cheever continued. "Killed in Afghanistan when the jeep she was driving ran over an IED. When my mother—her sister—found out, I thought she was going to run out of tears and start crying blood. Sometime after the funeral—Aunt Lucy's at Arlington now—my mother comes to me and hands me this piece of paper, a certificate. It's from the Department of Veterans Affairs. Honoring the memory of; grateful service to the nation; etcetera. And it's signed, by Barack Obama. And being young, you know, I imagined that even if someone had put a stack of these things on his desk and he signed them without reading them, then at least he signed them.

"But then my mother showed me a sheaf of five of them, and an order form that would let us get as many as we wanted—one hundred, two hundred—for free. They were signed by a machine, you see: it could mimic the movement of the President's hand. The technology had been around for two centuries: Thomas Jefferson had even used a much more primitive version. But somehow, knowing this did not matter. The certificate did not seem cheap, or fraudulent, because of this. It still had its aura of honor and fame. Strange. But also wonderful."

■

"Felix," Mr. Cheever said. "To business. We love your work. I want to say that right off the bat. Very impressive."

"Thank you." For the past few months he'd been working on avatars for the most viable candidates in the upcoming presidential election, which was still over a year away. That might have seemed like a long time, but when the new president came into office, the transition between avatars had to be instant and seamless, and the animation quality of the new one had to be just as good as that for the outgoing chief executive. And the presidential avatars needed to be convincing for hours at a time, in high definition, and their movements needed to be so lifelike that they could convince you to suspend your disbelief without making you acknowledge that you were being asked to do so. There could be no public beta test: the launch had to go perfectly, which meant many months of prior planning. And since there was no way of accurately predicting the election this far out, the best course of action was to start work on the avatars of the two or three candidates most likely to win, and hope that your luck held.

Lately Felix had been assigned to develop the avatar of a moderate midwestern governor, and he liked the guy in spite of himself—you couldn't help but become at least a little intimate with a man after you glued motion-capture dots to his face a few times. Though there were points on which they strongly disagreed—civil liberties; immigration; the proper alcohol content of beer—he seemed like he could at least be reasoned with. Felix's guess was that the guy didn't have much of a chance, and even though the candidates wouldn't get to use the avatars that were being worked up unless they actually got elected and the federal government licensed their likenesses, Felix had tried to help him out a little, giving his weak chin slightly less of a slope and diminishing the scars that had been left behind by a bout of teenage acne.

"You've got a real craft," Mr. Cheever said. "I've seen the before and afters, when you come in to do that polish on the early work of others. Before, the avatars are dead ringers for their sources, but after . . . well, I'd actually be hard put to point at exactly what you do to change them, but . . . they look less realistic, but more *real*. Which is why I want to loop you in on something."

"He's *very* good at what he does," Gaia said, and Mr. Cheever shot her a glare that seemed borderline hateful. Felix got the impression that just as Gaia viewed him as a person who was good for pouring water, Mr. Cheever viewed Gaia as a person who was good for carrying keys, and nothing more.

"We have been running simulations," Mr. Cheever said, turning his attention back to Felix. "We have been predicting possible futures, based on which of the most promising candidates wins the upcoming election, whether they adhere to their currently stated policy positions, whether the composition of the legislative branch of the government changes significantly, and whether the newly elected president is able to work effectively with the legislative branch to enact the policies he champions. I will spare you the details, but . . . if the current president gets another term, it does not look good for . . . us." Mr. Cheever let that last word hang in the air, leaving Felix uncertain whether he was referring to the nation, or to his employers; perhaps Mr. Cheever saw them as one and the same.

Mr. Cheever got up from his seat, walked over to the plate-glass window through which he could see the pilots of the presidential avatars, and stood there with his hands clasped behind him. "I would not want you to defame or betray your country in any way," he said, and to Felix his voice seemed to come out of the ceiling: he thought it was just him who had that idea at first, but then he saw Gaia look upward in startled confusion, and try to play it off by swatting before her face as if some kind of a bug were hovering around her. More weird tech that looked like magic tricks or sleight of hand. It'd be nice to have this in conference rooms, though, whatever it was.

"I want to put you in charge of day-to-day maintenance of the current president's avatar," Mr. Cheever said through his thrown voice. "You won't be able to work with him firsthand, I'm afraid, though we'll provide you with a daily supply of candid reference photographs."

"This is a real honor," Gaia said to Felix, as if he were not aware. Mr. Cheever continued to stare out the window. Five of the avatar pilots outside raised their arms in the air, as if they were in a roller coaster car that was heading down its first steep drop. That would be the President's daily fitness program for wheelchair users: Felix's grandfather watched it religiously.

"It would be interesting," Mr. Cheever said (and now Felix had the strange feeling that Mr. Cheever's voice was coming from inside his own chest, as if Felix himself were speaking with it), "if the President, in the next couple of months, were to begin to appear . . . not entirely in the pink. Skin a little ashen; posture starting to droop."

"That would be interesting," Felix said cautiously, resisting an urge to put his hand to his stomach, as if Mr. Cheever's voice were causing him indigestion.

"It would be interesting," said Mr. Cheever, "if in a year or so, the President's appearance became slightly more . . ." He paused. "*Other.* You understand."

Felix looked at Gaia, who had suddenly become deeply mesmerized by the conference room's carpet.

■

So that was the game, then, Felix thought later that evening as he sat alone in a booth in the nightclub on the roof of his hotel, watching the crowd of people knocking back weak, brightly colored drinks and grimly insisting on their own happiness. An aura of power once granted could be revoked. The mediation that made a man what he was in the eyes of the people could also unmake him, and there was little he could do about it. If this was managed properly, he wouldn't even be able to indicate what had altered in the visage of his proxies; perhaps he'd confuse the slow degrading of the computer-generated image with the inevitable decline of his own appearance. Everyone knew that being the president did a number on your looks: you went into the job an Adonis and came out broken, having aged a decade for every term you served.

Felix didn't quite get Gaia, he'd decided. Mr. Cheever, he got—that guy was The Man, and didn't mind if you knew it—but Gaia was more of a puzzle. When he'd first started working on the romantic avatars, Gaia had given him the same talk that Felix later found out she had given Rebecca, about how it was a mistake to confuse people with the data they generated. But she also seemed to think that most people *did* actually confuse themselves with the data they left behind as they made their way through the world; that the corporations that powered social networks and suggested love matches and generated credit scores tacitly encouraged that deception; and that if you fell for that deception, it was your own fault, and you should have known better. Furthermore, Gaia also seemed to think that it served the greater good of humanity for *most* people to view themselves as assemblages of quantifiable traits, so that their lives could be better managed by those few who had the power to aggregate huge volumes of data and draw conclusions from it. Gaia seemed to think that access to Big Data automatically made you into some sort of benevolent philosopher-king.

Was that okay? Maybe it actually was okay, and Felix was just worrying about nothing. Gaia seemed to think it was okay, and she was doing just fine. Mr. Cheever would probably say it was okay, if you asked him.

The server brought out the bottle of vodka on its tray, right on cue, placing it down just as the bass punched Felix in the chest, the way Mr. Cheever's voice had. She leaned forward over the table to pour the vodka into a shot glass, giving Felix a generous glimpse of cleavage that was part of the whole ceremony: to him her breasts looked hard and hemispherical, with none of the give of real flesh. He figured they'd feel like stress balls in your hand.

She stood up and handed him the glass, nearly filled to the brim. "Drinking alone tonight, are we?"

"Looks like it." He carefully took the glass from her and sipped.

"Well, with this booth and a big ol' bottle, I'm sure a pretty girl will be along soon enough." She winked and strutted away.

Felix gulped the vodka, feeling its chill in his throat. He put down the empty shot glass and slouched in the booth, looking out at the crowd. One guy in a black shirt and a skinny leather tie that he must have inherited from his dad was leaning over a woman in a short shimmering sequined dress, gently getting in her personal space, punctuating his sentences with movements of his hands that stopped just short of touching her, backing her up as he spoke until she'd soon be against the wall with nowhere to go. Nearby a group of four thick-necked former frat boys in tight T-shirts were clinking together newly opened bottles of beer, but the bottles were made from plastic that muted the sound of their collision. The men looked like they all went to the same gym together, with hypertrophied upper bodies balanced precariously atop legs like sticks. When they tipped the necks of the bottles to their lips they flexed their arms for each other, as if they were holding dumbbells. Funny how you could tell the difference between a man who worked out by lifting weights after a day in the office and a man whose muscles resulted from a naturally strenuous daily life: the former was bigger, and served as an effective advertisement of one's ample leisure time, but the latter was more beautiful, lean and ropey, honest in its strength. Real.

Felix pulled the bottle of liquor to him. He held it over the glass and, with one quick motion, he upended it. He watched the vodka fill the glass, and splash over its sides, and pool on the table, and pour onto the floor. He watched Mr. Cheever's rounding error waste away, observing the rising bubbles in the bottle that displayed warped, inverted versions of the nightclub scene beyond, attempting to catch the furtive gaze of people who were turning their backs to him and trying not to look.

34

QUAIL TROUBLE

In Rebecca's dream the skies have been raining quail for seven days, and the town of Stratton is in a state of emergency. The flocks flying overhead are so thick that they block out the light of the sun. Whole coveys of the birds come dive-bombing down at once, snapping their own necks on impact, shattering car windshields and felling pedestrians with concussions. Sometimes the birds hit the ground already plucked and trussed and seasoned, needing only twenty minutes in a hot oven to form the centerpiece of a delicious meal.

This is YHWH's fault, of course: Rebecca's parents have been renting her old room out to the God of the Old Testament, and according to Woody, He is "the worst tenant ever." At night He goes out into the backyard and becomes a pillar of fire, scorching the lawn and garden, shining His light into the windows of neighbors who are trying to sleep, baking the paneling of the house's exterior until it blackens and warps. By day He becomes a cloud, and retreats indoors to suffocate the Wrights with His holy miasma. "He just *sulks* all day, like a big baby, because no one will do what He wants," Woody complained. "He sulks and He pouts and He pulls these petulant little pranks. Like last week, your mom and I were having a little tiff— she thought I was going to do the grocery shopping; I thought she was—and it turned out that the only thing in the house to eat around dinnertime was a bag of oyster crackers that I think had been sitting in the back of the cupboard since the year before last. We're having a little argument about this, and YHWH overhears because He listens in on *everything* going on in the house, and He says, *What is wrong with oyster crackers? Oyster crackers are a perfectly adequate source of nutrition for mortals.* I say, But what about texture, flavor, color, succulence, surprise, all those things that make a good meal? And He gives me this look, like, *Be careful what you wish for,* and that's when the quail start coming down. For the first couple of days it was great, but now this is really starting to wear thin."

Rebecca and Woody were sitting in the kitchen having coffee, and as if in riposte to Woody's grousing, an irregular drumming on the roof signaled that another flock had fallen. "He's been going on about you, commanding me to send Him my firstborn," Woody said. "So could you just, you know, go back and talk to Him? And maybe He'll quit with the quail."

Rebecca could see YHWH's smoke leaking from under her bedroom door when she knocked. The door swung open of its own accord, slamming shut behind her when she entered. When YHWH spoke to you it was like listening to a thousand-dollar pair of headphones whose speakers were slightly out of phase: the words you heard just inside your right ear were far clearer than you'd realized speech could be, and echoed a quarter second later in your left. "All-knowing, all-powerful, all-good," He said. "The theologians say you must give up one of these if you are to explain the existence of both evil and Myself. But they do not take the longer view; they do not understand My total plan.

"I am fully cognizant of the present, but I cannot reliably predict the future. Chance is the cancer in Me. Hence My creation of humans, who, given enough time, would invent time travel, therefore gaining the ability to circumvent the deleterious effects of chance on history, and thereby curing that cancer. Time travel would give humanity the ability to alter the past and prune the tree of all possible futures of those branches that had been infected by evil; with enough revisions humans would eventually bring about the one version of history that was fully good. Thus would they fulfill their reason for existence; thus would evil be forever eliminated; thus would My omnipotent, omniscient, and omnibenevolent nature be made fully manifest for all to see, on Judgment Day, at the end of time."

Something changed in YHWH's voice, some kind of strange downshifting, making it not deeper or louder, but wider and taller;

Rebecca put her hand to her ear, felt a wetness, and saw that blood had painted her fingertip when she drew it away. "But I did not account for human selfishness. I did not account for your lack of ambition. I did not account for your inability, your unwillingness, to see the full arc of history. I have spoken to thousands of time travelers, have begged and pleaded with them to rid Me of the randomness that cripples Me, and every last one of them has suffered from the same poverty of imagination. You have the power to change the very shape of My face and you fritter it away. On one little life. On another little life."

■

"But that *is* what matters," Rebecca said as she began to tremble and blood ran from both her ears. "One life and another: that's what matters. You have to understand: history can change people, but people can change history too. Because what is history made up of, if not people's lives and stories and memories?"

■

If she did not exactly know what she had to do when she awoke, she knew how to figure it out, how to begin.

■

First, she was going to do something she'd been putting off for years: clean out Philip's office. There was no point in leaving it as a shrine to the past, or pretending he was coming back after an unusually long time spent in the lab. It was Saturday morning and she was unexpectedly bright-eyed, having decided for some reason not to drink the night before (and it would dawn on her, later in the day, that that weird, lightheaded feeling she had was the absence of her usual slight headache). There was no better time than now to get to work. She needed that space to make the future.

There was a lot, a *lot*, of stuff in here. Fortunately, none of it would be too heavy for her to move by herself: there were some pressed-wood bookshelves that could be dragged out once they were emptied of volumes, and a desk that could be moved with Sean's help as long as she bore most of the weight.

She sorted things by their appearance, more or less. She filled a Pyrex measuring cup with USB sticks found in various drawers. A rat's nest of chargers and adapters lay in the bottom of a closet. In a pile she placed several corkscrews of different designs: the kind with two wings that extract the cork from the bottle when you press them down; the slim Swiss-army-knife kind that waiters carry around; a strange one that was made of nothing more than a handle and two thin metal prongs. Each one had a handwritten number taped to it somewhere on the handle; Rebecca had no idea what Philip had intended to do with these, and probably never would.

A copy of a textbook, *Mathematical Methods in the Physical Sciences,* had every other page dog-eared: it seemed to hail from Philip's undergraduate days. On the same shelf was an English-German dictionary; a two-inch-thick paperback titled *Canopus in Argos: Archives;* an equally long book called *Gravity's Shadow* (this appeared to be a mix of physics and sociology, from what Rebecca could tell); and a copy of *Ulysses* that, Rebecca found, had been inscribed on the flyleaf with a woman's handwriting: "And I thought well as well him as another. Enjoy: let me know what you think when you're done. —A." Its spine had never been cracked.

More stuff of a life, the enigmatic evidence of abandonment and half-completed thought and thwarted intent. A leaf severed from the stalk of a plastic houseplant, taped to an index card next to a desiccated sample of the plant it was meant to mimic. A credit card, still unsigned. An unopened bag of almonds. An old iPod with a heavily scratched finish and a cracked display. A metal tin that held a half-dozen Earl Grey tea bags, and an open box of Domino brown sugar whose contents had transformed into a single crystalline brick. Three rolls of duct tape in different colors: red, black, and navy blue. In a picture frame, a ticket stub for a Rush concert at Madison Square Garden in 1994 (the price a mere thirty-five dollars). A napkin that had a telephone number in a handwriting that Rebecca didn't recognize; beneath the number Philip had carefully printed *CALL THIS IF SOMETHING WEIRD HAPPENS.* A shoebox that held a collection of receipts for hotel rooms: Taipei; Marseille; Darmstadt; Valencia; Kansas City; Birmingham; Paris; Cambridge; Dallas; Leiden.

All of this went into boxes and garbage bags, which Rebecca ferried piecemeal to a storage facility she rented in North Brunswick. Sean rode along on the trips back and forth: he found something inexplicably pleasurable in the idea of a room that was completely empty, whose primary and only purpose was to hold things, a space full of pure potential. For ten minutes after they first arrived at the storage facility she shut him inside and let him experience the bare space, with its cold cement walls and the single bulb hanging from the ceiling; after that, he seemed disappointed when she began to sully the room with Philip's possessions. She saw his pouting, and the way he performed his whiny exhaustion after assigning him the lightest of burdens to carry out from the car, and said, "How would you feel if I made a room like that for you at home? If we took everything out of your father's office and gave that room to you?"

"That would be *awesome*," Sean said, and though Rebecca knew the meaning of that word had been diluted through decades of overuse to something closer to "pleasant" or "agreeable," she felt that Sean was using it in its ancient, literal sense, and that the idea of his father's once-forbidden secret space, transformed into a place where he could traipse with impunity, was in fact something that truly inspired awe.

"What am I supposed to do with it?" he said.

"I want you to make a new world in it," Rebecca said. "When the space is ready for you. Give me some time."

■

Even after the week it took to get the office emptied out, it took two more weeks to get the room in the condition that Rebecca wanted. In the meantime she kept Sean out "on pain of death" (pronouncing those last words of warning in a fake Cockney accent that tickled Sean whenever he heard it). Sean was not one to spoil his own surprises, though—fidgety as he could be, he had that peculiar and rare kind of patience, and understood the delicious pleasure of anticipation. When she went into the room and shut the door to work, he respected the boundary just as she had when Philip had been in there, huddled over his desk, working away.

She painted naked: it was the best way. Skin dealt with stray drops better than fabric, and it was freeing to feel nothing but the motion of her muscles as she drove the roller up and down the wall. The paint was expensive and tricky to apply. It came in two buckets, and you had to dump the contents of the smaller one into the larger; after that you had two hours to get the stuff on the wall before it congealed to a hard hunk of plastic. Then the paint took three days to cure: during that time Rebecca kept the door locked and mysteriously said that it needed to stay that way because "magic was happening." That drove Sean bonkers. He had trouble sleeping after that.

Finally, when she got home from work one Wednesday evening, Sean was waiting for her, and the time had come. There was no point in waiting for dinner: he'd be too excited to eat anyway. She went into her bedroom, retrieved two gifts from a drawer where they'd been concealed beneath underwear, and presented them to him: a key attached to a golden ribbon, which she placed around his neck as if it were a medal of honor, and a box of dry-erase markers in a dozen different colors. Then she beckoned him to approach the locked door.

■

The room was white, a gleaming white, both walls and floor: Rebecca was proud of how it had turned out. Sean touched a wall, puzzled by its strange slickness and the way it reflected the late-afternoon light from the window.

"Write on it," she said.

He hesitated, perhaps flashing back to toddlerhood chastisements, but she pointed at the box of markers in Sean's hand, and then at the wall. "Write on it," she said again, half inviting, half commanding.

He selected a marker from the box—its color "Granny Smith." He removed its cap and sniffed the tip—Rebecca gathered that it was supposed to smell like apples—and then, with some hesitation, wrote his name in his plain, neat script. Then he got it. "It's a whiteboard! The whole wall is. All the walls are, and the floor is."

He wiped his hand through his name and, with a grin, showed Rebecca his palm, dyed green.

Rebecca dropped to one knee before him. "I made this for you, and this is what I want you to do. First: I gave you this key because this space is yours. No one can come into it that you don't want to. Including me."

Who else at school had a room with its own key that their parents couldn't go in? No one, that's who. Sean beamed.

"I want you to use these markers, and I want you to draw me a new, imaginary world, the world that you want to see the most. Then, when you're done, I want you to show it to me."

He looked at the walls, seeing past their surfaces, looking deep into all their possibilities.

"I want you to do this alone. I can't help you do this, and neither can any of your friends."

Sean nodded earnestly, though Rebecca could still see a glint of childish glee in his eye. He didn't have any intention of letting any-one but him mark a single square inch.

Rebecca stood. "I'm going to make us dinner now," she said. "This is the last time I'm going to come in here until you ask me to. I'm going to leave you to it."

"Thanks, Mom," Sean said, distracted, looking at the blank wall over her shoulder and not into her eyes. Good.

She left, shutting the door behind her. A few seconds later she heard the quiet click of the lock.

■

Father came screaming into the room as soon as Mom was gone, clothed in all his holy hellish splendor, holding a newborn star in his hand. "Now!" he shouted. "I made all the lions learn to march in a row and do just what they're told! But the robot that looks like me is staying in my place to lead the lion army. So I can come here to be with you. So that you can record all my adventures.

"Now: let's begin."

35

AUTONOMOUS GRIDLOCK

Okay: who's on deck this afternoon?" Rebecca said as Felix applied motion-capture tracking dots to her lips. This close to him, she could see his baggy, bloodshot eyes. She caught a whiff of last night's vodka wafting from his pores.

"Whoever it is," he answered listlessly. "You know." He blinked and shivered as the name popped into his head. "Catalina. Yeah."

"This is something like our fifth People Peek with her, isn't it?"

"Fourth. No—you're right. Fifth."

"You doing okay, Felix? Partying on work nights lately? I have some Siestalert if you need it."

He placed the last dot on her face. "Nah, I'm good. But every night's a rough night for me, lately. And every night's a party."

■

He loaded up Marcus, who today was wearing an outfit inspired by Morpheus's clothing in the virtual-reality sequences of *The Matrix Reloaded:* a forest-green vest and tie paired with a violet shirt, along with brass-framed pince-nez spectacles. "You look perky today," he said to Rebecca.

"I *feel* perky! I don't know. It's a weird thing lately. Wide awake all day, and I sleep like a dead woman as soon as my head hits the pillow at night. I haven't been drinking that much, either. I pretty much quit drinking."

"Huh." Felix kept his eyes on the monitor as he tweaked the color of Marcus's vest to match the tie, and pushed his eyes just a touch away from brown, just a touch toward hazel. "Twelve-step?"

"No, not at all," Rebecca said, wondering why that was the first place his mind went to. "I just . . . haven't wanted it. You know? Haven't even been thinking about it. I'm not *quitting* quitting: I'm just not feeling it right now."

"High on life, are you?"

"No, I wouldn't say that. I . . . I just have this good feeling, like I haven't had in a while."

She smiled.

"I really feel like things are going to work out, Felix. For you and for me and for everyone."

"Well, keep those warm thoughts in mind and try to let them show in Marcus. Three minutes, and you're up."

■

"Marcus!" Catalina said as soon as the People Peek's intro screen dissolved and the ten-minute clock hovering in the corner began to tick down.

"Catalina!" Rebecca said. "You know, I have to tell you, I've been looking forward to this People Peek all morning. I have had an absolutely crazy day at work so far—just managing everybody's little problems—and it'll be great just to take ten minutes out of my day to relax and talk—"

"I've been looking forward to this, too," Catalina cut in. "And the fact that we were *both* looking forward to it so much tells me that you have *finally* realized that it's time for your wishy-washy self to put up or shut up. Here's how it is. Three days from now, at twelve sharp, I will be at a table for lunch at the cafeteria in Alice Tully Hall, in Lincoln Center. I am either having lunch by myself, or with you."

"I—"

"Oh, I know, you're not sure if your all-powerful secretary has you scheduled for Kobe steaks with a captain of industry for lunch that day. You can move that to one o'clock and eat two meals. Because one of two things is going to happen. Either you and I are going to have a spectacular lunch together and really get to know each other—don't worry, I'll buy, if your wallet's feeling light—or I will have an equally spectacular lunch alone, after which I will head across the street to check out the American Folk Art Museum. Either way, my time will not be wasted, and I'll know whether I need to waste any more time with you. Now."

Rebecca looked over at Felix, who shrugged in confusion as Catalina said, "What are you looking at, over there? Is your secretary over there offscreen? Put her on so I can ask her if it's okay for you to go on a lunch date."

"Um, uh, you know . . . you know what, Catalina? You drive a hard bargain. And my mother always told me that assertive women were the best women. Tell you what. I'll clear my calendar. And I'll be there. Twelve o'clock, Alice Tully Hall cafeteria. I've been blowing you off for too long, and I've been stupid. I'm looking forward to seeing you, finally."

"Apology accepted. And I'm looking forward to meeting you, too. And you'd better be there." The tone was half tease, half threat. "Goodbye, Marcus."

The People Peek ended, with six minutes left.

"What in the hell," said Felix.

"I know, right?" Rebecca laughed gaily.

Felix looked at the monitor as if he was hoping that Catalina would reappear. "Are you just going to stand her up? That's crossing a line, isn't it?"

"I'm not standing her up. I'm going to meet her."

"I don't. Uh. W—wait now. Do you have, like, some kind of plan? One that isn't publicly embarrassing, or incredibly offensive, or self-evidently doomed to fail?"

"I told you. Everything's going to work out for everyone. I've got a good feeling."

She took off her helmet and wiped a hand across her face. "Are there any more of these things to do today? Can you just tell them all that Marcus and Helen and Beauregard and whoever have family emergencies? I don't really feel like being at work. It's too nice a day."

"Well, okay, sure, but—"

"But nothing. See you, Felix." She shrugged into her coat and removed her purse from a hook on the cubicle wall. "You should head up to Central Park and people-watch. One of the last decent days of fall. People will be doing their little mating dances so they can get someone to warm their winter beds: always fun to see. Work to live, don't live to work."

∎

On the way back to Stratton in the early afternoon there was, strangely, a traffic jam, the first one that Rebecca could recall having been in in quite a while. When these self-driving cars glitched out, they did it in ways that would have seemed inexplicable to twentieth-century drivers, ways that would have been entertaining if you didn't have to deal with the results. All of the cars around her were at a dead stop, their engines shut down to save gasoline and electricity. The most likely cause was that a few cars ahead of her had gotten stuck in infinite loops when attempting to determine their movement priorities: that sort of thing could crash your system so hard that manual override wouldn't even work. Since self-driving cars decided when and how quickly to move based on the information being broadcast by the cars around them, the immobilizing effect of the infinite loop had cascaded backward along the highway, and would continue to do so until someone in Seattle or Nashville or Phoenix looked at his monitor, saw the problem, and rebooted the offending vehicles via satellite signal. Until then, these cars would all be stuck here, neatly packed together.

The car in front of Rebecca had actually tried to turn around and head down the road in the opposite direction before Rebecca had blocked her in. Rebecca and the woman who was facing her behind the wheel of her own vehicle had shared a mimed shrug and laugh— *these crazy computers; what can you do*—and were now assiduously attempting to avoid eye contact with each other.

The news projected on Rebecca's windshield was of coming civil war: quadracopters were flying in phalanxes over the Badlands, carrying who knows what manner of devilish nanotech payload. This battle was going to be quick and nasty, and though Rebecca was sure she would not be spared the incessantly repeated bloody details of what had convinced the President to bring the hammer down, she was certain that whatever violence was meted out in return would be seen through a scrim at best, portrayed as mechanical and bloodless.

Whatever happened, it was all going to work out. It was weird to know that she was one of the few people, perhaps the only person, who understood, and was willing to accept, that this was merely a rough draft of history, one that could be revised by those who could step outside of time. Outside of time you could see the whole structure of things: Rebecca was certain of this. While you were inside time, the past was distorted by your memory, and the future was doomed to be a mystery. But outside time it would be easy to see the irregularities of history's warp and woof. You'd just have to pull at a thread here and there to straighten things out.

Her phone rang with what she still remembered as the core group's "special chime": through all these intervening years she'd dutifully transferred the ringtone from one phone to the next. She looked at the screen: Kathryn. At three o'clock? She should be working. But maybe they could play hooky together. "Guess what," she said as she answered.

"What," said Kathryn, her voice strangely heavy.

"Chicken butt," Rebecca replied, but did not get the childish giggle in response that she was gunning for. "Are you crying? I'm talking about the hind end of a fowl: that's just funny, in and of itself."

"Carson and I broke up," Kathryn said. Then: "Carson broke up with me." Then: "Carson dumped me."

"Oh!"

"You sound . . . happy about that?"

"No not at all: it's awful!"

Kathryn hesitated. "Should I call you at another time?"

"No: now's a perfectly good time. I knocked off work early: I'm in the car on the way back to Stratton. But stuck in traffic."

"I've been trying to hold it together at work, and I'm not really holding it together."

"You should leave work," Rebecca said, and then she felt a jolt as her car suddenly accelerated to sixty-five along with all the other cars around her, including the one in front of her that was driving in reverse. "Look at that." It had been given to her to be attuned to the true nature of space and time: she merely needed to speak and the world did her bidding. "I should be back in town by three thirty. Wanna meet up for coffee?"

"Will the coffee be spiked with Everclear? Stop being silly. Tell Jeeves to get you to a bar."

"It's your party. I probably won't drink, but okay, wherever."

"We'll see about that. There's that hotel in downtown Stratton, and it's got the bar? Let's meet there at four. There'll be no one there, and we can get soused and talk things out. They have those sludgy craft beers that are like eleven percent alcohol, and I'm making a dinner out of them."

"Okay. There in a bit." She hung up.

Out her windshield, through the projected footage of combat drones in neat rows, she could see the car in front of her peeling off at an exit, presumably so it could point itself in the right direction for the rest of the trip home. As nearby vehicles in the traffic stream smoothly parted to make way, the woman behind the wheel waved at Rebecca, offering her a last weak smile as she receded, and disappeared.

■

"That's mighty virtuous of you, mighty virginal," Kathryn said as she gestured at Rebecca's drink, orange juice dosed with a spritz of carbonated water. Rebecca detected an unexpected edge of anger to her mockery. She'd bought Kathryn a beer that was served in a brandy snifter: the handle affixed to the tap had been a replication of one of those brightly colored skulls you see during Dia de los Muertos celebrations, with roses inserted into each of its eyeholes.

Kathryn made a face as the beer's hoppiness bit her tongue. "Hoo yeah." She drained half the snifter straight off, scrunching her shoulders and shivering like a wet cat; by the time Rebecca had wordlessly gotten up, gone to the bar, ordered a second glass, and brought it back to the table, Kathryn had finished the first. "You're letting me lap you," she said. "Shit, with that stuff you're not even in the race: you're like watching from the stands and cheering." Rebecca pushed the newly poured beer toward her in silent response.

"Now I'm ready to talk," Kathryn said after a few more sips. "This happened over the weekend. This happened Sunday afternoon. He calls me and he says, I want to come over, it's important. And he'd just stayed over the night before and we'd gone out for brunch, so I didn't know what the emergency was that had cropped up during the past few hours. Anyway, I say, Sure, come over.

"So he comes over, and this is when I get the idea that something isn't right: I let him in, and I go sit on the couch in the living room like I always do, and I'm expecting him to come sit next to me like he always does, but instead he just stands there looking down at me. And he's still got his coat on, and he's got this backpack slung over one shoulder, like he's halfway out the door before he's even gotten halfway in.

"And he says, I guess you're not expecting this, or I guess maybe you are, I don't know, but I don't think we should see each other anymore. This isn't working out for me.

"And I think, Fuck no I wasn't expecting it! I thought things were great! I didn't *say* that, but I thought it. But I do say, What's wrong? You know, sit down, we can talk about it.

"And he says he doesn't think it'll help to talk about it. And the hurting thing is that he kept his coat on the whole time. Like he was trying to escape, and he knew if he sat down and got comfortable he never would.

"And I said, I think we have something good here, and it's a shame to throw it away when whatever problem this is is something we can probably solve in ten minutes if we just sit and talk.

"And he doesn't say anything at all: he just stands there, in his coat, like the cat got his tongue.

"And I say, Well are you just going to stand there like an idiot? And I wish I hadn't said that.

"And he says, real quiet, I guess I'd better go then. And he turns and leaves and lets himself out. Not even, let's talk in a few days, or I'll call you, or anything. That's it."

■

"That's terrible," Rebecca said. "I'm not sure what to say."

She drank her orange juice. She was sure that this was all going to turn out okay, but it would probably be a bad idea to tell Kathryn this—those words would sound like empty consolation. And if Kathryn had any idea of the degree of boundless optimism that Rebecca was feeling right now, she'd think she was crazy. Best to be a good listener and let Kathryn talk her own way through her problems.

"I'm not young," Kathryn said. "I'm thirty . . . what. I have to think about it and add it up now."

"You look dry," said Rebecca. "Let me get you another."

■

"You know," Kathryn said when she was deep into her third beer, "you want closure. You want everything to make sense in the end; you want explanations for things. And I don't feel like I'm getting that here. That's why what he did seems so rude. Not providing people with endings is an asshole thing to do."

"I know how you feel, sort of. But life isn't neat in the way a story is. And if you try to pretend it is, then you just make yourself unhappy, or screw yourself over. Because of wanting something that can't be. I'm saying, maybe he doesn't even know exactly why he wanted to call it off, you know? People don't really know the reason why they do things, a lot of the time. You make up a story after the fact to explain to yourself why you slept with that guy you met in a bar who had a band of pale skin on his ring finger, or why you spent five hundred dollars on a dress instead of getting groceries, but the stories are just lies. Your mind doesn't make sense to you the way you like to pretend it does, and the world can't, either."

"That doesn't stop me from *wanting* an explanation, though," Kathryn said, and there was that rough edge to her voice again. "I wouldn't be human, if I didn't want that."

■

Halfway through her fourth beer, Kathryn said, a little loudly, "You don't think it was the race thing, was it?"

"The race thing?"

"Get the fuck out. I'm not going to lie, okay, I had one or two issues, maybe, and I know they were stupid issues but knowing they were stupid doesn't mean I didn't have them, I maybe had a couple of issues. And it only stands to reason that he'd have the same issues, too, you know? And more reason than me to have them, because, I mean, history, right? So I would try to engage him on this stuff, through humor, because that's what humor does, it breaks these barriers down between us, I would talk about this stuff to let him know it's okay for him to talk about this stuff whenever he wants, that it's not a serious thing, that it's a *jokey* thing, but whenever I brought it up he'd get quiet or change the subject to science or something. And I guess that whatever it was got bottled up in him and got worse and worse until he just couldn't handle it anymore."

"I don't know," Rebecca said. "But I wouldn't beat myself up about it. If you keep worrying about it it'll drive you nuts, and there's nothing you can do."

"Goddamn," said Kathryn. "If everyone could get on the same page and realize that we live in the future, we wouldn't have to deal with this bullshit."

■

At the end of Kathryn's fifth beer, when Rebecca had decided to herself that she was cutting her off, Kathryn said, "Something else I wondered about. Something."

Rebecca said nothing, and waited for her to speak.

Kathryn looked at Rebecca over her empty glass with bleary-eyed suspicion, and her eyes focused and narrowed. "There was that mean little woman in Carson's lab. When he took me to visit the lab and show me this thing he was spending all his time on, she kept giving me these dirty looks the whole time, trying to make me feel stupid. And I saw her a couple of other times like when Carson would bring me to these physicist parties. I know you two became friends eventually, but I never got along with her, to be honest. I never liked the way she acted, like anyone who wasn't a scientist wasn't worth her time to talk to.

"There was this way. She and him. When they stood next to each other. I mean. You know how you see a woman and a guy around each other sometimes, at a party, just talking, and from out of nowhere this question pops in your head: *Are they banging?* And it's just a question, but the fact that you thought to ask the question means the answer is probably yes? Maybe I'm wrong about it, I don't know, but I got that feeling a couple of times when I saw them together. You know: *Are they banging?*"

Kathryn sat back in her chair and slumped. "And the embarrassing thing about it is that if it were true then everyone would know. Everyone in the lab would have known, or guessed, that something was going on, and they just would have not said anything, would have looked at me and said not a single word, would have stayed out of it like a bunch of bystanders."

"That's a little paranoid, don't you think? Even if that *were* happening, it's not like these people were *colluding* against you or something. Besides, you can't expect someone you don't know to just walk up to you and say hey, guess what—"

"Did you know?"

Rebecca paused. "Did I what?"

"You heard me. Did you know. Because you and Alicia are pretty tight, going on runs and all that. Did she tell you and did you not tell me? Because—"

"Kathryn! I—"

"Because it was something you thought I'd be better off not knowing? Because—"

"Kathryn. Kathryn." Rebecca gently pried Kathryn's hand away from her empty glass and clasped it in her own. "How close have we been, for how long? You know I wouldn't pull something like that. If I'd found out anything like that was going on, I would have let you know. Without hesitation. You have to believe that."

Not meeting Rebecca's gaze, Kathryn nodded. She tried to pull her hand away, but Rebecca tightened her grip. "Kate. Look at me."

Kathryn raised her head, a tear sliding down her face.

"Do you believe me?" Rebecca said.

She gripped Kathryn's hand harder still.

"I said: do you believe me?"

"I believe you," said Kathryn.

"Okay," said Rebecca, letting her go.

36

FIRST DATE

Wasn't it all moot, at this point? If this was in fact history's mere rough draft, why bother to do what Rebecca was doing instead of, say, spending her afternoon at the Steven Soderbergh retrospective going on at the Film Society of Lincoln Center, or marching into Gaia Williams's office without an appointment to tell her off, or mooning strangers in front of the Metropolitan Opera House? And yet there was still something pleasurable about even an ephemeral act of altruism, a little ego boost that you couldn't get from hedonism or rank self-interest. Plus, if her ambition was to change the world for the better, there was no harm in a little practice.

She was sitting at a tiny table in the Alice Tully Hall cafeteria, with a tiny cup of espresso in front of her along with an equally petite biscotti. She'd sat down three minutes after noon. Catalina, whom she had to stop thinking of as the "mark," was two tables away from her. She was pretty: no, *handsome* was a better word, meant in the old twentieth-century way used to describe women who'd traded the beauty of youth for another. Her hair was shorn close to the scalp, with a slight reddish tint to it, the sort of sexily androgynous look you could carry off if you were blessed with a nicely shaped head and the courage to reveal it; gold-framed eyeglasses matched simple gold earrings and a gold necklace. She was draped in bright swaths of bold autumnal colors, and was reading a book, a printed book: *The Guns of August*, by Barbara Tuchman. She stared at the volume intently, turning the pages with appreciable speed; her eyes stayed fixed to the words as she ate the salad in front of her and drank her sparkling white wine. She did not have the half-attentive look of a woman who was waiting for a date, whose existence she would not fully accept until he appeared in the flesh before her; she was not glancing up from the book at the end of every paragraph in naked expectation. She had the sort of easy solitude in public that men often mistook for longtime loneliness. Rebecca would not have been surprised if some guy approached her and tried to use Archduke Ferdinand's assassination as a pretext to sit down and join her. It almost seemed a shame to interrupt.

Rebecca collected her possessions—the half-finished espresso with the biscotti balanced on its saucer; her purse slung over a shoulder; the manila envelope she'd prepared, which was full of very interesting documents—and walked over to Catalina's table. "Excuse me?" she said, her voice sounding high and thin in her own ears, not rich and sonorous, not Marcus-like.

Catalina did not look up.

"Excuse me?" Rebecca said again, but Catalina's attention appeared to be focused intently on Clausewitz's ideas about the use of terror in war.

"Catalina?" Rebecca said, and this finally got her attention, her eyes first looking up at Rebecca over her glasses, then her head following. "Yes." The way she pronounced the word reminded Rebecca unexpectedly of the way Philip had acted when you interrupted him, of the manner in which he treated his time as one of the world's rarest and most valuable resources, which it would not do for you to waste away.

"I'm Rebecca. Rebecca Wright. From Lovability." She thought to offer a hand, but her hands were already full, with the coffee and the biscotti and the manila envelope. "The website. Lovability. I work there."

"Really."

The biscotti slid off Rebecca's saucer and fell to the floor.

Rebecca placed her espresso on Catalina's table—she had to nudge her plate of salad slightly to do this, which Catalina observed with an eyebrow cocked in incredulity—pulled out the extra chair at the table, and seated herself. The table was too tiny for the envelope, so she kept it clutched in her hands. Then she realized that she'd left her coat hanging at the other table. "Excuse me," she said, lifting a finger; then she got up again, retrieved the coat, and hung it over the back of the chair at Catalina's table. Then she sat down again.

Catalina's brow furrowed. "Are you sitting down?"

"I have something important to tell you," said Rebecca.

"I have a question, first."

"Oh geez you must have lots of questions—"

"How. In the hell. Did you know. I was here."

"Okay, this is going to sound really crazy to you, but—"

"Excuse me, ma'am."

Rebecca turned to see a server standing above her with a slight, solicitous bow. On his outstretched hand lay a napkin; on the napkin lay an almond biscotti.

"I saw that you dropped yours," he said. "This is a fresh one."

"Thank you." She took the napkin from him and placed it on the table.

"Would you like me to transfer your tab to this table?"

"Yes, that'd be fine."

"Please go away," Catalina said, and though Rebecca was unsure whom she was speaking to, herself or the server, she had committed to a course of action, and was resolved to stick it out.

"Ma'am," the server said, retreating.

Rebecca turned back to Catalina. "Anyway. Okay. You're supposed to meet a guy here. Marcus. He was supposed to show up at twelve o'clock. Right?"

"You sound like you've been snooping. This is frankly unbelievable—"

"Okay. Here we go. I told you this is crazy. I'm Marcus. Me."

Slowly, Catalina placed a bookmark in *The Guns of August*, closed the book, and placed it in her lap. She took a moment to look through the brightly lit windows of the hall, letting the noonday sun shine on her face; then she looked at Rebecca.

"I expect people on dating sites to lie a *little*," she said. "But damn."

"I know, right?" Rebecca suddenly found herself feeling a pint of blood short.

"You are not making sense to me, Rebecca. You need to start making sense."

"Okay! So here it is." She held up the envelope before her. "Some of the people you see on Lovability . . . aren't actually real. They're computer simulations. We control them with these motion-capture rigs. So I sit in front of a camera, with this helmet on, and when I move Marcus copies the move, and whenever I say something Marcus says the same thing, in his voice."

"Imagine that."

"We do it because we want everybody to have a positive experience with—"

"Be quiet for a second," said Catalina, and Rebecca decided to be quiet.

Rebecca watched Catalina eat a few more bites of her salad and drink some more of her wine, with the same solitary ease she'd had before Rebecca came over. It was not as if Catalina were deliberately attempting to give her the silent treatment—nothing as malicious as that—but that Catalina had decided to find her *uninteresting* for a moment. She was not particularly enamored of the idea that her existence, at least temporarily, depended on Catalina's acknowledgment of it. But she waited, feeling her own invisibility.

"You know," Catalina said eventually, "I had it in the back of my head that there was something weird about that guy. I was on the phone with my girlfriend and I told her the night before: I've been talking to this guy on the Internet and he seemed like he *might* be a catch except, one, he keeps trying to string me along like he's afraid to meet me in public, and two, everything he talks about is blackety blackety black. And okay, the Internet does that to people. They can't squeeze every little bit of their personalities through those thin little cables that connect computers together, so they end up acting out their authenticity to try to let strangers know they're real. Being what they think black people are supposed to be, what white people are supposed to be, what women are supposed to be, what gays are supposed to be, what the President is supposed to be. This guy, he's going overboard: everything out of his mouth is P-Funk or Paul Robeson or *The Conjure-Man Dies*. A guy like that, I was sure that once I got him out from behind that computer and in front of me, after a couple of drinks the next thing you knew he'd be in a karaoke bar singing 'The Wreck of the Edmund Fitzgerald' or something."

"We use Wikipedia a lot. To work up the profiles of the romantic avatars. They're all experts in one thing or another. I've learned a lot, driving them. I have to know enough to give the impression that the avatar knows more than he can talk about in ten minutes."

"Avatars, you call them," said Catalina.

"Yeah."

"Driving, you call it. Like a truck."

"Yeah."

Catalina returned to her salad, and Rebecca felt herself vanish again. The salad looked pretty good—arugula, cherry tomatoes, and prosciutto, lightly dressed with olive oil—and Rebecca made a mental note to come back and try it here, before realizing she probably didn't need to make that note.

"What's the point?" Catalina said, her voice granting back to Rebecca her provisional existence. "It seems like so much work to do this. That's not just typing: that's special-effects stuff."

"We had it lying around? Lovability is one arm of this huge, huge company, and all the arms just kind of share resources sometimes. But any more than that is beyond my pay grade, so to speak."

"Hm."

"I came here to apologize, I guess. Not for the company: just for me. You're not the only person we did this to. I've driven about six of these avatars. White, black, Asian, male, female. All different."

"Very . . . diverse."

"Yeah!" Rebecca said. "Look. I want to show you something." She opened the manila envelope, extracted its contents, and placed them on the table in front of Catalina. They were printouts, some in color, some in black and white: profile photos of Lovability customers, and next to them the avatars that had been assigned to them. Somehow the still images of the avatars had an unsettling, uncanny-valley effect that disappeared when they were in motion: here you could see their doll-eyed, unearthly perfection more clearly. Columns of data dangled beneath the photos: period of membership; average time of a visit to the site; number of profiles viewed; price if a company wanted to acquire the profile's data or place a targeted ad on the member's page.

Catalina leafed through the printouts until she saw the page that featured her own profile next to Marcus's. She lifted it before her so that Rebecca could not see her. "I'm expensive," she said.

"It's because people like you, in your particular demographic, I mean, are hard to reach reliably, hard to get solid information about, and the company, we leverage that. They leverage that."

Catalina lowered the paper and put it back on the stack.

"You must feel really humiliated," Rebecca said. "I'd understand if—"

Catalina threw back her head and laughed, her merry chuckle echoing in the high-ceilinged hall. "Oh goodness. Oh goodness no. Humiliated. What a strong word."

Rebecca disappeared again for a few moments as Catalina finished off her glass of wine. Attempting to relax into her own invisibility again, she let her gaze fall on the documents that were supposed to blow the lid off this whole thing, but in which Catalina apparently had very little interest.

Catalina looked at Rebecca and tapped the paper before her. "This is not me. This is a picture of me and some numbers. You pretended to be a picture and a bunch of numbers so you could run a game on another picture and another bunch of numbers. Aren't you embarrassed?"

"Hey, hold on a second—"

"The only way I would be 'humiliated,' as you say, is if I did not believe I was actually real. Do you believe you are real and alive? Here in the world, sitting here? Able to be more than a bunch of ones and zeroes? It doesn't sound like it. If you would think that I would be *humiliated* so easily."

"Now hold on a second, you're being *totally* unfair. You made a date with me! With Marcus, I mean! And you're here! If I hadn't shown up here you'd have been totally stood up!"

"That's not true at all," Catalina replied. "I allowed it to be inferred that I would be at a certain place at a certain time, where I would embark on a certain course of action. I am doing this. I'm having a satisfying day so far: it's good to have a salad and a glass of wine in the middle of the afternoon. And now I am off to look at some outsider art."

Catalina stood and gathered up her things. "I don't know who you are," she said. "You told me your name, but I don't know who you are."

"I'll, um, get the check?" Rebecca said.

"That's very gracious of you." Suddenly a smile broke across Catalina's face as she looked down on Rebecca, and Rebecca suddenly felt *real*, like a puppet that had had life breathed into it by a blue fairy.

Catalina patted Rebecca's shoulder then, cocking her head sideways in a gesture that seemed to be half bemusement, half pity. Then she turned and left the cafeteria.

■

The server appeared a couple of minutes later, presenting Rebecca with the bill. She looked it over: twenty dollars more than she expected, but it could have been worse. *I try*, Rebecca thought to herself as she riffled through her purse for her phone, using it to send a squirt of data to the payment device the server kept in a holster on his belt, tacking on a thirty percent tip. Then she said to him, "You know what? Believe it or not, I really am trying to do the best I can."

She sighed, and the server nodded at her as if her non sequitur made perfect sense. With a high-pitched whirr his device spat out a flimsy receipt, which he ripped off and handed to her with a practiced flourish. "Aren't we all," he said.

37

MIDNIGHT MONOLOGUES

1. CARSON

My father had terrible circulation—he'd wake up in the middle of the night with his toes and fingers tingling, and would have to clap his hands and stomp his feet on the floor to get the blood going in them again. My mother was always trying to feed him spinach and kale, thinking the nutrients would help. A fleeting look of shame would cross his face when someone offered to shake his hand, for he'd anticipate their shock when they found his palm to be unpleasantly chilled and damp. "Cold hands, warm heart," he'd say, trying not to glance down to watch the man wipe his hand on his shirt. Not just an apology for a faulty body temperature, but a plea: *Do not believe this deceiving first impression. I am just as good a person as you believe yourself to be.*

Alicia reminds me of my father in that way, though apology isn't in her nature. I wouldn't mislead myself by believing that there is a secretly bubbly and weepy girl inside her that she will reveal to me in her own time, or if I chip away at her exterior for long enough. She is, as they say, what she is. But her sense of humor, though brittle and sharp-edged, must come from a kind of joy, and whatever relationship we have surely deserves the name of "love," though I'm also sure that "love" is a word that would make Alicia wince, were I to speak it.

Often when I am in her bed I find that I dream of ice. I am marooned on the Europa of my adolescent fantasies; I have lost one of my mittens in the snow. And I awake to find that Alicia, in her sleep, has twined her fingers into mine, or flung one of her legs over me. There will be a slow but certain transfer of heat from one body to another, then. Physics will speak where voices won't, and this, I think, is best.

2. SPIVEY

Terence. Put that book down, whatever it is, and talk to me. I have some good news for you!

Yeah, I know: you're thinking, "Spivey? *Good* news?" But it's true! Listen.

So I went over to visit Rita this weekend. And to be honest, I haven't said much about it, but lately she's been getting down in the dumps, worse and worse. But on this day I ring the bell, and I hear her holler *Come in*, like she always does to save herself the trouble of getting up. And when I come into the living room, the TV is off, for one thing, and she never gives that thing a rest, and I see her sitting on the couch with this big smile on her face and a blanket draped over her lap. And she has this black headband on, too, that looks like it's made out of plastic or something, but I don't think anything much about that at first.

So I say, "Hey, Rita," and she says, "Guess what," and I say, "What." And she smiles even bigger and says, "I got a new leg." And she whips off the blanket, and she picks her new leg up and puts it on the table in front of her.

And I will not lie: I was kind of horrified at first. It looked like a Terminator leg! Not flesh and bone, but this shiny metal skeleton, with cables wrapped all around the rods. Real elaborate. It had a metal rod and joint for just about every bone and joint in a human leg, a human foot. Definitely not a make-do, half-assed job.

Listen, though. Rita says, "Look at this." And she frowns her face up and starts *staring* at this metal leg.

And I say, "Rita," because I don't understand what's going on. And she says, "Shut up, I'm concentrating." And get this: the big toe, this metal big toe, it starts *moving*. Then the one next to that, then the one in the middle. And pretty soon she's wiggling them all, even the little toe, and I've never been able to do *anything* with my little toe except break it playing football.

Turns out that's what the headband's for. This thing reads her *brainwaves*, and sends signals to the electronics in this mechanical leg. And even though her old leg is gone, the part of her brain that controlled that leg and told it what to do is still there. Soon, Rita says, with enough practice, she'll be able to walk without looking at it or even thinking about it, just like you don't think about your real leg. Then they're going to wrap it in this plastic sheath—apparently they have this plastic that feels just about like skin if you touch it, it's got hair and everything, though Rita said she told the doctors not to put any hair on it if they could help it, because she didn't want to look like she hadn't shaved. Then it'll be like her old leg again: not exactly, but ninety percent. As long as she wears that headband. But that's no trouble at all, considering. I'd never take that headband off if I was her: they'd bury me with it.

This company that makes prosthetic limbs made the whole setup for her. Taligent Industries. The rig is kind of experimental, so they want people to try it out, so they can gather data. And Rita got picked to try it out. I bet it tells the company where you are and what you're doing all the time, but I guess that's the cost of doing business.

She was so happy! I haven't seen her that happy since I don't know when. She said, "You know, day after day I sit here and I think, Well, I guess this is going to be as good as it gets. And I still think that. But now the meaning has turned around for me. I say to myself, This *is* as good as it gets. And I have to thank God. Because I'm amazed."

We're in a time machine, Terence, you and I, right now. It's stuck in one gear and it's slow as hell, but it works. It's bringing us into the future. And I think that future might actually be good. I think it might be okay.

You should see that thing, Terence. Give her a couple of months and she'll be playing guitar with it.

3. ALICIA

I have an interesting idea. Why not go back to basics: a double-slit experiment. I'm surprised I didn't think of this until now. Mount an electron gun in the top of the causality violation device, behind a metal plate with two slits. Install a screen in the bottom. Fire the electron gun for an hour while the CVD is activated. Take a look at the screen and see if there's any deviation from the expected diffraction pattern.

I can give that to my grad student Adam to do. It'll give him some hands-on time with the CVD, and he probably won't screw it up. He's smart, but he needs to build up his confidence if he's going to become the kind of scientist who can run his own lab. This is a good task for him. I can tell him what needs to be accomplished and leave him to figure out how. The method should be self-evident, but if he gets it done without any handholding, he'll have that good feeling that comes from taking point on a project and seeing it through to completion. Even if the results are negative, which they probably will be. Negative results: something else he'll need to get used to.

I like Adam. He reminds me of me, when I was a graduate student. Though I think he got into physics because he wants to have that eureka moment that scientists always have in movies, when they're looking at a blackboard full of equations, and the music swells, and then they say *A-ha!* and dance a jig. I hate to tell him what I had to learn for myself: it almost never works out that way for any of us. If you are expecting that from physics, it will almost certainly disappoint you.

There was a graduate student in my cohort, this guy I dated, who told me he came to realize that doing physics is like this: there's a concrete wall twenty feet thick, and you're on one side, and on the other side is everything worth knowing. And all you have is a spoon. So you just have to take a spoon and start scraping at the wall: no other way. He works in a bookstore now.

But I think of it this way. There is a jigsaw puzzle. It's infinitely large, with no edges or corners to help you out. We have to put it together: it's our duty. We will never finish, but we have to find our satisfactions where we can: when we place two pieces together that suggest we may have found the place where the sky touches the sea, or when we discover a piece that is beautiful in and of itself, that has an unusual color or a glimpse of an unexpected pattern. And the pieces that do not join together also tell you something. If there are very few eureka moments, then at least there are a thousand little failures, that point the way toward a hundred little joys.

I like Carson. I really like Carson. I can hand an idea to him that's still a little rough, and he can turn it over and tumble it and hand it back to me shining. And I can do the same for him.

He could run his own lab if he wanted to. He's going to have to look for positions soon. We will either have to split up, or become one of those long-distance academic couples that are the rule rather than the exception. There will be ethical issues when I have to write a recommendation letter, but this is a special circumstance—it's only a bad accident of fate that I'm running this lab anyway.

He could get out of physics. I don't think he's as happy doing physics as I am. But he seems to have talked himself around to a kind of contentment. Still, if he left, I wouldn't complain and I wouldn't judge. It would make things easier for us.

He likes to wake up at eight. That's a ridiculous time! I get up and go for a run and come back and he's still in bed. We need to fix that. It would be better for both of us if he made a habit of waking up at six fifteen, like I do.

I'll wake him gently tomorrow morning, so I don't startle him. Then I'll tell him about my new idea.

4. THE PRESIDENT OF THE UNITED STATES

Hello, Tracey Wilson, from the great state of Illinois! I think *Fanny and Alexander* is a great choice for a weekend rental. It's one of the best Christmas movies because it's about so much more than Christmas. But I'd go with the five-hour cut instead of the three-hour theatrical version: the longer cut is far superior. Don't worry: it has three intermissions, so it's not too taxing on the attention.

Hello, Bernard Gregory, from the great state of Oregon. It would be my honor to say a soothing word to your father in his final moments. Please hold your phone next to his ear.

Muriel Fox, from the great state of Utah: you definitely want to use bleached flour for your angel food cake, not unbleached. I'm glad I stopped you before you made a fatal mistake!

Matthew Reichl, from the great state of Maine: I want to share a story with you, in these tough times. I wasn't the richest kid growing up: you're certainly better off now than I was back then. When other kids were getting PlayStation 2s for Christmas, I had to make do with a PlayStation Negative One. So one day my father gave me a piece of advice that I'd like to pass on to you: it may be cold comfort, but it's true. He said, *The man who has learned to be happy with what he has is the man who lives in the best of all possible worlds.* It's true! Think about it!

To the insurgents in the great state of North Dakota: I ask you one final time to lay down your arms. Those who have committed no crimes against America will be welcomed back with pleasure into this nation's embrace. You have my personal guarantee.

Grace Lanier, from the great state of New Mexico: one of the elementary strategies of go is expressed by the statement "A group with two eyes lives." But a group of stones can have what's called a "false eye": a group with a false eye is vulnerable, and can be captured if surrounded. May I show you some examples?

Rebecca Wright, from the great state of New Jersey: hey, I don't have a lot of time. Just: I've noticed that you've kind of changed a little lately? The past couple of weeks you've had this kind of couldn't-care-less, go-for-broke attitude? And . . . look, I'll just say it. If you're about to do, you know, something, stop and make sure it's the right thing first, alright? Okay I gotta go: someone's coming.

To all the citizens of all the great states of America: good night, good night, good night. Know that I continue to work while you sleep, continuing to act as the manifestation of your collective will.

Sleep, citizens, and dream the American dream.

5. WOODY

Lord, I come to You in silent prayer, honest in my doubt, uncertain of Your shape.

I believe I could bear almost any of the hundreds of versions of what the stories say You are. The benevolent father; the Three-in-One; the blind watchmaker. I could even bear Your absence or Your nonexistence, or the possibility that You are an artifact of humanity's collective imagining.

But I cannot accept a vision of You as an engineer who spends His days maintaining the machine of morality. I cannot take the idea of You as an optimizer, introducing evil into human affairs in an attempt to create the best of all possible worlds. I cannot bear this cold mathematician's God who sees all the universe as nothing more than an elaborate problem to be solved. Such a world is a world with no meaning, one in which one history is no more or less preferable to any other.

Let us find our own paths; let us make our own attempts at fashioning this world; let us bear the sting of our own inevitable failures. To do otherwise would be to fail Yourself. And the only thing You cannot do is fail.

6. SEAN

My father keeps telling me new stories, stories inside other stories, stories on top of other stories. And I draw them in this place. I could stay here and draw forever, but I can't. I have to show my mother soon.

This place is mine. The sky over me is mine, and the jail underground is mine. The jail has fire and water. But if you end up there you can't have both, only more than you want of one. And that's too bad for you: you should have stayed out of jail.

In the forest there is a tiger. He has needles for claws and his teeth are made of knife blades. He says and does whatever he wants, and if he doesn't like you, he'll bite into your throat and shake you all around. But when my father appears the tiger puts his head down, and covers it with his paws, and does whatever he's told.

The forest is my mother's hair. The tiger lives in her hair.

My father is here in a thousand shapes. My mother is made of the earth and the sky.

I'm going to show her now.

7. REBECCA

Nothing is as it should be. Everything is upside down.

But I know I can fix this. I can do it.

38

GRAND DESIGN

The first unusual thing that Alicia noticed when her retrofitted, autonomous VW Beetle pulled into Rebecca's driveway on Saturday morning was that Rebecca had apparently left the driver's-side door of her car wide open the last time she got out of it. As she passed the vehicle on the way to Rebecca's front door, Alicia peeked inside: the car stereo was still there, and the door of the glove box hadn't been forced. She shut the car door, which looked as if it had been left ajar overnight: the dashboard showed no electronic signs of life, suggesting a depleted battery. Wouldn't Rebecca have heard the car's insistent beeping?

Another odd thing was Rebecca's eagerness to have Alicia come over so they could go for a morning run. Alicia usually got up before sunrise anyway, and so she didn't necessarily mind phone calls at six fifteen, and was in fact liable to forget that most other people did. So when Rebecca had said that she wanted Alicia to drop by her place first to see "something cool that Sean had made" before they went for a run at eight, Alicia assumed that the professed need to display her son's juvenile artwork (when she could just as easily have snapped a picture of it on her phone and shown it to Alicia later) had been a pretext to begin their usual Saturday-morning run from Rebecca's apartment, instead of a place Alicia would pick that would lead to challenging terrain. Which was fine: not every run needed to kick your ass. Gentle slopes and asphalt were okay sometimes when you needed a break.

Rebecca answered her door, clad in running gear: she looked quite cheerful. "Come in," she said, ushering Alicia inside with a gentle hand on her shoulder (though Rebecca usually didn't touch her). "Come on in the kitchen: I made us some smoothies to have before we run, like you suggested. I whipped them up last night and put them in the fridge so they'd be cold."

"Hey, you left your car door open last night," Alicia said.

Rebecca paused in the entrance to the kitchen door. "Oh shit. I . . . I'll guess I'll figure out what to do about that after we go running. I won't need it today." She shrugged. "Some trouble I couldn't use, I guess. But whatever."

In the kitchen, Rebecca removed the smoothies from the fridge: two glasses covered with Saran Wrap. "Papaya, mango, and coconut water," she said, tearing the cellophane off each glass and inserting a stainless steel straw retrieved from a drawer. "And I mixed some of that cricket powder in yours."

Weirdly chatty, this woman, this morning. Alicia tasted her smoothie: it was good, and refreshing. Rebecca had added a dollop of honey to it as well: thoughtful.

"So how are you *doing*," Rebecca said, as if she hadn't seen Alicia in a while. Alicia was doing quite well, all things considered: she told Rebecca that she'd come up with the idea of mounting an electron gun in the roof of the CVD to perform a double-slit experiment, and even if it didn't explain why the CVD wasn't behaving as theories and simulations said it should, maybe it would tell them something interesting. There was always hope.

"But what about that idea you told me about in the diner?" Rebecca said. "That if the time—the CVD, I mean—that if it actually worked, you might not be able to prove that it worked?"

"That's just conjecture, at this point," Alicia said. "Elaborate conjecture, with some decent reasoning behind it, but conjecture just the same."

"But it's still on the table."

"Until we find some evidence that proves otherwise, of course it is. But if we're talking about unprovable propositions, lots of things are on the table."

"But out of all these possible but unprovable propositions—"

"Of which there are an infinite number," Alicia interrupted.

"Okay, got it. But this is the most plausible out of those."

"Yes, I suppose it is," Alicia said. "But that's why we have to keep working, and trying to find evidence to prove otherwise. Because I'd really prefer it to not be true. You can see why."

"I can," Rebecca said. "And I'm glad you're keeping at it. Hey, how's your smoothie?"

"It's nice. I . . . I appreciate it." Alicia smiled and looked at Rebecca, who looked back at her as if she expected her to keep talking, or sought a more convincing demonstration of her approval. "This is . . . a good mix of nutrients? Good for running, once we take some time to digest it."

"Well, while that's digesting and filling us with nutrients, I want to show you what Sean made. He's sleeping, still: he sleeps in on Saturdays. But I'll show you his . . . installation, I guess you'd call it. It's amazing."

Installation? Alicia thought.

■

"Sit over there," Rebecca said, indicating a plush footstool on the side of the room opposite its single door. "That's the best place to see the overarching pattern. Look how he's divided the space into four quadrants: earth, air, fire, water. There's not a clear line between each element, but you can start to see the boundaries if you pay attention to the way he uses color. Greens and browns in that corner, mostly; reds over there near you; blues on your other side; and air is suggested by his use of negative space. See?"

Feeling like she could have stood an extra half hour in bed—this whole random situation with Rebecca was starting to make her tired—Alicia sat on the footstool and looked out at the room before her. The artwork covered the entire floor from wall to wall, except for a narrow stripe in the middle that was clearly intended to spare the rest from being smeared by footsteps. The colors also crawled about four feet up the walls: Sean must have started there, working back toward the middle of the room, always leaving himself a path out.

"See how he's integrated a history of technology into the four elements," Rebecca continued. "That goes counterclockwise, starting with the earth: the people in that section are using rocks and spears and things. Then someone discovers fire and you've got cooking and kilns and gunpowder; then the water section is dedicated to the steam age, all engines and gears. And see that plume of steam drifting upward? That draws your eye from water to air: that last section represents the Information Age. See those dotted lines that are connecting those two heads together? See how one is standing on a miniature outline of the U.S., while another is in Australia?"

Alicia continued to stare at the riot of hues before her. "Sean did all of this?" she said.

"He's been working on it for about a month, pretty much nonstop. Though I called him out sick from school for a week, near the end."

"Did he explain this . . . interpretation to you?"

"Well, *no*, obviously, but it's easy to see what you're looking at if you pay attention. Look: there are some things I haven't pointed out yet, but it'd probably take you a day to see everything, and we don't have much time."

Alicia yawned. *Don't have much time?* What was the hurry?

"Okay," Rebecca said. "See all these men here who are building these machines? These are all representations of Philip. He's been drawing Philip over and over again, in different shapes. You can see that if you look up close. But from where you're sitting, if you take in the whole thing at once, you'll see something else entirely. Look: see it?"

Alicia gazed at the drawings before her and, despite Rebecca's mounting excitement, she quietly, almost imperceptibly, shook her head.

"It's my face!" Rebecca said. "Sean made a portrait of me!" She walked down the central aisle toward Alicia, gesturing at one part of the mural, then another. "See that image of Philip entering the dark cave, in the earth section? The entrance to the cave is the pupil of my left eye. And this part in the air section, where the spaceship that's crewed by a bunch of Philips is observing a black hole: that's the pupil of my right eye. And near where you're sitting, where those six Philips have joined hands and they're singing a hymn to a steam engine: they make up an outline of my lower lip. Focus on those details and the rest will snap into place. I screamed when I saw it."

"Rebecca," Alicia said. "This is . . . something."

"It is!"

"But . . . I have to be honest," Alicia continued. "I . . . I am *really* not seeing what you're talking about here. These people that Sean drew are all supposed to be Philip . . . but they all look like stick figures to me. I mean, they've got eyes and noses sure, but there's nothing about them that says *Philip* so much as just *vertebrate*. And I don't really see a larger pattern in all this, either. I certainly don't see your *face*."

Alicia paused for a moment. "Though I guess I can see how different parts of the room are decorated in different colors," she said. "I can give you that. But even that might be because he used a marker until it ran dry, and then switched to another. Are you sure that all that 'negative space' in what you're calling the 'air section' isn't just because he didn't have any more ink?"

"I think you should keep looking," Rebecca said, backing away from Alicia to lean against the door.

■

Then, as Alicia's eyelids fluttered, the pattern began to reveal itself; the more she looked, the more details she saw, and the grander the design became. She saw a *Homo erectus* version of Philip learning to control fire, the sparks flying from the stones he struck together doubling as a gleam in Rebecca's eye. She saw Philip as Galileo, on trial for his heliocentric heresies; as Darwin on the deck of the HMS *Beagle*; as some other future scientist, answering questions about the nature of the universe that were as yet unasked. The arc of a boulder thrown by a catapult followed the helix of Rebecca's ear; the miniature globe that floated in the outstretched hand of Philip-as-Pythagoras was also a dimple of Rebecca's cheek.

Alicia saw all this, but doubted her seeing: she saw her eyes and mind not as purveyors of fact but as instruments of observation, instruments that might be in error, might even be inexplicably failing. How could a child Sean's age have done this? What would he know about the designs in Da Vinci's notebooks, or the Roman Inquisition's hostility to Copernican theory? Why, suddenly, was she having so much trouble staying awake?

And then the drawings before her began, in subtle ways, to

move, the water before the prow of the *Beagle* rippling as it parted, the wheels of the difference engine spinning as Philip-as-Charles-Babbage turned its crank, and she knew. She rose, unsteady on her feet. "What have you *done*?" she asked. Then: "The *smoothie*?"

"Siestalert," Rebecca said. "I ground up three pills and put them in, along with the cricket powder. You're tripping because you're fighting them. Sit down and go to sleep: you'll probably be out for an hour and a half or so."

Alicia's knees began to give out, and she plopped back down onto the footstool. "But!" she cried.

"Look," Rebecca said, crossing the room again to sit down next to Alicia. "There's something I have to do. And I'd ask your permission for it, but I figured when I told you what it was you'd want to have a big debate about it, and you're really good at arguments and I don't want to deal with all that. I need to go back into the time machine. And the easiest way I could think of to do that was to drug you and borrow your keycard so I could get back into the lab."

Alicia shook her head. The half-dozen Philips that were praying to the steam engine were singing now, and it was becoming difficult to hear Rebecca's voice over the harmonies of their hymn.

"There are two possibilities here," said Rebecca, placing her hand on Alicia's. "Either the machine works, or it doesn't. If it doesn't, I step in and step right out again, and the world is the same as it ever was, except I guess you're going to be super pissed at me now. But if it does work, then I have the chance to correct history. Because it's all wrong here. This is what Sean is telling you. That it's wrong and it needs to be made right."

Alicia waved her arm before her. "But it's just scribbles! Nothing! No." Her head bobbing around on her shoulders, she fumbled at Rebecca as if she meant to push her over. "You don't have the *right*."

"I do," Rebecca replied calmly. "I didn't ask for it, but it was given to me by accident when I stepped inside the machine the first time. And if I've already gone back into the past once, the history we're living shows that I failed to do the thing I must have intended to. I failed to save my husband's life. And I have the right to correct that error. I have the right to replace this history with a better one."

"You do not," Alicia said. "You . . . do not."

"I'm sorry," Rebecca said then as Alicia tipped over, her head resting in the crook of Rebecca's neck as she went under.

■

Terence was about to end his shift when Alicia Merrill's car pulled up, right at the door to the building. He figured that maybe Alicia needed to offload some equipment from the trunk, which is why she didn't park in the lot, but it turned out that the woman who got out of the car was not Alicia. She seemed familiar to him, but he couldn't quite place her—hadn't she come this way before?

Whoever it was, she was dressed in running clothes, like Alicia often was on weekends. But Terence couldn't get why this woman had Alicia's car. And when she badged into the building, the ID showed up on Terence's monitor as Alicia's, too. Why would Alicia loan whoever this was her car and her ID? Terence had this quickly blooming feverish itch at the back of his brain, like you get when your instinct is trying to tell your reason that you're being hustled.

Terence was on shift this morning with the Brazilian lady, and when he looked at her she just gave him this blank look and a shrug, like she wasn't expecting this job to require more than sitting behind a desk. The woman was bypassing security and heading straight toward the entrance to the lab, with the ease of someone who knew where she was going. Who on earth *was* that?

"Excuse me, ma'am?" Terence said, and the woman turned, giving Terence the first clear look at her face. She smiled and said, "Hello! Everything's okay," and then continued on toward the lab. Then Terence *knew* he was being hustled, and the penny dropped. It was that woman who'd gotten in here before, drunk with that other woman who'd been going out with that one guy for a while. The wife of that physicist who'd died in the car accident a while back.

"No no: excuse me, ma'am," Terence said, rising, and then Rebecca broke into a run, shouldering the door to the lab open, heading down the corridor, toward the machine.

■

There was only one person in the chamber that held the causality violation device, a young guy who was sitting at a desk, peering intently at his laptop's screen. He looked up startled when Rebecca burst into the room, breathing heavily. "You," she said. "What's your name?"

"Adam?" the kid said, as if uncertain.

She pointed at the hulking column of machinery in the center of the room. "What are you doing with that?"

"I'm running the double-slit experiment," Adam said. "You aren't here about that, are you?"

"Sure I am," Rebecca said as she approached the CVD.

"Well, what we're seeing here isn't that interesting yet. We need to do another couple of runs before we have enough data to look for a variance in the diffraction pattern, and then it'll be days before we can process—hey, what are you doing? You get away from there! Alicia said no one's supposed to go inside there!"

Rebecca yanked open the door to the device just as Terence entered the room, with Carson, who'd come in from another office, just behind. "Ma'am! Stay *away* from that!"

"Everything's okay," said Rebecca.

"I've already called the cops," said Terence, who, for a painful moment, was feeling his total lack of power in this situation: the magic of a badge could only go so far before it needed to be backed up by a weapon. "Think about it: where are you going to go?"

Hell: maybe it doesn't work, Rebecca thought.

She remembered what Alicia and Carson had told her, about the rules that would govern the machine's behavior. If the machine worked, and it allowed her to leave, she would have to return to this moment in time, to this exact place.

But it couldn't be as simple as that, could it? There had to be a way to cheat that, if you were committed enough to do what needed to be done.

Was she?

She looked into Carson's eyes. She thought of Sean waking up now, finding the house empty, going to the room in which he'd recorded the history of another world, and opening the door.

Hell: it's got to work. No other option.

"I don't know where I'm going to go," Rebecca said.

She entered the device, shut the door, and consigned herself to darkness.

EXTRAORDINARY EVIDENCE

Everything is as it should be; all is in its place. This is what Philip Steiner thinks.

When he wakes, the opposite side of the bed is empty, as it always is in the morning. He stretches beneath the sheets, clenches and unclenches his toes, rolls out of bed, drops to the floor, and knocks out a quick set of push-ups. These days he stops at thirty. Most men Philip's age can't knock out thirty push-ups. His morning routine used to involve bringing his muscles to failure, doing reps until his triceps gave out and he unceremoniously crashed to the carpet, but he's decided there's no point in that anymore. And he'd been able to see the evidence that his body had begun its long, slow slide toward senescence in the trend line of his daily maximum repetitions, sloping downward.

It is satisfactory to know that you are stronger than most men your age. It is nice not to have that lingering ache across your chest all the time.

■

Philip moved out of Stratton a couple of years ago: he now lives in a cozy home on one of Princeton's green, secluded side streets, away from its tiny but bustling downtown. Here the only early-morning noise is that of landscapers hired by neighbors. At autumn's end they are not content to let leaves decay and return to the soil in their own time: the leafblowers start their engines at eight sharp, daily. But most of the families around here have two incomes in order to make the mortgage: the few adults who remain behind to hear the din carried on the morning air are nannies and au pairs; people who are somehow able to eke out a living working at home; and those, like Philip, who are at long last easing into retirement.

Shrugging into a wrinkled polo shirt and putting on a pair of faded jeans, he goes out to the garage, where his bicycle waits propped against a wall. This is the second part of his newly dialed-down regimen: a ride past the Theological Seminary and along back roads to the Institute for Advanced Study, where he will have breakfast.

■

In the IAS dining hall the fellows have quietly segregated themselves by general discipline. Physicists are seated nearest the end of the buffet line: after they load up their trays they sit right down at the first chair they reach and start eating without a word. Chemists must walk past the physicists to find a table; biologists have to walk past them both. There are a few humanities types at IAS, too, a couple of historians and even a writer of short stories that regularly appear in the *New Yorker:* when they do come for breakfast, which isn't often, they tend to sit alone in the corners of the hall, where the dust is thick and the light flickers.

Philip does not sit with the physicists, though he supposes he is entitled to, if he wishes. He sits in the balcony that overhangs the floor of the dining hall, with the physicists' wives and partners, and watches the fellows from above. He brings with him a copy of *Ulysses*, along with a second volume, a collection of annotations of Joyce's novel, keyed to page and line number. He reads a few pages a day while he eats his regular meal of scrambled eggs, turkey sausage, and black coffee. The reading is slow, but he enjoys it, though he's never spent much time reading novels: *Ulysses* is not a story, so much as a system of the world. A place for everything, and everything in its place. Joyce would have made a good physicist, Philip thinks: he has that same yearning to make sense of existence that the best physicists do.

Occasionally, Philip peers over the railing at the long rows of diners below. While the fellows of other disciplines are dressed more casually, the physicists wear tweed jackets, and dark coats, and neatly ironed shirts, and solid-colored ties; even now, in the way they dress and groom themselves, they silently pay tribute to their predecessors of the Atomic Age, the heyday of physics in the public imagination. Amid the men is a single woman, holding court. Her black top displays bare biceps that flex as her hand gestures gloss her monologue. This is Philip's wife, his second wife, Alicia Merrill. She is an IAS fellow while he is not; her name is on the card that Philip presents to the cafeteria's cashier when he wants his breakfast.

Alicia is aware that Philip bikes out to the Institute for breakfast after she arrives there at seven; she knows they eat at the same time, and that he eats in the balcony. But she has never invited him to join them. Philip figures that the reason why is best not to know. He sometimes considers inviting himself into the group, but he can imagine the collective stinging look that would appear on the faces of the other physicists, and he fears that the same look would appear on Alicia's face as well.

Or perhaps she just wants to leave him alone with Leopold Bloom and Stephen Dedalus.

He is content to sit in the balcony. He likes observing from a distance the workings of the field in which he once played a daily part. He enjoys reading the copy of *Ulysses* that Alicia had given him years ago. Only now has he made the time for it, and each day it reminds him of all the things and people he failed to make time for, and how little time he has remaining. Even if he lives for decades more, decades are not enough.

■

Though Philip and Alicia are happily married, he still thinks of his first wife, Rebecca, every day. He still wears the mechanical wristwatch she gave him, which now runs nine hours slow.

You rarely ever know that the last words you say to someone will be the last. Philip had been at the lab when the phone rang and derailed his train of thought, the line of code he was typing left half finished. He was short with Rebecca when he answered.

"Hi, honey," Rebecca said. "I have something to tell you."

"What?"

"Sean's gotten into some trouble at school. And I've got to go pick him up."

"Good. Because I'm busy."

"I know, honey."

They listened to each other breathe in silence for a moment.

"Okay, then," said Rebecca. "I gotta go."

"Goodbye," said Philip.

"I love you."

"Goodbye," said Philip.

Two hours later he got the call about the accident.

■

"No father wants or expects to bury his own daughter," Woodrow Wright said, leaning on the pulpit as if he feared his legs would give out. "But I can tell you this: that I am deeply, deeply proud of Rebecca. That she made a split-second decision to save the life of her son, turning the wheel of her vehicle so that her side of it would be impacted by an oncoming car instead of his. She gave her life in the exercise of that greatest gift that God grants us—the ability to change the trajectory of history."

Sitting next to Philip in the front pew, Sean fidgeted uncomfortably: he could feel the eyes on him of the mourners seated behind him, as if their gazes were trying to drill into his head.

"Ashes to ashes, dust to dust," Woody said. "But for a brief and precious time, our souls can bind ashes together, and give them a shape and the will to act.

"May I ask you to honor my daughter's memory?

"May I ask you never to be content with simply being? May I ask you always to strive, to change, to *do*?"

■

Philip found the wake exhausting—the endless expressions of sympathy from those who had no common frame of reference for his grief—and eventually, when the last few stragglers were sitting in the living room of Rebecca's parents' house, talking shop, he retired to the kitchen to do some dishes. He was not habitually a doer of dishes—plates, he thought, were best disposable—but he wanted to do something with his hands, and he wanted not to worry about whether he had the correct expression on his face.

As he scraped congealed cheese with a sponge, he sensed rather than heard Alicia appear in the kitchen doorway. "It was a nice funeral," she said. "As nice as funerals can be, I guess."

"Yes," said Philip. "It certainly was."

"We didn't need the God stuff, though. In the eulogy. To explain why she did what she did. She did it because she was good, and brave. You don't have to introduce the idea of God into it to make sense of that."

Philip closed his eyes for a long moment, and then quietly returned his attention to the dishes soaking in the kitchen sink.

He felt Alicia's hand on his back. "I'm sorry," she said. "That was inappropriate. I shouldn't have said that, right then."

He turned toward her again, and she silently took his hand between both of hers. He choked back a sob. She had a faint smell of vanilla.

■

Philip is working his way through Wandering Rocks, watching Dublin's citizens cross each other's paths from a God's-eye view. At a table nearby a woman dandles a cheerfully babbling toddler, who hasn't yet learned that the strings of noises coming from human mouths aren't music made for its own sake.

From the balcony he can hear the murmur of physicists in conversation, though he can't exactly make out what they're saying. He doesn't need to know the lyrics to hum the tune, though. The words are about science, but the music is about the people who do the science.

The volume at the table drops for a moment: one person has been yielded the floor. Alicia. She accents her speech with sharp, precise hand movements, like an orchestra's conductor; the rest of the table is silent and attentive. When she stops they are all quiet for a second; then the entire table bursts into a laugh that is long, and from the gut, and laced with a touch of poison.

That is the kind of laughter that finishes careers, though science moves slowly, and whoever they are speaking of will not discover for two or three years that his fate has been decided. Over time his citations will dwindle; new papers that feature his name prominently will have trouble finding homes. His versions of the truth will go unheard, no matter how loudly he proclaims them. Then, as if it is his own idea, he will think to himself that, at last, it is time to get out of science: perhaps he is not too old to change careers, to try something else, before it is too late.

∎

He finishes the chapter of *Ulysses* just as Alicia appears in the balcony. "Hey, sweetie," she says, rubbing his back and pecking his cheek.

"Hey," Philip says. "Lively talk this morning, sounds like."

"Oh, you know: just deciding who's going to get the next Nobel. Don't worry about it." She bent over and hugged him. "Today's your big day!"

"Papers in Honor of Philip Steiner. Who would have ever thought."

∎

After Rebecca's death, Philip saw no other choice but to throw himself wholeheartedly into the Great Work. There was no other option! He could not let the effort he'd put into it go for naught. The child he'd been left with was entrusted to a succession of nannies, babysitters, and au pairs. He spent all the time in the lab that he could, and the giant machine never failed to reward his unceasing attention with inscrutability, or with the tantalizing promise of a solution, or with the promise of a solved problem that would in turn produce a yet larger conundrum that would be an even greater pleasure to solve. Sometimes he wondered what would happen if he ever actually figured the whole thing out: it'd be like a longtime lover announcing unexpectedly that her dependable ardor had finally flagged. It'd be the end of him.

The thing that happened with Alicia: it was more complicated than it looked. It really didn't have anything to do with loneliness, or bereavement. She was brilliant: that was the plain fact of the matter. And when the two of them were alone in the lab at night, speaking the private language that had sprung up between them after years spent in the company of the great machine . . . there was nothing like it. Even though grief draped his heart in a cloak of black velvet, he could still feel that joy, the simple happiness that came from expressing an original idea and being understood.

Those in the lab who noticed something was going on between Philip and Alicia appeared to turn a blind eye, even when the two of them gave up their pretenses and stopped being quite so circumspect. Alicia eventually applied for job positions elsewhere as her post-doc appointment approached its end. Her publications and her assiduous social networking paid dividends: in the field she'd made a name for herself as someone who would soon make a greater name for herself, whose success was a foregone conclusion, merely lying in wait for the right time. She got three job offers: Berkeley; Harvard; the Delft University of Technology.

Philip selfishly hoped she'd take the Harvard spot, only a few hours away. But one evening Alicia and Philip went out for dinner, and she mentioned that Dutch had some surprising linguistic similarities to English, and the language would be easy to pick up.

■

Though she left the country, she didn't leave his life: they kept in touch, daily, via e-mail and phone and webcam. They talked mostly about work, and though Alicia was pursuing her own projects in Delft, she still had ideas to offer Philip that could provide new directions for research. Philip could not help but notice that once Alicia left, his research efforts began to slow and stall: he would have liked to chalk it up to the possibility that Alicia's presence had boosted lab morale, but he suspected, in his heart of hearts, that she was just smarter than he was. He'd come up with the idea of the CVD, but she'd been able to take it and run with it, farther than he ever would have without her.

He got the feeling that she was losing interest in it. While her work on her own projects showed significant promise, Philip could tell from the tone of her voice during their daily talks that she was beginning to see his work as undead science, still soldiering on in ignorance of its own demise. Nonetheless, it was Alicia who half-heartedly gave Philip the idea that, instead of sending a robot into the causality violation device, he should go back to basics, install an electron gun in the roof of the machine and perform a double-slit experiment. He didn't think there'd be much of a result, but any promise of something interesting happening was better than none at all, and if there was any kind of anomaly in the resulting diffraction pattern, such an anomaly might show the way forward.

He installed the electron gun himself: it was the kind of easy task he'd normally farm out to a grad student to let him get his hands dirty, but to his shame, he hadn't been able to attract any grad students to his lab this year, and he'd been carrying out most of his work alone. Even the DAPAS money had begun to dry up as the pie-in-the-sky defense folks found other pipe dreams more promising.

Philip completed the installation early one Saturday morning and, after taking a quick break to brew a cup of tea, began the initial run. He set the gun to fire for an hour, planning to spend the interval writing a grant proposal. He began work, cutting and pasting paragraphs from other failed proposals, attempting to ignore the sinking feeling that though all these proposals were going to different addresses in the United States, they were all being read by the *same person*, when from the causality violation device came a strange, muffled sound that shouldn't have happened, an inexplicable *thump*.

Had he improperly mounted the electron gun? Had it come loose from its housing? Surely not: a glance at his screen showed that it was still firing. Nonetheless, that sound needed investigation, even if it ruined the run. He shut the gun down, approached the causality violation device, and opened its door. And out tumbled the body of his first wife, Rebecca Wright, looking as if she'd passed away in her sleep just seconds before.

■

In the intervening year between the day when the chair of Stratton's physics department announced a symposium in his honor and today, Philip had allowed himself fantasies of what the event would actually be like, and slowly reined in those fantasies as he watched plans for it come together. Instead of a full day, the program is half a day, from noon to five. Instead of the proceedings being published in a hardcover book to be sold to libraries at no small expense, they will occupy the back half of a special issue of a journal that is well regarded, but not top-tier. Instead of Stratton University's largest auditorium being booked for the event, the symposium is being held in the physics department's second-largest classroom, which seats about fifty. Instead of a golden throne, Philip sits in a wooden chair in the front row, where he must, for five hours, perform the act of close attention.

Sean is slouched in the seat next to him, and clearly feels the need to perform nothing except his constant teenage discontentment.

Though this boy shares Philip's home and half his genes, he is a stranger to him. He has made a pro forma attempt at dressing for the occasion: a suit jacket paired with faded jeans and dirty sneakers, and a tie knotted loosely around his neck, striped green and silver. Beneath this is a white T-shirt that features David Bowie's downcast face, a pink and blue lightning bolt painted across it. Though Philip does not quite get David Bowie, he has tried to use Sean's newfound love of classic rock as a means of creating a father-son bond. But when he bought Sean a recording of Rush's *Signals* (thinking that he'd dig "Subdivisions" in particular: *be cool or be cast out!*), he said it had "too many synthesizers" and dismissed the band's entire corpus as "Randroid horseshit." This was the first time Sean had used a swear word in Philip's hearing, and unprepared for this sudden testing of boundaries, Philip had chosen to let the moment pass in silence. That had probably been a mistake, he thought: the occasion called for parenting, called for discipline.

Alicia is sitting on Philip's other side, and occasionally she reaches out and places her hand on his. He can read her face, and can tell that she agrees with the opinion that he himself is too politic to speak aloud: that the papers being delivered today are not that good. They are not very interesting. They are parsimoniously doled out fingernail parings of thought, bloated into full length by badly written prose and extensive recapitulations of material with which an audience of this kind would already be familiar. They are evidence that the desire to bide one's time in order to do good science has been sublimated to the constant drive to publish; as the saying goes, the committees that hand out funds and grant tenure cannot read, but they can count. The colleagues and former students presenting today—a couple of whom he still remembers; some of whom he shared a credit with on a paper as one of forty authors—are here primarily to get yet another line on their CV.

Though there are good intentions here that should not be discounted. Philip's career is not one that will be long remembered—his most famous paper, the capstone of his labors, is famous for the wrong reasons. But he has given good service to Science for many years, and if there is a hint of *there but for the grace of God go I* in the eyes of younger physicists at this afternoon's symposium, they are doing what they see as their duty to a colleague who has reached his

career's end without turning his back on the field: they are providing
the final cadence that signals a happy ending, despite the tragedy or
the impermanence of all that came before.

■

There is a newly hired assistant professor at the back of the hall who
is not on the same page as everyone else, who does not realize that
the function of this symposium is largely ceremonial. His snorts and
harrumphs land like spitballs on the back of Philip's head. He seems
considerably annoyed by the talk given by the high-energy physicist
who came up from Louisiana, on the current efforts toward gravitational wave research: there are plans under way to launch three
spacecraft equipped with lasers, which will work together to function as an interferometer that will be several orders of magnitude
larger than the interferometers currently running on earth. Surely
everyone in the room is imagining what wonders they could accomplish with the funding necessary to undertake such a project. But the
money goes where it goes.

The young, arrogant assistant prof saves his biggest raspberries
for the last talk of the afternoon, given by a former post-doc of Philip's who left the field to teach high school physics. It's Carson Tyler!
Philip always liked Carson, and recalls that Alicia was fond of him,
too. Carson's talk isn't about the cutting edge of physics so much as
it's about how what he learned in Philip's lab about the day-to-day
details of scientific research helps him to get kids interested in physics and related fields. "Kids are natural-born experimenters," he says.
"You don't have to encourage their desire to do science: you just have
to not discourage it." He displays a chart at this point that causes
some uncomfortable stirring in seats: it shows that while the raw
number of women and ethnic minorities applying to physics graduate programs has been rising over time, the attrition rate once they
get inside the gate is still alarmingly high.

Rather than gloss the chart and suggest conclusions that one might
draw from the data, he takes it down after a few moments without
comment, and quietly segues into homilies about the fulfillment he
gets from seeing his students' faces when they experience a "sense of
wonder." This calms people down. Everyone in the hall has heard
this stuff before, but it is still comforting: it reminds them of when

they themselves were young, of the parts of their minds that have still remained youthful.

When he concludes his talk to polite applause, the assistant professor says, a little too loudly, "That wasn't science." Alicia has had enough. She turns and shouts, "It *was. Shut* it."

■

When Rebecca's body fell out of the causality violation device, aged several years since he last saw her alive, dressed in the sort of tank top and leggings that implied that she'd been about to go for a run, Philip went insane, for a little while. There was some screaming. When he came to his senses briefly, he found that he had somehow gashed the back of his left hand, though the cut wasn't bleeding heavily. Then he remembered what Mr. Cheever had told him, long ago: *If something weird happens, and I mean only if it's really weird, call this number. I might not pick up, but the message will get to me fast.*

He had the number written on a slip of paper folded up in his wallet: he'd copied and recopied it from the original napkin that Mr. Cheever had given him years ago, the napkin that he had since lost somewhere in his home office. (Multiple backups in multiple places: it pays off.) He dialed the number and a woman's voice answered, curt and English. "Speak."

The command startled him. "Rebecca," he stammered. "She's here. She's: I think she's dead? She's here—"

"Is your name Philip Steiner?"

"Y-yes,"

"Don't move." He was pressed up against the wall, looking at the body that lay inert in front of the door to the causality violation chamber, one of its legs folded awkwardly beneath its back. He looked up at the ceiling-mounted camera that hid behind its hemispherical dome, and presumed that the camera was looking back at him.

"Please stop wailing," the voice on the phone said. "You're panicking. Don't move. Stay on the line."

Philip clamped his mouth shut.

"Leave this room and enter your office," the voice said. "Then close the door."

Philip walked past the body (she doesn't look like she did the last time he saw her; her hair is longer; she looks thinner; there are no signs of an accident or an autopsy; it is her; it is her; it is her), through the double doors of the lab's entrance, and into his office, the first door on his left. He shut the door behind him, locking it for good measure, as if the body in the lab, once disgorged into this world, might get up, might begin to articulate questions best left unspoken.

"Sit down in the chair behind your desk," the voice said, "and remove your shoes."

"Why should I—"

"Do not ask *questions*! You're panicking; you will be calmer without your shoes on. Remove them!"

Philip, chastened like a schoolboy, kicked his shoes off. "Okay: done."

"Now. My name is Sidney. I'm here to help. But you must do *exactly* as I say. First: I will be disconnecting from you without warning, and calling you again sometime later. When I call, answer immediately; answer by saying *Hello, Sidney.*"

"Okay."

"Don't move. Don't turn on your computer! Stay calm. Relax."

"Okay," Philip said, but there was no further response.

■

Ten minutes later the phone rang again. "Rebecca," he said. "Rebecca—"

"Say *Hello, Sidney.*"

"Hello, Sidney."

"Hello, Philip. You will notice some noise outside, of conveyances and personnel. Stay in your office. Do not be curious."

As Sidney said this, Philip heard what sounded like two large vehicles pulling up outside the building, perhaps the size of garbage trucks. There was a commotion of men barking commands.

"Mr. Cheever says hello," said Sidney. "He will be in Stratton in three hours."

"Oh, good," said Philip, but Sidney was already gone.

■

Fifteen minutes later, the phone rang again. "Hello, Sidney," Philip said.

"In a moment a man in uniform will knock on your door. He is bringing you a slice of chocolate cake and some hot tea. Eat the cake. Drink the tea. Relax."

She hung up just as Philip heard a rap on the office door's frosted window.

He opened it to reveal a soldier in full camouflage gear looming over him, corn-fed and twenty-four, his red hair cropped to a buzz cut, his uniform free of any insignia that would indicate name or rank. An assault rifle was strapped to his back, the end of its barrel peeking over his shoulder. In one hand he held a steaming Styrofoam cup; in the other, a slice of dark chocolate cake in a clear plastic container, along with a plastic fork.

"Cake, sir," the soldier said, proffering the food.

Philip took the cake and the tea, but the soldier remained standing there. "I just wanted to say," he said, "that it's a real honor to meet you, face-to-face."

Behind the soldier Philip could see four people in white hazmat suits, pushing a gurney into the lab.

"Thank you," he said. Don't you tip people when they bring you food? It seemed to Philip like a good idea. He pulled out his wallet and extracted a twenty-dollar bill, fastidiously folding it in half so that the crease cut across the face of Theodore Roosevelt, with its shining spectacles and its Cheshire Cat grin. He held the money toward the soldier, who politely waved it away with a nervous laugh: "Nice, but this one's on us."

The soldier stepped backward with an unexpected bashfulness. "I gotta get to it. But I'm gonna remember meeting you forever." He left, shutting the office door behind him.

As Philip sat back down at his desk, the phone rang again. "Hello, Sidney."

"Don't burn your mouth on the tea. Let it cool."

She disconnected.

■

He nibbled at the cake (which was, to be honest, quite good: not too sweet, the frosting rich and dark) and drank the tea while he listened to the clamor outside: *Okay, on one. Lift. Go. Move it. We want to be out of here by ten o'clock, like we were never here. Get Evie in here to switch out the security recordings and fudge the logs. Come with it. Move move move! Get her into the dry ice. Get—what the* fuck *we don't need this now. Get him away from here: give him the cover story, scare him to death.*

Was Sidney even English? Philip suspected she wasn't: they were probably exploiting the American instinct to hear a female voice that sounded like a BBC newsreader as one of prim authority that ought not be questioned. They probably wanted him to take off his shoes so he wouldn't run, or do something stupid: even if he wasn't really immobilized, they wanted him to *think* he was, and wanted him not to mind. The cake and the tea probably had mild tranquilizers in them or something, for all he knew. If anything, he was not as concerned about what in the hell had just happened not half an hour before; he was not even too worried about the possibility of bull-necked military types and people in hazmat gear rummaging indiscriminately around his laboratory. He was content to wait, to let the causality violation device be someone else's problem for once.

The phone rang. "Hello, Sidney."

"Mr. Cheever is about to knock on your door. He is going to take you to a safe place. Alicia Merrill is on her way from the Netherlands: we've sent a plane for her. She didn't have much time to pack, but we've provided her with a suitcase full of necessities: she'll be okay. She should arrive in Stratton by this evening. Then we'll go from there."

"Thank you, Sidney."

"No, thank *you*," Sidney replied, and Philip could have sworn he heard her accent slip a little, revealing something midwestern beneath the surface. "It's been a pleasure, Philip. Goodbye."

As she hung up for the last time, Philip answered the knock on his office door to see Mr. Cheever, immaculately dressed in a navy-blue suit and powder-blue tie, offering his hand in greeting and, Philip suspected, congratulations.

"It's good to see you," he said. "Everything's okay. Come with me."

■

The next time Philip saw Mr. Cheever, thirty hours later, was when he appeared at the door of the hotel suite in which he and Alicia had been installed. "You," Alicia said, walking around Philip as he opened the door, standing between him and Mr. Cheever, "have kept us imprisoned here for a day."

"You're not imprisoned," Mr. Cheever said, stepping past them both and seating himself in the center of the couch in the suite's living room.

"When I go to get ice, from the ice machine, a man in a suit stops me after I'm five feet out the door. He's got a suspiciously heavy pocket. He says *he'll* get the ice for me. I want to get my *own* ice."

"I want to see my son," Philip said.

"He's fine: he's being looked after. You'll see him soon. You're not imprisoned." Not looking at either of them, Mr. Cheever opened his briefcase.

"We haven't done anything wrong," Philip said. "Though, to be fair, I can see how past events might pose a serious problem of appearances—"

"We know you haven't done anything wrong." Mr. Cheever removed a manila folder from his briefcase. "We've looked at the tapes. A body comes out of the machine, but a body doesn't go in. That's one thing we can't explain. Here's the second." From the folder he extracted two documents and laid them out next to each other on the coffee table in front of him. "We disinterred Rebecca Wright's body last night. By which I mean the *first* one." He tapped one paper. "The DNA matches, a hundred percent. But here's what's even weirder." He tapped the other paper. "Our forensics team wanted a second confirmation of the . . . similarity of these two bodies. The first body shows the expected signs of decay as well as the trauma from the automobile accident that caused her death. But there's something really strange about the teeth. Their enamel is . . . it's just *gone*. And there's no evidence of any tool being used to strip it away. It's just vanished, as if it was never there."

As Alicia and Philip seated themselves in chairs opposite him, he said, "What we seem to have here are two . . . instances . . . of the same person: more or less identical, except that one instance has had its teeth mysteriously altered. None of this makes sense at all. That ought to be impossible."

He looked at them in confusion and, Philip thought, horror. "Shouldn't that be impossible?"

■

"You two told me last night that you have a theory about how causality violation might work, one that means there wouldn't be any evidence left behind that it *did* work," Mr. Cheever said. "But here we've got evidence that *something* happened. And you also said that causality violation is subject to principles of conservation of mass and energy. A body that leaves a particular point in spacetime has to return to the place it left.

"But here we have two instances of the same body. The same mass. That can't be right. Can it?"

"Humans are different," Alicia said.

"What do you mean?"

"Be quiet and let me think."

■

They sat silently, while Alicia thought. Mr. Cheever got up to use the suite's coffeemaker; once it finished brewing, he poured himself a cup, sipped at it cautiously, grimaced, and placed a call on his phone, mumbling so that Alicia and Philip couldn't hear. A few minutes later, one of those guys in heavy-pocketed suits arrived, bearing three mugs of steaming joe on a silver platter, along with a few sugar packets and a tiny glass bottle of cream, stopped with a cork. He placed the platter on the table, nodded at Mr. Cheever in greeting, and retreated.

"Humans are different," Alicia announced, after a half hour. "They're different from the robot we sent into the device in important ways. First: because humans are sentient, and can make a conscious decision to alter history. Arachne is too rudimentary to be able to do that. That's one thing. It's important, given that we're dealing with an experiment whose intention is to violate the normal order of causes and effects.

"Second: the mass of a human isn't constant. Humans aren't just masses: they're patterns of information that organize masses. Atoms are constantly leaving your body and being replaced: as you breathe, and eat, and expel waste, and slough off dead skin. Your hair grows, and you cut it, and more hair grows back in the same pattern. Most of it, anyway. Same goes for your fingernails. But this is also true for your muscles, and your blood, and your brain, and your bones. With an important exception, none of the molecules present in your body right now has been there for more than a few years.

"So it's not quite correct to say that we have two instances of the same person. What we have here are two *masses* that were organized by the same *pattern*.

"The theory still holds. We have a person who, in a previous version of history that is now erased from the record, went backward in time. Suppose she corresponded with a prior instance of herself. The same *pattern:* same identity, same personality, same childhood memories. But the time-traveling version is several years older than the earlier version. They are two different *masses*.

"The future instance of the time traveler does . . . something. We don't know what. Acts in a certain way; gives a tiny piece of advice. Exercises her ability to cause an effect. The future instance of the time traveler says or does something that leads to the death of the past instance: either deliberately, or accidentally. We can't know.

"When the past instance of the time traveler dies, the pattern that holds her mass together dissolves and cannot be re-created. Which naturally means that the future instance of the time traveler must also die, or, more accurately, must be wiped out of existence. But the laws of physics still have to be satisfied. A mass that leaves a certain point in spacetime has to return to the place it left."

■

"A proposition. In the history in which we're now living, in the moment just before the second instance of Rebecca's body appeared in the causality violation device, the particles that composed it were scattered everywhere: in a rock quarry in Pennsylvania, in a loaf of bread for sale at a grocery store in Detroit, in a water reservoir in Newark. Then, the causality violation happened, and those particles were . . . translocated. They became part of what, in our history, we see as Rebecca's second instance. How did this happen?

"That body that showed up in the causality violation device. I don't think calling it a corpse is the right word. I don't even think calling it Rebecca is the right word. It's wrong to say that it's dead, because from our perspective that body was never alive: all of us here agree that Rebecca Wright died in an automobile accident, years ago. That second instance is just a . . . failed homunculus. A shape. An inert mass. The result of the universe pulling a little sleight of hand in order to correct its balance books. But because of a unique set of events that took place in a prior version of history—one in which Rebecca lived to the present day, entered the causality violation device, traveled backward in time, and somehow brought about the death of her younger self—we were able to watch that sleight of hand happen. We saw it.

"And the reason that the enamel has disappeared from the teeth of the past instance of Rebecca is that tooth enamel is nearly the only part of the human body that doesn't constantly replenish itself. The molecules that make it up couldn't be in two places at once: they had, so to speak, to make a choice. And they chose the future instance.

"I realize this is an extraordinary claim," Alicia finished. "But you must admit that we have the required extraordinary evidence."

■

A day after their conversation about Alicia's explanation for what Mr. Cheever, and the other heavily beribboned military types who were constantly tromping in and out of the physicists' suite, had come to refer to circumspectly as "the phenomenon," Mr. Cheever arrived with two lunch boxes: a couple of sushi rolls for Philip and Alicia, along with Styrofoam cups of miso soup. As usual, he sat in the center of the suite's lone couch, while Philip and Alicia pulled up chairs to the coffee table between them. For his own meal, Mr. Cheever produced an orange, which he began to peel with a paring knife he pulled from a worn leather sheath that he kept in his pocket: though the knife had clearly seen much service, it still cut cleanly.

"Philip, we want you to publish a paper," Mr. Cheever said as he kept his eyes on the physicists. His hands continued to peel the orange as if of their own accord, the rind unspooling in a perfect spiral. "We are already working on the content. But you will be the sole credited author."

"What, exactly, is this paper meant to state?"

"In this paper, you will report the results of your attempts to create a causality violation. You will conclude that to do so is impossible. I feel certain that the paper will be published in a prominent place. It would be best if it's the last article you write."

The curled rind dropped to the table, leaving the orange naked.

"Oh, hell no," said Alicia. "Oh, hell no. You're not taking that away from him. You're not taking that away from me."

"Wait," said Philip, his heart sinking. "Let's hear him out."

■

"Look," said Mr. Cheever as he placed the unsheathed paring knife on the table. "It's clear that the history of the world has been altered in some way, small or large. But we don't know what the history was like that was, as you call it, overwritten. Maybe it was better than this one, or worse. Or better for some people but worse for others. We can't know. We have speculations, but they're only that. But whatever happens, the existence of this thing, behaving in the way that it does, presents a severe existential problem. We think it's better that no one know that this device exists.

"Human behavior—of individuals, of families, of nations—is predicated on accountability to the future, but it is also predicated on the persistence of memory. We act as though we may not be able to evade the consequences of our actions. And it is our memory of our past that forces this, if nothing else. A woman who does good will always remember the results of that goodness, and will choose to do more good. Or she spends a week in jail, but the memory of her time in prison lasts for the rest of her life. Do you see?

"But if this device functions as you believe it does, then a time traveler would not even carry a memory of past versions of history from one to the next. If he would not have the reward that comes from knowing that he has somehow made the world better by alter-ing history, he would also be free of the guilt of knowing he has made things worse. And a person who had access to time travel would act with impunity, committing crimes in plain sight with the certainty that the memory of his crimes would be obliterated by changing history—not just in his mind, but in *all* minds. Can you imagine what would happen if the wrong person got hold of this technology? If the wrong nation got hold of it? If *multiple* nations with different ambitions got hold of it? History would constantly be rewritten in an attempt to advantage one faction or another, and we would always be unaware of the changes. All we would know is that our own history would be anarchy and chaos.

"Given that, we believe that the knowledge that time travel is possible is best suppressed. We'd much prefer it if humanity believed that time travel could not, in fact, happen; we certainly don't want people to know that, in a sense, it already has. I wish I could forget it myself—I wouldn't have lain awake last night wondering what Rebecca Wright's previous version of history had been like, or those of any time travelers before her.

"There may have been dozens, you know? Hundreds of prior iterations. She was just the first one who managed to leave behind proof."

■

"That's one of our speculations, by the way. That the prior version of history that this one overwrote was horrible. Complete geopolitical mayhem; half of New York City is underwater. The United States is headed toward civil war, or ruled by an artificial-intelligence construct, or some such other thing. Real end-of-days stuff. That the instances of ourselves who existed in that history figured out what we have: that the invention of the causality violation device was the cause. That in that prior version of history, Rebecca did not die in a car accident. That she went back to the past on a mission, as a volunteer, well aware of her sacrifice."

■

"Both of you will be made whole," Mr. Cheever said. "We can't make a one-to-one restitution for the intangible benefits you'd get from publishing a positive result. But we can ensure you'll be well taken care of. Dr. Steiner, you'll receive an ample pension; Dr. Merrill, we feel certain that there's a prestigious position available for you in the United States. You deserve a top-tier spot on the merits, but that doesn't mean it wouldn't be our privilege to . . . smooth the way for you."

"I'm quite happy in Delft, thank you," Alicia said. "And I intend to return as soon as possible, if we're done here."

"We hope we can convince you to be content in the country of your citizenship," said Mr. Cheever, his index finger running along the timeworn handle of the paring knife before him. "I suspect that, given what you are known by some to know, free and easy foreign travel may become . . . difficult, for you."

■

"The device," Philip said. "What are you going to do with it?"

"I know how this sounds. But you'll have to trust us. We'll take possession of it. We're going to dismantle it; when we do so, the wormhole will close, making this the final version of history we live through. Then we're going to box up the device and forget about it. Lose it somewhere; burn the records. It'll end up in a warehouse right next to the Ark of the Covenant."

■

Alicia sat back in her chair, her eyes closed, slowly shaking her head. "We are getting owned on this," she said. "Absolutely fucking owned."

Mr. Cheever popped an orange slice into his mouth and chewed it thoughtfully. Then he picked up the paring knife and sheathed it.

"This is true," he said, with no small amount of compassion. "You are, as you say, 'getting owned.' But it's in the best interest of humanity. You and Philip have discovered the rare truth that it is inarguably best not to know. For this you have my sympathy, as well as my genuine admiration."

■

Alicia, Philip, and Sean return to the house late; for Philip it has been a satisfying, but very long, day. Tomorrow is a school day for Sean, and Alicia asks him conspiratorially if he wants her to call in sick for him. He says he'll be alright: he hasn't done his homework yet, but it's always super easy, it'll take like five minutes, he can do it on the way to school.

Sean has a habit of not looking Alicia in the eye when he speaks to her. Alicia does not like this, but also does not know what to do to convince Sean that she has the authority that is a mother's by right. He resists her attempts to get him to see her as anything more than a friend of the family. She sometimes thinks that she and Philip should have had a real wedding after she returned from the Netherlands to take up her position at IAS, even though neither of them wanted to deal with the expense and the fuss, and were happy to settle for signing a form in front of a registrar while a couple of close friends watched. But in retrospective that was perhaps needlessly furtive, and might have cemented the idea in Sean's mind that she was some sort of usurper.

Alicia had known Rebecca, Philip's first wife, though not that well—she'd never been in her company when Philip wasn't there. But she knew her to have been a good person. She had no intention of replacing her, or even trying; someday, perhaps Sean would understand that.

He is already expressing a desire to attend art school after he graduates. This is troubling. Down that path lies penury and parental dependency. They will have to have a serious talk soon, mother and father to son, and she will have to be a parent rather than an older pal who provisionally plays the part. But not tonight: it can wait.

"I'm going to bed," says Sean, and without another word, he heads down the hallway to his bedroom, leaving Alicia and Philip behind. Then he hesitates, turns around, comes back into the living room, and sticks out his hand toward Philip.

But when Philip takes it, he feels that Sean's grip is strong (and he realizes that Sean is tall, with a voice that has stopped cracking: he's nearly a man now). Sean pulls his father, and Philip feels himself being pulled, and now father and son are in an awkwardly masculine embrace, with Sean's arm loosely slung across the back of Philip's neck. Philip has not touched Sean in years.

"Dad," Sean says, his mouth at Philip's ear. "You did real good."

■

Now Philip is in bed, and drifting off to sleep. Alicia is snoring lightly in his arms, her hand slipped up his shirt to press against his chest, cold but becoming warmer.

It is always at this time, just before he slips into unconsciousness, when the voice comes to him: not as loud and snide and insistent as it once was, but still there, still hounding him from behind, still trying to drive him stumbling forward. *Is this the best you can do?*

Tonight, for the first time in many, many years, Philip chooses not to ignore it: he answers. *It is. It really is.*

Then say it, and shout down the darkness.

"It is," Philip whispers between clenched teeth as Alicia mumbles and stirs in her slumber. "It is!"

■

And as Sean climbs into bed and closes his eyes, Mother comes, riding astride a lion the size of a house, blowing a clarion from a horn made out of a hollowed-out elephant's tusk. Her eyes have a faint crimson glow from the lasers that are mounted behind her irises, ready to fire at will.

"I touched a prince's chest today and made his heart stop," she says. "I'll do it again if I have to: they'll see what happens if anyone gets in my way. Good night, my son. Remember that I will always keep you safe; that I am always everywhere and always here."

"Good night, Mom," Sean says, and falls asleep.

And Mother recedes, wise and beautiful and strong, a genius and a hero, a punisher of thieves and a slayer of wicked men, to watch over her son in all her different versions.

ACKNOWLEDGMENTS

I'd like to thank the following people:

At Pantheon Books: my editor, Edward Kastenmeier, and Emily Giglierano.

At Writers House: my agent, Susan Golomb.

Sylvia Smullin provided a number of helpful comments on an early draft of this manuscript.

Certain elements of the novel arose from conversations with Sarah Batterman, Christopher W. Morris, Kendrick Smith, and Meghan Sullivan. I am also indebted to the work of Harry Collins, Ilana Gershon, and Joseph Hermanowicz.

And thanks to my family for their support, as always.

—Dexter Palmer
May 19, 2008
July 28, 2015
Princeton, New Jersey

ABOUT THE AUTHOR

Dexter Palmer's first novel, *The Dream of Perpetual Motion*, was selected as one of the best fiction debuts of 2010 by *Kirkus Reviews*. He lives in Princeton, New Jersey.

www.dexterpalmer.com